While the City Sleeps

Books by Elizabeth Camden

WOMEN OF MIDTOWN

While the City Sleeps

ELIZABETH CAMDEN

BETHANYHOUSE
a division of Baker Publishing Group
Minneapolis, Minnesota

Published by Bethany House Publishers
Minneapolis, Minnesota
www.BethanyHouse.com

Bethany House Publishers is a division of
Baker Publishing Group, Grand Rapids, Michigan

Printed in the United States of America

Library of Congress Cataloging-in-Publication Data
Names: Camden, Elizabeth, author.
Title: While the city sleeps / Elizabeth Camden.
Description: Minneapolis, Minnesota : Bethany House, a division of Baker
    Publishing Group, 2024. | Series: Women of Midtown ; 1
Identifiers: LCCN 2023037662 | ISBN 9780764241710 (paperback) | ISBN
    9780764242731 (casebound) | ISBN 9781493445134 (ebook)
Subjects: LCGFT: Christian fiction. | Romance fiction. | Novels.
Classification: LCC PS3553.A429 W45 2024 | DDC 813/.54—dc23/eng/20230919
LC record available at https://lccn.loc.gov/2023037662

Scripture quotations are from the King James Version of the Bible.

This is a work of historical reconstruction; the appearances of certain historical figures are therefore inevitable. All other characters, however, are products of the author's imagination, and any resemblance to actual persons, living or dead, is coincidental.

Cover design by Dan Thornberg, Design Source Creative Services

Baker Publishing Group publications use paper produced from sustainable forestry practices and post-consumer waste whenever possible.

24 25 26 27 28 29 30   7 6 5 4 3 2

1

NEW YORK CITY • APRIL 1913

People were rarely in a good mood while in a dentist's chair, but Dr. Katherine Schneider's patient was singing. Vittorio had been terrified when he first arrived because he'd never been to a dentist before, but the sedative had finally taken effect. Nitrous oxide, sometimes known as laughing gas, often had the delightful side effect of euphoria.

"How are you feeling?" Katherine asked, and Vittorio gave her a wide smile.

"Life is wonderful," he said, then went back to singing "The Sugar-Plum Tree."

Vittorio had brought his brother along for moral support. The brother didn't share Vittorio's easy mood and interrupted the singing with a blunt, angry spiel of words spoken in Italian.

She glanced down at Vittorio. "What did he say?"

"Gino says he doesn't believe a woman can be a real dentist."

"I'm a real dentist," she assured him, pointing to the diploma on the wall from the Philadelphia Dental College, class of 1911.

She had been one of four women in her graduating class, but not a day went by when someone didn't question her qualifications.

"Gino doesn't believe it," Vittorio said. "He wants to know if there's someone else who can pull my tooth."

The only other dentist in the clinic this late in the evening was Dr. Alvin Washington. Alvin wanted to leave soon for his anniversary dinner with his heavily pregnant wife, but if a patient refused to be treated by a female dentist, Alvin would step in to do the job.

She opened the door of her compact treatment room to call down the hall. "Dr. Washington? Could you come introduce yourself? My patient might be more comfortable with a man."

Alvin had been chatting with the janitor in the lobby, but agreeably headed down the hall, past the six other treatment rooms that were closed for the evening, and into her room. He had to navigate around the narrow space between the dental chair and a table covered with gleaming surgical instruments already laid out for work.

Vittorio took one look at Alvin and blanched. "He's a dentist?"

"I'm a dentist," Alvin replied. "Harvard University School of Dentistry, class of 1906."

"But you're Black!" Vittorio said, his voice both shocked and bewildered. Laughing gas removed the filters people normally had in place, causing them to blurt out whatever thoughts floated through their minds. She and Alvin were both used to it.

"Yes, I'm Black," Alvin said. "And you're in a lot of pain from that badly infected tooth. If you want it fixed tonight, you can have me do it or Dr. Schneider. Or you can wait until tomorrow."

Tomorrow they'd have a whole crew of dentists staffing one of the largest and most forward-thinking dental clinics in the country. The owner, Dr. Edgar Parker, believed that not only should the office stay open late at night to accommodate working people's schedules, but patients could also be treated by dentists with whom they felt comfortable. Their office had dentists who were fluent in German, Russian, and Chinese. Dr. Parker also hired Black and female dentists. By hiring dentists who looked like the diverse population of New York City, at least one obstacle that made people reluctant to see a dentist had been removed.

Vittorio and his brother conferred in Italian while Katherine waited. Finally, Vittorio relaxed back into the chair. "I want the woman to do it," he announced. "Smaller hands."

"Excellent reasoning," she said, and Alvin sent her a smile of relief. His wife and their anniversary dinner were waiting.

Alvin left while Katherine began preparing the equipment to pull the tooth. The only real pain Vittorio would experience tonight would happen when she injected his gum with a numbing drug that Dr. Parker had invented. It was highly effective, making a tooth extraction merely uncomfortable instead of painful.

Though Vittorio was already feeling good from the laughing gas, she needed him completely relaxed before giving him the injection. She squeezed the rubber ball to feed another dose of nitrous oxide into his mask while he breathed deeply. He smiled and pulled the mask away and continued rambling his odd collection of thoughts, jumping from one topic to another with no logical sense.

"Cleopatra was a goddess of the Nile," he mumbled. "She might get mad when she sees what we did. What do you think, lady dentist, will Cleopatra be mad at me or is she good and dead?"

"Cleopatra is good and dead," Katherine assured him. "Open wide, and you're going to feel a prick. I need you to hold still."

The patient obeyed but still let out a wailing howl as she injected the pain-killing solution into his gum. This was always the worst part. He reared up a little, still squealing, but didn't fight her.

They both gave a sigh of relief when the injection was over. It would take a few minutes for the medicine to numb the area, and she set out cotton balls while Vittorio prayed to the Virgin Mary to have mercy on him. Then he added Saint Patrick for good measure because "good old Saint Patrick" was probably mad at him too.

"I don't like Saint Patrick," Vittorio said. "Sure, he drove the

7

snakes out of Ireland, but what did he ever do for the Italians? Nothing! I shouldn't feel bad. Saint Paddy deserves whatever he's got coming to him."

It wasn't unusual for patients under the influence of narcotics to ramble. Sometimes people got giggly, others became weepy. Tonight, it made Vittorio philosophical as he speculated about various people from world history.

She gave Vittorio a final breath of nitrous oxide. By now he was coming to enjoy the drug, and he clamped her hand holding the rubber mask to his face to suck it in deeply.

Katherine pulled it away, then rolled the table with the tools closer as Vittorio continued to ramble. "Lorna Doone," he said dreamily. "Have you ever read that book, lady dentist?"

"I've never read it."

"Sad, sad story. Oh, poor Lorna Doone. At least she wasn't an old lady. A boring gray lady who hates us. No, Lorna Doone isn't like the awful gray lady."

"Time to stop talking," she said in a soothing voice. "Open wide, we're ready to begin."

―――――――――――

There was no such thing as painless dentistry, even though the name of their clinic was Painless Parker Dentistry. That was her boss's idea, and it outraged the respectable dentists in the city.

Traditional dentists branded Dr. Edgar Parker a menace to the dignity of the profession, claiming that his large crew of dentists treated patients as though they were on a production line. They didn't like the way Edgar kept his clinic open during unconventional hours. They didn't like Edgar's low fees that dramatically undercut what other dentists charged. They didn't like Edgar's garish advertisements, his stable of dentists, or the fact that a man who started his career as a vaudeville tooth-puller was now the richest dentist in the country.

But nothing outraged the dental establishment so much as

the name of Edgar's clinic, Painless Parker Dentistry, which they claimed was false advertising. Edgar hadn't been to the office for a month because he was battling a lawsuit from the American Dental Association to force him to stop using the name. Edgar's chain of dental clinics on both coasts all used the name, and it brought customers beating a path to their doors. Most dentists used similar pain-killing drugs, yet Edgar was the only one who exaggerated his services with his clinic's memorable name.

After Katherine's work was finished, she helped Vittorio slowly rise from the chair, an arm around his back to steady him. He held a block of ice wrapped in a towel to his swollen jaw, but still managed a wobbly smile.

"Are you feeling okay?" she asked.

"Okay, lady dentist," he mumbled.

Katherine locked gazes with Vittorio's brother and gestured for him to take over. She waited until the brother had his arm firmly around the patient before she led them down the hall, through the waiting room, and out the front door into the warm June night.

Vittorio leaned heavily on his brother as they wandered toward the subway stop, loudly singing the refrain from "The Sugar-Plum Tree." To a casual observer, they probably looked like a pair of drunks, but the effects of the drug would wear off soon. Vittorio was walking on his own by the time they disappeared into the crowds of Times Square.

It was only nine o'clock and Katherine had another patient waiting. Birdie Jamison's hands were covered with the nicks and scars of someone who worked in a cannery. Birdie could never have afforded care at a fancy dental office with drapes on the windows and upholstered chairs in the waiting room. Katherine smiled at her next patient and led her into a treatment room.

Maybe the Painless Parker Dentistry clinic was little better than a production line, but New York City was home to almost five million people. One-third of them had been born overseas and lived close to the bone. Thank goodness there were dental clinics to bring relief to those who couldn't afford it elsewhere. Poor people suffered the same amount of pain as rich people, and they deserved access to a decent dentist.

Katherine prayed Edgar won his lawsuit, because if the courts ordered him to stop using his brash advertisements, this clinic would be forced to close. It meant patients like Birdie Jamison could no longer afford basic dental care, and Katherine would be out of a job.

Katherine's final task before closing the clinic at midnight was to peel off the white high-collared tunic she wore while treating patients. She traded it for a nip-waisted jacket, then smoothed her upswept dark hair, taking care to arrange a few tendrils to frame her face because . . . well, because she always liked looking nice for Lieutenant Birch.

It was mortifying to care so much about the dashing police officer's opinion, especially since he never showed the least amount of romantic interest in her. And yet why did he always show up after her shift to walk her to the subway? He'd been doing this for two years, and it wasn't part of his official duties. Still, he seemed very protective of her.

Katherine snagged a large pretzel from the break room before heading to the front lobby. Dr. Friedrich was from Germany and often brought a sack of freshly baked pretzels for the staff to share. The only other person in the clinic was Hector, their janitor, who was busy cleaning up.

"There are still some pretzels in the break room if you want," she offered to Hector.

"I've already had my fill," Hector replied, not looking up as he mopped the tile floor. It had been a long day for them both. "Good night, Dr. Schneider."

"Good night, Hector," she said before leaving through the front door. She turned to take in the dazzling view of Times Square at midnight, brightly lit by hundreds of streetlamps and theater signs. The night air shimmered with excitement, lively music spilling from the restaurants that catered to affluent crowds after the theaters let out. Even at midnight, Times Square blazed with radiant light.

It was why Edgar opened his clinic here. Patients wouldn't feel safe venturing out to see a dentist at night unless it was in a clean, well-lit part of town. Most people visiting Times Square saw only the glittering lights and the people carousing in an all-night party, but Katherine saw another side of the famed theater district of Midtown Manhattan. None of this could happen without the overnight staff who made it possible. Cooks and waitresses served food. Actors, dancers, and musicians put on the shows. Police officers patrolled the square, and streetcar operators drove people wherever they wanted to go. Janitors cleaned offices, and bakers were already kneading dough for tomorrow's breakfast. Across the street, the *New York Times* building was lit up like a Christmas tree all night long. Inside, journalists, editors, and printing crews were hurrying to get the newspaper ready for sale by sunrise.

Katherine's parents back in Ohio worried incessantly about her late-night hours, but she was twenty-eight years old and navigated the city with ease. Six years after fleeing the humiliation of a mortifying heartbreak in Ohio, she had fulfilled her improbable dream of becoming a dentist. Her heart had mended, for nothing healed a wounded heart faster than a crush on another man, even if it was unrequited.

She glanced both ways, then hurried across the street. The subway stop was three blocks away, and she started munching on the pretzel that was already a bit stale and brushed a few crumbs from her chin.

Like clockwork, Lieutenant Birch emerged from the crowd farther down the block and strode toward her. She admired the chiseled set of his jaw and quiet intensity of his expression, partially hidden beneath the brim of his police cap. Always alert, always cool and unruffled. He appeared to be in his thirties and attracted plenty of female attention whenever he walked her to the subway station.

He tipped his head in greeting. "Good evening, Dr. Schneider."

The way he said her name gave her a quick thrill. His tone was precise and polite, delivered in a smooth tenor wrapped in velvet.

"Lieutenant Birch," she greeted, trying to sound equally non-chalant. "How has your evening been?"

"Fine."

The fact that he didn't elaborate was not a surprise. Lieutenant Birch never talked about himself. Ever. He didn't merely draw a line around his personal life; it was more like a fortress topped with barbed wire and searchlights to keep out intruders. After two years, the only thing she knew about him was his deep apprecia-tion for Italian cuisine.

He glanced at the pretzel she held. "You don't really like pret-zels, do you? Pretzels are dry, lifeless bread. Try this. It's much better."

He handed her a paper sack, and she peeked inside to see a wedge of golden bread flecked with bits of herbs. It was still warm. She tore a piece from the soft loaf, inhaling an herbal fragrance that made her mouth water. She tossed the remnant of the pretzel into a trash can where it hit with a clang.

"It's focaccia," Lieutenant Birch said. He repeated the word and even spelled it for her. The freshly baked bread was an explosion of flavor with an airy texture beneath a golden crust.

"Why did you say pretzels are lifeless bread?" she asked as they continued walking, their footsteps in tandem.

"Pretzels are nothing but flour and yeast that's been boiled and salted. But *focaccia*," he said, his voice suddenly much warmer. "Focaccia is an Italian bread infused with the oil of olives that were cold-pressed just a few days earlier. It has rosemary and oregano baked into it. This bread is so fresh you can taste the sunlight in the herbs."

12

How did he know so much about fancy food? Katherine's friend Blanche had a brother who was a police officer, and he said Lieutenant Birch grew up at a spartan orphanage, where Katherine sometimes donated free dental care. It was *not* the kind of place where anyone could have learned to appreciate fine food. She once inspected the building, and the industrial kitchen had oatmeal and dried rice by the barrel, not cold-pressed olive oil or herbs that captured sunlight.

She wanted to tease him for waxing poetic about a loaf of bread, but her mouth was full, and yes, the way he had described it almost made her believe she could taste the sunlight. Over the years he'd taught her a lot about food during their late-night walks. Sometimes he brought her imported candy, sometimes wedges of cheese. He taught her the difference between the nutty flavor of pecorino cheese and the savory bite of aged parmesan. He claimed that his knowledge came from living above an Italian restaurant, where meals were included in the price of his rent.

A boisterous crowd loitered outside the well-lit opera house straight ahead. A tipsy gentleman wobbled off the side of the curb, spattering water onto his snowy-white dress shirt. Another man, also wearing a tuxedo, reached down to haul his companion upright.

Lieutenant Birch held his arm out around her shoulder . . . not touching, just shielding her. Jonathan Birch never touched her, but she liked being within his protective orbit as they strolled past the theatergoers. The women were probably chorus girls, still wearing stage cosmetics and spangled jewelry. Some might dismiss those girls as floozies, but Katherine saw hardworking women who rehearsed all afternoon and put on two performances each evening. They deserved her respect.

One of the young women straightened up when she spotted them. "Lieutenant!" she called in a singsongy voice. She skipped toward them and planted a smooch on Lieutenant Birch's cheek. It left a bright red lipstick mark. He swiped it with his handkerchief but couldn't wipe away the blush on both his cheeks. It was rather charming to see the famously staid Lieutenant Birch cringe under the risqué female attention.

"Isn't he a doll?" the showgirl said, twining soft white arms around his neck, but he gently disengaged.

"Run along now, Nancy," Lieutenant Birch said.

Nancy pouted. "How come you always tell me to run along? Why don't you ever come out for a drink with us?"

The staggering man in the tuxedo hiccupped. "He's on the job, Nance."

Not all the women were drunk. A couple of them looked tuckered out and ready to head home, but even they eyed Lieutenant Birch with interest.

He was a handsome man, with closely trimmed brown hair and pale blue eyes. He wasn't particularly tall or muscular. If anything, he was slightly built, but he had a clean-cut look that made him seem powerful. Maybe that wasn't quite the right word. Dangerous? Lethal? None of these words quite captured his restrained sense of tightly coiled energy. But he wasn't truly dangerous. Lieutenant Birch was the epitome of respectability. In all the time they'd known each other, he had never intentionally laid a finger on her. Sometimes their hands accidentally touched when he passed her a slice of cheese or piece of focaccia like he'd done tonight, but he always withdrew quickly, always left her wanting more.

He cared about her. She couldn't explain why, since he never tried to see her outside of these late-night walks to her subway stop. Lieutenant Birch worked a twelve-hour shift, from eight at night until eight in the morning, and during that time he spared ten minutes to walk her to the subway. It had been two years, and there was no sign he would ever push for greater intimacy. Katherine's crush was as hopeless as the chorus girls who called out in mock sorrow as he passed them by.

"Please tell me you aren't going to write about this in your

14

column," Lieutenant Birch said after the chorus girls were safely behind them.

"Not unless you want me too," she teased as they kept walking. Lieutenant Birch was one of the few outsiders who knew of her job penning an anonymous newspaper column called "While the City Sleeps." Each month she profiled various overnight occupations that helped make life in the city safe and civilized. So far she had profiled hospital staff, drivers, telephone operators, bakers, and postal sorters. Next month she had arranged to watch engineers who kept electricity working all through the night. Lieutenant Birch steadfastly resisted all her attempts to interview him. He was too closemouthed to share insight into his overnight world, but Katherine believed these nocturnal workers deserved to be seen and celebrated.

She lifted the hem of her skirt as they descended the staircase to the subway station beneath the street. She tore a stub from her booklet of tickets and headed toward the waiting area, where the coffered ceiling was held aloft by white columns. Lots of people got off work at midnight, so it was crowded. Rumbles from the 12:15 train sounded from deep inside the tile-lined tunnel.

Lieutenant Birch waited for her to board, then touched the brim of his cap. "Have a good evening, Dr. Schneider."

"You as well, Lieutenant."

The doors slid closed, and the train pulled into the darkened tunnel. Was this going to be all she ever had with Lieutenant Birch? For two years he had ensured her safety and asked nothing in return, and yet behind his calm, impassive face she sensed he hid a world of mystery.

2

Lieutenant Jonathan Birch arrived back at his station house as the sunrise began to light the city streets. The 15th Precinct was in the oldest and shabbiest station house in the city, yet he loved it here. The smells of weathered brick and hot coffee were comforting. The familiar thud of his heels on the aged wooden flooring, the rattling typewriter keys, and the endless ribbing from his fellow officers all made it feel like home.

His last duty was to write up his overnight report, most of which had been routine. He had surveilled the gambling rackets in Hell's Kitchen, where he arrested a pair of men caught shaking down a customer too drunk to protest. He gathered more evidence in an ongoing case against a cardroom that was engaging in prostitution. He'd also been monitoring the underworld activities of the Rinaldis, the notorious Mafia family in Brooklyn. Dante Rinaldi, the new ringleader, was starting to reach his tentacles into Manhattan, something Jonathan could not overlook.

The best part of his shift was always Katherine Schneider. Seeing her in the middle of his nightly rounds was a habit as engrained as fastening the buttons on his high-stand collar or adjusting the brim of his uniform's cap. When he first learned of a female dentist coming off duty each night at midnight, he instinctively showed up to watch over her. Rowdy elements tended to behave themselves when a uniformed cop was around, but over time it became obvious that the location for the dental clinic had been carefully selected. It was close to a subway stop, and security outside the high-end theaters kept seedy elements at bay. Yet this fact didn't affect Jonathan's instinctive urge to keep an eye on her.

He settled at his desk, which was one of three rolltop desks assigned to lieutenants. Each compartment of the desk was perfectly organized. After a chaotic childhood with no control over his life or surroundings, he kept his desk in rigid order. He could operate blindfolded and still know exactly where every pen or index card was filed.

The rattle of typewriter keys was in full swing, though Jonathan preferred writing his reports in longhand. He still had the Waterman fountain pen he'd been given for graduating from school. He took a good deal of ribbing over the pen, one he refused to lend to anyone. Over the years the nib had become worn to his style, and someone else might use it at a bad angle and ruin it.

His wooden office chair squeaked as he leaned back, fanning his freshly written report for a moment to dry the ink.

Jake Kendry, the officer manning the switchboard, looked over and met his gaze. "Did you hear Gallagher got a commendation yesterday?"

Jonathan froze, the report still clenched in his hand. He had only one enemy in the New York Police Department, and his name was Sean Gallagher. "What kind of commendation?" he asked, his voice deliberately casual.

"An award for exceptional merit," Jake said. "A little kid fell into the harbor yesterday and lost consciousness. Gallagher jumped in to save him. The kid probably would have drowned if not for Gallagher."

Jonathan said nothing as he started fanning the document again. "Who witnessed the event?"

"Tomaso Conti. They came back to the station house and filed the reports. Captain Avery pushed for a commendation because technically Gallagher risked his life by jumping in after the kid. It was a long way down and a dangerous dive."

"Good for Gallagher," Jonathan said calmly, rising to his feet and adjusting his tie. He filed the report on his way out the door, pondering what to do about Gallagher's commendation, for it was based on a lie.

Sean Gallagher couldn't swim. They had grown up together at the Clifton School for Orphaned Boys, where they competed in everything from grades to sports to girls, and in almost every competition, Gallagher had won. Swimming was the only area in which Jonathan had been able to triumph over the bully because Gallagher had a weird fear of getting his face wet.

Jonathan's day ought to be over, but in fact it was just beginning. He had a fraudulent report to investigate.

———

Jonathan waited until late in the afternoon to confront Gallagher down at the harbor. New York City was the largest port in the nation and had over a hundred miles of coastline. The police took shifts patrolling the waterfront on the lookout for smuggling, illegal dumping, and theft.

Or rescuing children who happened to fall into the water. Jonathan had no doubt that a kid truly had been in distress. Gallagher was too smart to have concocted a story like that out of whole cloth. But there was no way Gallagher could have been the one who saved him from drowning.

Jonathan strolled along the waterfront piers, watching gulls hover in the air. Water sloshed along the pilings, and a briny scent mingled with damp concrete and wet rope. Most of the piers were long industrial warehouses with room for ships to off-load their cargo, but Pier A at the base of Manhattan was different. The white neoclassical showpiece featured rows of arched windows and spacious walkways to take in the view. Inside, the Department of Docks collected revenue and handled administrative duties of the port, while outside was a prime spot to watch ships steaming in and out of port. Tourists and pedestrians strolled along the wooden boardwalk to enjoy the afternoon breeze, others sitting at one of the dozen tables to feast on treats from the pushcart vendors.

Jonathan bought a mug of coffee to sip while waiting for Gallagher to show up. This was Gallagher's favorite place to take a break because it gave him a chance to flirt with women. Gallagher was a good-looking man with blond hair, blue eyes, and a winning smile. Jonathan knew from painful experience how easily Gallagher could charm any woman he chose.

The tang of strong, bitter coffee was satisfying as he watched a ship pull toward Ellis Island. Most of the arriving immigrants probably didn't speak English and would have a rough few years ahead of them. He murmured a prayer for the immigrants, who had risked everything in making the journey to America, their new home.

He turned to scan the esplanade. Two men in uniform were headed this way. Jonathan squinted in the late afternoon sun. Yes, it was Gallagher and his young protégé, Patrolman Tomaso Conti.

Gallagher spotted him. It was obvious by the sneer as he leaned down to whisper something to Conti. Things were about to get interesting. Jonathan removed his cuff links and dropped them into his coat pocket before shedding his jacket and draping it over the rope fence that lined the pier.

"Nice day," he said as Gallagher and Conti approached him.

Gallagher grinned, his teeth flashing white in his tanned face. "Indeed it is, Sapling."

Growing up, Gallagher had dubbed him Sapling because of Jonathan's slim, shorter build. Five-foot-ten wasn't exactly short, but Jonathan was still several inches shorter than Gallagher's six-foot-two frame. Other kids at the Clifton School followed Gallagher's lead in calling him Sapling because most people wanted to be on Gallagher's good side.

Jonathan studied Conti, a new patrolman still learning the ropes. He seemed like a good man, but getting too close to Gallagher was not wise.

"Where did you learn how to swim, Conti?"

The young man answered without hesitation. "My dad runs a fishing boat near Cooperstown. I've always known how to swim."

"Interesting," Jonathan said, turning to face Gallagher. "I heard you had a little excitement yesterday. Tell me about it."

Gallagher shrugged and looked out at the sea. "You can read about it in the report submitted to Captain Avery."

"I'd rather watch you swim," Jonathan said calmly. "So would Conti. In fact, so would all these people on the pier today. Go ahead." He nodded toward the water. "Show everyone here how well you can swim."

"Shove off, Sapling. I'm on the clock."

Gallagher turned to walk away, gesturing for Conti to follow, but Jonathan blocked their path. He looked directly at the newly minted patrolman. "Who rescued the kid, Conti?"

The patrolman shifted nervously, swallowing so hard that his Adam's apple bounced. "Uh . . . it's in the report, sir."

The evasive answer confirmed Jonathan's suspicion. Even today, Sean Gallagher was both a bully and a leader whose goodwill was eagerly sought by the younger officers. Tomaso Conti might have felt as if he had no choice but to let Gallagher take credit for rescuing the child, although getting caught in a lie could end his career in a hurry.

Jonathan decided to have no mercy. He shifted his attention back to Gallagher. "I don't want Captain Avery to make a fool of himself by submitting an inaccurate report. I don't think you saved that kid; I think Conti here did it. Do you want to head back to the station house to correct the report? I'll go with you."

"I'll bet Charlotte would get a kick out of that," Gallagher taunted, and Jonathan stiffened. Charlotte Boroughs was the first girl Jonathan ever cared for, and Gallagher stole her away when they were sixteen years old.

"How did you rescue that kid if you can't swim?"

"I can swim," Gallagher insisted with a hard shove against Jonathan's shoulder. He managed to regain his footing and not fall into the harbor, but Gallagher didn't back away. Instead, the man stepped forward to bump chests with Jonathan. Gallagher towered four inches over him, outweighed him, and could win any contest of strength.

But Jonathan was always faster. A swift kick behind Gallagher's knee knocked him off-balance. Jonathan then tipped Gallagher over the rope fence and into the harbor.

Gallagher hit the water with a loud splash, and Jonathan reached for one of the life rings tied along the waterfront. He watched carefully, waiting for Gallagher to surface, which happened quickly.

"Hang on, sir. I'm coming!" Conti said, already shucking off his jacket.

Jonathan grasped his arm. "Wait," he ordered, then leaned over to toss the life ring to Gallagher, who grabbed it and shouted a string of obscenities.

"You're going down for this," Gallagher panted. "I'm going to see you drummed out of the police force."

"You'll have to confess what happened first," Jonathan called down.

As Gallagher continued to thrash and curse, Jonathan strolled toward a chest stacked with emergency supplies to get a rope ladder. People dining at outdoor tables stood to watch the drama, but Jonathan ignored them as he secured the rope ladder to a bollard post with a hitch knot. He motioned Patrolman Conti over to teach the younger man the procedure.

"See how I loop the end of the rope counterclockwise around

the pole? It's the best knot to use in a situation like this." He explained patiently, all while keeping an eye on Gallagher down below. There wasn't any danger, not from drowning anyway. Gallagher had an arm looped through the life ring, his other hand braced on a nearby piling. He'd be fine, but Tomaso Conti was headed for trouble if he got sucked too much deeper under Gallagher's influence.

Once both knots were securely tied, he looked up at Conti. "Ready?"

Conti still seemed thunderstruck. "I can't believe you did that, sir."

"And I can't believe you lied on an official report," Jonathan said quietly. "Don't *ever* lie on a police report, do you hear me? Captain Avery is a good man; Sean Gallagher isn't. Learn who you want to throw your lot in with, and don't waver."

Conti looked both alarmed and chastened as he nodded. Jonathan wished he didn't need to add this next part, but there was no avoiding it. Crime among the Mafia tarnished everyone with an Italian name or accent.

"You've already got a strike against you because you're Italian, and even in the police force, people make assumptions. You have to be twice as good. Twice as honest. Do you understand what I'm telling you?"

Conti sagged. "I know. My dad warned me."

"Your dad is a smart man."

Jonathan tossed the rope ladder over the pier, listening as Gallagher muttered curses the entire way up. One of the most important aspects of a fight was knowing when to end it. Jonathan stepped well away from Gallagher as the larger man emerged onto the pier, spattering water and glaring at him.

Jonathan wiped his face clean of all triumph as he looked at Conti. "I'm glad we could clear this up. Will you submit the amended report, or shall I?"

Conti shifted, looking uneasily at Gallagher.

"I'll do it," Gallagher grumbled. "It was just a stupid mistake. Isn't that right, Conti?"

"Right, sir."

"Don't submit sloppy work in the future," Gallagher told Conti in a castigating tone.

Jonathan gave a friendly cuff to Conti. "Congratulations, Patrolman. Once the clarification is submitted, I suspect a commendation for bravery is in your near future. Well deserved, I'm sure."

"Thank you, sir," Conti stammered, but Jonathan was already strolling away.

All things considered, Gallagher was getting off lightly by taking a quick toss in the harbor instead of a police investigation for lying on a report. Jonathan tried not to pick fights, but when he did, he always finished them.

There were going to be consequences for tossing Gallagher in the harbor, and they arrived the next afternoon in a summons to Captain Avery's office.

In the chain of command within the New York Police Department, Captain Avery was the top dog of the 15th Precinct, with the power to promote, demote, and set the rules. There were eighty-four precincts, each with its own station house ruled over by a captain. With over ten thousand police officers in the city, promotion to one of those eighty-four spots was a steep climb, and Captain Avery had the respect of all the men serving in his precinct.

Captain Avery's office reflected the age of the building with a maze of electrical and telephone wires anchored to the brick walls, but everything else in the office reflected Captain Avery's austere personality.

When Jonathan joined the force at age eighteen, Captain Avery was a trim man with sandy-red hair and a neatly clipped mustache. Now, sixteen years later, Captain Avery's hair was liberally sprinkled with gray, and he had a hard, flinty look as he stared Jonathan down.

"I've now heard an account of the incident at Pier A from both Patrolman Conti and Lieutenant Gallagher," Captain Avery began. "I'm ready to hear your side of the story."

Jonathan looked his captain directly in the eye and told the unvarnished, unflattering truth in a professional tone. "I suspected the official report describing Lieutenant Gallagher's rescue of a drowning child was inaccurate and asked for a demonstration of his ability to swim. When he declined the opportunity, I pressed the matter."

"You shoved him into the harbor in full view of two dozen civilians, all to carry out the unresolved schoolyard rivalry between my two best officers. I can't let this go unpunished for either one of you. I'm busting you down to desk duty and a reduction in pay for the rest of the month."

Jonathan expected no less, yet he didn't want Gallagher's attempt to cheat Conti of a medal to go unnoticed. "I hope the report of the child's rescue has been amended."

"It has. I'm also finished playing peacemaker between you and Gallagher. I'm moving him to police headquarters."

Jonathan nearly choked. "You're doing *what*?" An assignment to headquarters was tantamount to a promotion. It was where all the elite task forces met in a spectacular new building on Centre Street that looked like a palace. The gleaming, five-story citadel in the heart of Manhattan had a laboratory to analyze poisons and bombs, a shooting range in the basement, and a gymnasium to keep the police force in fighting shape. It was the finest police headquarters in the nation.

"I'm docking Gallagher two weeks' pay for that stunt with the report," Captain Avery said. "I've also added a written reprimand to his file, but we can't afford to lose him. The brass at headquarters want him for an elite new team called the Bomb Squad. Only the smartest and bravest of men are selected for it, and Gallagher has earned it."

"What's the Bomb Squad?" Jonathan asked. If it resulted in his climbing a few more rungs on the ladder with the department, he wanted to join it.

"Just like it sounds," Captain Avery said. "Men will receive specialized training to investigate and diffuse bombs. It requires knowledge of chemistry, physics, and electrical circuits. We need men of outstanding self-control, attention to detail, and excellence under pressure. They must be able to improvise solutions and have nerves of steel. Gallagher has it all. You don't."

His chin jutted up. "Sir, with respect, I can demonstrate all those criteria."

"No, you let a schoolyard grudge get the better of you. You and Gallagher can't both serve on an assignment this sensitive, and we need Gallagher more than we need you."

Captain Avery tossed a file onto the desk and gestured for Jonathan to sit and open the report. "Read it."

Jonathan tamped down the impulse to keep battling for superiority over Gallagher and flipped open the case file documenting a bomb that went off at a private home last week. Alberto Torricelli was the millionaire owner of a sugar refinery in Brooklyn. He'd been having trouble with his labor union for years, but when he refused their last set of demands, a bomb exploded at his house. Mr. Torricelli escaped injury, but the maid who picked up the package on the mansion's doorstep lost her left hand when it detonated in her arms.

The most unusual document in the file was a printed page bordered with red ink. "Copies of that document were mailed to Mr. Torricelli and to police headquarters the following day," Captain Avery said.

Jonathan scanned the text, a repetitious jumble of anarchist philosophy, political grievances, and monetary demands. The letter was signed *Achilles*.

"Achilles is the leader of a group called the Sons of Chaos," Captain Avery explained. "It's a revolutionary group, and once someone joins, they can never get out. He uses that nickname because he cuts the Achilles tendons of anyone who betrays him."

Shaking his head, Jonathan let go of the red-bordered page, letting it drop to the desktop.

"We don't know who Achilles is or if he's associated with the Mafia or an anarchist organization, but that document is the first time he's gone on record with his ranting." Captain Avery nodded to a stack of boxes on the far side of the office. "Those are complaints that have been filed with the New York Police Department over the past two years. I want you to go through each one, looking for similarities either in the tone or the content of this manifesto by Achilles."

"Yes, sir," Jonathan replied.

He didn't care for the tedium of desk duty, especially since it meant he'd no longer be able to squeeze in a chance to see Katherine Schneider each night. So be it. There was going to be a cost for exposing Gallagher's lie, and he was willing to pay it.

So Jonathan spent the next two weeks at his desk, methodically reading two years' worth of complaints about everything from stray cats to accusations of police bribery. He practically went cross-eyed by the end of each day. Nevertheless, he felt a strange sort of enjoyment from reading the letters. They reflected the character and diversity of the city. Some letters were terse, direct complaints, while others were written by people struggling with the English language. Some were littered with obscenities and threats, others showing great formality. A few even closed with prayers for the safety of the police officers.

At the end of his assignment, he hadn't found any similarities between the Achilles screed and earlier letters of complaints, but he did learn a few things about Achilles.

The manifesto reflected a well-rounded education, containing references to anarchist philosophy and classical allegories. He probably had a college education, his intent was to tear down the ruling classes, and he probably wasn't Italian. No Italian would have consistently used Greek classical references when there was a Roman equivalent.

And yet the note concluded by warning Mr. Torricelli to expect more bombs unless he deposited $5,000 into a bank in Sicily. That sort of international extortion was a classic Mafia technique used to block the police from following the money trail. It was easy to understand Captain Avery's confusion about whether Achilles was part of the Italian Mafia or an anarchist group since his behavior seemed consistent with both.

Jonathan submitted his conclusions to Captain Avery at the end of his two-week punishment but was no closer to identifying this new and terrifying criminal element beginning to take root in the city. Serving on the police force was the greatest privilege of Jonathan's life. Maybe Gallagher had beaten him on a promotion to police headquarters, but Jonathan would redouble his efforts to track down Achilles and the Sons of Chaos.

Keeping the forces of darkness and corruption at bay was a never-ending battle, but Jonathan would pay any price to keep his city safe.

3

While the Martha Washington Hotel was not without its flaws, the place had been a godsend for Katherine. Her parents would never have consented to letting her venture into the urban wilds of New York City were it not for the existence of the female-only apartment building that catered to career women. The Martha Washington had a few rooms that could be rented by the week, yet most of the twelve stories were apartments occupied by single women such as herself. It opened in 1903 and was immediately filled to capacity with five hundred female teachers, stenographers, nurses, and other professional women who could afford the rent.

Katherine's eighth-floor apartment had a bedroom and a compact sitting area complete with a wash sink and a view across 29th Street. A bathroom at the end of the hall was shared by all forty-five women who lived on the floor. Everyone who lived here was gainfully employed, but Katherine was one of the few women who worked a late shift. That could cause problems, like this morning when Florence Barlow exercised her considerable lung power to berate whoever used the last of the hot water.

It was seven o'clock in the morning when Florence started making a racket. Katherine rolled out of bed, darted across the cold tile floor, and cracked open the door. "Flo, some of us are still sleeping."

"I need to wash my hair before work this morning, and how am I supposed to do that when someone used up all the hot water?"

"However you manage it, please do it quietly," Katherine said before closing the door and hopping back into bed. She pulled a mask over her eyes to block the light and waited for sleep to claim her. It was best to sleep at least until ten o'clock, which could be a challenge when most of the people on her floor were up and out right after breakfast.

Sleep wouldn't come because thoughts of Lieutenant Birch kept intruding, triggering a thrill of anticipation. After a two-week absence, he suddenly appeared again last night, this time with a paper sack filled with almond biscotti.

How long had he carried around that sack of biscotti before handing it over to her at midnight? He *had* to care for her, even though he refused to explain where he'd been for the last two weeks.

Katherine tucked her nose inside the paper sack and breathed deeply. The scent of almonds and amaretto smelled divine. Residents were forbidden from storing food in their apartments because Mrs. Blum feared pests, and it wasn't worth upsetting the building's notoriously strict chaperone. Still, the biscotti was too delicious to waste, and Katherine could smuggle it to Blanche, who had another half hour on her overnight shift at the building's front desk.

Katherine dressed and wrapped a shawl around her shoulders to hide the biscotti from the elevator attendant during the long ride down to the first floor. Most of the hotel's staff were women, including the elevator attendants and those working the front desk. Shortly after opening, there were some sketchy incidents when male staff tried to get overly familiar with the residents, and the Martha Washington couldn't afford to let that sort of thing tarnish their reputation. The men were let go, and women were hired in their place. The ground floor of the building had a restaurant, a library, a hair salon, and a newsstand—all of them staffed by women who lived in the building.

The lobby was as elegant as any high-end hotel, with coffered ceilings and Persian carpets warming the tiled floor. Hand-carved walnut paneling covered the walls and front counter. Even the hundreds of cubbyholes behind the desk for residents' mail were made of walnut.

"You're up early," Blanche said when Katherine arrived at the front counter.

"Guess who showed up again last night?" Katherine confided in a low, excited voice.

Blanche's eyes widened. "Your long-lost lieutenant?"

Katherine pushed the paper sack to Blanche with a grin, all the response that was needed. Blanche peeked inside.

"Well done!" she said before hiding the sack behind the counter. "Did he say where he'd been all this time?"

Katherine rolled her eyes. "I asked, but he launched into a monologue about the history of biscotti and how it dated all the way back to when Roman legions took the hard cookies with them on their campaigns."

It was typical of Lieutenant Birch's reluctance to talk about himself, and yet she was so relieved to see him again that she hadn't pressed the matter.

After Blanche finished her overnight shift, the two of them headed outside to a bench opposite the building to share the rest of the biscotti and watch people hurrying on their way to work. The clang of streetcar bells mingled with clopping horse hooves as hundreds of people geared up for a busy day ahead.

It didn't take long before Katherine spotted the skinny man on the corner, wearing a painter's cap and wiggling a cup. The same man had been loitering on that corner for almost a month. Katherine patted her skirt pocket, feeling about for a few coins.

"Don't you dare," Blanche said. "Sometimes I think he shows up there just because he knows you're an easy mark."

"He needs money for his baby girl's operation," Katherine said. How could she refuse a man trying to help his child? He once told her that he didn't earn much as a house painter, and his little girl would walk with a limp forever if she didn't get an operation.

"Look at him!" Blanche scoffed. "That man is at least sixty—he doesn't have a baby girl. You need to quit being so gullible."

Katherine paid her no mind. She had but a single quarter in her pocket, and she hurried over to drop it into the man's cup.

"Thank you, ma'am! My boy really needs that operation, and you're an angel walking this earth."

Katherine returned to the bench, hoping that Blanche hadn't overheard. But the glint in her friend's eyes said otherwise. Katherine shrugged it off with a good-natured smile. Maybe she was too trusting, but wasn't that better than being cynical and suspicious? Yes, sometimes she still felt like a green girl from Ohio, but she loved New York with all its hustling businessmen, shifty beggars, and mysterious cops. She didn't believe God led her to New York to make her hard and cynical. Katherine would continue to cheerfully help people wherever possible and wouldn't let the darker side of the city get her down.

Would that attitude get her into trouble someday? Probably not, but even if it did, she'd face whatever came at her with faith and good cheer.

Saturday afternoons were a special treat for Katherine. It was the day she and her fellow residents who worked late shifts enjoyed a leisurely afternoon luncheon at the Martha Washington's rooftop café. The spot overlooked Midtown and included a lovely promenade featuring flower-box planters brimming with geraniums, marigolds, and vines of ivy.

Everyone brought something to share as they relaxed and talked about their week. These women had been the first people Katherine interviewed for her "While the City Sleeps" column. Blanche was the overnight desk clerk at the hotel, and Midge Lightner worked at the hospital. Midge was seventy-three years old and had been a nurse during the Civil War. She never married and had no children but was like a grandmother to everyone who lived at the Martha Washington. Inga Klein was the fourth member of their little group. She worked as an overnight wireless operator at the port, but she was strangely absent today.

"Here, have a pear," Midge said as she finished slicing the fruit. "Pears are good for your digestion and will offset those wonderful cookies you brought, Katherine."

"Lieutenant Birch told me they're healthy cookies and don't have too much sugar," Katherine said. He'd brought two dozen of the toasted hazelnut cookies to her last night when he walked her home. "I think he made them because dentists are supposed to hate sugar, but I love it."

"You really think that policeman bakes these cookies himself?" Midge asked, skepticism in her voice.

"I think he does," Katherine said. "He knows too much about baking to have learned it any other way."

"How could he bake if he lives in a rooming house?" Blanche asked.

"There's an Italian restaurant on the first floor of his building. Maybe they let him use the kitchen."

"I think you're letting your imagination run away with you again," Midge said. "The man surely buys everything from a bakery, and you're filling in the gaps with all sorts of fantasies."

Maybe, but he was so secretive, it was hard not to speculate about Lieutenant Birch's life story. She shrugged and reached for a section of the newspaper they shared each Saturday. The *New York Journal* was their favorite newspaper because it was scandalously fun and had lots of pictures. Plus its owner supported Edgar in his quest to keep advertising their clinic as "Painless Parker Dentistry."

Blanche liked it for the juicy scandals. She was in the middle of reading them a story about a murderous widow suspected of killing a string of husbands when the door to the rooftop café opened and Inga finally joined them.

"Sorry I'm late," she said, dropping a round of cheese on the table so abruptly that the silverware jumped. Inga's blond chignon was messy, her typically cheerful demeanor absent. "Bad night down at the harbor."

Midge frowned. "What happened, dearest?"

Inga's work as a wireless operator required communicating with ships as they neared port. She was originally from Germany but had lived in America since childhood. She was perfectly fluent in both English and Morse code. No ships were scheduled to dock or depart overnight, so Inga usually didn't have much to do in the long hours after the sun went down. On the rare nights when things got busy, it was often an emergency.

"A ship caught fire about ten miles off the coast," Inga said. "It was the *Lorna Doone*, an old wooden schooner that's been making cargo runs to Miami every week for the past twenty years. They wired in a little after midnight to report a fire in their hold, and they couldn't put it out. The harbormaster told them to head back to port, and he sent the fireboats out to meet them."

The only time Katherine had seen the harbor's fireboats in action was during a parade to welcome the arrival of President Wilson last year. The sturdy boats were fitted with pumps and nozzles to shoot huge arcs of water toward shipboard fires, although they could also be used for festive displays during a parade. The fireboats pumped out fantastic twirling arcs of water to the delight of the crowds during the president's welcoming ceremony.

The true purpose of a fireboat was far more dire. Inga looked destroyed as she continued speaking. "I took their distress messages for almost an hour. The wireless operator on the *Lorna Doone* was named Clyde. I had taken a lot of messages from him over the years."

Katherine caught her breath. The way Inga referred to Clyde in the past tense had an ominous ring.

"Clyde reported that they couldn't put the fire out no matter how much water the fireboats threw at it. New fires kept starting. He said they might have to abandon the ship, and then he stopped communicating. I sent message after message, but he never answered."

Inga was silent for a while, staring at her hands clenched in her lap. Then she continued, "Both fireboats got back to port an hour later with everyone from the *Lorna Doone* because the ship had to be abandoned. They said that sometime during the night, Clyde got hit on the head by a falling timber in the control room. Everyone thought he'd be okay. He kept wiring messages to me for a long time after he took that blow, but then he stood up and collapsed. They loaded him onto a fireboat, but he was dead by the time they got him back to port."

Inga looked at Midge. "I don't understand how that could happen. The other people on the crew said he had been fine after he got hit. He kept sending messages for an hour. How could he just drop dead?"

"Oh, my dearest," Midge said, a world of hurt in her old voice. "It sounds like he suffered a concussion. Sometimes people are fine, but sometimes the damage builds up inside their skull and then they are taken."

Inga went back to staring at her hands. "I never knew he was hurt. I was one of the last people he ever talked to. I feel like it's my fault I didn't spot it."

How could Inga possibly have known? Wireless operators communicated through Morse code. The electronic pulses wired through the air carried no emotion.

"I never met him in person, but I've been trading messages with him for years," Inga added. "He must have been a brave man to have kept at his post while the ship was burning all around him."

"Yes, a very brave man," Midge echoed. As a Civil War nurse,

Midge surely had been at the bedsides of countless brave men who passed away, but this sort of thing was new for the rest of them.

Inga glanced at the newspapers spread out on the table. "I suppose it happened too late to be reported in the morning papers?"

Katherine nodded. "I didn't see anything about a ship fire."

"I'll have to buy the late edition," Inga said. "I expect the sinking of the *Lorna Doone* will make the front page."

Katherine paused. Where had she heard that name before? A patient from a few weeks ago had babbled something about a person named Lorna Doone, but the details were fuzzy. Could her patient have been a sailor on the ship that sank last night? If so, what a terribly strange coincidence.

———

Katherine's parents always teased her for having an overactive imagination. As a child she was convinced the postman was actually Santa Claus in disguise who was checking up on her. Later, when her fiancé, Paul, repeatedly delayed their wedding date, she invented all sorts of innocent explanations to excuse his behavior. Even now, her lively imagination led her into an infatuation with a taciturn police officer when she knew literally nothing about his private life.

So yes, she had an active imagination, and yet the afternoon edition of the newspaper reported that the fire aboard the *Lorna Doone* was considered suspicious. The inability to quench the fire had been odd, and sailors reported that new fires continued to break out during the three-hour period before the ship sank.

Maybe it was sheer coincidence that a ship named the *Lorna Doone* sank a few weeks after her patient bemoaned something about "sad, sad Lorna Doone." The details of her encounter with the patient were starting to come back. He had been a big guy, and his companion couldn't speak English. She was pretty sure they were Italian because when they spoke to each other, they used that beguiling manner with lots of vowels and melodic, lilting cadences.

She remembered it was a little funny how such a big, burly man had been so mournful about a novel. *Lorna Doone* was the title of a novel, wasn't it?

After lunch, Katherine paid a visit to the library on the first floor of the Martha Washington. Elbow-high bookshelves ringed three walls, leaving plenty of space for windows overlooking 29th Street. Upholstered chairs nestled before a small fireplace, and the long table down the center of the room hosted card games and jigsaw puzzles over the two years Katherine had lived here.

A compact box atop a corner table served as a card catalog. Katherine flipped through the cards but couldn't find any books called *Lorna Doone*. Luckily, Delia Byrne was curled up with a book in one of the comfy corner chairs, and Delia was one of the best-read people Katherine knew.

"Dee, are you familiar with a book with the title *Lorna Doone*?"

Delia rolled her eyes. "When I was a kid, I read that novel so many times the spine fell apart. I was halfway in love with the hero, and I wanted to *be* Lorna Doone."

"Sad, sad Lorna Doone" was what the patient had mumbled. "Is it a happy or a sad novel?" she asked.

"Oh, it's both," Delia said, straightening in the chair, eager to summarize the tale of star-crossed lovers battling against the forces of evil. "But it has a happy ending, of course. Lorna survives to marry John, and the two live happily ever after."

Katherine gazed at the city outside the oversized window. Five million people lived in the city. Five million! The odds that someone involved in a suspicious shipboard fire had visited her clinic shortly before a crime and babbled about it while under the influence of nitrous oxide was ridiculously tiny.

She couldn't report it to the police. What other evidence did she have that those men might have had foreknowledge of the ship's fire? That they were Italian? Such a charge would be bigoted and irrational. If she tried to report this to the police, they would laugh her out of the station.

Lieutenant Birch wouldn't laugh at her. First of all, Jonathan Birch never laughed. Secondly, he knew her to be a sensible person and not a crackpot who saw conspiracies everywhere. What she overheard was probably nothing, but her conscience wouldn't rest until she confided in someone qualified to judge the situation correctly.

It was time to head to the 15th Precinct and ask for Lieutenant Birch.

4

Jonathan's strongest asset had always been his speed, and that skill transferred to his ability to handle a gun. It was why he'd been appointed to train an elite corps of Italian American detectives charged with taking on the Mafia. The Italian Squad had been formed in response to the ominous rise in crime among Italian communities that could no longer be handled through traditional means. It was led by Lieutenant Joe Petrosino, New York's most celebrated police detective, until a Mafia assassin cut him down a few years ago.

The city ground to a halt, and the mayor declared a day of mourning. The funeral was held in Saint Patrick's Cathedral, and over two hundred thousand people crowded the streets to pay their respects. Rather than discouraging the Italian Squad, the police department invested more money and training in the brave officers willing to serve.

Jonathan, the best sharpshooter in the department, met with squad members at the shooting range in the basement of police headquarters on Centre Street. He trained the men on long range, short range, quick draw, and sniper work using paper targets.

Today's lesson was on quick draw of a concealed weapon when the officers were on undercover duty.

"You can hide your pistol tucked into your trousers at the small of your back, but you'll be better off carrying it at your side," Jonathan said. All three of the officers he was training were skeptical a pistol could escape detection there, even though Jonathan repeatedly showed them how a loose jacket could disguise the weapon.

"Get used to carrying at all times," Jonathan stressed. "The street gangs you'll be infiltrating will be armed and won't think it strange for you to carry a weapon. The trick is to be faster than they are."

"What about accuracy?" the youngest and newest member of the squad asked. Sergeant Matteo Sizmetti, or Smitty as everyone called him, was a nice kid. Probably *too* nice for this line of work.

Smitty had married at eighteen, was a father by nineteen, and now at twenty-four he was like the younger brother Jonathan always wished he had. With bulging eyes and a weak chin, Smitty was possibly the homeliest man this side of the Mississippi, but he had a heart of pure gold, along with a wife and three kids who adored him.

"Being fast is no excuse for poor aim," Jonathan said. "You'll be going into some crowded neighborhoods, so accuracy is essential."

"Sean Gallagher said you're a lousy shot on the quick draw," one of the other officers said. "Yesterday he shot a ninety-two at target practice. Three inner rings plus a bull's-eye."

Jonathan skewered him with a withering glare. "I don't believe it."

If Gallagher would cheat to win a commendation, he'd cheat in a shooting contest. Smitty headed over to the front counter and asked the clerk for Gallagher's paper target. Gallagher was so vain, he wanted it pinned up behind the counter for all to see, the highest target score all month.

"Set it up at the end of the range," Jonathan said.

Smitty looked at him in surprise as all the men gathered around to watch. The rivalry between him and Gallagher was about to enter its next phase. A better man would congratulate Gallagher and return to the lesson, but Jonathan wasn't in the mood. Besides, it was important that the men in the Italian Squad implicitly trust him as the department's authority on marksmanship.

An eerie calm came over him as he loaded six bullets. He waited until Smitty returned from setting up Gallagher's target before he carefully holstered his pistol at his side. He wouldn't make this easier by taking the time to carefully aim; he would beat Gallagher using a quick draw. All eyes were on him. Gallagher wasn't even in the building and yet the next sixty seconds would be a man-to-man contest between the two of them.

In a flash, he drew the gun and fired. Two inches to the left of Gallagher's bull's-eye. There were a few sympathetic murmurs as he holstered the gun. He shook his hands out, stilled, then stared hard at the target. He drew and fired the next shot so quickly that everyone in the room jumped.

Exactly two inches to the right of Gallagher's bull's-eye.

His next shot was two inches above, and his fourth shot two inches below. He cast a cocky look at Smitty. "What do you think? Should I aim for his bull's-eye?"

A roar of affirmations met his challenge. "Do it," Smitty said, a wide grin spreading across his young, homely face in anticipation.

The clerk at the front counter stepped forward. "Excuse me, sir. You just got a message sent from the 15th Precinct. Do you know someone named Katherine Schneider?"

He lowered his pistol. "Yes," he said cautiously.

"She came by the station house looking for you. She needs to report something."

His mouth went dry. People rarely sought out a police officer for good reasons. "Did she say anything more?"

"No, sir. Just that it wasn't an emergency, but she wants you to call on her when you go back on duty. She's at the Martha Washington."

In the two years since he met Katherine Schneider, this was the first time she had turned to him for anything. He wasn't officially back on duty until eight o'clock tonight. It was time to regain his concentration and blow a new hole straight into Gallagher's bull's-eye. He drew the pistol and fired.

Five inches wide of the mark. It barely even hit the paper target.

"Better luck next time," one of the men said, and Jonathan grimaced. This was likely to get back to Gallagher and give the bully just one more reason to gloat.

Katherine spent her Saturday evening at home awaiting the arrival of Lieutenant Birch. Her apartment had a small sitting nook adjoining the bedroom, where she curled up on the chair, a pad of paper on her lap, while she toyed with ideas for professions to feature in her "While the City Sleeps" monthly column.

Her column began shortly after she arrived in New York as a project to get her mind off a broken heart. It had been an impulsive decision, inspired by the people she met during her late-night employment. Until she started working at night, she had no idea about the huge range of jobs people carried out while the rest of the world slept.

All her articles for "While the City Sleeps" were flattering. She deliberately looked for the valiant and admirable aspects to highlight. Yes, some of the people who worked the graveyard shifts might be maladjusted or odd. Even so, they deserved to have their hard work recognized.

To her surprise, the public was hungry for her optimistic articles that celebrated ordinary New Yorkers carrying out their unique jobs in the middle of the night. Amid the never-ending articles about crime and corruption, Katherine's monthly column made people feel good about their city.

It was nine o'clock when the telephone in Katherine's apartment finally rang. She tossed her pencil down to answer the call on its first ring.

"There is a policeman here to see you." The disapproval in Mrs. Blum's voice snaked up through the phone line. The Martha Washington did not welcome men who called on residents after dark, and visits from the police or anything else that carried a whiff of scandal were especially unwelcome. Mrs. Blum was a busybody who justified her spying and eavesdropping on telephone calls by claiming she was safeguarding the morals of the residents.

"I'll be right down," Katherine said, instinctively smoothing a few loose strands of hair into the chignon at the back of her head. She adjusted her collar on the elevator ride down and spotted Lieutenant Birch at the front of the lobby once the elevator doors slid open. She closed the distance between them.

"What's going on?" he asked, his face tense with concern.

Mrs. Blum glowered at her from behind the lobby's front counter. Katherine didn't want to blurt the story out with the apartment's fustiest matron within earshot.

"There's a private dining room where we can speak," Katherine said, gesturing toward one of the three rooms that could be rented out by ladies who wished to host private gatherings.

Mrs. Blum hurried over to intercede. "We don't permit men to be alone with our residents after dark," she insisted. "If you need privacy, you may speak in my office."

"Thank you, ma'am," Lieutenant Birch said. Unruffled. Polite. Alluring.

Katherine pushed the thought away as Mrs. Blum opened the wooden gate to allow them behind the counter and into her back office. There wasn't a lot of room, as two desks, the telephone switchboard, and a wall of filing cabinets took up most of the space.

Mrs. Blum insisted on leaving the door open. Lieutenant Birch sat on one of the desk chairs and gestured for her to take the other.

"Tell me what you need," he said. Though his expression remained calm, the intensity in his gaze was disconcerting.

"Did you hear about the fire on a ship named the *Lorna Doone*?"

"I did, yes. What about it?"

"I'm probably overreacting, which is why I didn't want to file a report with the officer at the police station. I might have witnessed something, but I don't want to accuse anyone without good cause."

"I understand." He nodded slowly. "Just tell me what you know."

Katherine relayed everything she could remember that the patient said about "sad, sad Lorna Doone," and his odd comment about Lorna Doone not being a boring gray lady. Then she told him about the other strange things the patient had rambled about, how Vittorio wondered if Cleopatra might get mad at him, mentioning something about Saint Patrick, and that he'd been singing "The Sugar-Plum Tree" when he staggered off into the night.

Lieutenant Birch took careful notes as she talked, writing everything down in a little notepad. What extraordinary penmanship he had. Did they teach that at the Clifton School for Orphaned Boys? Somehow she never expected a police officer would have such beautiful handwriting. Each word was written at a perfect slant, the capital letters given elegant loops and flourishes. She almost didn't want to stop talking because then he'd stop writing, and the way his hand wielded the pencil . . .

He was watching her. "Anything else?"

She jerked her attention away from his hands. "No, that's all. I know it's not much to go on."

"No, it's not," he agreed. "That's all he said?"

"I'm afraid so. I'm sorry to have called you over something that's probably of no account."

He gave a dismissive wave as he closed the notepad. "It's not a problem at all. Here, I brought you something."

For the first time she noticed the brown paper bag, and a guilty thrill surged. Maybe he would forever keep her at arm's length, but these little presents were a sign that she was special to him. The bag crinkled as she peeked inside, a grin spreading across her face. "Chocolate biscotti?" she said.

He gave a single nod. "I know you like it."

She loved it. He first brought it to her on a rainy night shortly after they met. He told her it was best with coffee, making biscotti the perfect excuse to have a cookie for breakfast.

"Thank you!" she said. "I went to an Italian bakery looking for something like this, but the lady said she'd never heard of chocolate biscotti."

"It's hard to find. My grandmother made the world's best chocolate biscotti. Nobody else could make it with that same crumbly, crisp perfection. She used to bribe me with it. Anytime I didn't want to do my chores or study for school, she'd promise chocolate biscotti if I did a good job."

Katherine hung on his words. This was the first glimpse into his life he ever offered. She didn't want to pry, but . . .

Actually, she *did* want to pry. She wanted to know everything about Lieutenant Jonathan Birch's life and where he grew up and how he learned so much about baking. She wanted to know if he had a woman in his life and why he went out of his way to escort her to the subway stop for the past two years. Why he never let her get close to him. Now he was about to leave her once again, so she scrambled for an excuse to prolong their time together.

"How old were you when she died?"

He looked surprised, but only for a moment. "My grandmother? I was fourteen." He tucked the stubby pencil back into his pocket and prepared to leave.

"How did she die?"

"She died in her sleep, so I don't really know. One day she was alive and healthy and baking up a storm, and then the next morning she didn't wake up. That's when I went to live at the Clifton School for Orphaned Boys."

"I'm so sorry," she said quietly. Fourteen was far too young to be left all alone in the world. How different her own life had been, growing up with two doting parents in idyllic Hudson, Ohio. They lived in a sprawling Queen Anne-style house with her father's dental practice on the first floor, where she grew up showered with love. During the summers she helped at her father's clinic, and when she said she wanted to become a dentist too, they paid for her to attend the shockingly expensive Philadelphia Dental College. Her parents still bombarded her with letters, care packages, and even a monthly long-distance telephone call that was obscenely expensive but something they all enjoyed.

It wasn't fair to probe into Lieutenant Birch's painful past when hers had been so perfect. Still, she didn't want to let him get away. Not yet.

She broke off an end from a rectangle of biscotti and offered it to him. He agreeably popped it into his mouth while she snapped off another for herself. It melted on her tongue, first the chocolate flooding her with contentment, then the collapse of the sweet, crisp biscuit. This might be the most perfect recipe since mankind invented bread thousands of years ago.

Lieutenant Birch licked a crumb from his thumb and started heading toward the office door.

She sprang to her feet. "Where did you get this biscotti?" she asked. "It's so delicious, and I've visited every bakery within miles and haven't been able to find one that makes it."

He turned, leaning against the doorframe, the hint of a smile on his lips. It reached all the way up to his eyes. "It's tough to find. Sometimes you need connections with a good baker."

"Tell me where I can find this special baker. I can't keep depending on your generosity."

He glanced over her shoulder, watching Mrs. Blum file cards at the front counter. He was stalling for time, but finally answered, "I got it downtown, near the police headquarters. I can't remember the name of the place."

She didn't believe him. He didn't look her in the eye, and he knew so much about baking, whether it was focaccia or biscotti or the million different varieties of flour. Bread flour, almond flour, semolina flour—what sort of man knew such things?

He baked it himself. He had to have.

She stepped a little closer and took a risk. "Will you give me the recipe? For chocolate biscotti?"

"I don't have it," he said, glancing over her shoulder again. He was a terrible liar, but he'd always been so thoughtful and generous, and it wasn't any of her business why he wouldn't confess to baking for her. Yet it sent a secret thrill knowing that he had. He was blushing. Actually blushing!

She stepped even closer to whisper, "If I'm ever on my deathbed, I hope you will cave in and give me the recipe."

He lowered his head until his nose almost touched hers. His eyes gleamed, and his voice was soft, almost velvety. "I don't know the recipe, but I promise . . . if you are ever on your deathbed, I will personally deliver as much chocolate biscotti as you like."

She locked gazes with him, uncertain whether to laugh or to rise up on her tiptoes to steal a kiss. For he was flirting with her, and there might never be a better—

"Katherine!" Mrs. Blum called out from the front room. "A little decorum, please!"

Lieutenant Birch jerked away, and all hope of a kiss soon evaporated. Mrs. Blum had the heart of a python and seemed savagely pleased to catch a resident on the verge of falling into temptation. Katherine swallowed back her frustration as she followed Lieutenant Birch into the lobby.

He paused to stare at a portrait in the foyer. "Who's she?" he asked.

"That's Martha Washington, the lady the building is named after. I gather she was a wonderful woman, but . . . " Her voice trailed away. Everyone who saw the reproduction of the famous painting by Charles Wilson Peale had the same reaction. The old woman looked stern, frumpy, and distinctly unappealing with her gray hair peeking out from an unflattering mobcap.

Lieutenant Birch's mouth curved a tiny bit in his version of a smile. "She looks rather daunting," he said of Mrs. Washington. "My grandmother was just such a woman. She could bake cookies and distribute hugs, but she could also have led the charge at Gettysburg. Both old ladies would be a good role model for the women who live here."

Katherine wanted to tear her hair out. Jonathan had been within an inch of kissing her until Mrs. Blum butted in, and now he compared her to Martha Washington? She raised a brow and gave him a pointed look. "I hope you don't consider me in the same category as your grandmother."

"Never," Lieutenant Birch said. His voice was warm with admiration as he met her gaze. "I consider you to be the kind of woman who makes poets burn the midnight oil."

He gave her a respectful nod of farewell, then retreated. Katherine remained motionless as he crossed the lobby, exited the hotel, and disappeared into the night.

Perhaps she had an overactive imagination, but the yearning she just saw in Lieutenant Birch's eyes could have set the building on fire.

The first thing Jonathan did after leaving Katherine was to head down to Pier A to follow up on what she told him about the *Lorna Doone*. A team of fire inspectors were already looking into the sinking of the ship, and Katherine's strange tale was too much of a long shot to distract them with, especially since Jonathan could follow up on it himself.

Most of the employees who worked for the Department of Docks were long gone for the day, but a night clerk was still on duty. Jonathan's footsteps echoed down the vacant halls as he approached the main office.

"May I please see the schedule of ships slated to anchor here in the next month?" he asked the clerk. Jonathan was in uniform, which tended to earn immediate cooperation.

The night clerk led Jonathan to a cluttered office, where the port inspectors worked. He clicked on an electric lamp and opened the logbooks, scanning the names of the ships scheduled for arrival and departure.

Nothing named Cleopatra, Saint Patrick, or The Sugar-Plum Tree. He breathed a sigh of relief. Dr. Schneider had probably let her imagination get the better of her, but he liked that she had confided in him. It was flattering.

She was too good for a man like him. He ought to feel guilty for letting her believe he was as clean-cut and wholesome as she was. Nothing could ever come of their fleeting interactions, and yet those few minutes after midnight were the best part of his day.

It was two o'clock in the morning when he left the waterfront. He nodded to a couple of patrol officers, moving along quickly. Unlike the well-lit and well-traveled area in the theater district, the waterfront was a dicey part of town this late at night. Few people had any legitimate business being down at the wharves so late, yet plenty of people congregated outside the taverns or strolled drunkenly along the streets. They were mostly sailors and long-shoremen, with prostitutes, gamblers, and grifters also in the mix.

He walked along the esplanade, staring at the man ahead of him. The clothes were a little sloppy, but he wore very fine boots. New, with no wear in the heels. The man's gait was familiar, as was the broad set of his shoulders and the way his dark hair curled at his nape.

Jonathan quickened his pace to catch up to him. He kept his hand on his service revolver, even though people rarely picked fights with cops in uniform. He risked a quick glance as he drew alongside the man, frowning as his suspicion was confirmed. Dante Rinaldi was the kingpin of the most corrupt Mafia family in Brooklyn, and he had no business being in Manhattan.

"Hello, Dante," Jonathan said.

Dante slanted him a quick glare. "I'm not doing anything wrong. Mind your own business."

"What are you doing on this side of the river?"

Dante's jaw tightened. "Minding my own business, just like you should be doing."

Maybe, but they had a deal, and Dante was breaking it. "I'm just here to say hello and point out that I've noticed you," he said calmly. "I'm heading back to my precinct. I suggest you get back to your side of the river too."

Instead of being decent, Dante spat on the ground. Jonathan managed to step away in time, but the message was clear. Dante Rinaldi was a nasty piece of work and that would probably never change. The gangster turned and headed toward the Bowling Green subway station. The subway ran around the clock and would soon take Dante back to Brooklyn where he belonged.

"And don't come back," Jonathan called after him.

Dante gave him a rude gesture but kept walking.

Jonathan didn't mind. Instead, he headed toward the stairway leading up to the elevated train. Once on the platform, he had a bird's-eye view of the harbor and was relieved to catch sight of Dante stepping down into the subway.

The fact that Dante was in Manhattan wasn't good, and Jonathan was going to be forced to resurrect old rivalries to keep an eye on him.

5

Of all the men serving on the Italian Squad, Jonathan feared for young Smitty the most. Last night's brush with Dante Rinaldi brought back ugly memories of how tough the Italian underworld could be. The Mafia thought any Italian who cooperated with the police was a traitor who deserved a swift execution, which was why Jonathan went out of his way to provide extra coaching to Smitty.

They were the only two men in the station house dormitory as he showed Smitty how to hide knives in various parts of his clothing. Switchblades weren't standard gear provided by the department, but if Smitty's life was on the line, Jonathan would be sure the young man knew how to fight hard and dirty.

"You don't need much of a blade," he told Smitty. "Two inches will be enough so long as you get it out quick and have a good grasp."

He showed Smitty how to hide it on his ankle, drawing on shadowy memories of watching his father teach his older brothers how to hide weapons in their clothes. Knives, brass knuckles, steel batons, his father had all sorts of underworld tools. During one particularly brutal snowstorm in the dark of night, Jonathan remembered watching in wide-eyed fascination as the men of the family suited up.

"Where are you going?" he had asked his father in bewilderment.

"Never you mind," he gruffly replied. "In a few years you'll understand about payoff nights and want to come along too."

Jonathan straightened in righteous indignation. "No! I'll stay back to protect Grandmother."

The men had all laughed, and by the time Jonathan was old enough to know the meaning of a payoff night, his father and older brothers were all dead, so it never became an issue. He had absorbed his father's lessons, though, and now had a duty to pass them on to Smitty.

"Always avoid a fight if you can," Jonathan said. "If you can't, be sure to throw the first punch. Make it quick and hard. While the other guy is reeling, reach for a knife."

"I don't know if I can use a knife on another person," Smitty said, and Jonathan tried not to wince.

"You're too nice for this job. The Mafia is ruthless, and they have a special hate for any Italian who joins the Italian Squad."

"I need the money," Smitty said with a shrug. There were a lot of reasons the men serving on the Italian Squad got paid more. They had to be fluent in Italian, willing to investigate their fellow countrymen, but the biggest issue was the shortened life expectancy.

"Do you value money more than a long life?" Jonathan asked.

Smitty sighed. "I've got a wife and three kids."

"Which is why you shouldn't be on the Italian Squad."

Smitty rambled a long and explosive stream in Italian, ending with "*Il denaro apre tutte le porte*."

Jonathan shook his head. "What does that mean?"

"It means I'm broke, and money opens doors. I'll get a big bonus in my paycheck after I complete my first year on the squad. I can't afford to turn it down. Wait until you get married and have kids. Then you'll understand about needing to earn a little extra."

Jonathan said nothing as he continued showing Smitty how to draw a switchblade, but his mind wandered to Katherine Schneider. The few minutes when he walked her home at night were a tiny glimpse into what his life could have been like if he were an ordinary man. If things were different, he would have liked to court her. She was pretty and smart, but mostly it was how wholesome she was that attracted him to her. Katherine was the most sunny, optimistic person he'd ever met. He liked the way she looked at him as though he was an aboveboard, straitlaced police officer.

He wasn't, and he cared too much for Katherine to ever let her see the other side of his life.

―――――――

The residents of the Martha Washington were professional women ranging in age from their early twenties all the way through gray-haired ladies like Midge. But one of the quirks of living there was the necessity of chaperones. The Martha Washington couldn't afford to let their reputation slip by allowing women to entertain men inside the building or indulge any of the thousands of temptations offered by the city. Mrs. Blum threatened to evict anyone caught violating the rules for ladylike comportment and cleanliness in all aspects of their lives.

Strict building rules were why the women of the eighth floor had a tight sisterhood protecting their guilty secret. They named her Celine, and she was a barn owl who'd built a nest on the ledge outside the eighth-floor communal room window. Pets were strictly forbidden in the hotel, and Celine made quite a mess.

Like all barn owls, Celine had a white heart-shaped face, yet her wings were a golden brown flecked with darker spots. Why she chose to nest on the ledge below their window was a mystery, but she was now incubating a clutch of three eggs, and Katherine liked to peek at their illegal resident a few times each day. Celine usually slept during the day, which gave Katherine a chance to huddle in close for a good view of the owl without alarming her.

Someone was already curled up at the window seat when Katherine tiptoed into the common room at noon. "What are you doing here?" she asked in surprise.

Delia Byrne had a demanding job as a stenographer, so it was odd to see her here in the middle of the afternoon. Normally, Delia spent her days keying verbatim transcripts of depositions at the law firm where she worked. Her slender fingers moved across the keyboard of a steno machine with amazing speed and could accurately record hours of conversation without ever having to look down at the keys.

"I have the day off," Delia said, pulling away from the window so Katherine could look at the owl. Celine's head was tucked close into her body, eyes pinched shut in a deep slumber.

Katherine perched on the windowsill while Delia moved to the upholstered sofa. The communal room had plenty of comfortable seating and tables where the residents could relax and socialize. It was usually empty during the days, and Katherine hesitated to ask why Delia wasn't at work. The law firm that employed Delia was currently suing Katherine's employer, and it made their friendship a little awkward.

"Why are you off?" she asked carefully.

"Work has dried up," Delia answered. "I was supposed to spend the week recording depositions, but the person we wanted to depose is mysteriously missing."

"Ah." Katherine nodded. That was because Edgar was in California, where he went to avoid being served papers demanding his testimony in the ongoing lawsuit against Painless Parker Dentistry. She hoped he stayed out there. The longer Edgar could draw out the lawsuit, the longer Katherine would be assured of a job. Edgar had already announced he would close their clinic if he lost the lawsuit. There weren't many places that would hire a female dentist, and returning to her father's dental practice in Ohio wasn't a possibility.

"My boss has been trying to locate Dr. Parker for weeks," Delia said. "You don't know where he is, do you?"

"Nope." After all, California was a big state and Edgar could be anywhere. Maybe her blunt reply sounded a little chilly because Delia's tone was apologetic.

"Katherine, I'm sorry we have to be on opposite sides of this mess."

Technically, they weren't on opposite sides, since it was the American Dental Association who was suing Edgar. Delia merely worked for the ADA's lawyer. The lawsuit was to force Edgar to stop using the advertising slogan that made him famous. He was accumulating hefty fines each day he continued to use the Painless Parker name. If the lawsuit went against him, he would never be able to pay those fines and would have to close most of his clinics.

Why couldn't the hidebound dentists at the ADA realize that Edgar was doing a good thing by easing people's fear of visiting a dentist? It seemed narrow-minded and intolerant, but it had been going on for years.

"What are they like? The clients from the ADA you're working for?"

"They're out for blood," Delia said with a worried look. "They think that if Dr. Parker gets away with how he exaggerates, all the other dentists will have to do the same to compete. They think Dr. Parker is stealing their business and want it stopped. And Katherine"—Delia looked embarrassed as she leaned forward to speak in a low voice—"they don't believe he's a real dentist. They think he's a charlatan who's no better than a snake-oil salesman."

Katherine bristled. "That's not true. He earned his dental degree at the same place I did."

Even so, the Philadelphia Dental College was too embarrassed to admit he was a graduate of their school. Katherine didn't care. Edgar treated patients nobody else would. He hired *dentists* nobody else would. He was a good man and she refused to believe otherwise.

"Why can't he tone the advertising down?" Delia asked. "The

ADA has a photograph of him walking around wearing a tuxedo, a top hat, and a necklace made of human teeth. It's disgusting."

Maybe, but it got people talking. Katherine had been appalled when she first saw that necklace with hundreds of teeth strung together, but Edgar said there was no such thing as bad publicity, and he loved wearing it to shock people.

"I'm sorry I brought it up," Delia said. "I just wanted to warn you that Dr. Parker is going to lose this lawsuit because the ADA won't settle for anything short of complete victory. You need to know in case you want to start looking around for another job."

Katherine sighed and gazed down at the sleeping owl nestled against the wall of the building. Poor little owl. Maybe neither one of them had any business trying to make a home for themselves in this city.

Delia joined her. "If Celine makes more of a mess, Mrs. Blum is going to notice and order the nest to be knocked down."

It seemed cruel but was probably true. Owls couldn't digest the fur and bones of the rodents they swallowed whole, and they coughed up the remnants in nasty brown lumps. Celine used some of the pellets to build the nest, kicking the rest over the side of the building where they mounded up in the alley below. Katherine had been cleaning up the mess lest Mrs. Blum discover it.

"If Edgar loses the lawsuit, could you go back to Ohio and work for your father's practice?"

Katherine silently cringed. "Not unless I want to see Paul every day."

She had loved working for her father when she was an apprentice, but that was before her heart had been trampled by the only other dentist in town and had her embarrassment held up for all to see. At least the wedding dress she'd planned to wear was no longer displayed in the seamstress's front window. The extraordinary gown showcased the seamstress's artistry, and she used it as an advertisement in her shop. Her parents finally convinced the seamstress to sell it to them last year, but they couldn't make Paul disappear so easily.

Maybe Katherine had been cowardly fleeing her hometown to get away from him, but so far it had worked.

"Did Paul ever get married?" Delia asked.

"No." For months Paul tried to lure her back to Ohio, but she could never trust him again. How could she trust a man who had looked her in the eye and repeatedly lied to her for a solid year? She no longer dreamed of the charismatic Paul Winslow. Now she longed for the enigmatic, trustworthy Lieutenant Birch, a virtuous man of principle and honor.

He almost kissed her on Saturday night. She couldn't be imagining the chemistry between them, and yet Lieutenant Birch seemed perfectly happy with their midnight walks. *He* might be content to keep things exactly the same for another two years, but she wasn't. Maybe he was just shy. Maybe he harbored an attraction for her too but needed a little prompting.

Or maybe she was fooling herself and nothing would ever come of her hopeless infatuation. One thing was certain: If Lieutenant Birch couldn't return her affections, it was time for Katherine to press on and find someone else.

6

It was exactly one week since encountering Dante at the harbor that Jonathan was asked to stay for the morning police briefing at nine o'clock. Something serious must have happened because he was rarely asked to stay for the briefing after his overnight shift unless there was trouble.

The first thing he did was to dart upstairs to the officers' dormitory on the fourth floor, where five men were already rousing and getting dressed for the day. That was good. Whatever had happened hadn't been serious enough to awaken the cops who slept at the station house in the event of an overnight emergency.

"Do you know what's going on?" Jonathan asked one of the bleary-eyed officers.

"I've got no idea," he mumbled as he rolled out of bed. None of the other guys knew anything either, so Jonathan headed to the lavatory for a quick shower. He had a rented room where he sometimes slept a few blocks away, but he preferred living at the station house. It felt like a family here. A large all-male family that bickered, teased, and competed for promotions. It was the closest thing Jonathan had to a family, and nobody complained that he had essentially moved into the station house.

After getting cleaned up and changed into street clothes, he used the half hour before the meeting to crack open the chemistry textbook he'd checked out from the public library.

He wanted a slot on the Bomb Squad. Understanding chemistry and physics and how explosives worked was going to be a challenge. And the fact that Gallagher had already been assigned to the Bomb Squad? Well, it didn't matter. Jonathan would buckle down, be the bigger man, and convince Captain Avery that he could get along with Gallagher.

Two minutes before the meeting, he returned the chemistry book to the top shelf of his metal locker, grabbed a tie to knot around his neck, and hurried downstairs to the briefing room.

To his surprise, Sean Gallagher was sitting in the front row. Whatever brought Gallagher out to his old station house was probably serious news. At least Tomaso Conti was now sitting on the opposite side of the room. The young patrolman had been awarded the commendation for rescuing the drowning child and hopefully had learned his lesson about the dangers of currying favor with Gallagher.

The briefing room was crammed with enough tables and chairs for fifty officers, and most of the seats were occupied. A blackboard hung on the front wall, where Captain Avery stood looking grim.

"For those of you who haven't heard, there was an incident at Central Park at six o'clock this morning," Captain Avery said. "A bomb went off, and a sixteen-year-old bystander was killed. Poor kid was helping his dad roll a pushcart selling bagels toward a spot near Fifth Avenue when the blast went off. He never knew what hit him. We believe the location was chosen for political reasons. The bomb was next to that tall monument outside the Metropolitan Museum of Art."

"Cleopatra's Needle?" Smitty asked.

"Yeah, Cleopatra's Needle," Captain Avery confirmed.

Jonathan froze. Cleopatra was one of the names Katherine

mentioned in the drugged man's ramblings. It couldn't be a co-incidence. First the *Lorna Doone*, now Cleopatra's Needle. He bowed his head and squeezed his eyes shut. He'd give anything to turn the clock back and spot this connection earlier. If he had raised the alarm, a sixteen-year-old kid might still be alive.

Captain Avery continued his briefing. Cleopatra's Needle was an Egyptian obelisk, the same shape as the more familiar Washington Monument, except Cleopatra's Needle was the real deal. It was more than two thousand years old and covered with Egyptian hieroglyphs celebrating the military victories of Ramesses II. The ancient monument had been a controversial gift to the United States by the viceroy of Egypt as a sign of friendship in 1877.

The monument was still standing despite the bomb blast. It was hard to knock over a two-hundred-ton monument, but the pediment had been damaged, and a young man who'd been minding his own business had been killed.

Jonathan's mind whirled with the implications. Katherine Schneider said the patient rambled a long string of people who seemed to have no connection with one another. The nonsensical ramblings had suddenly become vitally important.

"A stack of incendiary literature was left scattered around the bomb scene," Captain Avery said. "They are consistent with the flyer found after the bombing at the Torricelli mansion. There isn't much of the bomb left for analysis, just a few scraps of metal that were probably part of an alarm clock used to trigger the bomb. I'm turning the briefing over to Lieutenant Gallagher, who is now an official member of the Bomb Squad."

Gallagher looked impressive in his full dress uniform as he stepped up to the blackboard. He never missed a chance to show off the ribbons and medals pinned to the uniform. This morning he had a brand-new ribbon denoting membership with the Bomb Squad. His voice sounded suitably professional as he began his briefing.

"Remnants of a clock found this morning appear to be the

same make and model as the clock used to activate the bomb at the Torricelli mansion," Gallagher said. "This is almost certainly the work of the Sons of Chaos. The red-bordered notes left at the scene criticize the museum for accepting the monument and demand that the museum send a $5,000 payment to a bank in Sicily to avoid future bombs."

"Are they going to pay?" someone asked.

"Torricelli did, but it's too early to say if the museum will," Gallagher answered. "It's got them frightened, and they plan on hiring a crew to patrol the grounds. I'll come back with a formal report once we know more, but in the meantime, keep your eyes peeled as you go about your business today."

Chairs scraped, and a rumble from the men rose as the briefing broke up. Gallagher started glad-handing his buddies, and Jonathan angled around the group to reach Captain Avery.

"Captain," Jonathan called. He managed to catch up with the captain just before he disappeared down the hallway. "Captain, I might know something about what happened this morning in Central Park . . ."

A sickening pit widened in Jonathan's gut because there was no way he could reveal what he knew without bringing Katherine's name into this. And doing so could put her in profound danger.

Katherine had just sat down to a late breakfast of ham and cheese quiche with the other women who worked on the night shift when a clerk from the front desk arrived.

"A message was delivered for you a few minutes ago," the clerk said, handing Katherine a note:

> Update on the *Lorna Doone*. *Please come to the police headquarters on Centre St. as soon as possible.*
>
> Lt. Birch

60

There was no way she could choke down even a bite of the heavy quiche. It had been more than a week since she confided her overactive imagination to Lieutenant Birch. He'd walked her to the subway stop several times since then and never brought it up. What had changed?

Curiosity set her nerves on edge during the three-mile subway ride to the downtown police headquarters. Katherine had never been to this part of the city that was dominated by courthouses and government buildings. Two stone lions guarded the entrance of the police headquarters, a fortress built of white granite, trimmed with ornamental ironwork, and topped by a copper dome.

Inside, dozens of people crowded the main receiving room, all of them waiting for help. How was she to find Lieutenant Birch? Three clerks manned service stations at the front counter, and each had a long line of customers. She joined the shortest line, where a blustery man wanted the police to evict a family of squatters who had moved into a building that was under renovation. A pair of police officers hauled a drunken man through the crowd, presumably toward a lockup room somewhere in the building.

A young officer whose uniform looked too big for his lanky frame approached her side. "Dr. Schneider?"

"Yes, I'm Dr. Schneider," she confirmed.

"You're wanted in the commissioner's office."

What on earth could be so important? She followed the officer through the throng of humanity and down a hallway with vaulted ceilings. Noise from the main room still echoed down the hallway, but eventually she was shown into a wood-paneled office with a ceiling fan slowly rotating overhead. A group of men clustered around the commissioner's imposing desk. They stood when she entered, one striding forward to greet her.

"Thanks for coming," he said, and with a shock she realized it was Lieutenant Birch. She'd never seen him in anything but a uniform before, and how different he looked in ordinary street clothes. More approachable but just as handsome. In the light of day, she noticed that his brown hair had flecks of tawny gold throughout. It made the paleness of his blue eyes even more appealing.

"I almost didn't recognize you," she said stupidly, yet it was good to see a familiar face in this masculine world where she didn't belong.

His smile was brief. "I got word of something important this morning at the end of my shift." He directed her to the desk. "This is Police Commissioner Davis and Captain Avery. Please have a seat. We're interested in the patient you treated back in June, who had something to say about the *Lorna Doone* and Cleopatra."

Katherine sat, and Captain Avery spoke in a clipped voice. "I need you to tell us exactly what your patient said to you. Don't leave out a single word. It is a matter of life or death."

She blinked at the urgency in his tone and cast an uncertain glance at Lieutenant Birch. "I thought you said it was probably nothing."

"We've changed our mind," he replied tersely. "A bomb went off this morning at Cleopatra's Needle in Central Park."

"No!" It was unbelievable. And frightening. She'd just seen that monument a few months ago when her parents were in town and they visited Central Park.

Captain Avery went on to report that a sixteen-year-old boy had been killed in the blast. The weight of all these people looking at her made it hard to think. It was so hot. She wished the fan overhead would move faster because her entire body prickled with anxiety, and she needed to concentrate. That poor boy, only sixteen years old.

"You think the man whose tooth I pulled did it?"

"Maybe," Lieutenant Birch said. "We need to know everything you remember about him."

Her body felt hot and cold at the same time. She'd had her hands in that awful man's mouth. A murderer's mouth? A shiver came over her, and she stammered, "L-Lieutenant . . ."

"Call me Jonathan," he said, pulling his chair closer to her. He smelled like crisp pine soap, and his expression was reassuring. "Take your time," he added in a calm, soothing voice. "You did a good deed contacting me after the *Lorna Doone* sank last week. We need to know if there's anything else you can remember about what that man said or who he is. Does your clinic keep records of their patients?"

"Sometimes, but he walked in without an appointment." She remembered because Alvin had wanted to leave early for his anniversary dinner, and they'd both been disappointed when such a serious case arrived late in the evening.

"You said he mentioned both Lorna Doone and Cleopatra," the police commissioner said. "What else did he say?"

"Saint Patrick."

The name sent a ripple of concern through the group. The most obvious target would be Saint Patrick's Cathedral, but the man also mentioned the Virgin Mary and a boring old gray lady.

"No name for the old lady?"

Katherine closed her eyes, trying to remember exactly what was said. It was so long ago, and she'd paid scant attention to the strange ramblings.

"I don't remember a name, just that he disliked a boring old gray lady. Or maybe that the boring old lady didn't like *him*?"

Frustrated silence descended on the room as the men shifted in their chairs. The police commissioner finally came to a decision. "Put a guard to watch Saint Patrick's Cathedral. Dr. Schneider, I need you to work with a sketch artist to create a drawing of both men. Can you do that?"

It had been weeks ago. She had probably treated a hundred patients since that night, and they all blurred together in her mind.

"The companion had a big nose," she said. "The patient's name was Vittorio, and he was big because I needed to use a lot of laughing gas. That's really all I remember about them."

"You told me one of them didn't speak English," Jonathan prompted. "Were they Italian?"

"I think so."

"Get Fiaschetti on the case," the police captain growled. "This sounds like the Mafia, and I want him to lead the investigation and work with this woman."

"Can't you do it?" she asked Jonathan.

He shook his head. "I don't speak Italian. Michael Fiaschetti is in charge of the Italian Squad ever since . . ."

Jonathan's voice trailed off. He probably meant to say, *ever since Joe Petrosino was assassinated*. Everyone in the city had heard about it. The police force was still mourning the gallant police officer cut down in the line of duty. Detective Fiaschetti had been appointed to succeed Petrosino, and most people thought he would suffer a similar grim fate sooner or later.

"Can I stay anonymous?" She hated how cowardly she sounded, but the only brave thing she'd ever done in her life was to leave home to become a dentist. She wasn't the sort of person who could stand up to the Italian Mafia.

"There won't be any reason for your name to be associated with this investigation," the commissioner assured her. "You will be in no danger whatsoever. We will have you meet with an artist to draw some sketches of the suspects. If we catch them, we have a good track record of getting confessions, so you may not even need to testify in court."

Court! She slumped back in the chair, wishing she could sink through the floor, but the commissioner had more questions.

"Will Vittorio remember that he spilled information to you?"

"Probably not. His brother wasn't drugged, but he didn't speak English and so couldn't know what Vittorio was saying."

"Good." Captain Avery nodded. "If this fellow doesn't have a clear memory of spilling the beans, you should be entirely safe. Lieutenant Birch is going to take you to a sketch artist, and once we catch these guys, we can all breathe a little easier."

And yet Katherine feared she might never breathe easy again.

7

Jonathan loitered beneath the wrought-iron lamppost across the street from the Painless Parker Dentistry clinic. The police department didn't employ a dedicated sketch artist, and on those occasions they needed one, they hired the illustrator who worked for the *New York Journal*. He worked the overnight shift, and Jonathan would escort Katherine to meet with him tonight.

Katherine had good cause to be frightened. Though her name was to be kept out of official police reports, she was still taking a risk by coming forward with evidence against the Mafia, and it spoke well of her that she didn't balk.

The door at the clinic opened, and a sliver of light illuminated the street. He waited for a trolley car to roll past, then jogged across the street to meet her as she locked the front door.

"You haven't changed your mind, have you?"

She tucked the keys into her satchel. "I've changed it every twenty minutes since I met with you this morning, but I won't back down. I know it's the right thing to do."

Jonathan cocked an elbow, and she grasped it as they set off toward the nearest subway station. She was unusually quiet as they boarded a train and waited for the doors to slide closed.

"I've got a question," she said, her voice hesitant.

"Ask away."

"If the police catch the ones who planted the bombs, will they get the death penalty?"

"Probably," Jonathan said. "A kid died at Cleopatra's Needle. So did a sailor on the *Lorna Doone*. An eye for an eye and all that."

She clasped her hands and looked down at her lap. His words obviously brought her no comfort, and he could guess why.

"Hey, don't feel guilty for helping us track these guys down. So far they've killed two people and cost a housemaid at the Torricelli mansion her left hand. We need to stop these people before they strike again."

She sighed and looked out the window, where lanterns anchored to the tunnel walls cast amber flashes of light as they raced beneath the city streets. "I know they're bad men, but I'd like to think they can be redeemed."

He slanted her a look, but she kept staring through the window, the outline of her profile as pure and refined as the statues of saints he saw in church each Sunday. "Do you really believe that?"

"Of course," she said automatically. "If someone gives themselves over to Christ, all things are possible."

He smothered a cynical laugh. Her innocence was delightful but a bit naive. "What about Nero? Judas? John Wilkes Booth?"

She shrugged. "No person is so lost they can't be forgiven."

"Let me get this straight," he said. "If John Wilkes Booth, the man who shot Lincoln and derailed the reunification of our nation, managed to choke out an apology on his deathbed, you would say it's okay . . . that all is forgiven?"

She lifted her chin. "God would. Jesus would."

"But would Dr. Katherine Schneider?"

There was a long pause as she considered the question. The

lights scrolled across her face as the train continued hurtling through the tunnel.

"Yes, I suppose I would," she finally said, and a smile broke out across his face. "Please don't laugh."

"I'm not laughing." Her innocence was rather marvelous. Growing up he'd been surrounded by violence and vengeance. There had never been room for sunny optimism or sweetly forgiving women.

The train slowed to a stop at Newspaper Row. Technically, the street was named Park Row, but nobody called it that. This was where most of the city's newspapers were published, printed, and distributed. Pulitzer's *New York World* was here, as was the *New York Tribune* and the *New York Journal*. The papers chose this location because it was a mere stone's throw from City Hall and a ten-minute walk to the New York Stock Exchange.

It was well after midnight, but still there was plenty of activity on Newspaper Row. These were some of the tallest buildings in the world. During the day, their height blotted out the sun, while at night the streetlamps made the intersection glow. A larger-than-life bronze statue of Benjamin Franklin loomed over the intersection, holding a copy of the *Pennsylvania Gazette*, the newspaper Franklin once published long ago.

"Which one of these buildings houses the *New York Journal*?" Katherine asked.

He pointed to a tower with nineteen stories, a mansard roof, and ornate coffered windows. "You've never been here before?" After all, this was the newspaper that published her anonymous "While the City Sleeps" column each month.

"No, I send my column to them through the mail. I've met with my editor only once, and he works the day shift."

They went inside and boarded an elevator to reach the editorial offices on the top floor. He'd never been with Katherine in an enclosed space this snug. The back of his hand brushed hers as the elevator began lifting, and he took a step away. She mustn't misinterpret that touch. They'd grown close of late, but he wasn't a free man.

The elevator attendant cranked the doors open, and they stepped into another world. The rattle of typewriter keys, ringing telephones, barking of newspaper editors, and laughter among some of the staff.

"My word," Katherine breathed as she scanned the newsroom. Men with open collars and rolled-up sleeves huddled around the draft of tomorrow morning's front page while others banged out stories on typewriters. The scent of strong coffee emanated from a bubbling percolator, but mostly the air smelled of newsprint and cigar smoke. Overflowing trash cans and crumpled balls of paper littered the floor.

Rather than being appalled by the sloppy newsroom, Katherine seemed dazzled. A balding man tore off a strip off paper shooting from a rapid-fire teletype machine and carried it across the bustling room to a waiting journalist. They hunkered down close to discuss the message.

"It's like its own little microcosm," Katherine said.

He grinned. He'd never heard the word before, but could figure out what it meant. Yes, the newsroom had its own hierarchy among the dozens of journalists, typesetters, clerks, and editors who worked through the night to be sure people had something to read in the morning. And somewhere in this chaos was Dick Kelly, a sketch artist the police used for odd jobs, but whose bread and butter came from the *New York Journal*, where each night he cranked out drawings to illustrate lurid stories of murder victims, escaped criminals, Broadway starlets, or in this case, suspects in a major crime.

Dick was thin as a rail, with a lined, leathery face brought about by heavy smoking. He worked at a drafting table with a tilted surface, an oversized paper pinned to the board as he sketched a caricature of President Wilson bowing down on bended knee before the German kaiser.

"We need your services, Dick," Jonathan said.

"What's up?" Dick asked, a cigarette clenched in his tobacco-stained teeth.

"We need a couple of sketches of two suspects. Tonight. Can you do it?"

Dick straightened and looked around the newsroom. "Yeah, I can bang something out for you. The boss isn't here yet." He set the political cartoon aside and laid a clean piece of paper on the board. "Who am I drawing?"

This wasn't a discussion to be having on the main office floor. Katherine had already attracted the attention of everyone in the room. They needed to be discreet about this. "Is there a private office we can use?"

Dick scooped up his pens and art supplies and gestured to an empty room. It was probably used by someone during the day shift for billing or clerical work. The door had a window in it, and Jonathan twisted the Venetian blinds closed.

"This lady saw a couple of people we suspect have been involved in a spate of bombings." He'd refused to say Katherine's name. If the newspaper didn't know her name, they couldn't print it and she'd never be in any danger.

Dick sat at the desk while Katherine took the only other seat. With a wall of file cabinets and shelves filled with reference manuals, there wasn't even much room to stand. Jonathan didn't mind standing close to her. It gave him a good view of her swanlike neck and the appealing upsweep of her dark hair amassed atop her head. He liked the view. He liked it too much, in fact.

"I'll be right outside the door, talking to the editor, okay?" he said. She swiveled her head to look at him, the electric lamp illuminating the soft curve of her cheek.

"Okay," she said, but the reluctance in her voice was plain.

It didn't matter. He needed to maintain some distance from her lest this dangerous attraction continue to grow.

Katherine couldn't stop staring at the artist's teeth. Mr. Kelly was an articulate and educated man, but he'd never once visited a dentist. It was obvious from the buildup of tartar on his stained teeth. Too many people neglected their teeth until the pain of a howling infection sent them scurrying to a dentist.

"I'm afraid the only thing I remember about the brother was that he had a big nose. That can't be much help, can it?"

"It's a great starting place," Mr. Kelly said. "People almost always focus on a single feature when they meet someone. A big nose, bushy eyebrows, corkscrew hair . . . that's normal. My job is to ask you a ton of questions to coax your memory, okay?"

It probably wasn't going to help, but she agreed.

"First of all, there's no such thing as just a big nose. What kind of big? Bulbous? Wide? Hooked? Did it have a bump in the middle? Big all the way down or just at the end?"

Before long, he'd drawn a quick charcoal sketch of the nose, and from there it was easier to remember the shape of the brother's chin: It was narrow and had a dimple in the middle. And he had long sideburns and a five-o'clock shadow. As she talked, Mr. Kelly fleshed out the image using a bit of charcoal. Each time she voiced a correction, he rubbed a little putty over the marks and tried again.

Within a half hour he had created a remarkable likeness of the man, so much so that it triggered a hint of anxiety.

"All right, miss, let's move on to the next guy."

They used the same procedure for Vittorio, who was harder to remember because mostly she had been looking inside the man's mouth.

A soft knock interrupted her thoughts, and Jonathan cracked the door open. An imposing figure towered behind him, a good-looking man in a tuxedo with a keenly intelligent face. His white bow tie dangled alongside an open shirt collar, and he held a half-filled champagne flute.

"Ma'am, this is Mr. Hearst," Jonathan said. "He owns the newspaper. He'd like to talk to you."

The man offered his right hand. "William Randolph Hearst. And you are?"

"Don't answer that," Jonathan instructed. "I've already warned everyone here that they aren't to use your name or any identifying details. Mr. Hearst has agreed to run the story in tomorrow's paper. If Dick can get the drawings finished within the hour, we can print those with the article."

"You're the lady who saw the crooks?" Mr. Hearst asked, one hand hanging on to the top of the doorframe as he partially leaned inside the office, the champagne glass gripped in the other hand. The lackadaisical posture almost made him seem drunk, but the sharp-eyed way he peered at her indicated he was fully alert.

She stood. "Yes, it was me."

He raised his glass to her. "Thank you, ma'am. We shall print an extra twenty thousand copies of the morning edition. And I'll offer a thousand-dollar reward for information leading to these men's arrest."

It was amazingly generous, and a glimmer of hope took root that the drawings might help bring this awful string of bombings to an end. A team of New York's top detectives was on the case, and in the morning the city would be blanketed with sketches of the suspects.

The sketch artist delivered on his promise to complete the two drawings within the hour, and Katherine went onto the newsroom floor to watch the paper come together. By now Mr. Hearst had shucked his tuxedo jacket and rolled up his sleeves. He leaned over the proposed format for the morning's paper with a red pencil, rearranging the stories to accommodate a new headline.

He was full of opinions. A headline reading *Fire Destroys Three-Story Warehouse* was changed to *Flames Devour Warehouse; Millions Lost! Owner Crazed with Grief!* Reports of the tragic bombing at Cleopatra's Needle had dominated the two earlier editions of today's newspaper, but the story would be given new life tomorrow when sketches of the suspects would be featured on the front page.

"I want this boring story moved below the fold," Mr. Hearst demanded, drawing a red circle around an article about the president's budget. "Get the bombers on the front page."

"We can't be sure the men I saw were the bombers," Katherine said.

"Print first, apologize later," Mr. Hearst shot back. "They're probably guilty anyway, so don't worry about it." He spoke without taking the cigar from his mouth. He issued orders as if he were king of the universe, circling stories and drawing cut marks through others.

The editor was incensed. "This is the third night in a row you've annihilated my entire front-page layout."

"That's because it's the third night in a row you've been stingy with your verbs. I want drama! I want verve! Blood, sweat, and tears dripping off the front page."

"Lovely," the editor scoffed, but not in a bad sort of way. The two men bickered and sparred, but it was clear they respected each other. Her parents were the same way. Nobody loved more vocally, vigorously, or rambunctiously as Howard and Lilian Schneider, yet it was a teasing born out of decades of being joined at the hip in both business and marriage.

Katherine watched in fascination as the editors thrashed out the newspaper before her eyes. It took another hour before the stories were written, formatted, and sent to the typesetters.

At four o'clock in the morning, she and Jonathan left the newsroom. How different the city seemed. When she left work at midnight, the streets were still alive with the late-night crowd, but not now. The city seemed empty now, silent. She could hear the patter of their footsteps. Normally a person risked their life by trying to cross a downtown street choked with streetcars, horse-drawn buggies, bicyclists, and automobiles.

"I could walk down the middle of the street and no one would care," she marveled.

"This is typical for this hour," Jonathan said.

"Have you always worked the overnight shift?"

"Ever since I got out of training."

"Why?" Surely a man of his accomplishments could have his pick of shifts.

"I like the solitude. It suits me."

A surge of energy began building inside her despite the late hour. It felt like they were the only two people in the world, and there was a strange sort of intimacy in that. She'd been battling fatigue at the newspaper office, but now all her nerve endings were alive.

Jonathan understood. "My grandmother would say you have your second wind. You may have trouble unwinding once you get home."

"What was she like, your grandmother?"

Maybe it was the moonlit night, or maybe the last few hours spent together working on a common mission, but Jonathan was unusually chatty. He laughed affectionately for a moment before answering.

"She always wore these long black gowns and looked like she came from a different era. She was tough. She taught me the meaning of the word *grit*. But she could also bake and hug and kiss away tears from a scraped knee or any other childhood trauma. I really loved that woman."

"You lived with her?" she asked.

He sent her a knowing glance, as if he sensed she was prying. "Yes, I lived with her until she passed away. Then I went to the Clifton School."

It was eerily quiet in the subway station. It was one of the nicer stations, with carved woodwork and fine wrought-iron benches. The lampposts had frosted globe shades that looked like they came from a craftsman's studio. They sat in companionable silence until the rumble of a coming train sounded from deep in the tunnel. The breeze came next, heralding the arrival of the near-empty train.

"Are you coming with me?" she asked in surprise as he boarded the train with her.

"Yes, ma'am. It's a little too late for you to go all the way back home alone."

The only other person in the carriage was a priest near the front, so they headed toward the back. The train began moving, sliding into the dim tunnel, which made her feel unusually bold. There was only a sliver of electric light coming from the top of the carriage, and she mustered the nerve to ask her question.

"Are you here as Lieutenant Birch the police officer, or as Jonathan Birch the man?"

Jonathan took off his officer's cap, holding it loosely on his lap. "We're the same."

"No, you're not," she pointed out. "Lieutenant Birch is fulfilling a duty. But if you're escorting me all the way to my apartment as Jonathan Birch, the private citizen, that's a different scenario. I need to know which man is sitting here beside me."

"I'm a police officer, Katherine. It's all I've ever wanted to be."

A fluttery sensation gathered in her chest. It was time to give Jonathan a gentle nudge and let him know that she was wide open to more if only he would reach out for it. She touched the side of his leg. "Don't you want more out of life? A girlfriend? A family?"

Passing lights anchored to the subway tunnel flashed across his face, giving her only momentary glimpses of his expression, but it seemed frozen. Sad.

"No, I don't want a girlfriend or a family. Being a member of the police force is enough of a family for me."

She jerked her hand back as if it had been burned. "O-okay," she choked out, but every cell in her body cringed. This was the most mortifying moment since the collapse of her relationship with Paul. The difference was that she had lost respect for Paul, whereas her admiration for Jonathan Birch grew by the hour.

And he had just made it abundantly clear that he would never consider her in a romantic light.

Jonathan escorted Katherine back to the Martha Washington Hotel, even though the walk was exquisitely uncomfortable. It was obvious that he'd hurt her feelings. He wished there was something he could say to mitigate her embarrassment, but that would likely make things worse for both of them.

Katherine barely even acknowledged him as the doorman moved to let her inside the building.

It was just as well. His entire life was built on a shaky foundation of lies and deception. He wasn't free to invite a woman into his world. And if the truth about his past ever came out, he'd be banished from the police department, the only real family he had left.

That didn't mean he wasn't a normal man. He'd had his first crush on a girl when he was fourteen years old, having spotted Charlotte Boroughs tending flowers at the house across the street from the Clifton School for Orphaned Boys. The way she mothered the geraniums growing in the window boxes was entrancing. Even from across the street, he could see that she was talking to the plants. She fussed and clipped, watered and weeded the blooming flowers that brought a splash of color into the gray, urban environment. There was a birdbath near the flowers, and every morning she filled it with water. Sometimes he saw her watching birds from behind the window of her house, and he watched along with her.

One night he filled a jar with birdseed and tucked it into the flower box. He watched her find it the next morning, examining the jar in surprised confusion. She poured a little of the seed into the birdbath, and for the rest of the day the birdbath was visited by robins, goldfinches, and cardinals.

He'd been too shy to ever approach her, but he started leaving other little gifts tucked inside the flower boxes. Sometimes a tin of candy or more birdseed. Once he left her a bright blue ribbon for her hair, and she wore it the next day. He loved finding gifts to leave for her. Then one day she caught him in the act as he hid another jar of birdseed beneath a petunia.

"Why do you do it?" she asked, and he swallowed hard. He couldn't tell her the real reasons—that he was lonely, enjoyed watching her take care of the birds, and secretly liked everything about her.

"I-I don't know," he stammered, feeling himself blush furiously. She blushed too. "I'm glad that you do."

He courted Charlotte for two years after that. Most days after school they filled the birdbath and tended the flowers. Her parents had a fine kitchen, and he taught Charlotte the secret to baking perfect cannoli using his grandmother's time-tested recipe.

As much as he liked Charlotte, he liked her parents even more. They welcomed him into their home that smelled of vanilla and sunshine and compassion. They asked about the Clifton School and seemed genuinely interested in his life. One day Mr. Boroughs asked for his help replacing the aging roof tiles on their building, and for that single afternoon it felt as if Jonathan had a real dad. He spent Christmas and Easter dinners with them, even though he was never able to offer more than the Italian cookies he and Charlotte baked in their kitchen.

In all that time he never once kissed her. He respected her too much. He'd read in an etiquette book that a man shouldn't kiss a woman before a betrothal, and he intended to do everything exactly right. Yes, he had a shady and shameful start in life, but going forward he would live on the straight and narrow. He was lucky to have found Charlotte and would never do anything to bring shame to her.

Then Sean Gallagher figured out how much he cared for Charlotte, and he swooped in like a hawk snatching a prize away. Charlotte responded. What woman wouldn't? By then Gallagher was well over six feet tall, funny, and smart. He wasn't ever tongue-tied like Jonathan could be. Gallagher could lay on flattery with a trowel, and Charlotte fell for it all. When Gallagher bought her a beautiful red knit cap and a matching scarf for Christmas, she let him take her ice skating in Central Park.

Jonathan tried to win her back. When he asked her what he'd done wrong, Charlotte said she didn't think he cared. That he never told her with words that she mattered, and that Gallagher treated her like a princess. She'd been crying when she said it, like it was breaking her heart to hurt him, so of course he smiled and wished her well. He told her he would be fine.

Gallagher dropped Charlotte after a month. Jonathan would have taken her back, but she was too ashamed to even look at him.

That had been eighteen years ago. He'd heard through the grapevine that Charlotte eventually married a pharmacist and moved to Queens. He hoped the pharmacist knew how lucky he was and that Charlotte was happy, for there was nothing worse than being alone in the world.

Sometimes in the dark of night, Jonathan imagined that he had a companion, someone who didn't mind that he had no past and that he preferred to work in the nocturnal world of shadows. Someone who could understand the terrible half-life he led. He wanted to think of himself as a good man, but he lived in the twilight between good and evil. Honesty and corruption.

He rarely thought of Charlotte anymore, but one thing was certain: He wouldn't ever lose a woman to Sean Gallagher again.

8

ormally Katherine tried to sleep in at least until ten o'clock each morning, but two things jerked her awake early and refused to let her sink back into slumber: embarrassment over her rejection by Jonathan, and excitement about this morning's newspaper.

She got up early, dressed, and arrived downstairs at eight o'clock to buy a copy of the *New York Journal*. Mrs. Blum refused to stock "that scandalous rag" at the Martha Washington newsstand, so Katherine had to walk a few blocks to find a newsboy. She gave him a nickel and snatched a copy of the paper, drawn to the sketches of the two men and Hearst's typically sensational headline: *Dastardly bombers on the loose! One-thousand-dollar reward!*

A hint of pride straightened her spine. She didn't mind the melodramatic packaging of the article so long as it helped bring the bombings to an end. She hid a smile on her walk back to the Martha Washington, then took the elevator straight to the eighth floor to pore over every line of the article.

As soon as she stepped off the elevator, Delia Byrne descended. "There you are!" she said in a breathless whisper. "Katherine, the owl eggs are starting to hatch. Come quickly!"

An involuntary squeal leaked out. Katherine followed Delia to the common room, where a cluster of women huddled near the window.

"Celine is crazy with worry," one of the women said as she stepped aside for Katherine to see.

Celine was strutting and circling her eggs. The owl dipped and bobbed and hovered closely over the eggs, making it hard to get a good look. Finally, Katherine managed a glimpse of one egg with a distinct chip in its smooth surface.

"I think it's better to leave them alone," Midge cautioned from the far side of the room. The elderly nurse was still dressed in her white uniform, having just gotten off the overnight shift at the hospital. "I don't think birds like people hovering nearby, especially at a sensitive time like this."

"But we watch her all the time," one of the women replied.

"You watch while she's sleeping," Midge pointed out. "She's awake now and can probably sense you watching her."

Katherine pulled away from the window. That poor owl was in for a tense and uncomfortable few hours. Celine's eyes were pinched into little slits against the blinding morning light. "Come away," she urged the others. It took some coaxing, but most of the women needed to prepare for work and soon headed out to their various jobs.

Katherine took a seat at the far side of the room to study the newspaper again. There were no clues about her identity in the article, merely the fact that the police had good reason to suspect the two men shown in the drawings of having foreknowledge of the sinking of the *Lorna Doone* and of the bomb at Cleopatra's Needle.

She read the article three times just to be certain, and everything was exactly as Mr. Hearst promised. She was safe. No one could learn her identity from the article.

Before leaving the common room, she closed the curtains over the window to protect Celine from more prying eyes. Then she returned to her apartment, put on her sleeping mask, and settled in to sleep, secure in the knowledge that she'd done the right thing in speaking with the reporters and that all was well.

Jonathan arrived at the police headquarters for a meeting about the Sons of Chaos because tips about the sketches in the newspaper were already flooding the department with potential leads.

Now the hard part would begin. Hearst's generous reward had a downside because culling legitimate leads from the deluge of wild-eyed guesses was going to be a problem. A dozen patrol officers had already been given a list of addresses to start checking out tips submitted by the public. So far, the Sons of Chaos matched the profile for both an anarchist group and the Italian Mafia. Which were they, and where would these tips lead?

A letter from Achilles himself had arrived at police headquarters a little after four o'clock this afternoon. Captain Avery didn't know its contents yet, but both of them had been asked to attend the strategy meeting at headquarters. Long tables arranged in a U-shape dominated the center of the strategy room.

Jonathan took a seat at the table that was already filled with representatives from the Italian Squad, the Bomb Squad, and two police detectives. Several copies of the *New York Journal* were passed around the room with people commenting on the sketches, but all Jonathan wanted to know was what Achilles had to say in his latest missive.

"Why didn't the article report the list of possible future targets?" Smitty asked.

"It would be premature," Detective Fiaschetti replied. As leader of the Italian Squad, Michael Fiaschetti would be overseeing the investigation since most evidence pointed to Italian mobsters. Fiaschetti had a strong build, shiny black hair, and a trace of an Italian accent. Like every other man on the Italian Squad, he had been born in Italy and was completely fluent in its language and customs. He stood before a blackboard with a list of names scrawled on it that Vittorio had rambled during the night Katherine pulled his tooth: Cleopatra, Saint Patrick, Lorna Doone, Sugar-Plum Tree, and Boring Old Lady.

"I'd bet my last dollar that Saint Patrick's Cathedral is next on the list," Captain Avery said.

One of the other men wasn't so sure. "The Metropolitan Museum has got a big statue of Saint Patrick on loan from the Vatican. They could be going after that."

"Or we could be thinking too literally," Detective Fiaschetti said. "What if the target is Saint Patrick's *Day*. There's always a parade that day, which would make for a dangerously attractive target."

"When is Saint Patrick's Day?" someone asked.

"March," Captain Avery answered.

"We need to solve this thing before March," Jonathan said. "Can we move on now to the latest screed from Achilles?"

"All in good time." Detective Fiaschetti turned his attention to the blackboard again. "Who do we think the boring old lady might be?"

Jonathan ground his teeth in frustration. He wanted to get his hands on concrete new evidence, not speculate about such cryptic clues.

Detective Fiaschetti wrote down a list of suggestions about who the boring old lady might be: the president's wife, the mayor's wife, a steamship named *The Old Maid*, and the Statue of Liberty. "Gentlemen," the detective said, stepping back from the blackboard, "it is natural to want to warn a potential victim, but as you can see from the many possibilities, releasing a list of potential targets would serve little good other than alarming the public. That would give Achilles exactly what he wants, which is attention." He opened a file and held up a document with the familiar red border. "This is the latest letter we've received, sent in response to the *Journal*'s sketches. I've had a secretary prepare copies of the text."

Jonathan snatched a copy from a stack of pages circulating among the men and began reading:

> *Childish sketches will not stop us. I have an army at my command. If you cut off one head, we grow ten more. If you are thirsty, I will stop your water. Hungry? I'll deprive you of food. Frightened? I will burn down your refuge. I will be inside your head, your heart, and in every breath of air you inhale.*
>
> *The police, the government, and the church are nothing but foot soldiers of the ruling class. They are agents of oppression and must be destroyed before decent men can experience the breath of true freedom.*
>
> *Achilles*

"That's it?" Captain Avery asked. "No ultimatums? No ransom or extortion demands?"

Detective Fiaschetti tossed the letter onto the table. "That's it. In the past he's made demands for payments to be directed to a bank in Sicily, but he knows we're on to him with those two sketches of his associates. It took him by surprise and provoked him to write this letter. It's the hot-tempered action of a young man whose ego can lead him to become reckless."

"Could Achilles be one of the two guys in the sketches?" Smitty asked.

Detective Fiaschetti shook his head. "I don't think so, but my hunch is that they're related. The Mafia is organized around family units, so once we catch these guys, it probably won't be long before we find Achilles."

Jonathan shifted uneasily. Ever since Detective Fiaschetti took command of the investigation, all their efforts were focusing on

Italians, and it felt like they were jumping to conclusions. He raised his hand and said, "There's nothing in this letter that implies the Mafia is behind this. The patient Dr. Schneider treated that night was Italian, but this letter doesn't sound like the Mafia."

"Are you an expert on Italians, Birch?" the detective challenged.

Jonathan dipped his chin and immediately conceded the point. "I didn't mean to stomp on your territory, but this doesn't have the hallmarks of extortion or ethnic infighting. And the payments to Sicily? It could have been a diversion to throw us off the scent."

Captain Avery nodded to the letter bordered in red. "Red has always been the color of the Marxists, symbolizing the blood of the laboring classes. We could be dealing with an anarchist group. Look at the targets that have been hit. So far, they have all been either a symbol of power or wealth."

Cleopatra had both. The Torricelli mansion had been the home of a robber baron, even though a kitchen maid got the worst of it. The *Lorna Doone* cargo ship was owned by a millionaire.

He stared at the possibilities for the boring old lady. They didn't have a logical suspect for this one, and it bothered him. It could be a symbol for someone or an actual person targeted for assassination. The mayor's wife? The president's wife?

A chill passed through him.

Martha Washington.

A portrait of Martha Washington hung in the lobby of the hotel named for her. Would someone really bomb a building filled with women?

"What about the Martha Washington Hotel?" he asked. "That building has five hundred rooms, most of them rented out as apartments for single women. Maybe Achilles doesn't like the idea of women who can support themselves."

Detective Fiaschetti added the Martha Washington Hotel to the growing list of potential targets.

It was impossible to know if the string of bombings was being driven by an anarchist or an Italian gang, but it wasn't something Jonathan could afford to ignore. He knew of a lead he wasn't free to share with the other men in this room, and it was time to track him down.

9

Jonathan took a streetcar across the Williamsburg Bridge, mentally analyzing his options. He had been abiding by the unwritten truce for years, but Dante broke the rules when he ventured across the river a few weeks ago. All bets were off now. Initiating a sensitive conversation with Dante Rinaldi was risky, but it couldn't be avoided. Even if the Rinaldis weren't behind the bombings, they might know who was. The prospect of the Martha Washington being a target gave the case a heightened sense of urgency. Jonathan needed to solve this crime before a bunch of defenseless women fell victim to a cowardly bomber. Katherine deserved that.

So yes, Jonathan intended to break the truce. He wore street clothes with an ordinary straw boater hat. Police uniforms were looked at with suspicion in this part of town, so it was best to try to blend in.

A hazy glow of the setting sun cast the old neighborhood in a warm light as Jonathan arrived at his destination. Or was it just fond memories that infused the crowded street with a rush of nostalgia? The buckled cobblestones were the same, as were the vendors selling oranges and apples from wagons lining the curbs.

The rails embedded in the streets were new, however, allowing city trolleys to roll through with ease. The sounds were quite familiar: children playing in the alleys, peddlers hawking their goods, the distinctive clopping of horses' hooves. A beleaguered mother stood on a fire escape and hollered at her children in the alley below.

All of it summoned long-ago memories of a happier time. He had been one of those scrawny kids, playing stickball and running errands for the vendors to earn enough to buy penny candy. He had never been lonely when he lived on this side of the river.

He doubted anyone would recognize him, but it was best to play it safe, so he turned down an alley to travel farther north using the narrow lane behind the tenements. He walked for two blocks, then headed back to the main street.

Rinaldi Grocers still occupied the corner lot, but the sign above the grocery store was new. A vegetable stand overflowing with onions, carrots, and turnips stood in front of the establishment's plate-glass window. Nobody manned the table because only an idiot would try to steal from a Rinaldi.

The door was propped open to encourage a breeze, though inside the air still carried the scents of coffee and old wood. His footsteps thudded on the planked floor, which hadn't changed at all. Almost everything else looked different, improved. Floor-to-ceiling shelves had been added to one side of the store, brimming with tins of cocoa, tea, and coffee. Rows of assorted canned vegetables were stacked beside sacks of flour and sugar. It seemed times had been good for the Rinaldis.

Dante stood on a ladder, setting bottles of olive oil on the shelf behind the counter in a quick rhythmic motion. The door to the back alley was open as well, the mechanical whir of a fan pushing outside air into the store. There was at least one additional man at work in the alley, which shifted the odds against Jonathan. At least he'd come well-armed if things went badly.

"Hey," Jonathan greeted.

There was a break in Dante's stocking of the shelf as he recognized him, but only for a second. He grunted and continued his work until the crate of olive oil was empty. Then he climbed down the ladder with slow deliberation.

"What do you want?" Dante asked.

"Just some information," Jonathan said.

Dante didn't break eye contact as he reached for a rag. He wiped his hands clean, then flipped the rag over his shoulder. He was the most feared of all the Rinaldis. Just a few years older than Jonathan, but bigger and meaner. With his shirtsleeves rolled up, the corded muscles of Dante's forearms testified to a life of manual labor and back-alley brawls. Judging by the fresh scabs on his knuckles, it looked like Dante still liked to settle a score with his fists.

"I'm fresh out of information." Dante reached for a stick of licorice from a jar. "You'll have to go somewhere else."

"Hey, Papa, that Morelli guy sold us the wrong size of bags again." The voice came from the alley. The mechanical whirring had stopped, and a lanky teenager with a pile of canvas sacks entered the store. "See?" the young man said, holding up an empty sack. "Five pounds, not ten."

"Keep bagging the sugar anyway," Dante said. "I'll clear it up with Morelli later."

The boy had Dante's square chin and dark coloring, and the hint of innocence in his expression probably wouldn't last much longer.

"Carlo, come inside and watch the store while I talk to Jonathan out back."

The boy turned to look at him, his eyes widening. "Are you *that* Jonathan?"

Dante barked out a string of angry words in Italian, but the boy didn't seem dissuaded. He looked a little awed as he gaped at Jonathan.

"I heard about you," the boy said. "The word is that everyone in the family is supposed to turn around and walk the other way if we see you."

There were more harsh words from Dante, and this time the boy obeyed, stepping around the counter and tossing the stack of canvas bags on the shelf behind him.

Jonathan followed Dante to the alley behind the store, which held the moldering stink of damp cardboard and rotting vegetables. A heavy-duty sewing machine, the kind used to make upholstery, sat on a table next to the back door, along with barrels of sugar and coffee. When he was a kid, Jonathan's mother used to sit out here and hand-stitch bags for sugar from the barrels. While it was cheaper to buy in bulk and repackage into smaller bags, it appeared the Rinaldis were selling so much that they had invested in a machine.

Since Jonathan was about to ask a big favor, he decided it wouldn't hurt to lower the temperature a bit. "The store is looking good. No more hand-sewing the bags?"

Dante nodded. "I bought the sewing machine last summer, and it's already paid for itself. I'm planning on adding iceboxes so we can start selling milk and cheese too. Now, what do you want?"

Jonathan took a step farther into the alley, his only escape route. Dante probably wouldn't try anything dirty with his son around, but caution had been bred into Jonathan since infancy. Which was why he never took his eyes off Dante. "I want to know if you've heard anything about the bombing at Cleopatra's Needle and the sinking of the *Lorna Doone*."

"Most people have heard about it," Dante said with a shrug.

"Do you know who did it?"

Dante ripped off a hunk of licorice with his teeth and began chewing. "Nope," he said casually, the licorice staining his teeth black.

"Are you sure? I couldn't help noticing you were in the vicinity about the same time the *Lorna Doone* sank."

Dante threw the licorice aside, and the casual demeanor vanished. "I just *told* you I don't know anything about what happened. That's the end of it. Get away from my store, get off my street, and don't come back."

Jonathan held up the section of newspaper folded open to the two drawings. "Do you recognize either of these guys?"

"Nope," Dante said, but he hadn't even glanced at the paper. It didn't surprise Jonathan. No Rinaldi would tattle to a cop unless something was in it for them.

"What about another bombing involving an old lady? Maybe the Martha Washington Hotel?"

"I'm fresh out of news."

Jonathan waved the newspaper at him. "It's only a matter of time before we catch these criminals. If you help us, there will be a reward. I can be sure your name won't ever be linked to it. No one will know. You're one of the best-connected men in the city, and I think you know which family is behind this."

Dante let out a hearty laugh. "Do you think I'd tell you anything? *You?* I don't want anything to do with you or your weasel-faced police force. I've got a good thing going at the store, and my wife is pregnant again. Having a cop come see me in broad daylight doesn't look good, so get out of here and stay away from my family. Got it?"

Dante was a good liar, and yet Jonathan had a hunch he truly didn't know anything. He nodded. "Yeah, I got it."

He strode back up the alley, monitoring what was going on behind his back the entire way. It had been naive to believe Dante might help, but it was impossible to leave that stone unturned.

He left Rinaldi territory but wouldn't cross the river quite yet. He had enough time to squeeze in another visit before heading back to meet Katherine at midnight. Instead of walking her home tonight, he had promised to escort her to the substation, where she planned to conduct another interview for her "While the City Sleeps" column. As much as he disapproved of her nocturnal prowling, he liked the way she had taken an interest in the city around her. Tonight's subject would be the engineers who kept the electricity flowing around the clock.

It took ten minutes to reach the church, where the Wednesday evening recitation of the rosary was nearing an end. It was cool inside the vestibule, and the tiled floor caused each footfall to echo off the vaulted ceiling. He dipped his fingers in the holy water and crossed himself before slipping into the last pew. There weren't many people gathered this evening, only a few dozen older women near the front. The priest spoke in Latin, the congregants murmuring their responses.

Even from the back row he could pick out Nonna Rinaldi, a black lace veil covering her head and draping over her bent shoulders. He lowered his head and let the priest's ritually chanted prayers and devotions wash over him. Though the Latin was incomprehensible, he hoped it was a holy blessing because he needed all the help he could get.

The novena came to an end, and the priest switched back to English. "Glory to the Father, and to the Son, and to the Holy Spirit. As it was in the beginning, is now, and ever shall be forever and ever. Amen."

Clicks and thuds echoed as most of the congregants rose and began funneling down the aisle. Nonna didn't. Jonathan waited until most of the others were gone. A few people remained in their pews, kneeling, heads bowed in prayer. Nonna was too old to kneel anymore. Instead, she sat quietly, a rosary clasped in her wrinkled, knobby hands.

Jonathan slid into the empty bench next to her. She looked over, her eyes widening in pleased surprise. "Giovanni," she greeted, reaching both hands out to him.

He smiled and took her hands in his. "Good to see you again, Grandma."

10

Katherine had years of experience riding the New York City subway, but she had never seen the inside of an electrical substation that powered the trains. A substation was located nearby in Times Square, only it was almost impossible for visitors to access it. The first time she knocked on their front door, a blunt mechanic told her they were closed to outsiders. Her letters to subway management were similarly dismissive. It wasn't until she enclosed a copy of her latest "While the City Sleeps" column, promising she would write a celebratory profile of their overnight workers, that they agreed to an interview, and tonight was the night.

She shrugged out of her high-collared dental tunic and into a walking jacket. It was her favorite, a robin's-egg blue jacket tailored to show her long neck to its best advantage. She wasn't wearing it specifically for Jonathan, but if he happened to notice that the jacket made her look exceptionally willowy and pretty, that would be fine by her. Maybe he had no romantic interest in her, but she wanted him to get a good look at what he was passing up.

He was waiting beneath the lamppost across the street when she stepped outside at midnight, and they set off for the substation two blocks away. It was housed in a splendid building with a Beaux-Arts façade to blend in with the other fancy shops and hotels along the street. Who could imagine that hidden behind the charming façade were the machines and generators that powered so much of the city?

She and Jonathan mounted the wide front steps leading to the substation entrance, where Jonathan pressed the buzzer. A gentleman in shirtsleeves and cheerful red suspenders answered the door and introduced himself as Rudy Pane, the lead engineer.

"Sorry I had to be so tough about letting you inside," he said. "We have to worry about busybodies from the press complaining about the way we do our jobs. Even spies from overseas trying to steal our technology. It's all patented."

"I'm more interested in you and the other workers than the technology," she replied.

The engineer grinned and looked at her curiously. "That's what I don't get, but come on in. You too, Lieutenant."

"I can't stay," Jonathan said. "Can you make sure Dr. Schneider gets escorted safely to the subway when she's done?"

"Sure thing, we'll take care of it," Mr. Pane assured Jonathan, then led Katherine into the odd interior of the building. While the outside looked like an ordinary town house, inside were three stories of open, cavernous space filled with gigantic rotating turbines and generators, each about twenty feet tall. The walls were rimmed with iron filigree skywalks and staircases that overlooked the turbines below.

"I thought it would be louder in here," Katherine said as she looked around. She heard only a low, steady hum.

"That noise isn't even from the generators," Mr. Pane said. "You're hearing the pumps downstairs. You wouldn't believe how much water seeps into the tunnels every day. Those pumps run around the clock to suction it out and send it into the storm-water system."

Katherine nodded as he continued with the tour, pointing out the electrical switchboard panels of dials, levers, and breakers. All of it controlled the generators that funneled high-voltage power to the subway trains running beneath the city. Mr. Pane was so enthusiastic it was hard for her to explain she was more interested in him and the other engineers than the intricacies of how the subway worked.

She noticed his gold ring. "Does your wife ever wish you worked normal hours instead of overnight?"

"She loves it. My working the night shift allows us to see each other more. Hey, how do you know Lieutenant Birch?"

"He usually walks me to the subway after I close up the clinic at midnight."

"Yeah, he's good as gold," Mr. Pane said. "I once saw him jump down onto the subway track to toss up a kid who fell in. He risked his life to do that, but then shrugged it off like it was no big deal. I asked him why he did it, and he said that all kids deserved to be protected. That his grandma sacrificed a lot for him, and he owed it to her to pass it on."

Katherine pondered the statement as they descended the staircase into the basement, where noise from the pumps increased in volume. Mr. Pane opened the door and gestured her inside. "You see that pipe? That's the one that funnels all the excess water into the storm drains."

There was a gothic beauty to the industrialized machinery upstairs, while the basement was a dank, subterranean world. Cinder-block walls, a clammy smell, and loud, unending chugging from the pumps made her ill at ease.

"Is anyone stationed down here?" She had to shout to be heard over the machinery.

"Nope, these things run all on their own," Mr. Pane shouted

back. "No one needs to come down here unless things are going haywire."

The oppressive environment would be a dreadful place to be trapped for an eight-hour shift. Mr. Pane must have noticed her distaste.

"I don't much like it down here either," he said. "Come on. Let's head back upstairs."

Katherine breathed a sigh of relief as she emerged into the spacious substation above, glad to have escaped the perfectly horrible basement. She hoped never to see it again.

Two weeks after Jonathan escorted Katherine to tour the substation, he read her column about the experience in the *New York Journal* during his 3:00 a.m. break at the station house. Her voice was obvious in every line as she praised the engineers who worked in the nocturnal world of the substation, operating massive generators that made it possible to keep electricity operating throughout the city.

Like all of Katherine's columns, each line radiated with her sunny optimism. Her descriptions of nighttime city life, the dedicated workers, and their jobs looked beyond the dingy back alleys and seediness to see the positive in everything. A part of him feared for her, but deep inside he hoped her joyful buoyancy would never change. New York needed people like Katherine Schneider.

He clipped the article from the paper to add to a file of all the others she'd written over the years. Someday when they'd gone their separate ways, her essays would be a window back to the magical, moonlit nights they had shared.

His break ended at 3:30, and it was time to head to the gambling den on 39th Street, one of the sordid establishments in the city where prostitutes and pickpockets loitered. The owner sometimes shook down his inebriated customers, none of whom was ever featured in Katherine's column. Still, they were every much a part of the city's nightlife as the admirable ones she chose to write about.

He was halfway to 39th Street when a boom shattered the night air. The hair on his arms stood on end as vibrations shook the pavement. An orange glow lit up the sky to the north.

He raced for the nearest police telephone call box. It was four blocks away, and he was breathless as he ran up to it, inserted his key, and grabbed the receiver that automatically connected to the nearest station house.

"Something just blew up around Midtown," he bit out. "Do you know what's happening?"

"No, sir. We're still trying to figure it out."

Jonathan stared at the skyline to the north. The orange glow was gone, and he heard a siren in the distance. He was tempted to drop the telephone and rush to the scene, but he needed to wait for orders.

Seconds later, the police dispatch operator came back on the line. "A bomb went off at Saint Patrick's Cathedral," he said. "Get to the scene as soon as you can."

Jonathan sprinted toward Madison Avenue, battling the wave of guilt threatening to choke him. They knew the cathedral might be a target. Yes, there were a dozen other targets in the city, but the cathedral was the jewel in the crown, precisely the kind of high-profile target guaranteed to attract attention.

An acrid stench tinged the air as he got closer. How bad was it going to be? The cathedral was made of solid granite, so a single blast surely couldn't bring the building down, but a partial collapse was possible.

A crowd had already gathered by the time he arrived. The pale stones of the gothic cathedral looked ghostly and pure in the moonlight. The building looked to be unharmed. Police officers had set up barricades on the other side of the edifice.

Jonathan approached a uniformed officer, who relayed what little they knew.

"The bomber got blown up," the officer said. "A cook who had just gotten off her shift saw him carrying a box toward the church. He tripped, and the box exploded. The guy is a goner, blown to pieces. It's a mess over there."

"What about the police officer who was supposed to be guarding the church?"

The officer scowled. "Headquarters wouldn't authorize another month of guard duty. We haven't had a guard all week."

Jonathan cursed beneath his breath, then hurried toward a cluster of officers near a police van. The south transept entrance to the cathedral was already blocked off. Officers were now putting up wooden barricades around a dairy wagon. A skittish horse harnessed to the wagon pranced and nickered, the whites of its eyes showing its distress. The bomb had exploded only fifty yards from the animal, which was still alarmed and restless.

Detective Fiaschetti was already on the scene and gesturing for Jonathan to come around the barricade. "Gallagher and Richter are both on their way over. We sent for the stable master from the mounted police division to get over here to unhitch the horse. The bomber used that wagon to get here, and we don't know what else is inside it yet."

Jonathan glanced back at the wagon. "I could probably do it." He had spent a month working with the mounted officers when he first joined the force and knew the basics.

Fiaschetti shook his head. "We can't risk that horse getting nervous and bolting before it's unharnessed. A single bomb wasn't going to take down a cathedral, so there are probably more in the wagon. In the meantime, I want you to go inside the church and start looking for bombs. There's a good chance the guy managed to place other bombs before he tripped and blew himself up."

Jonathan nodded, even though he wasn't sure what he was

looking for. Sticks of TNT attached to a lit fuse? A wad of nitroglycerine-soaked rags? Before he could ask, another police officer intruded.

"Bad news," he told Fiaschetti. "There are more bombs in the wagon. I hear a bunch of ticking clocks too."

Fiaschetti went pale, then quickly flew into action. "Clear the streets!" he shouted. "Go door to door and evacuate all the buildings around the cathedral. Now!"

Jonathan didn't move. "Sir, we've got to get the horse away from the wagon."

"Forget the horse! Human lives are what matters most, Lieutenant."

An eerie sense of calm settled over Jonathan. A cool head was always his best weapon whenever danger loomed. "Sir, if that horse panics and bolts, we'll have a bomb-laden wagon careening through the streets. Please order me to unharness the horse."

Fiaschetti blew out a breath of air. "Good point," he said. "Go ahead and separate the horse from the wagon."

Jonathan made the sign of the cross as he carefully approached the horse, one hand snaking behind his back to remove the switchblade he kept there. The quickest way to disconnect the horse from the wagon was to cut the leather traces. The three-inch steel blade was honed to perfection and could do the job.

"Easy, girl," he said as he approached the skittish mare. This would be easier if the approaching police wagon didn't have its air siren blaring, but at least the horse wore blinders.

"Easy now," he said again as he began cutting the first of the traces. He sawed the blade along the thick leather strap, continuing a stream of soothing words during the full minute it took to slice the strap free.

The mare shifted and stamped, its chains jangling. She probably didn't realize she was partly free, and he wanted to keep it that way as he moved to the other side of the horse and began the same sawing motion on the remaining leather straps.

He was dimly aware of a pair of bystanders approaching from behind. "You need to stay well away," he ordered. "This wagon contains a bomb."

"Pipe down, Sapling. It's just me."

Gallagher. Jonathan ignored him and kept sawing with the blade, making steady progress until he severed the two-inch strap. He dropped the harness to the ground. "I'm going to lead her to the stables behind the church," he said in a calm, measured tone. A halter tie still dangled from the horse's bridle, and he held his breath while reaching for it.

The blast of an air horn shattered the night, and the horse reared up on her hind legs. Jonathan staggered back. The horse bolted then, galloping down Madison Avenue at full speed. But the wagon remained.

"Brilliant," Gallagher taunted.

Jonathan turned away, blotting the sweat from his forehead. This wasn't the time to get angry. Every pore in his body was sweating, his heart pounded, and the wagon was still loaded with explosives. He turned toward Gallagher and the other man with a thin mustache and intent expression. It was Captain Richter, head of the Bomb Squad. Both wore civilian clothes, hastily pulled on after being dragged out of bed most likely. "Something is ticking in the wagon," he told Richter. "Fiaschetti thinks they're time bombs."

Richter nodded. "Gallagher and I will handle the wagon. You check out the cathedral to see if other bombs have been planted. Listening for the tick of the clock is probably the best way to find something."

Jonathan nodded, heading toward the front of the cathedral and averting his eyes from the side entrance, where body parts of the bomber still littered the walkway. He stepped over a shoe with a foot still inside it.

Detective Fiaschetti approached him with a young officer whose nametag read *Brewster*. "We need the entire cathedral searched inside and out," Fiaschetti said. "It's dim inside, but we can't risk switching on any of the electrical lights. Have you ever been in there before?"

"Every Sunday morning, sir."

"Good. Brewster and I will go in with you."

Brewster glanced at the severed foot and went pale. "I c-can't, Detective," he stammered. "I just can't. I got kids."

Fiaschetti's mouth compressed, and he turned his hard gaze on Jonathan. "You got kids, Birch?"

"No, sir."

"Good. You're coming with me."

The calm descended again. This was what he was born to do. He and Detective Fiaschetti walked side by side as they mounted the steps.

It was indeed dim inside the church. A few votive candles from late Mass still flickered in their clear-glass holders. Jonathan breathed a silent prayer, then paused to listen. After a moment, his eyes adjusted to the darkness, the cathedral's interior coming into sharper focus.

"Do you hear anything?" Fiaschetti whispered.

Jonathan shook his head.

"You go left, I'll go right," Fiaschetti instructed. The clicking of their heels on the marble floor echoed and bounced in the silence. Jonathan removed his shoes, and Fiaschetti did the same. Socks were slippery, so he pulled them off too, the stone floor cold against his bare feet. They needed absolute silence to hear the ticking of a clock.

He held his breath as he walked slowly down the left aisle, pausing briefly to scan each pew. Every few yards he stopped and listened, hearing nothing but the pounding of his heart.

He continued moving forward. Each side of the cathedral had alcoves, shrines, and smaller altars—excellent places in which to plant a bomb. Stations of the cross were grand and elaborate, another perfect hiding place. Three life-sized statues of female saints stood behind a bank of votive candles. Half a dozen candles still shone, lit by some congregant earlier in the night, but now providing a little blessed light.

A crack interrupted the silence. Jonathan startled, then spotted Fiaschetti, who had mounted the wooden steps leading to the huge pipe organ in the front corner. More creaks and pops continued to emanate from the organ as Fiaschetti checked the towering pipes, keyboards, and pedals.

Jonathan released a ragged breath and continued tiptoeing closer to the main altar. It felt disrespectful to approach the sacred place in bare feet. He mounted the stairs anyway, constantly looking, listening. A maze of guide rails lined the altar, with a short flight of stairs leading down to a pair of copper doors beneath it. Behind the doors was the crypt. He knew about the cathedral's crypt but had never actually seen it.

Curious, he stepped forward . . . and heard the ticking clock.

He held his breath, listening intently. There was no mistaking the steady, rhythmic ticking.

The bomb was placed outside the doors to the crypt. It was in a milk crate, filled to the brim with sticks of dynamite and wired to a clock. If it went off, it would blow the altar to kingdom come.

He glanced over to Fiaschetti, still inspecting the organ. "Bomb," he said quietly, pointing, and Fiaschetti met his gaze.

Neither one of them was qualified to do anything about it. It was impossible to know when the bomb was set to blow. Now, or tomorrow morning when the church was filled with worshipers?

Fiaschetti motioned for them both to walk away. Jonathan hurried down the central aisle, through the nave, and out the door onto Fifth Avenue. For the first time since seeing the bomb, he dragged in a lungful of air and crossed himself.

The area around the church had been cleared of bystanders. A police photographer snapped pictures of what was left of the bomber. The dairy wagon was still in place, with members of the Bomb Squad carefully unloading its contents. Rimming the cathedral at a safe distance were fire trucks, ambulances, and police vans.

Lieutenant Richter motioned him over, his face intent. "Tell me exactly what you saw," he said, and Jonathan relayed every detail of the bomb. The color of the dynamite wrapping, the wires, the positioning of the clock.

Richter gave assignments to each of his men as they prepared to enter the church. A priest, who'd been standing with the firefighters, came to join them and offered general absolution to any who wanted it. Jonathan clenched his fists, watching four members of the Bomb Squad line up before the priest, who said a heartfelt prayer for their souls' safekeeping.

For once, Sean Gallagher wasn't gloating. He accepted absolution from the priest, straightened his shoulders, then strode toward the cathedral alongside the other three men going inside. As always when a crisis arose, some people fled from danger, while others walked toward it.

Jonathan bowed his head, wishing each brave man well. Half the Bomb Squad was now inside the cathedral, the other half still working on the dairy wagon to disarm the bombs inside. This had been a major operation. Had all these bombs exploded, it could conceivably have brought down part of the cathedral.

"Come on. Back behind the barricades," Detective Fiaschetti prompted, and Jonathan was quick to obey.

The next thirty minutes felt like the longest of his life. Newspaper reporters had arrived, as had more bystanders awakened by all the commotion. Through it all, Jonathan watched the men working on the dairy wagon. He should be helping them. He shouldn't be standing on the sidelines or patrolling the streets at night. It was time to aspire to the next level, and the only two elite squads within the department were the Italian Squad and the Bomb Squad.

He could never join the Italian Squad. It was hard enough covering up his Italian roots, and if the police ever learned he'd lied about his past and was actually part of the biggest crime family in the city, he'd be fired on the spot.

But the Bomb Squad? He had the intellect, the cool head, and the willingness to serve.

No matter what it took, Jonathan intended to win a spot on that team of brave men.

11

A joint meeting of the Bomb Squad and the Italian Squad was scheduled for three days after the incident at Saint Patrick's. Word of Jonathan's willingness to get the skittish horse unhooked from the dairy wagon had spread, and plenty of men lined up to shake his hand as they gathered in the strategy room at police headquarters.

Gallagher didn't. He parked himself near the front of the room beside the blackboard, a scowl on his face. Word had already gone out that all eight men on the Bomb Squad would be awarded medals for their service at the cathedral. Jonathan was to receive a medal as well, and to Gallagher, that was an insult.

There hadn't been enough of the bomber left to identify. The wagon had been stolen from a dairy company that reported its loss earlier in the day, so they were no closer to finding Achilles. But rumor had it that a major breakthrough in the investigation had surfaced, which was why this meeting had been called.

The strategy room had tables arranged in a U-shape facing the blackboard. Oversized maps of all five boroughs covered one wall, while another had diagrams of New York Harbor, the city's streets, and the subway system. Detective Fiaschetti began the meeting by outlining the events at the cathedral for the officers who hadn't been at the scene.

"According to the cook who witnessed the explosion, at least four other men, possibly more, fled the scene after the first bomb accidentally detonated. We were able to defuse the bomb planted in the cathedral plus four additional bombs in the dairy wagon. This is the first time we have an unexploded bomb to study, and we've made considerable progress in tracing the materials used to build the bombs. Thanks to the work of Lieutenant Gallagher, we also have our next significant lead in the case. Lieutenant, take it away."

Gallagher stepped to the front of the room, holding a clock aloft. It was the size of a baseball, with a plain dial and alarm bell on top.

"My friends, this is the beating heart of a time bomb," Gallagher began, and Jonathan fought the urge to roll his eyes at the needless dramatization. "It is the clock I personally defused at four o'clock in the morning at Saint Patrick's Cathedral."

A low murmur of approval was followed by applause. There was no way to deny Gallagher's bravery, but it would be nice if he'd refrain from milking every last drop of glory to be had. Gallagher patiently waited until the applause died down, then continued his analysis.

"This clock has a patented crown wheel that is unique to the Hollingsworth Clock Factory in Queens. They're the only company allowed to make this particular clock."

Gallagher set the clock on the front table, then reached for two small evidence boxes on the table. The contents rattled as he tipped the first box to display fragments of twisted metal and shards of glass. He performed the same procedure with the other box.

"These fragments were all that was left from the bombs at the Torricelli mansion and at Cleopatra's Needle. We couldn't identify the make of the clock from them, but now that we have an undamaged sample from Saint Patrick's, we have verified that this was the same make and model at all three bombings."

"What about the *Lorna Doone*?"

Captain Richter, head of the Bomb Squad, stood. "The bomber used a different device on the *Lorna Doone*. Time bombs require someone to physically plant the bomb, but cylinder bombs can be slipped into the cargo and carried aboard by unwitting crew members."

Captain Richter approached the blackboard, grabbed a piece of chalk, and drew a cigar-shaped outline on the board. "Cylinder bombs cause fires, not explosions," he explained. "One side of the metal tube gets packed with potassium chlorate. It's then sealed with an aluminum disk. And the other side is filled with sulfuric acid. When the acid eats through the aluminum disk, it will ignite a fire."

Jonathan leaned forward, studying the crude drawing. "And you think that kind of bomb was on the *Lorna Doone*?"

Captain Richter nodded. "The *Lorna Doone* probably had a dozen of these things stuffed into its hold. That's why the fires kept igniting, and why they were so hard to put out. They were chemical fires, not the normal kind you start in a kitchen grate."

Richter rattled off a bunch of chemical equations and atmospheric conditions that made the cylinder bomb uniquely challenging to find and extinguish. It was an inexact science, and the bomb could take hours or days to ignite, depending on how long it took the sulfuric acid to eat through the slim disk of metal and generate enough heat to trigger a fire.

"How can we be so sure these bombs came from the same group?" someone asked. "It seems strange to use two completely different types of bombs."

Captain Avery supplied the answer. "We know they're from the same group because our witness heard the *Lorna Doone* included in a list of possible targets."

Jonathan shifted in his chair as frustration mounted. The police were still keeping Katherine's name secret. It had been three weeks since the sketches had appeared in the newspaper, and no new credible leads had emerged. Fear of Achilles might have compelled silence among the people who could identify the two men.

Captain Avery stood at the front of the room, holding the Hollingsworth alarm clock high. "This clock model is our best lead so far," he said. "Our next step is to locate everyone in New York who bought this model of clock and start tracking them down."

The 15th Precinct had been playing friendly weekend baseball games with the nearest firefighter division for years. The Coppers and the Smoke Eaters played eight games per season. Cops who weren't on the nine-man team always came out to cheer from the stands, along with the wives, kids, and friends of the players.

Jonathan had Smitty's eighteen-month-old toddler on his knee. Smitty's wife sat with her older two kids directly behind the police bench so her boys could get the best possible view. Those boys gazed at Smitty as though he'd walked on water. It was humbling.

Captain Avery must have felt the same. "I don't know how a man as ugly as Smitty ever got such a beautiful family."

Jonathan smiled and kept bouncing the toddler. Smitty deserved it. For years, Smitty's wife had let Jonathan snag one of her kids while she huddled up behind her husband. Down on the field, Gallagher stepped up to the plate and assumed the familiar crouch as he prepared to bat. The crowd stirred in anticipation, cowbells and whistles from the police side geared up, while a few on the Smoke Eater side grumbled. Gallagher was one of the strongest players in the entire police force, and when he was transferred to police headquarters to serve on the Bomb Squad, he ought to have left the Coppers. Headquarters had their own amateur team called the Finest, but they had a losing record and so Gallagher petitioned to keep on playing with the Coppers for the rest of the season. After all, winning was always the main thing with Gallagher.

The crack of the bat sent the baseball soaring. The crowd rose to their feet, screaming wildly. Jonathan remained seated, keeping his hands cupped over the toddler's ears.

Gallagher made it to third base. The bleachers squeaked as the crowd settled down again, and Captain Avery slanted him a disapproving glance.

"When are you going to get over it?" he demanded.

Jonathan nodded to the toddler on his lap. "Ricky doesn't like the noise," he said defensively, but this was a good opportunity to bring up a sore subject.

"I'm ready for a bigger challenge," he said to Captain Avery. "The Bomb Squad doesn't have anyone assigned to the overnight shift. I could be that man."

Avery folded his arms across his chest. "If you want a bigger challenge, transfer to the day shift. You'd make a good detective."

He would, but he liked the night shift. Ever since he was a kid, it was hard to excel in school because he was drowsy and lethargic for the first few hours, but at night he came alive.

"The city gets bigger every year," he said. "There are five million people here, and you've got a Bomb Squad that works during the *days*. You think criminals will play by the rules and only set off bombs during the day?"

The captain glared at the field. Smitty was up to bat, so they both put the topic on hold to watch. Smitty passed on the first two pitches but smacked the third in a high arc deep into right field. It was a sacrifice fly. As soon as the ball was caught by the right fielder, it was thrown to home plate in hopes of stopping Gallagher from scoring. Gallagher ran full steam with his head lowered as he took a diving slide to capture home plate inches ahead of the ball.

The crowd erupted in cheers, and even the Smoke Eaters gave a quick pump of a fire siren in reluctant admiration. Gallagher raised both arms in triumph and accepted the cheering while Smitty returned to the police bench and his wife, who gave him a glorious kiss as a consolation prize. The teenaged kid tending the score-board changed the card to reflect another run for the Coppers.

"Well?" Jonathan asked as soon as the crowd settled down again.

Captain Avery frowned. "I don't know if I can ever trust you and Gallagher to serve on the same team together, but you make a good point about needing trained men working overnight. Before I do anything, you need to prove that you can work alongside Gallagher without coming to blows. I'll put you on a couple of assignments together. See how you do. If I hear of bellyaching or backstabbing, the deal is off. Work with him for a while and then maybe I'll consider recommending you for the squad."

Jonathan patted the toddler's back, enjoying the chance to imagine having a kid of his own someday, but annoyed that his future was going to be linked to winning Gallagher's approval.

Jonathan avoided Gallagher during the ferry ride across the East River. The chance to enjoy the sunshine on his face and the cries of gulls wheeling above was far better than sitting belowdecks with Gallagher. Their mission was to identify suspects who had purchased large orders of clocks from the Hollingsworth Clock Factory. But there was no need for Jonathan to share a bench with Gallagher during the twenty-minute ferry crossing. They would soon arrive in Queens where they'd board a streetcar to take them the final three miles to the factory. With luck the owner would supply them with a concise list of their major customers, and then Jonathan could get back to the station house and begin the painstaking process of analyzing the list.

It wasn't to be. Ten minutes into the ferry ride, Gallagher drew up alongside him at the railing. "How does it feel to be out in the daylight, Sapling?"

"I'm ignoring you," Jonathan replied casually. No heat, no in-terest. Just trying to keep the peace.

"Why do you always act like you're better than me?" Gallagher demanded.

"Because I am."

Gallagher wasn't likely to let that pass, and he didn't. "No way, Sapling. I study, train, fight, and don't ever give up. I was better than you back in school, and I am today. I'll beat you in any honest competition, and I'll get my captain's bars first. I'll get every medal in the department, including the Medal of Valor."

Jonathan smirked. "Most people are dead if they get that one."

"Not me. I'll figure out how to get it so I can enjoy women falling over themselves to congratulate me."

Gallagher's ridiculous quest for glory had always been a mystery. Why should a man so accomplished be so aggressive? Back in school, Gallagher had always been surrounded by a ton of kids who were either intimidated by him or wanted to bask in his reflected glory. Not much had changed, even in the police department.

Meanwhile, Jonathan held himself aloof, partly because he was a natural loner but also because keeping secrets had been drilled into his head since childhood. Wallowing in painful memories served no purpose, so he scrounged around for a needle to prick Gallagher's sense of superiority.

"Was cheating Conti out of a commendation an example of how you fight and win honestly?"

"Shut up, Sapling," Gallagher said. "You always had everything so easy. You were lucky. You had a mother until you were fourteen."

Jonathan blinked. He hadn't expected Gallagher to remember a detail like that, but it was true. Jonathan had a loving mother, who did her best to keep him safe until she passed away from tuberculosis. Sofia Rinaldi had struggled and sacrificed throughout her dying years to ensure her only remaining child had a decent future. Shortly before she died, his mother humbled herself to call across the river for help pulling strings to get Jonathan admitted to the Clifton School for Orphaned Boys. He never considered losing his mother at fourteen to be "lucky," but Gallagher apparently did.

Jonathan knew nothing about Gallagher's life before they arrived on a collision course at school, nor did he care. He wouldn't believe anything Gallagher said about his history if it came notarized on a silver platter.

"Tell me more about this dentist who got the scoop about the bombings," Gallagher said.

Discussing Katherine wasn't comfortable, but Gallagher was a lead investigator on the Achilles case, so he had a right to know. "One of her patients babbled while under the effects of laughing gas," he said simply.

"Yes, but why did she come to *you* with the details?"

He shrugged. If Gallagher sensed Jonathan cared for Katherine, he'd figure out a way to exploit the situation.

"Does she mean something to you?" Gallagher pressed. "You're blushing."

"Get your head out of the gutter," he replied. "You're imagining things."

Tension crackled between them as they left the ferry and boarded a streetcar to take them to the clock factory. It took twenty minutes to arrive at the nondescript brick building in an industrial part of town, where noise from a passing elevated train blotted out the rumble of wagons leaving an upholstery warehouse next door.

Jonathan let Gallagher take the lead once they found the front office of the factory. With his imposing height and natural air of command, Gallagher was good at projecting the right blend of intimidation and authority. They were both in uniform, and it didn't take long to be shown into Mr. Hollingsworth's cluttered office. There was barely any room to navigate around the file cabinets and boxes of spare parts. Mr. Hollingsworth cleared a crate off the only guest chair in the room. Gallagher quickly took the chair, while Jonathan remained standing in the corner.

The police couldn't demand Mr. Hollingsworth's help in their investigation without a judge's search warrant, but if he willingly opened his business records to them upon a simple request, they were within their rights to look.

Mr. Hollingsworth blotted a handkerchief on his bald head as he took his desk chair. Behind his half-moon spectacles he looked nervous, but unexpected visits from police officers sometimes caused that reaction. It wasn't necessarily a sign of guilt.

Gallagher set the clock taken from Saint Patrick's Cathedral on Mr. Hollingsworth's desk. "Tell us about this clock," he began.

Mr. Hollingsworth picked it up. "This is the Reveille model. We designed them for the Army. They're sturdy and will keep working even if they get wet or covered in mud. No money is wasted on frills or extra gadgets that might break down after hard use."

Gallagher took the clock back and affected a casual tone. "You are to be commended for making such a sturdy timepiece. Did you know that it is the preferred clock for making time bombs?"

Mr. Hollingsworth turned pale, his eyes widening. Once again, the factory owner blotted his head. "I-I didn't know," he stammered. "When the Army asked me to design a reliable, no-frills clock, I did my best to strip the components down to the bare minimum. Fewer parts, less probability for breakage."

"Yes. Perfect for time bombs to withstand all sorts of conditions," Gallagher rapped out, this time using his bully voice.

"You have to believe me . . . I had no idea."

"Perhaps you can help us," Jonathan interjected politely. Gallagher had succeeded in frightening the factory owner, and now it was time to lower the temperature a little. If the man was innocent, he would probably cooperate.

"I'll help however I can," Mr. Hollingsworth readily agreed. "Just tell me what you need."

"We'd like to see a list of every store and distributor you've sold the Reveille model to in the past year."

Mr. Hollingsworth stood. "I'll show you the archive."

The archive was in a windowless basement room that smelled of old masonry and mildew. It was hot too, which made Gallagher's musky cologne especially overpowering. Jonathan itched to make a snide comment about Gallagher's need for perfume to cover his natural stench, but kept his mouth shut. It was more important to prove to Captain Avery that he could work with Gallagher without coming to blows.

He and Gallagher quickly divided the work, but this was no easy task. The receipts were arranged by name of the purchaser, not the clock model. It took hours of hot, grungy work going through each page of customer orders in search of Reveille purchases. Over sixty thousand of the Reveille clocks had been sold in the past year, most of them to the War Department. For now, those could be dismissed.

Gallagher concentrated on customers beyond the New York City area and handed the local orders to Jonathan. All sorts of organizations bought them. Hardware stores, prisons, even the New York Zoological Park had ordered two dozen of the clocks.

"Why would a zoo need so many alarm clocks?" he asked Gallagher.

It only took a moment to come up with a reason. "The animals probably need to be fed on a routine schedule," Gallagher replied.

Even so, twenty clocks seemed like a lot for a zoo, and whoever had placed such a large order might have held several back for nefarious purposes. Jonathan put the order slip on the pile of customers who warranted further investigation. He went on to the next document in the stack and sucked in a quick breath.

Rinaldi Grocers.

His mouth went dry, and his skin tingled. What would Dante want with three dozen Reveille clocks? Dante sold groceries, not hardware.

Gallagher noticed Jonathan's sudden interest. "What have you got?"

"Nothing," he instinctively said, but Gallagher yanked the page from him.

"Rinaldi Grocers," he said in a pondering tone. "Interesting. The Rinaldis are scum. They've been extorting the canneries and the produce markets for decades. They should probably all be deported."

Jonathan schooled his features to remain neutral. If Gallagher learned of his connection to the Rinaldis, it would ruin his career with the police force.

And Gallagher knew enough to suspect. Jonathan's grandmother used to pay him occasional visits to the Clifton School. Nonna was one of the few good Rinaldis, yet she could be sharp and cunning if necessary. Whenever she visited him at school, Nonna acted as though she could barely walk, stooped over and leaning heavily on a cane. The ruse was to show why she couldn't provide him with a home, and the school gladly accepted hefty donations from her trembling hands without asking too many questions.

Jonathan had lied about his past when he applied to the police academy. If they'd known he was a Rinaldi, they would never have trusted him to join their ranks. He intended to go to his grave with the name he adopted at age twelve when his mother and grandmother conspired to get him safely away from the family.

Jonathan gathered the receipts for all the customers who'd bought more than a dozen Reveille clocks and pretended to randomly divide them into two groups. "You look into these, and I'll take the rest," he said to Gallagher, making certain the receipt from Rinaldi Grocers was in his stack and would be his responsibility to investigate.

12

Twenty-two years after leaving the Rinaldi name behind him, the moment Jonathan dreaded had finally arrived. His allegiance to the police force was about to be tested against his loyalty to his birth family.

It shouldn't be a hard choice. Deep in his soul, Jonathan was a police officer and a God-fearing man who strived to keep on a straight and narrow path in life. He thought of himself as a real American.

And yet it was all an illusion. Jonathan Birch was really Giovanni Rinaldi, born in Sicily, where the Rinaldis got rich providing "protection" for families who worked in the olive groves and lemon orchards. When competition among warring families became too great in Sicily, the Rinaldis moved to greener pastures in America. Giovanni was seven years old when he boarded the ship, but the move from rural Sicily to urban New York hadn't been all that difficult. They lived in an Italian enclave in Brooklyn, so Giovanni continued speaking the language of Italy. He ate, sang, and prayed like all the other Italians.

Those were the good things his family brought from Italy, but they brought over the bad too. Extortion was a filthy business, and the Rinaldis were good at it. They strong-armed honest Italian businesses for protection money and pressured the canneries to sell them merchandise at cut-rate prices. The extortion racket demanded constant vigilance, as rival families tested them, ready to encroach on another's territory if it wasn't vigorously defended. All the Rinaldi boys were raised to be fierce, tough, and loyal. Allegiance to the family was the first commandment.

Giovanni didn't go to school in those days. His mother wanted him to, but his father insisted that learning the family trade was more important. As soon as Giovanni arrived in America, he joined his father and older brothers in setting up business at the Wallabout Market down near the Navy Yard.

In hindsight, Jonathan's affinity for working the graveyard shift was probably born during those exciting nights down at the wharves, when ships off-loading fish and fruit pulled into the harbor. The Wallabout was at its liveliest in the middle of the night as ship captains haggled with vendors to buy their cargo. Lanterns flickered, and men laughed as a bounty of food arrived. They hefted silvery fish more than ten feet long. Tropical fruits arrived by the packing crate. Vats of ice came tumbling down conveyor belts to keep it all fresh. By morning the market was ready to sell to the canneries, grocers, and fishmongers. Giovanni watched it all, eager for the day he'd be old enough to start talking business like his dad.

He was twelve when his father and two older brothers had been killed by a rival family during a battle for control of the Wallabout Market. It had been the last straw for his mother. Sofia had hoped their move to America would be a fresh start for her family, but after losing her husband and two eldest sons, she grabbed Giovanni and fled across the river.

Giovanni was renamed Jonathan. He learned to speak English without an accent. He acted, dressed, and pretended to be an American even though it hadn't come easily. His mother cuffed him in the face whenever he slipped and spoke Italian, not because she was cruel but because she was afraid. The Rinaldis had enemies everywhere, especially after Jonathan's uncles and cousins took revenge against those who had killed his father. The cycle of revenge and retribution was likely to continue for years, which was why Sofia was determined to scrub all traces of Italian heritage from her son.

The other Rinaldis considered Sofia's decampment to be a slap in their face. Her shocking disloyalty was allowed only because Nonna Rinaldi had condoned it. Nonna funneled Sofia enough money to keep a roof over their heads and provided homemade chocolate biscotti for Jonathan. Every now and then, his mother received letters from the cousins, some saying they were proud of Giovanni for going to school and becoming confirmed in the Catholic Church.

But when Jonathan entered the police academy, the truce cracked. It was one thing to decline membership in the family business, but siding with the police was unforgivable. Jonathan agreed to stay in Manhattan and ignore whatever the Rinaldis were up to across the river. He never considered joining the Italian Squad. If the police department knew he was a member of one of the largest crime families in America, they would either kick him out of the police force, or worse, force him to infiltrate and inform on his own family.

The discovery of the alarm clocks changed everything. If the Rinaldis were setting bombs on this side of the river, they were the ones breaking the truce, not Jonathan.

That meant it was time to confront Dante and figure out why he'd bought three dozen Reveille clocks.

A queasy ache knotted Jonathan's gut as he headed to Brooklyn the following morning. Italian housewives didn't shop before the day's produce had a chance to be delivered, and the early morning was when storekeepers swept, straightened, and awaited deliveries from the Wallabout Market. Jonathan's first job was helping unload wagons with his brothers. Crates of spinach and kale from New Jersey, bundles of asparagus from Long Island, and baskets of peaches from Georgia. Unloading those wagons had been his first lesson in American geography.

Jonathan strolled through the front door of the store, which was empty inside. The rear door was open, so someone was probably around back getting ready for the day.

He scanned the shelves and spotted the Reveille clocks almost immediately. They were displayed high on a shelf with other goods that were new additions since Jonathan left Brooklyn. He hadn't noticed them when he was here before—nonfood items like lanterns, rolling pins, and cleaning supplies. He picked up one of the clocks and weighed it in his hand. It was one of two Reveille clocks on the shelf.

Dante came into the store from the back alley, carrying a basket filled with Italian bread.

Jonathan set the Reveille clock on the counter. "When did you start selling clocks?"

Dante walked past him to set the basket on the front table. "Your presence isn't wanted here. I thought I made that plain the last time you came around."

"That was before I learned you were selling Reveille clocks from the Hollingsworth Clock Factory."

"Yeah?" Dante looked genuinely curious. It was possible he didn't know. There were twenty-five other wholesalers and hardware stores in the city that needed to be checked, but the Rinaldis were the most obvious suspects.

A newsboy walked into the store and grabbed a stick of licorice. He clamped it in his teeth while rooting around in his pocket for a coin.

Dante waved the boy away. "Forget about it, kid. Free today."

The newsboy flashed a grin and tore out of the store lest the notoriously hard-nosed Dante Rinaldi change his mind.

"Let's not talk about this here," Dante said once the kid was gone.

"Name the time and place. I'll be there."

Dante's eyes narrowed. "Why do you care what we sell?"

"The Torricelli mansion, Cleopatra's Needle, and Saint Patrick's Cathedral."

Dante stared at him for a moment, then whirled away and let out a string of curses in Italian. He punched a bag of rice so hard that it split open, spilling a cascade of white grains onto the floor.

"And the clocks were part of it?" Dante asked, his voice lashing out like a whip.

Jonathan nodded, and Dante cursed again. He paced in the small space near the front of the store, rubbing the back of his neck, his face purple with rage. He stomped to the far side of the store and banged on an old drainpipe anchored to the brick wall. "Micky, get down here and man the store!" he shouted.

"Uncle Mick is still alive?" Jonathan was genuinely surprised.

Dante grunted. "Worthless old sack of garbage. All he does is eat and complain about his bunions."

Mick finally staggered down to the store, shorter and balder than ever. "Giovanni!" he enthused, grabbing Jonathan's shoulders and giving him a kiss on each cheek. Then he grabbed a bit of his cheek and pinched it. "Look at Nicco's fine boy—all grown up, a man now. We're proud of you, Giovanni."

"Speak for yourself, Mick," Dante growled.

Mick waved Dante away. "We're all proud of you, Giovanni. Your grandmother especially."

"That's enough talk down here," Dante said. "Gio, follow me up."

Most of the Rinaldis still lived upstairs in one of four apartments above the store. It was why they'd all been so close growing up, and why Jonathan felt so alone after he left with his mother to live in a building where they didn't know a soul.

The scents of basil and garlic in the stairwell summoned a

flood of memories. The wooden staircase and brick walls were as familiar as the back of his hand . . . and yet everything seemed so small. This flight of stairs had been steep and immense in his childhood memories. Now he had to duck his head to climb it.

Dante led him into the apartment that once belonged to their uncle Stephano before he'd been killed in a knife fight down at the harbor. Jonathan read about it in the newspapers. The police never solved the crime, although Jonathan wondered whether the family had balanced the scales, because a couple of Mazzinis ended up dead in the river shortly afterward.

Dante's apartment looked different from what he remembered. The cast-iron stove had been replaced by a white-enameled one. The redbrick walls had been painted a warm yellow. A pretty woman with a long dark braid stood at the counter chopping tomatoes. She wore a loose gown to accommodate a pregnancy.

"Angie, take the kids and go over to Nonna's place," Dante ordered.

Jonathan bit his tongue at the brusque command, and at the way Dante's wife obeyed without question. Not all Italian men were like that. Jonathan's father treated Sofia like a queen.

Angie led two girls with long braids and shy smiles out of the apartment. Dante watched them go, then closed and locked the door.

"Quit asking about the clocks," he said. "I didn't have anything to do with Cleopatra's Needle or Saint Patrick's. None of us did."

"But you know who did," Jonathan said.

"No, I don't. And you're asking me to be a snitch. Did you see that woman who just walked out of here? Who's going to take care of my family if I get snuffed out for talking to the cops?"

"Nobody needs to know."

Silence stretched in the room, except for the sound of Dante's ragged breathing as he paced before the window.

Jonathan dialed up the pressure. "A sixteen-year-old kid was killed at Cleopatra's Needle. That makes it a death-penalty case.

Someone is going to swing for that kid, and if the Rinaldis were involved, it's not too late to walk some of it back."

Dante remained adamant. "We didn't do it."

"But you do know who was responsible, don't you? Your store took an order for three dozen Reveille clocks. That's a lot of bombs, and sooner or later whoever is setting them will make a mistake. The police will catch them, and when that time comes, the trail is going to lead back to your store and those clocks."

Dante blotted the sweat on his forehead with a handkerchief and continued to fume, his jaw clamped shut into a frown.

"I'll keep your name out of everything," Jonathan promised. "No one needs to know. Just tell me the name of the family who's behind this."

Dante shook his head. "It's not an Italian thing. You're barking up the wrong tree."

"And yet an infamous Italian grocery store sells the clocks that were used in the bombings—Rinaldi Grocers. It won't look good, Dante." Jonathan went to the window overlooking the alley, and sure enough, Dante's teenaged son was there manning the sewing machine, earning a few extra pennies by repackaging sugar. "You've got a hardworking kid there," he said. "I know what it's like to grow up without a dad. Don't do that to your boy."

Dante dragged a hand through his hair, already starting to gray at the temples. They grew up together. Used to play stickball in the alley. They were on opposite sides of the law now, with mutual distrust thick in the muggy air.

Dante opened the front door and looked both ways before locking up again. He moved to the window and slammed it shut, then turned to Jonathan. "I'm only telling you this because I always liked your dad. The Rinaldis cut a truce with the Mazzinis about five years ago. The families got tired of killing each other, so we divided Brooklyn up. We agreed to let them control the cotton and sugar mills in Brooklyn and Queens, and we've got the fish and vegetable markets at the harbor. We've each been minding our own business, and life is pretty good. Both families are doing well."

This news was a surprise. As a kid, Jonathan was taught to fear the Mazzinis like he should fear cholera or leprosy. They were a big, bad lot, but they hadn't been causing the police much trouble of late. Maybe the truce was the reason for that.

"Some of the Mazzinis are starting to get a little snooty," Dante continued. "Putting on airs and dressing all natty. They're sending their kids to college." He snorted as though college was as bad as becoming a cop. "Mick said he heard one of those Mazzini college brats got an accounting degree and was mouthing off about politics and philosophy like he was better than the rest of us. Marxist claptrap about pulling down the capitalist overlords."

"Was he the one who bought the clocks?"

Dante's expression darkened. "A kid bought the clocks. He was probably ten years old. He came in with an ad torn out of a newspaper for the Reveille clocks and asked us to order a few dozen. He had a toothy smile and a Saint Adrian medal like all the Mazzinis wear. I didn't want to rock the boat, so I ordered the clocks. The same kid came in a week later to pick them up. He paid in full."

"And you didn't ask any questions?"

"He bought some clocks," Dante said. "What was I supposed to do? Call the cops and report a customer for keeping good track of time?" He balled up the handkerchief in his fist and went back to pacing.

"You have no idea who the kid was?"

Dante rolled his eyes. "You know the Mazzinis. Each one of them has six or eight kids, hundreds of the little scamps running around. *No*, I don't know which kid it was, and that's everything I know."

It appeared the Mazzinis had gotten the better of Dante, sending a puny child to lower the man's defenses, and he'd fallen for it. No wonder he was furious.

Minutes later, Jonathan headed back to Manhattan and retreated to his rented room above the restaurant to write an anonymous letter to Detective Fiaschetti. Instead of his normally graceful penmanship, he printed in crude block letters. He kept Dante's name out of it, merely suggesting that the Mazzinis had recently bought a large number of Hollingsworth clocks, and the family should be watched. He slipped the letter into an envelope, sealed it, and deposited it in the nearest mailbox.

Pointing the Italian Squad in the direction of a strong lead was the right thing to do, even though it felt like he was betraying his family.

Jonathan took a long, steaming shower when he returned to the station house, but it couldn't scrub away the taint of disloyalty.

13

The weather was miserable, with sheets of rain spattering the windows and ruining everyone's Saturday. Katherine curled up on the chair in the eighth-floor communal room, watching the baby owls with concern. Normally Celine was there with her chicks nestled beneath her, but the mother owl hadn't been around all day. She was simply *gone*. The three-week-old chicks were awake and sopping wet, their scanty white feathers plastered to their pink bodies. Something was wrong. Never had Celine left her chicks for hours on end, especially not in the middle of the day.

The telephone in the communal room rang, and Katherine abandoned the window to answer it.

"That police officer is here to see you again," Mrs. Blum said in her sour voice.

"Lieutenant Birch? What does he want?"

"He wouldn't say, but come downstairs immediately. I don't like police officers loitering in our lobby."

Katherine took one last look at the baby owls, praying Celine would return soon, then hurried downstairs to see Jonathan because it was odd for him to show up unexpectedly like this. She took a moment to glance in the mirror, releasing the top few buttons on her collar and folding them down, as her long neck made her look willowy and pretty.

Jonathan looked dapper in his police uniform with his tie perfectly knotted. He carried a dripping umbrella in one hand, a stack of books in the other.

"Thanks for coming down," he said. "I'd hoped to take you out for lunch, but the weather is a little daunting today." Rain battering the pavement outside fell so hard that the hissing sound could be heard from where they stood.

She was taken aback by his offer. "I've just had lunch," she said a little reluctantly. "Was there a reason you wanted to see me?"

He gave her one of those pained half smiles. "I've come to ask a favor. Is there anywhere we can meet privately?"

The rain had trapped everyone inside today. The lobby and both dining rooms were crammed with residents, but there might be space in the library. A glance through the window in the library door showed it was crowded with women playing cards and occupying all the best seats. Only a small table in the back was still vacant.

"A corner table in the library is the best we can do," Katherine said. "Mrs. Blum would tar and feather anyone who tried to smuggle a man upstairs."

He nodded and followed her into the library. Jonathan received plenty of admiring glances from the women at the game table, but he didn't seem to notice as they crossed to the back table.

"What's going on?" she asked once she was seated opposite him, for something was making him distinctively uncomfortable. He set his books on a table and propped the umbrella in the corner. It gave her a moment to glance at the spine of one of the books. *Chemistry?*

He scooted his chair a little closer and spoke in a low voice. "You once told me about the chemical reactions that happen when someone inhales nitrous oxide."

"Yes," she cautiously replied. The dentists at Edgar's clinic had been warned not to discuss their sedatives with outsiders. Everything they used was perfectly legal, but Edgar had enough trouble without the authorities looking into his "painless" claims.

"You probably had to take a lot of chemistry classes in college to understand those drugs, right?"

Of course she did, but this discussion was making her uneasy. "Why do you ask?"

"I want to know if you can help me understand how chemical reactions work."

She folded her arms across her chest. "If the police are trying to get Dr. Parker banned from using drugs, I won't help. Neither will anyone else from the clinic."

"That's not what this is about," he hurried to say. "I just . . ." He glanced at the women playing cards at the nearby table, his mouth turned down. "I never went to college," he confided. "I'm street-smart, not book smart. I checked out all these books from the public library, but they're like a foreign language to me. I need to learn about chemistry and don't know how to get started."

Provided Jonathan's curiosity wasn't leading toward getting Edgar in more hot water, she'd gladly help. "What sort of chemistry do you need to learn?"

"I'm aiming for a promotion to the department's Bomb Squad. They find and defuse bombs, so I need a better idea of how they work."

"A Bomb Squad?" she asked in horrified wonder. "I should think that any sane person would run away from that kind of assignment rather than fight to get on it." A low rumble of thunder in the distance echoed her ominous thoughts.

A glint of humor lightened Jonathan's features, but he sobered quickly. "You heard about the bombing at Saint Patrick's Cathedral?"

"Of course."

"I was there. I helped, but when the real work happened, I

retreated with all the other bystanders to safety behind the barricades while the guys on the Bomb Squad headed the other direction. They walked straight toward the danger, a band of brothers united in a cause. Not many people have the guts to handle a crisis like that, and I want to be one of them."

He would probably be good at it. In all the time she'd known him, she had never seen Jonathan become rattled. His cool, measured intelligence was probably ideally suited for such a job.

"If you got on the Bomb Squad, wouldn't they provide you with all the training you need?"

He gave a wry shake of his head. "I've already been turned down for the slot. I have a feeling, though, there's going to be a vacancy pretty soon. One of the guys on the squad is so insufferably arrogant that he'll get kicked off eventually, and when he does, I want to take his slot. Look, this is the kind of stuff I need to understand." He opened a textbook to a marked page. It contained charts and tables for how different chemicals react depending on the conditions.

"Wasn't it scary being that close to the bomb at Saint Patrick's?"

"A little," Jonathan admitted. Then a spark of energy lit his eyes, giving him an intensity that made him impossibly attractive. "I still want it, though. Being a cop is dangerous, but I love everything about it. The risk, the camaraderie. Even the failures and backbiting and disappointments. It's in slogging through the hard stuff that we find the satisfaction of a job well done. I want my life to matter."

"But, Jonathan, you could *die*."

He gave a reluctant tip of his head. "I'm aware of that fact. The prospect of dying is . . . well, terrifying actually, but sometimes I think that life on earth might be a dry run for life in the hereafter. We all have the freedom to choose what kind of person we want to be, what kind of character to show to the world, and I want to be brave."

Jonathan was a man of shining integrity, heart and soul. She wished he had picked a different path to prove his valor, but this was the first time he had asked anything of her. "I'll help you, but I've got a much better chemistry text in my apartment. I'll get it, and we can go through it together."

What began as a dreary, rain-soaked day was suddenly turning bright. For two years, Jonathan had been doing her a favor by walking her to the subway after work. Now she could return his kindness.

She had just settled back at the corner table with her old chemistry textbook when Delia Byrne came hurrying into the library. Delia sometimes did extra stenography work on the weekends at City Hall and was still dressed for work as she rushed to Katherine's side.

"Celine is dead," Delia said in a shattered voice. "I found her in the alley when I got back from work. It looks like she tangled with a racoon and the racoon got the better of her."

Katherine stood. "Are you sure she's dead?" If Celine was gone, who was going to look after the baby owls?

Jonathan stood too. "Who is Celine?"

"Shhhh!" Delia said in a harsh whisper. Katherine quietly filled Jonathan in on the barn owl and how they needed to keep her a secret because the building's supervisor had no tolerance for the messy creatures. Now the baby owls were more vulnerable than ever.

Once he understood the situation, Jonathan offered his umbrella as the three of them headed outside into the alley. Midge and a few other women from the eighth floor were gathered around Celine. The owl lay on her side, her talons curled and lifeless, a little blood on her tawny feathers.

"She's gone," Midge said, rain dribbling from her umbrella.

"What should we do with her?" Delia asked. "I can't bear just leaving her here."

To Katherine's surprise, Jonathan stepped forward and said, "Give her to me. I'll take care of her."

"You won't just throw her away, will you?"

His face was full of compassion. "I'll take her to the same place where we bury the horses from the mounted police. I'll be sure she is buried with respect."

There were discarded boxes near the wastebins at the end of the alley. Katherine huddled beneath the umbrella as Jonathan wrapped the owl in newspaper and lifted her into a box.

Katherine craned her neck to peer up at the ledge outside the eighth-floor common room. "How are we going to feed those chicks now that their mother is gone? They don't eat cooked meat, do they?"

Midge wasn't sure but didn't think so. "Maybe one of the cooks will give us some raw meat scraps," she suggested.

"Mrs. Blum would fire any cook who helped us smuggle raw meat upstairs."

Once again, Jonathan came to their rescue. "I live above a restaurant. They've always got leftover chicken gizzards. I'll bring you a jar of them."

She beamed at him. A jar of chicken gizzards wasn't the most romantic gift ever offered to a woman, but it was perfect because it was exactly what she wanted, and Jonathan had gallantly provided it for her. Maybe she was the eternal optimist, but somehow, someday, she was going to crack through the wall of reserve Jonathan hid behind. And then?

Katherine drew a deep, fortifying breath as she gazed at him. Jonathan Birch was everything she wanted, and she was determined to find a way to win him over.

———

Jonathan felt like a hero as he handed a jar of minced chicken gizzards to Katherine an hour later. None of them were sure the baby owls would accept food from a human hand, and Jonathan wasn't allowed upstairs to help. The rain had stopped, and he now stood in the alley to watch Katherine and the old nurse appear in the eighth-floor window.

Katherine leaned out the window to dangle a sliver of glistening meat above the nest. Jonathan held his breath as she wiggled the scrap of gizzard. It seemed to be taking awfully long, and Katherine's face was getting red from hanging partially upside down, her arm extended to dangle the gizzard between her fingertips.

Suddenly her face blossomed with joy, and she beamed at him from eight stories up. She reached back into the jar for another scrap of meat. It didn't take so long this time. She met his eyes, gratitude shining in her face, and he gave her a thumbs-up.

The group of women huddled at the window all smiled and waved down at him. He offered them a quick salute before heading back to the station house.

Jonathan began bringing a jar of kitchen scraps each morning as he came off his shift at eight o'clock. Katherine was always asleep, but the old nurse got off her overnight shift around the same time as him. Midge waited for him in the lobby to receive the contraband jar of raw meat. Sometimes he brought gizzards, sometimes scraps of tripe or liver. The baby owls enjoyed it all. One jar lasted the entire day, and he brought a fresh one the following morning. It had been ten days, and Katherine reported the owls were thriving.

After making his daily morning delivery, he usually stopped at a corner market to buy a salami or a bagel for later in the afternoon when he woke up. One morning, as he waited to pay, he glanced at the latest edition of the *New York Journal* on a stack of papers a delivery boy had just dumped on the stand beside the front counter.

Hearst was running the sketches of the two men Katherine saw, along with another announcement about the reward. The initial flurry of leads hadn't come to anything, so Hearst took the initiative to run the story again. The checkout line was moving slowly this morning, and Jonathan started scanning an issue while waiting to pay.

He felt the blood drain from his face as he read.

A terrible mistake had been printed, one that was going to put Katherine in grave danger.

14

The ringing of her telephone jerked Katherine awake. She nudged her sleeping mask aside to peek at the clock, annoyed to see that it was only eight-thirty. Every limb felt sluggish as she shuffled to the telephone, lifting the receiver.

"Sorry to wake you," Blanche said. "Lieutenant Birch is down here, and he said he needs to see you right away."

"Tell him I'll be down in a couple of minutes," she replied, the fog of sleep vanishing. Jonathan wouldn't wake her up unless it was important.

She hurried to the sink to splash cold water on her face, then pulled on a pink cotton day gown, laced up her pumps, and was on her way to the elevator within five minutes. There was plenty of time to finger-comb her hair on the ride down because the elevator stopped on almost every floor. She started fixing her hair into a loose braid over the front of her shoulder, but then had to abandon the task when the elevator reached the ground floor. The attendant cranked open the doors.

Jonathan stood waiting on the opposite side, leaning against a column with a newspaper folded under his arm. He pushed away from the column the instant she stepped off the elevator.

"Is something wrong?" she asked. Not that Jonathan's expression was any more somber than usual, but for him to call at this time of day meant that something was either very right or very wrong . . . and he looked pretty grim.

"Let's step into the library," he said. "It's empty."

She nodded and followed him into the library, too nervous to sit as Jonathan took the time to carefully close the door before turning to face her. "I've never seen you with your hair down," he said. "You look different."

It was the first time he had commented on her personal appearance in two years. She touched the half-completed braid lying on her shoulder. "I have to keep it pinned up at work," she said, wishing she didn't find the way he gazed at her so appealing.

He nodded, the admiration on his face fading, replaced by sympathy. "Katherine, I'm sorry to have to tell you this, but the *New York Journal* has rerun the sketches of the two suspects you saw." He unfolded the newspaper to show her. The headline once again asked for the public's help in catching the "dastardly criminals" and touted the generous reward.

"That's good, isn't it?"

"The text of the article isn't good. Read this passage here." He pointed to a paragraph midway down the article. She carried it to the window and tilted it toward the sunlight to read:

> While under the influence of mind-numbing nitrous oxide, the criminal let slip a number of details that indicate the recent bombings are but the tip of the iceberg. More innocent businesses or beloved landmarks are likely to fall victim to the bombers unless the public can bring them in. Can you help?

It took a moment for the pieces to fall into place. A chilling sense of dread felt like steel bands around her chest, making it impossible to draw a full breath.

"Oh dear," she finally said. The article made it clear that it was a dentist who had overheard Vittorio spill the details of the crime, and Vittorio had never seen a dentist in his life before the night he sat in her chair.

They knew who she was; they would want to silence her.

Her stomach curdled, and she braced a hand against a bookshelf. The police had promised her anonymity, but this article had included enough information to give her identity away.

"Katherine, I'm so sorry," Jonathan said.

The gentle concern in his voice ratcheted her anxiety higher. "So I'm not imagining things if I think this article is extremely bad?"

"You're not imagining things."

She paced in the narrow space between the tables and the bookshelves. By now, thousands of copies of the newspaper were already in circulation. Hearst's newspaper, with its scandalous stories and colorful language, was the best-selling paper in the city. She grasped in vain for hope. "Would it be possible to recall the issue?"

Jonathan looked pained. "They might, but doing so would call even more attention to the story. People would want to know why it was being recalled, and thousands of them have already been sold."

"Police protection?" she asked, and the answer was what she expected.

"They won't provide the kind of protection you need. If this place permitted animals, I'd suggest a mean guard dog, but . . ."

But the Martha Washington Hotel didn't allow guard dogs, nor could she have one at the dental clinic. It had been two months since she pulled that tooth. So much had happened that it felt like a year, and all of it started with those two awful men. Now she had to live in fear that they'd come for her.

"We'll figure something out," Jonathan assured her. "Until I've got something in place, I will escort you to and from the clinic. Whenever you leave this building, you must never be alone."

Katherine was a little dismayed when Jonathan arrived that afternoon still wearing street clothes. Somehow she'd have felt safer if he was in uniform.

"Don't worry, I'm armed," he assured her as they stepped out onto East 29th Street. He wore dark trousers with a matching jacket. The flaps of his coat were open, revealing an ordinary shirt, necktie, and a pair of maroon suspenders. She saw no gun holster or weapon of any kind.

"Are you sure?" she asked.

Amusement lit his eyes, and he struggled not to laugh. "I'm sure, Katherine. Some armed men like to flaunt everything they're wearing, while others prefer to hide it. Guess which kind I am?"

She ought to have known. His low-key confidence helped calm her nerves as he rode the subway with her and accompanied her all the way to the clinic's front door. A new set of advertisements covered the plate-glass window, touting a sale on tooth extraction with the best painkillers in the city. Jonathan scanned the lavish promises with a skeptical eye.

"Can I offer you a dental filling or an extraction as thanks for coming all this way?"

"No, thank you," he said, trying to suppress a smile.

"Root canal? I've been told I'm very good."

This time the smile broke through, the white of his teeth looking exceptionally nice against his flushed face. "My teeth are fine," he said, then sobered. "Will you be all right until I come for you at midnight?"

He was standing close enough for her to smell the pine scent of his soap. They were nose to nose. "I'll be okay," she said. "Thanks for everything."

After he saw her safely inside, she watched through the window as he disappeared into the crowd of people in Times Square. From a distance he seemed so ordinary. Just another man in a dark suit, blending seamlessly into the throng of other dark-suited men. And yet there was something different about him. Beneath the suit lay a world of bottled-up emotions, which for some reason he kept hidden from others.

She needed to tell everyone who worked at the clinic about the threat looming around her. They deserved to know what was happening. The lobby was crowded with patients. She asked Josephine, the receptionist, to tell each dentist to come see her in the break room as soon as they finished with their current patients.

She set today's issue of the *New York Journal* on the table in the center of the windowless break room. Normally she liked this cozy space, complete with a dining table, upholstered chairs, and colorful folk art on the wall that Dr. Friedrich had brought all the way from Bavaria. Today these homey touches just made her feel guilty for putting their workplace in danger.

Alvin Washington was the first to arrive, which was good because he'd been here the night the two suspects showed up and might even remember something. He must have just finished with a challenging procedure because he shrugged out of his bloodstained smock and grabbed a clean one from a wall hook.

"What do you need?" he asked congenially as he fastened the high buttons on the collar of the fresh smock.

"Do you remember these two men?" she asked, showing him the newspaper.

Alvin glanced at the drawings. "No. Should I?"

"They were here two months ago. It was the night of your anniversary."

Alvin studied the sketches, his face drawn in concern. "They don't look familiar."

"Try to remember," she prompted. "One spoke English, but the other couldn't. They didn't believe either one of us were real dentists."

Alvin nodded. "Yeah, I think I remember. But why are they on the front page of the newspaper?"

The door opened, and Dr. Friedrich arrived, along with a couple of other dentists and Hector, the building's janitor. She gestured them all inside before closing the door and starting the story from the beginning, filling them in as quickly as possible.

Alvin was appalled. He rubbed the back of his neck and walked in a circle around the dining table. "Katherine, I was here that night. I should have stayed. I shouldn't have left you alone with two men late at night."

"I wasn't alone. Hector was still here."

Hector stared at the newspaper drawings, but he couldn't remember the men. All of them had seen hundreds of patients since that night. "Now they know that someone in our clinic is working with the police."

Dr. Friedrich scowled. "We need to report this to Dr. Parker at once," he said in his thick German accent. Everyone else in the clinic called Edgar Parker by his first name because he was such a friendly man, but Dr. Friedrich insisted on old-fashioned formality and called everyone by their surnames. Rumor had it he even referred to his wife as Mrs. Friedrich.

"I hate to bother Edgar," she hedged. The man was currently avoiding a lawsuit by hunkering down in California. He had enough on his mind without having to worry about her.

"Dr. Parker has invested considerable resources in this clinic," Dr. Friedrich said. "It is now in jeopardy. We have an obligation to warn him."

What was it about that German accent that made everything Dr. Friedrich said sound so reproachful? He was actually a kind man, but the last thing she needed this afternoon was to feel guilty for putting Edgar's business in jeopardy.

Alvin and Dr. Friedrich returned to their treatment rooms to prepare for their next patients. Katherine still had a few more minutes before her first appointment, so she remained in the break room. This room was usually a mess. Katherine had inherited her father's fastidious nature and began collecting coffee cups, then setting them in the sink to soak. Why did they have four canisters of the same brand of tea? She sighed as she combined them.

A loud crash split the air, immediately followed by screaming.

She ducked and covered her head. *A bomb?* Panicked voices came from the lobby. She raced into the hall, slamming into Alvin as he left his treatment room. They both hurried toward the source of the noise.

The large window in the front room was shattered, shards of glass everywhere. A brick with a note tied to it lay in the middle of the waiting room. Half a dozen customers huddled on the far side of the room, but one woman must have been sitting close to the window when the brick came through because she stood there frozen, flecks of blood on her face and chips of glass covering her gown.

Alvin darted out the front door, probably looking for the brick thrower.

"Call the police," Katherine said to the receptionist, her voice oddly calm.

Josephine looked too petrified to move. Katherine crossed to the receptionist's desk, glass crunching beneath her shoes. She was too angry to be frightened. The telephone box was mounted on the wall. She lifted the receiver, cranked the metal lever on the side of the box to alert the operator, and waited.

The lady with scratches on her face started crying. There was glass all over her, and she stood motionless as Dr. Friedrich pulled a few shards from her hair.

It didn't take long for a cheerful voice on the other end to answer.

"Please send the police to the Painless Parker Dentistry clinic in Times Square," Katherine said and hung up the telephone. She then grabbed a broom from the supply closet and began sweeping up the broken glass, wondering how to tell Edgar about the incident with the brick.

Curious pedestrians gathered outside the window to peek inside. "You folks okay in there?" one of them asked.

She only nodded, too angry to say anything more. The gaping

void where the window should have been exposed them to the breeze and noise from the street. The clopping of horses' hooves and the rhythmic ding of a streetcar bell rolling down the street sounded clear as day.

Katherine continued sweeping the shattered glass into a pile, all the while keeping an eye on Dr. Friedrich, who dabbed peroxide to the cuts on the injured woman's face. The only area Katherine refused to tidy was that awful brick lying in the middle of the floor. She didn't want to touch or look at it.

A police van pulled up to the curb outside the clinic. It was loaded with a handful of uniformed officers, including one she didn't expect to see. Jonathan raced ahead of the others, dressed in a plain white shirt, his trousers held up with suspenders. He looked a bedraggled mess.

"Are you okay?" he asked, his steady voice a contrast to his disheveled appearance. His shirt collar was open, his hair uncombed.

"I didn't expect to see you," she said. After all, he worked the night shift, and it wasn't even dinnertime yet.

"I was sleeping in the station house dorm just in case . . . " His voice trailed off, but she knew what he intended to say. He stayed at the station house in case she needed him, and at this moment there was no one she'd rather see.

Jonathan seemed like a different person as he took charge of the crime scene. He was the highest-ranking officer there and directed two patrolmen posted outside to search for witnesses while the third began interviewing those in the lobby when it happened.

Jonathan picked up the brick with the note tied to it from the floor and carried it to the reception desk. He untied the string and opened the note. There was no change in Jonathan's expression as he read, but his complexion turned pale. Quite remarkably so. He folded the paper and tucked it into his breast pocket.

"What does it say?" she asked, holding her breath.

"Nothing to worry about," he said as he glanced around the interior of the lobby. "Who's in charge of the clinic?"

Dr. Friedrich stepped forward. "This is Dr. Parker's business, but in his absence, I am in charge."

Jonathan's voice was calm and businesslike. "We'll be interviewing those who witnessed what happened. It won't take more than an hour, and I'll appoint an officer to patrol the immediate vicinity for the rest of the night. I don't see any reason you can't go about your normal business."

A trickle of relief unknotted the tension in her neck. Edgar would need every dime this clinic could earn if the lawsuit went against them. Shards of glass dangled at the rim of the smashed front window, making the prospect of staying open daunting, but a cowardly action like this shouldn't force them to close down. Today's appointment register was completely booked with clients.

"Yes, let's stay open," she said. "We mustn't let them close us down. Hector can run to the hardware store and buy the materials needed to board up the window until it can be replaced."

"I agree." Dr. Friedrich nodded. "We mustn't allow the brick thrower to score a victory."

Katherine took courage from the old dentist's words and consulted the appointment calendar on the reception desk.

"Katherine, I think you should go home," Jonathan said, and it felt like a slap in the face.

"Why? If there's an officer patrolling outside, we should be perfectly safe. I have appointments tonight."

Jonathan simply repeated himself. "You should go home. As soon as I finish examining the scene, I will escort you."

Something in the quiet intensity of his tone was alarming. She glanced at the corner of paper peeking out from his shirt pocket. "What did the note say?"

"We can discuss it on the way home."

It felt wrong to let this wicked incident drive her from work, but Dr. Friedrich overheard the conversation and agreed with Jonathan. "If the police believe you should go home, you must go home," he insisted. "I will stay late. Dr. Washington and I can cover your appointments."

Minutes later, Katherine was riding in the back of the police van beside Jonathan as he escorted her home. A pair of patrolmen sat opposite them on the long benches that lined either side of the vehicle. Stashed beneath the benches was a fascinating array of equipment: batons, folding barricades, ladders, and first-aid kits.

"We need to talk about the note attached to the brick," Jonathan said.

Fear raised goose bumps on her arms, but she tried to sound calm. "Okay."

He handed her the note, and she read:

> We know where you work, live, and pray. Go back to Ohio and shut your mouth or it will be shut for you.

Her heart thudded. "Oh dear," she said faintly. How did they know she came from Ohio? And did they really know where she lived and where she went to church? Her hands began to tingle.

Jonathan took the note back and slipped it in his shirt pocket. "We need to inform the management of your apartment about this. I'll do my best to arrange for extra security to patrol the area where you live. Now that there has been a direct threat, it shouldn't be difficult."

This seemed so unreal. If those horrible people knew she came from Ohio, did they know where her parents lived? What else did they know about her?

"Do you think I should leave the city?" she asked, a chill racing through her. She loved it here. She would be letting Edgar down if she left.

"You don't have to leave," Jonathan said instantly. "We can't force you to remain, but I don't want you to leave."

She caught the subtle change of wording, but this wasn't the time to ask why he in particular didn't want her to leave. Staying might endanger the women who lived at the Martha Washington. It was such a splendid building, towering over its neighbors with its grand pediments, lintels, and inset windows. It was a rare place for like-minded women to live in a safe environment. It wouldn't be fair if she stayed.

"I should probably move to another hotel," she said, but Jonathan disagreed.

"It would be harder for us to guard you at a regular hotel with hundreds of people coming and going each day. You live in an all-female building where it will be easier to spot someone who doesn't belong. Whoever is doing this is almost certainly a man. That alone will make him stand out if he loiters too long around the Martha Washington. We won't have that sort of advantage anywhere else in the city. I'll call a meeting tomorrow with a team of police officers assigned to the case, and we'll figure out our next steps. You should be at that meeting."

Katherine's gaze strayed out the narrow window as the van turned onto Madison Avenue, where thousands of workers were leaving their offices for the day. The normal sights and sounds of New York abounded. People shopping. Mothers tugging children along by their hands. How could it be possible that at any minute a bomb could upend their world?

Lorna Doone, Cleopatra, and Saint Patrick. It felt as though her name had been added to that list, and she needed to do whatever the police recommended to bring this string of violence to an end.

Jonathan wanted better protection for Katherine than what the police department would authorize, and he knew where to get it. A mistake at the newspaper had put a woman he cared for in danger, and William Randolph Hearst needed to pay for it.

At ten o'clock he headed back to Times Square, where Hearst was probably dining at Murray's Roman Garden, the richest, splashiest restaurant in the city. Roman columns framed the entrance designed to look like a grotto with jetted fountains and vines of ivy. The lavish interior was a fanciful recreation of an ancient Roman palace with a barrel-vaulted ceiling two stories high. Live trees strung with fairy lights filled the interior that glittered with crystal, diamonds, and laughter.

Jonathan showed his badge to the maître d' and was quickly escorted to Mr. Hearst's private dining room. Nothing put a damper on a party quite like the sight of a uniformed police officer, and women poured into silk gowns watched as he wended through the tables and around potted palms to reach the private suites. The maître d' knocked discreetly, then showed Jonathan inside.

"An officer to see you, sir."

A dozen men and women clustered around a table brimming with platters of food and open bottles of wine. A showgirl still wearing stage makeup perched on Mr. Hearst's lap. Luckily, the millionaire appeared in a jovial mood.

"Lieutenant Birch!" he called out in welcome. "Hop off, Nancy, and bring a chair for my favorite brave man in blue."

The showgirl hurried to obey, and a moment later Jonathan was sitting beside Mr. Hearst with a plate of stuffed olives and brandy-soaked figs before him.

"What can I do for you, Birch?" Mr. Hearst asked, reaching for an olive. Velvet draperies helped muffle the lively band music coming from the main room, but the festive atmosphere inside the private room continued. That was about to change.

Jonathan leaned in to speak quietly to the millionaire. "The morning edition of your newspaper had a big problem in it."

Hearst immediately stilled. Jonathan set a copy of the newspaper on the table and pointed to the line stating that the suspect in the sketch babbled details about the crime while under the influence of nitrous oxide.

"That line has put a Good Samaritan in danger," Jonathan stated.

"No one can identify your witness from that one line."

"Somebody did, and my witness has already been threatened because of this article. I want you to provide her with around-the-clock security."

Mr. Hearst frowned, then began the elaborate procedure of clipping the end from a cigar, lighting it, and slowly drawing a series of quick puffs to get it going. The pungent aroma tinged the air as Hearst leaned back to skewer Jonathan with a shrewd look. "Isn't around-the-clock security a little much?"

Jonathan stood. "Please follow me," he said in a tone that made it clear it wasn't a request. Hearst pushed away from the table and followed Jonathan to an area behind some hanging ivy several yards from the others.

"If my witness dies as a result of your newspaper article, there is no road or bridge or mountain I won't cross in seeking justice. When a woman as pure as the driven snow risks everything for a cause, the least she should expect is that the men around her will be just as honorable to ensure her safety."

Mr. Hearst started to cave. "I'll post a guard at her clinic."

Jonathan shook his head. "Not good enough. They know where she lives."

"Oh, very well," Hearst conceded. "Two guards, twelve-hour shifts."

It was the normal schedule for this sort of thing, and Jonathan dipped his head to accept the offer. "Thank you, sir."

Jonathan left the private dining room and was halfway to the front door when a woman hurried up beside him. It was Nancy, the showgirl who sometimes threw herself at him during his evening rounds. She had an open bottle of champagne with her. "Why are you leaving so fast?" she asked. "Sit with me and have a drink. Just one." There was a glassy look in her eyes, and she'd probably already imbibed plenty.

He was used to shrugging her off, but the note of desperation in her voice concerned him. He led her to a small table and sat opposite her. "What's wrong?" he asked.

She hiccupped and poured champagne into a glass. "I've been hankering after Willie for almost a year, and he hasn't taken me up on anything."

"He's married, Nance."

"So? Where's his wife? And there are plenty of other girls he squires around, why not me? I'm done with him. Finished."

"Good."

She leaned forward, offering a generous view of her bosom. "What about you, Lieutenant? I know you're not rich like Willie, but I don't mind. We could be good together."

A woman like Nancy would be bored with him in ten minutes. Besides, she wasn't anything like the wholesome, idealistic woman who'd had him captivated for two years now.

"No, you and I would be a train wreck," he said, not unkindly.

She sighed and slumped back into the chair, the picture of dejection. "How am I ever going to make something of myself if no decent man will look at me?"

Jonathan looked around the restaurant. Many of the women there were respectable wives glittering with gemstones, but plenty were showgirls like Nancy. Impulsively, he leaned forward and squeezed Nancy's bicep. It was well-muscled just as he suspected. "Nance, you're a strong woman. You dance and train and memorize during rehearsals, then show up for performances six nights a week. Why are you selling yourself short?"

The compliment seemed to take her aback. She blinked her eyes a few times before speaking. "I don't know."

"Half the dancers on Broadway come to places like this after work, and the other half go home and get a solid night's sleep. Those are the ones who are going to do better in life. Go home, Nance. The answer you're looking for isn't here."

She gave him a watery attempt at a smile. "It seems easier here."

Lively band music and boisterous laughter filled the gaudy restaurant, such a contrast to the despair in Nancy's eyes.

"So-called easy roads can often become very hard," he said

gently. He stood, then leaned down and whispered in her ear, "The hardest step is usually the first one, but you can do it, Nance."

It was up to Nancy if she wanted to change her life, but no one knew better than Giovanni Rinaldi that it was possible to switch courses in life. It wasn't easy, but it was possible.

15

K atherine's meeting with the team of police officers assigned to handle the threats against her took place in the
Martha Washington's library.

Normally she loved this room. Last weekend it hosted a lively
contest for who could assemble a jigsaw puzzle the fastest. Katherine teamed up with her fellow night-shift employees to finish
ten minutes ahead of a group of telephone operators in the first
round, but lost to the teachers' group in the final.

How long ago that seemed now. Instead of laughing women
gathered around the table, there were eight police officers, two
bodyguards hired by William Randolph Hearst, and a hatchet-
faced Mrs. Blum.

The matron's eyes turned to flint as she read the threatening
note that implicated the safety of the Martha Washington. Guilt
rained down on Katherine, adding to the queasy feeling she'd suffered ever since reading that awful threat.

Jonathan did his best to reassure both Katherine and Mrs. Blum
as he outlined the plan to keep the building safe. "The police will
patrol the perimeter of the Martha Washington several times a
day using both uniformed and plainclothes officers. Mr. Hearst

will provide Katherine with a dedicated bodyguard around the clock. Surveillance will begin immediately."

"I have a better solution," Mrs. Blum said primly, then turned her glare to Katherine. "I want you out of here. Our residents are required to be women of exceptional moral character, not people mixed up with the sort of riffraff who threaten violence. Take this problem of yours somewhere else. You are to pack your things and leave at once."

Katherine flinched at the fury in Mrs. Blum's tone, but Jonathan came to her rescue. "Hold on there, ma'am. No one is going to get evicted over this."

"No? I should think Dr. Schneider is getting evicted. Today, in fact."

Captain Avery stepped in. "You don't want to do that, ma'am, do you?"

"I most certainly do."

Captain Avery gave a mournful nod. "I suppose I can understand, but if Dr. Schneider has to move somewhere else, I'll be obliged to move my patrol officers wherever she goes. *All my patrol officers*. Permanently. You wouldn't want that, would you?"

The threat was clear, even though it was delivered politely. The Martha Washington was in a respectable neighborhood, but they still had periodic incidents to remind them they were in the middle of a huge city. Only last weekend the police had been called when a man staggered inside and passed out in an alcoholic stupor in the lobby. A patrolling officer arrived within minutes to handle the situation.

"How many additional officers will be on patrol?" Mrs. Blum asked.

It was the first hint of a concession, and Katherine met Jonathan's gaze across the table. She could drown in the gentle compassion she saw there. Captain Avery introduced the officers who would be patrolling the area; then the bodyguards provided by Mr. Hearst introduced themselves.

The daytime guard was a young man with a blond crew cut and easy grin. "I'm Jake Sullivan from Upstate New York, and I'm happy to be here. The last time I was on undercover duty, I was inside a prison." He faked a shudder, then tossed a wink Katherine's way. "Keeping my eye on Dr. Schneider and all the other ladies in the building will be a pleasure."

The nighttime bodyguard was an older man with a thick neck and the face of a bulldog. "Knock it off, Sullivan," he growled. "There won't be any flirting with the residents." He proceeded to introduce himself as Sergeant Michael Hood, who still used his retired rank from when he served in the Army, although most people simply called him Sarge. "Sullivan and I will be working twelve-hour shifts," he added. "We usually insist on close proximity to the person we're guarding, but we'll respect the rules of the Martha Washington by remaining in the lobby or patrolling the access points outside the building. No man will get in or out of the Martha Washington without one of us being aware of it."

Sarge's plan of protection did little to calm Mrs. Blum, who still kept a smoldering glare pinned on Katherine. "One month," she warned, pointing a finger at Katherine's nose. "If the police don't find and arrest these men within one month, you need to pack your bags and leave the building."

The meeting was upsetting, and Katherine had never been good at masking her emotions. Jonathan crouched down beside her chair after the meeting concluded. Everyone had left except for Mr. Sullivan, the young guard who would now be her permanent shadow during the daytime shift.

"Let's go across the street for a nice egg cream soda," Jonathan suggested.

She instantly recoiled. "Yuck."

"You don't like egg creams? Have you actually *had* one?"

She'd seen them on the menu boards but had more respect for

her digestive tract than to assault it with the vile-sounding drink. "Never," she said, and apparently that triggered something inside Jonathan because he laughed and insisted she try it.

His laughter was a balm. It was a reminder that while life around her had been turned upside down and riddled with fear, there were simple joys all around if only she paid attention. Vittorio and the other bombers had robbed her of so much. She would not let them rob her of a lovely afternoon with a handsome police officer who wanted to treat her at the deli across the street.

Mr. Sullivan walked on her other side, and soon they arrived at the deli.

"Three egg creams, please," Jonathan ordered from the man standing behind the front counter. The cramped deli had a single row of booths along the wall and only a narrow aisle separating them from the service counter. She and Jonathan slid into a booth while Sullivan took a barstool at the counter across from them. He pretended to scrutinize the menu to give her a bit of privacy, yet it was disconcerting to have a stranger following her everywhere. Was this what her life was going to be like now?

"Egg creams are what make life worth living," Jonathan said after the waitress delivered the tall, frosty glasses to their table. Katherine had mistakenly assumed that the drink was simply raw eggs beaten into milk, but Jonathan taught her otherwise.

"Nobody knows where the name came from," he said. "Most people think it's a corruption of Yiddish because it's a staple in all the Jewish delis. But there aren't any eggs in it—just milk, chocolate, sugar, and soda water."

She lifted the glass and sniffed. It smelled good enough to take a cautious sip through the straw. It was a delightful explosion of flavor. Jonathan watched in expectation, but she didn't want to confess he was right and fought the temptation to laugh. His smile grew wider, and she gave up the battle.

"It's delicious," she conceded, grinning back at him. "I still think it is a dreadful name, but now that you've shown me the light, my life will never be the same."

"Nobody can call themselves a real New Yorker until they've had an egg cream," Jonathan said.

"You've been in New York all your life?"

"Born and raised only a few miles from this exact spot," he said, and somehow that brought her comfort. She still felt like a green girl from Ohio, but how infinitely kind Jonathan had been to her from the moment he started walking her home each night.

Jonathan's foot nudged her ankle beneath the table, and she glanced up in surprise. "What can I do to make this easier for you?"

She sighed. "I'm worried about what my boss will do once he learns what's happened," she admitted. "I'm afraid he's going to insist that I quit when he hears about the threatening note."

"Then don't tell him," Jonathan said.

"I could never do that! Edgar calls Dr. Friedrich every Friday for a report on how business is going. It would be a lie if we told him everything was fine."

Jonathan leaned across the table. "Katherine, withholding the contents of that note would be an act of omission, not a lie."

"I don't see much of a difference." Honesty was important, and not telling somebody a vital piece of information was as deceptive as an outright lie. She had learned that when she was one month shy of her wedding day. "I can't tolerate liars," she said, and Jonathan's chin raised an infinitesimal fraction. She hadn't meant to offend him or imply anything, so she rushed to clarify. "I was engaged to be married once . . ."

Jonathan stilled, his face suddenly alert. His undivided attention was disconcerting as she braced to reveal the most embarrassing episode of her life.

"His name was Paul Winslow, and he apprenticed with my father for two years after he completed dental school. I was only fourteen when he started, but I was instantly infatuated."

Katherine's family lived on the second floor of a sprawling Queen Anne house on Hudson's town square, and the dental clinic took up the first floor. She used to peek out her bedroom window as Paul came and went each day. By the time his two-year apprenticeship concluded, Hudson had grown large enough for a second dental practice, and Paul opened a clinic on the north side of town with her father's full approval.

It broke Katherine's sixteen-year-old heart when the handsome young apprentice no longer came to their home every day. She took over as her father's assistant after Paul left, performing minor tasks like cleaning equipment and handing him tools during challenging procedures. Her father always narrated what he was doing, providing her with a keen understanding of dentistry before she even graduated from high school.

"When I was eighteen, the entire world bloomed into springtime because Paul began courting me. Then he asked if I'd like to help out at his practice by keeping the books in his front office."

It hadn't taken long for her overly active imagination to start filling in the end to their perfect love story. After all, her own mother was her father's front office assistant. It seemed natural to picture herself doing the same for Paul. They would get married, and when children arrived, she would set up a cradle in the office just as her mother did when Katherine was a baby.

They soon were engaged. She and her mother were over the moon and threw themselves into planning a grand wedding. They hired a seamstress to make the most spectacular wedding gown Hudson, Ohio, had ever seen. The lace was from Belgium, and the bridal veil looked like it belonged to a fairy-tale princess. Katherine and her mother wrote guest lists, planned menus, and even started stitching baby clothes for her hope chest.

Paul refused to set a wedding date until he could support a wife in style. Katherine would have been happy sharing his apartment above the town's hardware store, but Paul wouldn't hear of it. He earned additional qualifications in denture implants, and before long he'd saved enough for a fine house with a sweeping front porch and two fireplaces. There was nothing to stop them from getting married . . . and yet Paul still hesitated.

"That should have been my first clue something was wrong, but I was too blind to see it," she confessed. "He had a house-keeper named Jeannette Dean, and she was always so cold to me. I couldn't understand why. I just assumed she was a nasty and bitter person. It wasn't until much later that I learned she and Paul had been carrying on for years."

Jonathan's expression transformed into pained sympathy. "Oh, Katherine," he said gently, but she hadn't even gotten to the worst part.

"Paul didn't think he'd done anything wrong because he never actually lied to me. He said that since we hadn't taken our vows yet, there wasn't anything wrong with his secret affair."

Sullivan rotated on his barstool to face her. "What a bucket of scum!"

Heat flooded Katherine's face. Why hadn't she realized the bodyguard was listening to every word she had spoken? The harm was already done, so she turned to ask his opinion. "Do you agree that Paul lied to me?"

"Of course!" Sullivan replied. "He was groping the house-keeper! He probably went to a lot of trouble to keep the wool pulled over your eyes."

She shifted her attention back to Jonathan, waiting for his response. He didn't say anything. "Well?" she finally said. "Paul didn't technically lie about Jeannette, but it was 'an act of omission,' to use your term. Call it what you like, but I think he's a lousy, rotten liar and can't ever be trusted. I want more from life than being at the mercy of such a man, so I left Ohio to attend dental school in Philadelphia."

She didn't want Sullivan to hear this next part because it didn't speak very well of her character. She leaned forward to confide her terrible secret to Jonathan behind a cupped hand. "I may be the only person in the history of the world who went to dental school out of revenge."

Jonathan's burst of laughter was a mix of empathy and admiration, and she reveled in it. Maybe it was vain to be flattered by appealing to New York City's most attractive police officer, but so be it. She was proud of what she had accomplished and saw no need to hide it.

"I learned that I didn't need Paul to have a successful life," she continued, straightening up so her bodyguard could hear again. "I was fourteen when I started building castles in the air, and Paul was the handsome prince who would make it all happen for me. It took getting my heart stomped on to realize I'm more than capable of building my own castles. Getting my dental degree and moving to New York taught me that I could do it without him."

Jonathan pretended great concentration as he traced his finger through the droplets of condensation that rolled down the side of his glass. "Paul was selfish," he finally said. "I'm sorry you were hurt before finding him out."

It wasn't the ringing condemnation of her former fiancé she expected him to deliver.

Sullivan was far more vocal. "The guy was a lousy womanizer. Don't get me wrong, I adore the ladies, but I never lie about it. I'm an *honest* womanizer. Big difference," he said with a wink.

Across from her, Jonathan remained silent. He probably thought she was stupid for buying Paul's lies all those years, but her terrible experience was why she refused to deceive Edgar by withholding information about the threatening note.

She met Jonathan's gaze. "You've always said that I'm naive, and maybe I am. I want to keep believing the best of people and will always try to be completely open and honest. I'll tell Edgar about the note, even if it ends up getting me fired."

Jonathan said nothing, but his eyes looked achingly sad. It was sweet of him to worry about Edgar's reaction, and she reached out to touch his hand.

"Please don't worry about me," she said. "I'll be okay no matter what Edgar does."

Somehow, her words of reassurance made Jonathan look sadder than ever.

16

Dr. Friedrich telephoned Katherine at the Martha Washington that evening with good news. "I have spoken with Dr. Parker and told him the contents of that note. He is willing to allow you to keep working at the clinic provided you have a security guard with you at all times."

Relief flooded through her, and the next day Sullivan walked her to the dental office at four o'clock for the start of her shift. Workmen had already installed a new plate-glass window in the front of the office. The receptionist smiled as she handed Katherine her list of the day's appointments. Everything seemed like it was going back to normal.

Except that tonight Jonathan wouldn't be there to walk her home. That was now Sarge's job, the overnight bodyguard who would relieve Sullivan at ten o'clock. While she was grateful for Mr. Hearst's protection, it meant she wouldn't see Jonathan each night anymore.

The thought of losing Jonathan from her daily routine nagged her all evening as she treated her patients. She completed a tooth extraction and three cleanings, all while wondering if she should give up on Jonathan Birch. He hadn't acted on her first tentative overture a month earlier, and yet they'd grown closer than ever over the past few weeks. She was tired of waiting. She realized Jonathan might never act on the attraction between them, and she didn't want to be alone forever.

It was eight o'clock at night when Katherine finished with a root canal. It was one of the more challenging procedures offered by the clinic, and she was grateful for Alvin's help as they worked together on the patient because she was exhausted from the stress of the past few days. It took almost an hour, and at the end, Alvin helped the woozy patient out of the treatment room while Katherine stayed behind to clean up.

She swiped a rag treated with sanitizing solution over the table, then set the dental tools in a basin to soak. She laid out a clean set for her next patient and hoped he wouldn't be fussy because she was running almost twenty minutes behind schedule.

At least her next patient only needed a cleaning, which was the easiest task she performed. Katherine had already lowered the dental chair for the next patient when Alvin returned.

"I offered to take your next patient, but he insisted on seeing you."

"That's fine," she said, embarrassed that Alvin must have noticed how tired she had been. She stood in the doorway of the treatment room to greet her next patient, wondering why he had specifically requested her since she'd never seen him before. He was a handsome man, with blond hair, blue eyes, and a dashing smile.

"Sean Gallagher," he introduced himself. "Thanks for keeping the office open late so I don't have to take off work."

"That's why we do it, Mr. Gallagher," she replied. He settled into the chair and seemed remarkably cheerful for a man about to see the dentist. She cranked the lever to lower the back of the chair and put his head in the proper position. "Just a simple cleaning today?"

"Yes, ma'am." His appealing grin was full of mischief. "Before we get started, and in the interest of complete honesty, I'd like to say that you're far too pretty to be a dentist."

A snort of laughter escaped. Maybe she was overly tired to find such a comment ridiculously funny, but she did. "Why can't a dentist be pretty?"

"It robs the dental experience of the necessary gravitas. When you badger someone to do a better job flossing, do they take you seriously?"

"Indeed they do, especially since I can wave this around for emphasis," she said, brandishing a sharp descaling tool.

"Hmmm," he said, pretending to ponder. "I'll bet a pretty lady like you has already got a sweetheart. Am I right?"

"That sort of question goes beyond a dental exam."

"Not at all. I'm just worried that a lady like you leaving the clinic late at night might be putting herself at risk. Are you sure it's safe?"

For once he wasn't laughing. His face showed a note of concern, which was rather sweet. Besides, the only time she ever got into trouble late at night was from a patient who babbled about a bomb, not from street crime. The fact that she now had a bodyguard wasn't something she intended to share.

"I'm perfectly safe when I leave the clinic. Now . . . open wide."

She used a long-handled examination mirror to pull his cheek aside, but he stopped her hand. "I know the cop who has overnight duty in this area. Lieutenant Birch. Do you ever see him around?"

"You know Jonathan?"

"He lets you call him by his first name? He's usually pretty fusty about stuff like that."

She smiled and shook her head. "No, he's a sweetheart. Now open wide. I'm already behind schedule."

Mr. Gallagher finally complied. Overall, his teeth looked pretty good, which was a relief. Sometimes she encountered grown men who'd never had their teeth professionally cleaned, and scraping off decades of tartar was a miserable experience for both the patient and the dentist. That obviously wasn't the case for Mr. Gallagher, who had excellent teeth except for one small flaw.

"How did you get this chipped tooth?" The tiny chip on the left front incisor was barely noticeable until she started her examination.

He hesitated for only a moment before answering. "My dad used to hold my head underwater whenever I didn't bring home good grades. Getting your face slammed into the bottom of the kitchen sink can do that."

"Oh dear." It wasn't the first time she'd seen chipped teeth because of violence, but the idea of a father doing such a thing to his own child was appalling.

Mr. Gallagher shrugged it off. "Hey, I started bringing home good grades, so it all worked out okay."

Katherine's father treated her like a princess. Maybe she saw the world through rose-tinted glasses, but she assumed all men doted on their children.

She sighed, wishing the world was different. Mr. Gallagher must have noticed her somber thoughts because he laid a gentle hand on her wrist. The laughter had vanished from his face, replaced by compassion.

"Hey, don't look so sad. It's okay. I survived it just fine except for that one little chip. Overall, the world is a really great place, you know?"

How ironic that he was the one offering her comfort. Katherine shook away the gloomy thoughts and proceeded with the cleaning, taking extra care around the man's chipped tooth, a sad memento of an abused childhood.

After finishing, she walked Mr. Gallagher to the lobby. Instead of dutifully being on guard, Sullivan was flirting with Josephine outside the front door of the clinic. Maybe there wasn't any harm in it. Katherine was perfectly capable of collecting Mr. Gallagher's payment, and Sullivan could guard the building from outside. Still, she'd need to keep an eye on him.

Mr. Gallagher had just left when the front-desk telephone rang. She walked behind the counter to pick up the receiver and spoke into the mouthpiece. "Painless Parker Dentistry, may I help you?"

"Stand by for a long-distance call," the operator said. Katherine waited while a series of connections were made. While it wasn't unusual to receive late-night telephone calls from people in pain, such calls were usually local. She clenched the receiver, hoping it wasn't her parents calling from Ohio.

"Katherine?" a voice sounded on the other end. "Edgar here."

She let out a sigh of relief. "Edgar! Where are you?"

"Still in San Francisco. What's this I hear about a brick being thrown through our window? Dr. Friedrich said it had a note attached to it, threatening you."

"Yes, but please don't worry. I'll pay for the window. And I'm very safe. The police have been wonderful—"

He cut her off. "Right, Dr. Friedrich said you have a bodyguard."

"I do."

There was a long pause on the other end of the line. Normally it was easy to read Edgar because he was an open book, but this silence was alarming. At last he said, "Katherine, I'm worried about you."

"There's no need, really."

"Yes, but a bodyguard isn't going to solve my problem. I am paying top dollar to keep that clinic in a safe and well-lit location. If my clinic gets the reputation as a place that attracts crime, I lose that advantage."

She bowed her head and braced her hand against the counter. Paying for a broken window seemed so piddly now.

"I've just opened my third dental clinic in San Francisco," Edgar continued. "If you aren't safe in New York, you can come out here."

She gazed out at Times Square, ablaze with brilliant lights. The cafés were bustling, the night was alive. She loved it here. "But this is my home. I don't want to leave it."

"Katherine, the clinic you're standing in is a business, not your home. And it's *my* business. I'll do whatever I can to help you, but if the police can't solve who has been threatening you, I'm going to ask you to leave. I've got fifteen clinics in three different states, but the Times Square location is my crown jewel. Do you understand?"

"Of course I do," she said, feeling as if her world was crashing down around her.

"Look on the bright side! If things don't work out in New York, I'll be happy to put you on the payroll in San Francisco. You should taste the Dungeness crab out here. It's fabulous, far better than what they have in New York."

This telephone call must be costing Edgar a fortune, but how thoughtful he was to try to sell San Francisco to her. The call came to an end, but the message was clear.

Her days in New York were numbered.

17

The baby owls needed to be fed every six hours, and they were carnivores. Jonathan started delivering the jars of meat scraps to Katherine a little after midnight, which meant she still had a chance to see him even though he no longer walked her home. Katherine snipped the chicken livers, kidneys, and gizzards into slivers using a dental ligature cutter. Most of the women were squeamish about handling the glistening organ meat, but Katherine didn't mind.

This afternoon she shared the daytime feeding duties with Inga, a night telegraph operator at the harbor. She and Inga huddled at the open window, taking turns dangling a bit of chicken liver over the nest until a chick managed to stand on its wobbly legs to snatch it in its beak.

"Is it terrible to say they aren't cute?" Inga asked.

The owlets were actually a little bit hideous, with frizzy white feathers, bulbous eyes, and a screech that was bloodcurdling. How a creature only a few inches tall could make such an ear-splitting scream was a mystery. It meant she and Inga needed to be on guard throughout the day to promptly deliver a feeding before the screeching alerted Mrs. Blum to the owls' presence.

Katherine rooted around in a jar for another lump of meat and leaned over a chick, but her attention strayed to the sidewalk eight floors below, where Sullivan was supposed to be guarding entrances to the building. Instead, he was flirting with a lady selling pretzels from a pushcart. She now had a week of watching Sullivan on the job, long enough to know he couldn't be trusted near anyone wearing a skirt.

It was beyond frustrating. Mr. Hearst's men were supposed to guard the outside entrances of the building. Meanwhile, police officers patrolled the perimeter of the building several times a day, looking for suspicious people and signs of trouble.

So far, the police had held up their end of the bargain, but Sullivan was letting everyone down. He just coaxed the pretzel vendor to join him on a bench, and he hovered close enough to look straight down the lady's blouse rather than monitor the Martha Washington.

Katherine handed the jar of meat scraps to Inga. "Can you finish up?" she asked and started racing toward the elevator. It was time to confront Sullivan in the act.

Anger and frustration percolated as she waited for the painfully slow descent of the elevator that seemed to stop on every floor. She couldn't bring herself to exchange a greeting with the residents who got on and off. These were the women she had put in danger by continuing to live at the Martha Washington. The least she could do was light a fire under Sullivan and get him to do his job.

She crossed the lobby, pushed through the front doors, and stepped into the glaring sunlight of the August afternoon. By the time she arrived at the corner, the pretzel vendor had left and Sullivan was casually strolling along the street.

She drew up alongside him. "Mr. Sullivan, I understand that as a red-blooded American male, flirting with pretty street vendors is more invigorating than patrol work, but this building has four entrances to guard and over five hundred women, including me, who are depending on your ability to keep us safe."

"Dr. Schneider, I've been off duty for the last ten minutes. I've still got five minutes left on my break."

She blinked. "You have?"

He nodded down the street. "Lieutenant Gallagher took over at the top of the hour. It's his day to fill in on patrol duty while I'm on break."

A glance down the block proved the truth of his words. A tall officer in a spiffy uniform was walking toward them, the brim of his cap obscuring most of his face. Even so, she could see he was a handsome man. And on duty. She had no right to grouse at Sullivan, and the ire drained out of her, sapping her of strength. "You're entirely right," she conceded. "I'm sorry, Sullivan, you didn't deserve that. Can you please forgive me for being an ill-tempered shrew?"

Sullivan, who didn't seem to have a mean-tempered bone in his body, laughingly accepted her apology before heading off to chat with a group of ladies leaving the Martha Washington. It wasn't her business what Sullivan did with the last five minutes of his break, and she went to meet the policeman on duty.

The officer removed his cap as she approached, revealing a face she'd seen before. She couldn't place him until he smiled and revealed the tiny chip in his tooth.

"Hello, Dr. Schneider. Remember me?"

"Indeed I do. You've got the cleanest teeth I've seen all day. I should get the name of your dentist."

It turned out that Lieutenant Gallagher was a member of the Bomb Squad that had been assigned to the Sons of Chaos investigation. She hadn't realized when she cleaned his teeth a few nights ago and wondered if it had been a coincidence that he sought her out.

"No coincidence," he admitted when she asked him. "I needed to get my teeth cleaned anyway, and I figured I could take a look around your office just to be sure everything was as it should be."

His uniform looked quite different from Jonathan's, and it took a moment to spot why. "What are all those bars you've got pinned to your chest?"

He stood a little taller and pointed to a slim bar covered with blue-and-red silk. "That one is for being on the Bomb Squad, which is very dangerous work. Only the bravest of men are chosen for it." He acted lighthearted and amiable as he bragged, and it was oddly appealing.

"You don't have to convince me. And the green-and-gold bar?"

He touched it. "This is for the time I risked my life to stop a bank robbery in action. This one is for passing the lieutenants' exam with a perfect score. And this one is for helping dismantle the bomb at Saint Patrick's Cathedral."

"Very impressive." She couldn't recall Jonathan ever wearing any ribbons or medals on his uniform. "Is it normal to wear all your commendations on your daily uniform?"

He shrugged as they continued walking around the building. "There's no rule against it. I earned them, so I'm going to wear them anytime I get the chance. Heck, I wear them on my pajamas at night."

Lieutenant Gallagher's self-deprecating humor was delightful. None of the other officers wore medals on their everyday uniforms, and she pondered the question as they circled the building. His keen eyes scanned the windowsills, the ledges, and behind the bushes, always on the lookout for anything suspicious.

"Why are those commendations so important to you?" she asked.

"Well, Dr. Schneider, I grew up feeling like gum stuck to the bottom of my father's shoe. A medal is proof that I'm not a worthless piece of garbage after all. So, yes, I like collecting medals, and I like wearing them."

"What does your father think of you now?"

"Oh, he's long dead. He kicked the bucket when I was ten, but I still like collecting medals. Some men want a pretty girl or a pot of money. Me? I want to earn every medal under the sun."

She appreciated his shameless, openhearted honesty. "I expect that you shall, Lieutenant."

"Say, can I take you out to dinner sometime?"

The question took her by surprise. "I'm sorry, but there's somebody else." She avoided looking at him when she said it, even though it wasn't a lie because she'd been carrying a torch for Jonathan Birch for two years.

Lieutenant Gallagher was not easily dissuaded. "Really? I don't see a ring."

"That's because there isn't one, but I'm still not free."

The lieutenant's eyes gleamed. "Ma'am, if you ever get tired of waiting for that ring, you can find me at police headquarters. In case you aren't aware, that's where all the elite officers work."

"The modest ones too."

He grinned. "Oh, there's nothing modest about me, Dr. Schneider," he said with a dashing smile as they parted.

Her heart pounded as she watched him leave. Lieutenant Gallagher displayed more overt attraction to her in five minutes than she'd received from Jonathan in two years. It hurt to even consider, but perhaps it was time to look further afield to find a man who would care for her.

───────────────

Ever since Jonathan first came to her for help understanding chemistry, they had periodically met at the New York Public Library to go over another chapter in her textbook. Today marked Katherine's fourth tutoring session with him, and it was probably her last. She couldn't continue meeting him if her burgeoning feelings were never going to be reciprocated. She was halfway into her one-month time limit laid down by Mrs. Blum, and they were no closer to finding Achilles. Nor did they have any solid leads on the sketches of the two men. She couldn't depend on Mr. Hearst's bodyguards forever, and if something didn't happen soon, she'd have to take Edgar's offer and move to San Francisco.

Would Jonathan miss her if she had to leave? The biggest concession she'd wrung from him in the past two years was convincing him to use her first name. He was a huge part of the reason she wanted to stay in New York, but she was tired of waiting for him to make a move. It was time to force a change.

"I think we've reached the end of what I'll be able to teach you," she said as they left the library, walking down the wide front steps and onto the sidewalk.

"Why?" Jonathan asked. "The textbook you lent me is helping, but I've still got a lot to learn." He sounded both wounded and surprised. It hurt to hear it, and yet she mustn't let that dissuade her.

"Surely there are men on the Bomb Squad who could do a better job," she said. "I've met Lieutenant Gallagher, and he seems to be a fine man. Ask him for help."

Jonathan snorted. "Gallagher would rather help me plant my foot in a pile of manure before he'd tutor me."

She kept walking down Fifth Avenue. Sullivan trailed a few paces behind, probably listening to every word.

"I don't know why you can't get along with Lieutenant Gallagher. I think he's delightful."

"He's not delightful; he's a scoundrel."

"Then find someone else on the Bomb Squad to tutor you. I might be leaving New York soon."

It was an exaggeration, but she wanted to get a rise out of him. Wasn't he going to say anything? Offer to redouble his efforts to find the people who had threatened her?

Jonathan remained silent for several paces before he asked in an utterly calm voice, "How do you feel about that?"

She wanted to scream. She wanted to grab him by the shoulders and shake him until she could see behind the padlocked double-bolted door where he kept his heart hidden. Instead, she matched his measured tone. "I would rather stay here. California is too far away."

"What about going back to Ohio? Your father has a dental practice there. Surely he would give you a job."

Frustration boiled over. "I don't *want* to go anywhere else," she yelled, drawing the attention of some businessmen dining at a nearby café, but she didn't care. Jonathan blanched and took a step back.

She'd had enough. No more waiting. No more being polite and ladylike. "Don't you understand? I want you to tell me that you'd be devastated if I left, and you'll pull out all the stops so I can stay here in New York. I want you to find the bad guys and make it safe for me to be here, because for whatever insane reason, I actually care about you, Lieutenant Birch."

"You tell it to him, lady!" one of the businessmen chortled from the café. Katherine lifted her chin and kept her eyes locked with Jonathan's.

He flushed a brilliant shade of scarlet. He looked so stunned that she had to fight the temptation to apologize for yelling at him, but this had gone on long enough.

He opened and closed his mouth several times before finding his tongue. "I want you to stay, I would be devastated if you left, and I will pull out all the stops and pound on every door until you're safe. I will do whatever is humanly possible to keep you in New York because I am insanely, irrationally, and hopelessly infatuated with you. I think about you morning, noon, and night."

She could barely breathe. Her heart pounded so hard, it roared in her ears. "Prove it."

A gleam lit his eyes as he closed the distance between them and fastened his arms around her. He lowered his head and kissed her. It was a long, deep, and knee-weakening kiss. People across the street cheered, but Jonathan kept kissing her and it was glorious, and she didn't care that it was the middle of the day on Fifth Avenue. Jonathan Birch was kissing her, and the world had just become a more beautiful place.

She was dimly aware of Sullivan's voice intruding on the sheer perfection of the moment. "As her bodyguard, I should probably say something about this."

Jonathan broke contact with her lips. "Consider it said."

She had started to laugh when Jonathan smothered her with another kiss. Music from the buskers across the street was the perfect accompaniment to this joyous moment.

"I'm so happy," she said when he finally lifted his head.

Jonathan's eyes sparkled, and his face was alive. "I'm happy too. And, Katherine, no matter what, I will find a way for you to stay in New York."

Jonathan started sneaking into Katherine's building each night. He ought to feel guilty, but it was the only time they could be alone without a bodyguard hovering nearby. Sarge looked the other way when Jonathan climbed up the fire-escape ladder to Katherine's eighth floor, where he delivered a jar of kitchen scraps and took his one-hour break with her at midnight.

They met in the common room, where they shared a few quick kisses, flirted a bit, then fed the baby owls. The owls were now about six inches tall, and *loud*! As soon as the window opened, the chicks rose on wobbly legs and screeched loud enough to be heard all over the floor, which was why they had to hush them up quickly. Katherine never showed a bit of squeamishness as she snipped the livers and kidneys into slivers for the chicks. Other women from the eighth floor fed them throughout the day, but the hour after midnight belonged to him and Katherine.

For the first time in his life, he had a partner. He'd never allowed a woman to get close before because marriage and family seemed impossible for a man with no past and only a fake identity.

But was it really fake? In his heart and soul, he had become Jonathan Birch. His old life was a shadow left behind decades ago, and in all that time it had never once threatened to resurface. Why couldn't he become a normal man? His new identity was secure, and he wanted a life with Katherine. God willing, there would be children too. Ever since resolving that it was possible, he awoke each day with a lighter spirit. The first few moments after he roused were always a little hazy, questioning why he was so inexplicably happy, and then he remembered. Katherine! Their kiss, their newfound understanding. Sixteen years of dedicated police service and careful reserve in his private life had created a new foundation upon which he could build a normal life.

"Did you ever have a pet growing up?" Katherine asked one evening as they leaned out the window to feed the owls. He immediately went on guard. He didn't like talking about his past because he would forever need to be careful when discussing it with her, but this was an easy question.

"Never," he said. There were no rooms for pets in the crowded Brooklyn tenement where he grew up.

"Then how did you learn about taking care of birds?"

That had been because he and Charlotte Boroughs used to take care of the wild birds who visited the feeder she set out. She also had a parakeet they both looked after.

"For a while I courted a girl named Charlotte," he offered. "She had a parakeet."

Katherine dangled another piece of gizzard above a chick. "You've never spoken of her. Was she someone special?"

Charlotte came into his life after he left Brooklyn, so he could talk about her without lying. "She lived across the street from the Clifton School. She was pretty and kind, and I loved being around her. At first I was afraid her parents would disapprove of me because who wants an orphaned kid for their daughter? But they welcomed me into their home and treated me well."

There were times when he secretly pretended Mr. and Mrs. Boroughs were his parents too. They were wholesome people, always generous with affection and wise counsel. They said grace before meals, and their dinner conversations lingered long into the evening.

"Charlotte eventually found someone else, but to this day I miss her parents. I felt like a part of their family when I was with them."

"And now you've found a family within the police department."

He grimaced. "I can't stand half of them." They both laughed, but he sobered quickly. Katherine's eyes sparkled in the moonlight as she looked at him. "The family I was born into wasn't great. The Boroughs were the kind of people I wished I could have had for parents, and if I'm ever lucky enough to . . ." His mouth went dry, and he had to take a steadying breath. The chance to create a real family with Katherine had become a wonderous possibility so glorious that it took his breath away. He'd never dared to hope for it before, but now he couldn't stop praying for it. "If I'm ever lucky enough to have a family of my own, I hope I can be as good a husband and father as Mr. Boroughs was."

Katherine touched the back of his hand, and a shiver raced up his arm. "What's stopping you?"

A lifetime of lies.

He glanced down at the baby owls. They were snuggling down into their nest, still lively and awake, but no longer hungry. Soon they'd be big enough to leave the nest and rob him of the excuse to keep coming here each night.

He screwed shut the lid on the jar of scraps and turned to face her. "I'm far from a perfect man. I've made mistakes and have a lot of regrets. I don't know what sort of woman would want me."

She leaned in and kissed him. "I'm not perfect either," she whispered against his lips.

He squeezed his eyes shut and held her, praying they could be together forever and that she would never learn about his past. Katherine was the best, purest thing in his life, and he couldn't bear the thought of losing her.

18

Three weeks after someone threw a brick through the clinic's front window, Katherine received word that Edgar was in New York and had called for an emergency meeting with all of his employees at three o'clock.

Even more ominous, he ordered that all appointments for the rest of the afternoon be canceled. The notoriously thrifty Dr. Edgar Parker had never closed the clinic for anything before, and that worried Katherine. She arrived at the clinic an hour early, anxious and sick about Edgar's urgent meeting. The ongoing lawsuit was a constant threat looming over them. Though the Times Square office was his flagship clinic, if operating it was costing him too much money, Edgar wouldn't hesitate to close up shop.

Anxiety crackled in the clinic's lobby as the entire staff waited for Edgar's arrival. With nine dentists and five staff members, most of the seats were filled. Katherine was too nervous to sit and leaned against the back wall beside Alvin.

"Maybe we shouldn't have even bothered to replace the window," Alvin said in a low voice.

"Nonsense," Dr. Friedrich barked. "Dr. Parker owns this building, and if he wishes to lease the space to someone else, they must have a new window."

Katherine fidgeted. She'd always been a little intimidated by the gruff German dentist, yet she would miss him if this place closed. Wasn't that odd? They were almost like a family.

"Where will you go if he closes the practice?" Alvin asked.

She didn't want to think about it. Not many places would hire a female dentist, so she'd likely have to take Edgar's offer and move to San Francisco. "I don't know," she confessed. "You?" It might be even harder for a Black dentist to find work.

But Alvin didn't look overly worried. "I'll try to get a loan and start my own place. If Edgar has to close the practice here, there will be a lot of Black folks who'll have a hard time finding a dentist willing to treat them."

She fought the urge to cry. Didn't the people trying to drive Edgar out of business understand what he did for the community? Yes, Edgar was crass. Yes, he was gaudy and shameless and had gotten his start as a vaudeville dentist, pulling the teeth of elephants and tigers for the crowd's amusement. The dentists at the ADA despised that sort of thing, but Edgar also accepted clients other high-minded dentists wouldn't touch, and he set his prices low enough for them to afford.

"Here he is," Josephine said. Edgar's orange suit coat with a matching top hat were easy to spot coming down the street. He paused in front of the brand-new window, faced them all with a huge smile, and raised both hands high. One held a bouquet of flowers, the other a bottle of champagne.

Alvin opened the door. "Welcome back," he said a little cautiously as Edgar strode inside.

"Thank you, sir!" Edgar boomed. "You may all congratulate me. My friends, the lawsuit is over, and it was settled in my favor!"

The room was silent for approximately two seconds before the shrieks began. Edgar set the wine down and began shaking everyone's hand. Laughter mingled with a barrage of questions as Edgar popped the champagne cork and declared there would be no talk of business without a toast to his success. There were no drinking glasses so Katherine handed out paper cones used by patients to rinse their mouths. They all raised a toast to Edgar, who declared the lawsuit officially closed.

"Did they just give up?" Alvin asked.

Edgar shook his head. "Those dental busybodies wanted to drive me into bankruptcy and take away my license. 'There's no such thing as painless dentistry,' they kept accusing me."

Dr. Friedrich helped himself to another paper cup of champagne. "They've got a point."

Edgar grinned. "Indeed they do, so I decided to change my name. I am no longer Edgar Parker. I had my first name legally changed to *Painless*. As of this morning, my legal name is officially Painless Parker. My lawyer and the judge both agreed that the ADA cannot prohibit me from using my legal name to advertise my services. I shall use that name everywhere! Painted on the front door, printed on our stationery and in every advertisement and telephone directory. I am Painless Parker, and I will carry the name to my grave."

Josephine giggled. "Are we supposed to start calling you Painless instead of Edgar?"

"You may call me Edgar, or Painless, or Winner of an annoying lawsuit against the ADA. I will answer to them all!" Edgar raised the bottle, and everyone applauded.

The impromptu party continued until five o'clock when they reopened the clinic to patients. Katherine returned to her treatment room with renewed confidence that this clinic would continue to serve the people of New York for years to come. She was laying out her tools for the evening when Edgar appeared at her door.

She smiled and welcomed him inside. She was about to congratulate him again when she noticed what he held in his hands.

"These are brochures about California," he said, setting them on the table. "I also brought some fliers of apartments for lease and pictures of San Francisco. It's a marvelous city, Katherine. I'd very much like to lure you out there."

Her mouth went dry, and she took a sobering breath. "Are you telling me I have to leave?"

Edgar's expression was sympathetic. "I can't force you to move to California, but I think you'll like it there. And there's been no progress on finding the ones threatening you, correct?"

She wanted to bat the brochures off the table. Instead, she nodded and remained quiet.

"Well then," Edgar said, "take a week or two to decide. We'll revisit the subject soon, all right?"

She agreed. What other choice did she have? Unless the men behind the string of bombings could be found and brought to justice, she was going to be forced to leave the job she loved so well.

***

Climbing the fire escape to see Katherine each night never got old for Jonathan. He felt like the prince scaling the tower to steal a forbidden hour with Rapunzel. He and Katherine flirted, kissed, fed the owls, and feasted on whatever treat he found to share. Tonight it was chocolate biscotti, Katherine's favorite.

They sat on opposite sides of the window seat, where he had a perfect view of moonlight illuminating the side of her face. The owls had been fed, and he now cradled Katherine's bare feet on his lap, gently rubbing her ankles while she munched on the biscotti.

The tip of her toe poked him. "When are you going to give me this biscotti recipe?"

"Never, because I don't have it," he said honestly. Nonna Rinaldi guarded the secret of her chocolate biscotti like a general guarded battle plans. He had made a special trip to Brooklyn yesterday to pick up this latest batch.

"You made the lemon shortbread last night," she said.

He quirked a brow. "What makes you so certain?"

"Sarge saw you buy a dozen lemons at the market across the street."

"Hmm," he said, neither confirming nor denying her theory, but she was right. He made the shortbread because the owners of the Italian restaurant often let him use their kitchen to bake in the early morning hours before the restaurant opened. They knocked a few dollars off his room's rent in exchange for baking desserts they sold in the restaurant.

He continued massaging her ankles, peering at her through half-closed lids. "What would you like tomorrow night? If it's within my power, I'll bake it for you."

"Chocolate biscotti again."

"Not within my power. What else?"

"Focaccia bread, then."

He leaned forward to kiss the tip of her nose. "You shall have focaccia bread."

He returned to his side of the window alcove and pulled her feet back onto his lap. Then the door banged open, and a furious-looking woman strode inside.

"I *knew* it," she snarled.

He let go of Katherine's ankles and sprang to his feet. Katherine jumped down too, knocking over the glass jar of animal organs, which smashed on the floor.

Mrs. Blum didn't notice. She was too intent on stalking toward Katherine with a mix of fury and delight, pointing an accusatory finger at Katherine's nose. "Consorting with strange men, tawdry groping in the dark."

Jonathan stepped forward. "There's nothing tawdry about our feelings for each other," he said calmly. "As you can see, we are fully clothed and not doing anything wrong."

"No? The fact that a man has breached the sanctity of this home is a violation in and of itself. Dr. Schneider, you should be ashamed of yourself."

Before he could reply, an ear-splitting screech came from outside. Katherine slammed the window shut, but it was too late.

Mrs. Blum blanched, then rushed to the window, peering down at the baby owls in revulsion. "What are those filthy creatures doing on that ledge?"

"Breathing?" Katherine offered, which only incensed Mrs. Blum more. The older woman shifted positions, mashing her face against the glass to get a better angle.

"You might want to watch where you step," Jonathan suggested when the tip of Mrs. Blum's shoe dipped into the wet lump of chicken gizzards.

Mrs. Blum reared back, gaping in speechless horror at the glistening organs.

"We were feeding the owls," Katherine admitted. "They lost their mother and are dependent on a few scraps of food we provide. Lieutenant Birch has been very thoughtful in bringing us the kitchen scraps."

"This makes it even worse," Mrs. Blum hissed. "Those creatures are a health hazard to the building. I want them removed at once."

"They can't yet fly," Katherine said.

"I don't care. They're unsanitary and a violation of our rules. I shall ask the janitorial staff to dispose of them first thing in the morning."

"But you can't!" Katherine said. "They're helpless chicks. We love them."

"Then you may take them with you to your next residence. I was being generous by allowing you to remain for a month during the police investigation, and this is the thanks I get? You can pack your bags and be out of here tomorrow morning as well."

"Not without a written order of eviction signed by a judge," Jonathan said, grateful for his class in procedural law that police officers were required to pass. "Dr. Schneider has a lease, and it will be honored."

Being reminded of Katherine's legal rights did little to placate

Mrs. Blum, who turned her fire on Katherine. "*Six days*," she spat. "You have six days until the end of your allotted month, then you are out. As for the owls, they will be gone tomorrow morning. You!" she ordered, pointing that sharp finger in his face. "I want you out immediately or I shall call the police."

Jonathan was in uniform, but Mrs. Blum didn't recognize the absurdity of what she just said. Still, she had a right to be annoyed with him, and he was at the end of his dinner break anyway. He picked up his brimmed cap and placed it on his head, then turned to Katherine. "Don't worry about the owls. If you have any difficulty tomorrow morning with an attempted eviction, call the police station and we'll be back." He turned to give a respectful nod to Mrs. Blum before leaving.

Sarge was on patrol guarding the front door of the building. The bodyguard had been working for William Randolph Hearst for years and had a good sense of his employer's taste.

Jonathan approached the older man. "Do you think Mr. Hearst's newspaper might be interested in the story of some cute baby owls struggling to survive in the big city?"

Sarge gave a knowing smile. "Would those be the chicks up on the eighth floor that are causing a ruckus every few hours?"

He nodded. "They're likely to meet a grim fate tomorrow morning unless something can be done."

"Yeah, Mr. Hearst loves that kind of story. I'll bet you he's over in the newspaper office right now. Stop by and ask."

Within the hour, Jonathan had assurances that a reporter and a photographer would be at the Martha Washington first thing in the morning to start publicizing a story about the brave little owls struggling to survive in the big city.

Katherine waited in the lobby at eight o'clock the following morning. Jonathan was coming off duty and had sent word that he'd be bringing people from the *New York Journal* to write a laudatory article about the ladies at the Martha Washington who had been fostering some orphaned owl chicks. Mrs. Blum was not on duty, so getting the men upstairs to see the owls shouldn't be a problem.

Thank you, she silently mouthed to Jonathan as he stepped inside the lobby, followed by two men from the newspaper. He flashed her a quick wink, and then they all moved toward the elevator.

Dennis Keogh was a night reporter, and he'd already done some legwork researching the phenomenon of urban owls and the challenges they faced.

"Tell me about the owls here," he said.

"You'll have an excellent view of them on the eighth floor," she replied. "Their nest is right outside on the window ledge."

Mr. Keogh looked a little ill. "Ma'am, I'm not big on heights. I don't need to see the owls to do a story. We'll send Billy up to get a photograph, but can we talk down here?"

"No, you're coming up with us," the photographer said, and Dennis groaned but obeyed. She kept careful watch on him during the elevator ride up. Tiny pinpricks of sweat broke out across his brow, which he repeatedly blotted with a handkerchief.

How odd. She had often read Mr. Keogh's crusading stories in the *Journal*. He covered New York's underworld, writing about gambling and prostitution, stories that took him into the most dangerous sections of the city, and yet he feared riding an elevator.

"I've never been a fan of heights," he admitted as they approached the eighth floor. "These skyscrapers will be the death of me someday."

After they arrived at the eighth floor, Dennis took a quick peek at the owls before retreating to the far side of the common room. Even a fleeting glimpse overlooking the city was enough for him to tug on his tie and loosen his collar. She and Jonathan joined him at the table while the photographer started taking pictures through the open window.

The reporter opened his notepad, and Katherine recounted the story of how they noticed Celine building the nest, then her tragic death a few weeks after the chicks hatched. It didn't take long to complete her story.

Dennis was eager to change topics. "Why haven't the cops tracked down those two guys in the sketches?" he asked Jonathan. "It's been eight weeks since those pictures were first published."

She loved the way Jonathan's expression didn't change. The situation with the Sons of Chaos infuriated them both, but Jonathan remained calm and measured as he answered the question. "We've got only three officers following up on eight hundred tips. The numbers are against us, and that's half our problem."

"What's the other half?" Dennis asked.

"The fact that the city of New York is terrified of Achilles," he replied. "You know how he got that nickname, don't you?"

Dennis shook his head.

"Rumor has it that he punishes people who betray him by snipping their Achilles tendon, which renders the leg useless for the rest of their lives. Few people will risk that for a piddly reward. It's been more than a month since his last bombing, but I don't think he's given up. It takes a while to gather enough materials to make a bunch of bombs without attracting attention."

Dennis kept his pad open, scribbling Jonathan's responses. "Any idea where he'll strike next? The police think he's got a list of targets in mind. Who's next?"

Katherine shifted uneasily. There was only one left. "The suspect mentioned something about a boring old lady," she said. "I have no idea who that might be."

"The boring *gray* lady," Jonathan corrected. "The morning you first reported this to me, you claimed he said 'a boring gray lady.'"

There didn't seem to be much distinction to Katherine. "You're right. He said she was boring and gray. The boring gray lady. There are thousands of people who fit that description."

Dennis abruptly straightened. "The gray lady? That sounds like the *New York Times*."

"Holy cow," the photographer said as he turned away from the window. "You could be right."

"What are you talking about?" Katherine asked.

Dennis's face lit with a mischievous smirk. "People call the *New York Times* 'the gray lady' because the editor refuses to use pictures. Look at any issue. It's nothing but blocks of dreary, tiny text. No color, no verve, no pictures."

"Why would someone target the *New York Times*?" she asked.

"Because they're a threat to public health by boring the world to death," Dennis scoffed.

Jonathan wasn't laughing. "The *New York Times* is the most prominent newspaper in the city. Achilles wants to hit the city on all levels. Where we eat, drink, and pray. What we read and think. He wants attention, and attacking the *New York Times* would give it to him."

19

Jonathan took the tip about the *New York Times* being "the gray lady" seriously. The newspaper's building would be a wickedly perfect target. Not only did it house the city's most prominent paper, but its basement also contained a major hub of the subway system. A successful bombing of the building would strike at the city's transportation, information system, and cultural landmark all in one fell swoop. It was the most logical lead to date, and they needed to check it out.

The Bomb Squad assigned Sean Gallagher to be in charge of investigating the lead. Since the building was within the 15th Precinct, Jonathan was appointed to serve in a supporting role. Their task was to inspect the *Times* building for possible weak spots, then to come up with a plan for protecting it.

How did one keep a twenty-five-story building safe? With its stairwells, elevator shafts, and a subway station in the basement, the entire building was rife with possibilities for someone to hide a bomb and then disappear into the anonymous chaos of everyday life on Times Square.

Jonathan wanted a comprehensive patrol route to surveil the

building, complete with a list of vulnerable spots to be checked at regular intervals. Officers would be required to sign in at each point to ensure compliance.

Gallagher wanted the exact opposite. They were walking the length of the subway station beneath the building, assessing its vulnerability while Gallagher prattled nonsense. "Our cops need the freedom to follow their instincts. Obeying your rigid map will rob them of that."

"No, obeying my meticulously drafted route will ensure every vulnerable area is inspected each hour," Jonathan insisted.

An incoming subway train filled the tunnel with a wall of noise, so Gallagher indulged in a dramatic roll of his eyes to express his disdain. As soon as the noise subsided, Gallagher continued, "This subway stop isn't where anyone would plant a bomb. You're completely ignorant of what it takes to wire, position, and disguise a bomb. It's not a quick process, and this place is swarming with people. Trust me, this isn't where it's going to happen."

It was a good point, but Jonathan would never admit it. "Foot traffic down here dwindles to almost nothing between two and four o'clock in the morning. That's the perfect time to hide a bomb. It's when they tried it at Saint Patrick's."

"Oh, the time when I got a medal for distinguished service, and you got a ribbon for participation? *That* Saint Patrick's incident?"

The rumble of the departing train spared him the need for a response. Why did it always have to be about medals with Gallagher? Yes, Gallagher had received one of the highest awards possible, but Jonathan's service on the force was never about collecting ribbons or medals.

"Medals are about keeping the city safe, not personal aggrandizement," Jonathan pointed out. "Have you ever wondered if your insatiable need for medals is rooted in deep-seated insecurity? Sigmund Freud has theories about men's need to compensate for their physical inadequacies."

Gallagher shoved him. "You think I'm inadequate, Sapling?"

A cool, feminine voice intruded. "How nice to see the two of you getting along."

Jonathan blanched, embarrassed to have Katherine witness his petty spat with Gallagher. The younger bodyguard, Sullivan, was with her. "We're performing an inspection of the *Times* building," he said, as though he hadn't been completely intent on bickering with Gallagher.

Like a snake shedding his skin, Gallagher dropped the sarcasm and morphed into a tower of charm. "On your way to work?" he asked. When Katherine nodded, Gallagher offered his arm to escort her to the staircase leading out of the subway station.

Jonathan darted to her other side. It was a tight fit to walk three abreast up the stairs, but he'd eat nails before letting Gallagher steal her away. Sullivan walked behind them, and they all escorted Katherine to the dental clinic's front door.

"Please don't come to blows once my back is turned," she teased with a pointed look at them both.

Gallagher assumed an aura of exaggerated innocence. "Me? I'm the incarnation of goodness and mercy."

Jonathan blocked all expression from his face. Winning a spot on the Bomb Squad meant getting along with Gallagher, but enduring the man's arrogance was likely to kill him.

To Katherine's delight, newspaper coverage of the baby owls completely fascinated the city. Experts from the Brooklyn Zoo weighed in on the importance of predatory birds for keeping the city's rodent population in check. The newspaper hosted a contest for naming the chicks, and top submissions were published daily. Mrs. Blum proudly took credit for the survival of the chicks and became the spokeswoman for everything dealing with the owls.

Katherine was happy to let Mrs. Blum steal the limelight, especially since the surly woman relented about the eviction. Katherine now had too much goodwill from the newspapers and the police to enforce the eviction, even though she had to end her midnight rendezvous with Jonathan. To compensate, she and Jonathan started sharing breakfast together every morning at the deli across the street. Silverware clinked, coffee percolated, and frying pans sizzled with the scents of corned beef hash and eggs as she listened to Jonathan tell her about his overnight shift.

It was a little awkward to have an intimate conversation with her bodyguard listening to every word, but she didn't care. She was in love and savored wallowing in Jonathan's company and his dry sense of humor. It took her months to spot it beneath his sober demeanor, but now she caught glimpses of it all the time, like his teasing about her weakness for sugary sweets.

"You should be ashamed of yourself, Dr. Schneider. What sort of dentist dumps that much sugar into her coffee?"

She loved the way his face stayed serious while his eyes danced. It was rare to find someone she could bare her soul to, and amazingly, Jonathan seemed to feel the same way. They could talk about *anything*, for he wasn't a closed book anymore. He didn't even mind when she probed him on his irrational hostility toward Gallagher.

"Why do you hate him so much?" she asked one morning after taking her first sip of coffee. They sat in their regular booth, with Sullivan on a swivel stool at the service counter two yards away.

Jonathan's reply came instantly. "Because Gallagher is a vain, amoral cheat and always has been."

"I haven't seen that side of him," she said.

"That's because he's not interested in letting you see it, but trust me, it's there."

And yet the other men on the police force seemed to respect Lieutenant Gallagher. Everyone had different faces they showed the world depending on circumstances, and sometimes that could lead to errors in judgment. She had personal experience with doing so.

"I always disliked Paul's housekeeper because she was so cold to me," Katherine admitted. "I didn't understand that it was her love for Paul that caused her to resent me."

"Ha!" Sullivan chimed in as he rotated on his stool to face them. "She should have taken it out on Paul, not you."

"Amen," Jonathan said, and she scrambled for another way to make her point.

"Sometimes people show you their best side, but sometimes they only let you see their worst. Paul's housekeeper showed me her worst. I'm not excusing her behavior, but at least now I understand her better. I think you're seeing the worst part of Lieutenant Gallagher, and it's only the tip of the iceberg. There's a side of him you don't know."

"And you do?" Jonathan asked skeptically.

She thought of the chip in Lieutenant Gallagher's tooth. "Yes, I do."

Jonathan wore an amused expression as he took a long drag on his egg cream. "You're painfully naive, Katherine."

"Maybe, but I hope I never lose the ability to look for the best in people."

Jonathan's eyes warmed as he gazed at her. "I like that about you. I always have."

"Me too," Sullivan butted in.

Having a third wheel constantly intruding on a romantic moment was both frustrating and funny. Hopefully, the day would come when she and Jonathan would look back on these awkward dates with amusement.

Her childhood infatuation with Paul was such a pale, puny thing compared to the heft of what she felt for Jonathan. There were still dangers and uncertainties surrounding her, but so long as Jonathan was in her life, she would survive them. Edgar won his lawsuit, and the dental clinic was safe. The baby owls were thriving. She'd fallen in love with a good man, and life was almost perfect.

Katherine still savored the haze of euphoria as she dressed for work that afternoon. Her lilac walking gown with the bateau neckline always made her feel ridiculously feminine, and she paired it with a filigree choker her parents gave her after graduating from dental school. Tiny marcasite crystals were nestled in a wide band of platinum filigree, creating a lacy effect she adored. She usually wore it only for special occasions, but being in love qualified, didn't it?

A new Italian bakery opened only four blocks from the Martha Washington, and Katherine left for work early so she could pop in to ask if they had chocolate biscotti.

"I don't know why Jonathan denies that he's been making it," she confided in Sullivan, who ambled along beside her on the crowded sidewalk. "If he gave me the recipe, I could ask our cook to bake some."

"Maybe he's embarrassed to admit he knows how to bake," Sullivan said. "It's kind of a girly thing to do."

As if anyone could ever consider Jonathan Birch to be girly. He wasn't big or physically imposing like Gallagher, but his quiet masculine intensity attracted her from the moment she saw him. A group of sober-suited businessmen disembarked from a nearby streetcar. Their day was coming to an end just as hers was beginning, but life was good. With luck she would arrive at the dental clinic with a sack of chocolate biscotti for the entire office to share.

A sudden clattering of horses' hooves coming up from behind startled her.

"Watch where you're going!" Sullivan yelled at the wagon's driver because it was barreling toward the sidewalk.

Not at the sidewalk . . . the horses were barreling straight at *her*!

Sullivan dragged her out of the way as the horses veered onto the sidewalk. He reached for the bridle to gain control of the horses but fell beneath their hooves, and she screamed.

A man on the buckboard stood, his arms wide as he leapt out of the wagon. A knife flashed in his hand.

She ran, but he landed on her back, smashing her face into the wall of a store, driving the breath from her lungs. She couldn't breathe. Ice-cold pressure on her neck hurt as she tried to escape his weight.

Then the pressure on her neck was gone. *He* was gone. A flurry of bystanders dragged the man away, yelling and shouting. What had happened to Sullivan?

Her neck felt like she'd been stung by a bee, but that didn't make any sense. Had she been cut? She rotated, letting the wall hold her up as she reached for her neck. The choker fell off and hit the pavement, scattering marcasite crystals everywhere. There was blood on it.

The horses were gone, but Sullivan lay crumpled on the ground. She ought to go to him, except she didn't have the strength.

A man in a bowler hat approached, his face horrified. "Lady, you need help."

"I'm okay," she said, even though everything felt strange. Woozy. She touched her neck again, and it was warm and wet with blood.

She couldn't move. The man with the bowler hat grasped her shoulders and lowered her onto the sidewalk. Her head banged against the concrete. "Ouch," she whispered.

He apologized and pressed something against her neck, making it hurt even more. People gathered around her. How embarrassing to be lying in the middle of the sidewalk, flat on her back. The crowd of onlookers blotted out the sun as they huddled around. A voice hollered that the police were on their way.

Someone grabbed her hand. "Hang on, lady. I'm sure you're gonna be fine."

He didn't sound sure, and she didn't have the strength to argue. This might not end well. That awful man must have cut her neck. First he ran over Sullivan, then he cut her neck.

Tears blurred her vision. This was going to be hard on her parents. "Oh, Mama, I'm sorry," she whimpered. She tried to pray, but then the world went dark.

Somebody kicked the foot of his bed. "Wake up, Lieutenant. Your dentist lady is in trouble."

Jonathan rolled upright, wiping the sleep from his eyes to see Sergeant Jankowski standing at the foot of his cot. The blinds were drawn, and it was dim in the police dormitory, but there was enough light to see the somber expression on Jankowski's face. A couple other officers stood silently a few yards away.

All his senses went on alert. "What happened?"

"Somebody got to her down on East 29th. They cut her throat."

Jonathan remained motionless, staring at Jankowski, waiting for him to say this was a sick joke. But Jankowski's solemn expression didn't change, and this wasn't something he'd joke about. The others looked equally grim.

He glanced away, barely able to hear as Jankowski relayed the news. "Sullivan is down in the muster room, reporting everything to Captain Avery. He said a gang of men riding in a wagon ran him over and he got trampled pretty bad. Someone got to the lady and cut her throat. She didn't stand a chance."

Anger sliced through the fog of disbelief. Sullivan had been lax since the beginning. Everyone knew it. He shot to his feet and bolted from the room, racing down two flights of steps and toward the muster room. He flung the door open with a bang and made a beeline for Sullivan, who conferred with Captain Avery and a few others.

Jonathan grabbed Sullivan by the collar. "How could you let

this happen?" he demanded, but Captain Avery intervened, shoving him away.

"Pipe down," Captain Avery ordered. "They ran him over with a team of horses. He's lucky to be alive."

A swollen purple bruise marred one side of Sullivan's face, and his arm was in a sling. It looked like he'd been crying.

Jonathan took a step back. He still wanted to strangle Sullivan, but he was equally to blame. He had been *sleeping* when Katherine was attacked. *Sleeping* when her throat was cut, and life flowed out of her. For two years he'd been watching over her, and the one time she really needed him, he had been sound asleep. Remorse almost drove him to his knees.

Captain Avery remained firmly in command. "Sullivan was following protocol when the incident occurred, so shut up and go put some clothes on."

Jonathan wore only a nightshirt, his feet bare on the cold tile floor, but he wasn't leaving as long as they were discussing Katherine.

"I want to be the one to interview her first," Smitty said, and Captain Avery murmured something in reply, but Jonathan latched on to the word Smitty just used. He was barely able to hope.

"Interview who?" he asked, holding his breath and silently praying.

"Dr. Schneider," the captain replied. "They took her to the hospital on 29th. She's in surgery right now."

She was alive? He collapsed into a chair. *Dear Lord, thank you.* People rarely survived a cut to the throat, and he remained mute as he listened to Captain Avery report that although the cut was bad, the attacker's blade got tangled up in a necklace Katherine had been wearing. The cut was long but shallow, causing damage to some veins and the muscles in her neck, but sparing the major arteries.

"Bystanders caught the guy who did it," Sullivan said. "I waited until a bunch of cops got there and arrested him. The driver got away, but we've got good descriptions of him and the wagon."

That was something at least. He'd have to trust the police to start tracking them down because right now Jonathan needed to get to Katherine's side.

20

What sort of drugs had they given her? It was hard to fight her way through the sludge and drag herself to the surface. There was light behind her closed eyelids. She didn't have the strength to open her eyes, but she could hear nurses' voices, a cart with rattling wheels. Her throat hurt and thirst raged, but asking for a glass of water would be too hard. Not worth the bother. It was easier to sink back beneath this heavy narcotic fog than keep fighting it.

The thirst didn't go away. Every time she roused and tried to reach the surface, she was thirsty. A lot of time must have passed because the light was gone, and when she managed to get her eyes open, the room was dim. Just a single electric table lamp in the corner beside someone sitting in a chair, reading a book. She blinked, trying to focus . . . It was Jonathan.

Her tongue was dry and swollen, and when she tried to talk it startled Jonathan. He was by her side in an instant.

"Katherine? Are you awake?"

"Drink," she croaked.

He left, and there were some shuffling sounds and the sloshing of water into a glass. Then he came back and hunkered beside her bed. "Don't try to get up. Here's a straw." He held the paper straw to her lips.

It took a few tries to pull the water up the straw, but it was blessedly cool, the best sensation in the world. Some of it trickled down the side of her face, and Jonathan blotted it with the bedsheet.

"Don't try to move," he said. "You're going to be fine, but don't move, okay?"

Her neck hurt. Actually, everything hurt, though she didn't really mind. Was it the drugs that made everything seem so floaty? Someone had tried to kill her, yet she was still alive. How long had she been in this drugged stupor?

"My parents are going to hate this," she whispered.

"I know."

"Are they here?"

He nodded. "They got to New York two days ago. You don't remember seeing them?"

She didn't. Jonathan said that she had gone in and out of consciousness for two days, her parents hovering nearby the entire time. "Your mother said if you died and robbed her of the chance to plan your wedding, she would never forgive you."

A smile tugged because it sounded like something her mother would say. Jonathan said her father had brought special cleaning supplies because he wanted to personally disinfect the room. He and Jonathan sanitized the room from top to bottom yesterday. She'd slept through it all.

"Can I see them?" she asked.

"They're at a hotel now. It's two o'clock in the morning."

She closed her eyes, still floating on a narcotic cloud. "I always like this time of day. When the rest of the world is asleep, but not us."

"No, not us," Jonathan said, his voice infinitely tender. "I asked my grandmother to make you chocolate biscotti. It's right here whenever you want it."

"Tell her thank you," she murmured. Eating would take far too much effort, but Jonathan had been so sweet to get biscotti for her. "When are you going to kiss me again?" she asked.

"Not while you're under the influence of drugs."

"Such a rule follower."

"I want to earn the respect of your parents. I like them."

A hint of energy spurred her to open her eyes. "Everyone loves my parents."

"Your father is quite the stickler for cleanliness," Jonathan said. "I noticed your mother polishing his silverware before he would eat."

"He hates fingerprints."

Jonathan laughed, and it felt like warm honey. "He would never survive at the station house."

She made the effort to open her eyes to look at him. He'd drawn the chair up alongside her bed. He looked different. Softer. More normal. His shirt was open at the neck, and his sleeves were rolled up.

"You aren't in uniform."

"I've taken time off work so I can stay here beside you."

"Almost like you care about me."

Even in the dim light it was easy to see the affection on his face. "I *do* care about you. Quite a lot actually."

"Tell me how much."

His eyes gleamed in the faint amber light. "I used to wait for you across the street from the clinic and imagine the wonderful conversations we'd have if I could ever muster the courage to talk to you. I can tell you this because your father said you won't remember hardly anything when you wake up for good."

"That's a shame. I like seeing you all soft and agreeable."

The rattle of a squeaky wheel interrupted them as a nurse pushed a cart into the room. She stood over Katherine's bed, wearing one of the folded white caps and a surprised expression. "Is our patient awake?"

"As you can see," Jonathan said, back to his formal demeanor.

"It's time for another round of medicine," the nurse said in a cheery voice, holding a hypodermic syringe aloft.

"What is it?" Katherine asked.

"Morphine."

There were other drugs that weren't so strong. She couldn't think of their names because everything was still so foggy. "No more morphine," she said.

"It's doctor's orders," the nurse replied, moving closer.

"I don't want it."

The nurse pulled down the sheet to expose her arm, but Jonathan intervened. "She said she doesn't want it, and that's the end of the discussion."

The nurse seemed a little offended but retreated. How nice to have Jonathan here to protect her. After the nurse left, he stooped down to hold the straw to her lips again.

"Did you say my father was here?" she asked when he took the straw away. Everything was *so* confusing.

"Yes. Your mother and father have been here for two days."

Good. Her father would know a better drug she could take. "My father is very wise," she said nonsensically, and Jonathan laughed a little.

"Your father is wonderful. I wish I'd had a dad like him."

"Really? Tell me why," she prompted, since for once Jonathan's guard was down and he was unusually chatty.

"He's strong without being a bully. Smart without bragging. You're very lucky to have such parents. I envy you."

"I'll share them with you," she magnanimously offered.

He smiled. "Is that possible?"

"I'm a very generous person. Kiss me, please."

"We have already discussed this. I would like to earn your

parents' respect, and that means keeping my hands off of you while you're in a morphine-induced state."

"Why do you care about what my parents think?"

She didn't want to keep talking about her parents or the attack or anything but the way Jonathan's face hovered near, the light catching on the planes of his face. She could watch him forever.

"You won't remember any of this in the morning, so I suppose I can tell you. Good parents are the best and most important gift any child can receive. When I met yours, I knew instantly they were good people. And I wish in the deep recess of my soul that I had parents like Howard and Lilian Schneider."

"Oh, Jonathan, envy is a sin."

He smiled again. "I shall confess it to the priest on Sunday morning."

"Confess?" she asked in confusion. "Jonathan! You're not Catholic, are you?"

He continued stroking the back of her hand. "Shhh. You're talking nonsense now."

"Yes, I am. Kiss me again so I will stop talking nonsense."

He kissed the back of her hand. "That's the best I'll be able to do until you come to your senses again."

"Rule follower," she whispered, and he didn't deny it. She loved this conversation, but sleep was pulling her under again.

"Are you going to be here when I wake up?"

He leaned forward to stroke her forehead. The drugs swept her under again before he answered.

She awakened to see Jonathan slumbering in the bedside chair. What was Jonathan doing in her hospital room?

Disjointed memories of the amber-tinted night came back. He had been watching over her. She remembered him giving her a drink from a straw and how handsome he looked, but that was all. Sunlight streamed through the slatted blinds on the window, and it was probably far later than when he usually went off shift.

The pain in her neck was savage, and she was so thirsty. A pitcher sat on the bedside table, but she couldn't reach it and Jonathan looked so exhausted, slumped in the chair. Dear, sweet Jonathan. He must have been at her bedside all night long.

"You should go home," she said in a faint voice.

He snapped awake, straightening in the chair and quickly leaning toward her. "How are you feeling?"

Horrible, but she managed a weak smile. "Okay," she said, but it was hard to even speak when she was so thirsty.

As if reading her mind, he poured a glass of water and popped a straw into it. "Here," he said, scooting the chair forward and holding the straw for her. The sucking motion triggered pain across her neck.

"Maybe it was too early to lay off the pain medicine," Jonathan said when he returned the glass to the table.

"Maybe." Yes, memories were coming back. The nurse with the syringe, Jonathan helping her drink. Her attention shifted to a plate of chocolate biscotti on her bedside table. It had been here last night. Hazy memories continued to flit around, but she remembered the biscotti. "Did your grandmother make that biscotti?"

"No," Jonathan answered. "My grandmother has been dead for years. I bought them at the Italian bakery."

She searched her memory. Hadn't he said something about his grandmother last night? Remnants of morphine must still be clouding her mind. Strange. The drug could cause memory issues but rarely provoked hallucinations, and she remembered thinking him sweet for pestering his grandmother to bake for her. Why had her mind planted that false memory?

Maybe it wasn't false. She locked gazes with Jonathan. "I thought you said your grandmother made it. You wouldn't lie to me, would you?"

Jonathan didn't seem offended by the question. A little exasperated, but not offended. "No, Katherine, I wouldn't lie to you," he said with affection, gazing straight into her eyes.

She eased back into a doze, comforted by Jonathan's faithful, honest presence.

21

Jonathan sat with Captain Avery in a meeting room on the ground floor of the hospital, holding the mug shot of the man who'd attacked Katherine. The crook had a wiry build and a dark, thick mustache. He hated looking at the man who almost murdered the woman he adored, but it had to be done.

"He doesn't look like either man from Katherine's sketches," he concluded.

The captain nodded and took the photograph back. "Maybe not, but we still need to show it to her for possible identification. The guy is refusing to talk. He's so scared of Achilles, he won't even tell us his name."

Which was frustrating. All they needed was one member of the Sons of Chaos to roll over on Achilles. Katherine would have to leave New York unless they found him soon. She couldn't risk living here if Achilles could get to her even with a bodyguard at her side.

"Will she be up to looking at the mug shot?" Captain Avery asked. "It's understandable if it would be too upsetting while she's still so weak, though time is not on our side."

Jonathan couldn't be sure. Katherine had been steadily improving over the past few days, and her parents had been amazing. Instead of handling her with kid gloves, Lilian and Howard Schneider cracked jokes, teased, and brought a spirit of joy that was helping Katherine rally. "She'll want to help anyway she can."

Captain Avery nodded and slid the mug shot into a plain envelope. "I'd rather not conduct the interview with Dr. Schneider's parents in the room."

This made sense, for Lilian hovered over Katherine and constantly tried to speak for her daughter or instruct the police on how to carry out the investigation. "I'll go ask them to leave," he offered. "Give me a few minutes and I'll clear the room for you."

Jonathan set off down the hall, carrying a box containing the blueberry pie he'd made for Katherine. He decided to offer it to Lilian instead since she liked sweets too.

When he arrived at Katherine's room, a group of off-duty nurses had gathered to chat with the Schneiders, whose habit of slinging insults at each other kept the staff on the entire floor amused. Mrs. Schneider was in prime form as she recounted her challenges as a housekeeper.

"My husband requires an entire closet for his undergarments because he wants them ironed and individually stored on clip hangers. Can you imagine? I've been doing this for the past thirty-two years. Please don't talk to me about your problems." She grabbed a piece of chocolate biscotti and started munching.

"Cleanliness is important," Howard defended.

Lilian noticed Jonathan standing in the doorway and motioned him forward. "Jonathan, come inside and talk some sense into my husband. Please tell us you don't need your undergarments pressed and hung. I want better for my daughter."

A flush heated his face, and he met Katherine's laughing gaze, wishing he could talk about anything other than his undergarments. "No, ma'am," he said as he stepped farther into the room. Then he froze when he spotted Gallagher planted on the other side of Katherine's bed.

"Ha!" Gallagher laughed. "Jonathan keeps all his clothes crammed in his locker at the station house where they're probably a health hazard."

A rush of jealousy surged at the way Gallagher looked so comfortable sitting beside Katherine. She wore only a thin nightgown, and Gallagher's preening smirk rankled.

He handed the box to Lilian. "I brought you a blueberry pie. It's large enough to share with your husband and the other nurses. Captain Avery would like to interview Katherine, but it's too crowded in here for everyone. I think you'll be more comfortable in the waiting room."

Lilian's chin rose. "But what if Katherine needs help remembering things? I should be here."

Howard reached for his wife's elbow, all teasing now replaced with compassion. "Come along. We're leaving our darling child with strong and brave police officers. She'll be okay, Lilian."

Lilian reluctantly agreed, and soon the Schneiders and the nurses cleared out of the room.

"There's no need for you to stay either," he said to Gallagher.

"Oh, but I want him here," Katherine said. "Gallagher makes everything seem so much less serious."

Jonathan clenched his fists because it was probably true. If Gallagher helped Katherine, Jonathan wouldn't complain. He'd accept it with good grace until she was strong enough to get back on her feet.

Captain Avery entered the room, holding the envelope with the mug shot. Gallagher remained sitting at Katherine's bedside while Jonathan took a position on the back wall as the questioning began. Arms folded across his chest, he wiped his expression blank of the resentment simmering as Gallagher pulled his chair so close to Katherine that his leg was flush against the mattress.

Captain Avery passed the mug shot to Gallagher to show to Katherine.

"Is this one of the men in your dental office that night?"

"That's the man who attacked me?" she asked, her voice shaken. According to her earlier testimony, he'd leapt at her from behind and shoved her against a building's wall, making it impossible to get a good look at him.

"Yes, this was the man arrested at the scene," Gallagher said. "Was he one of the men you treated in your clinic last June?"

She cringed a little and looked away. "No. I've never seen that man before."

"Katherine, *think*," Gallagher prodded. "Look at the photo again and imagine him without the mustache. Are you certain it couldn't be one of those two men?"

Since when had Gallagher started calling Katherine by her first name? Jonathan knew her for two years before he took that liberty.

She glanced briefly at the picture before quickly looking away again. "I never saw that man before the day he came flying out of the wagon at me."

"You didn't really look," Gallagher said. "Take your time and look again."

Jonathan couldn't endure it anymore. "She said it isn't the guy. Let's move on."

Gallagher shot him a glare, but Captain Avery agreed and proceeded with another line of questioning. "When you met the two men at your clinic, did you notice anything unusual about their hands?"

Katherine considered a moment before answering. "Not really. It was so long ago that I don't remember anything about their hands."

"So they had all their fingers and thumbs?"

She blanched. "I would have noticed if they hadn't."

"No gloves?"

"No, it was June. I would have thought it very odd if one of them wore gloves."

Captain Avery nodded. "The man who assaulted you is missing two fingers on his right hand. We suspect he could be a bomb maker. Most amateur bomb makers learn the trade by trial and error, and missing fingers is a common phenomenon among a certain class of criminals."

Perhaps the attacker's damaged hand caused a lack of dexterity when his blade got tangled in Katherine's necklace. Those filigreed platinum wires could have prevented a cleaner cut and probably saved Katherine's life.

Katherine handed the mug shot back to Captain Avery. "I don't ever want to see that photo again," she said, looking ill.

Gallagher pounced on the opportunity to lean in close and take her hand, rubbing it soothingly. "No need to worry," Gallagher said. "I'm not going to let anything happen to you."

"Then why don't you let go of her hand?" Jonathan snapped.

Captain Avery intervened. "Gentlemen, this isn't the place for schoolyard chest-thumping."

"Jonathan, I'm okay." She withdrew her hand from Gallagher and reached for the plate of biscotti. "Have some cookies and let's all calm down."

Gallagher's eyes widened as he scrutinized the chocolate biscotti. There weren't many left, but he scooped one up to examine it closely.

Jonathan stiffened as recognition dawned on Gallagher's face. Every impulse wanted to smack the biscotti out of Gallagher's hand, but he kept his features carefully schooled.

"Is Grandma still baking cookies for you, Birch? Isn't that darling." Gallagher stuffed an entire cookie in his mouth and munched on it with ill-concealed delight.

"Jonathan's grandmother died when he was fourteen," Katherine said.

"Is that what he told you?" Gallagher's eyes gleamed in anticipation. "Nah! Jonathan has always been Grandma's golden boy. She used to come over to the school all the time, bringing him cookies and milk. Didn't she, Sapling?"

Confusion clouded Katherine's face, looking first at Gallagher, then at him. The foundation beneath his world was beginning to crumble. Katherine's troubled eyes begged him to deny it, but he couldn't. His tongue was stuck to the roof of his mouth, and he'd gone mute with panic.

Worse, Captain Avery was watching. When Jonathan joined the force sixteen years ago, he swore he had no living relatives. Interviewing family members was part of the vetting process for joining the police force, but Jonathan looked Captain Avery in the eye and swore he had nobody. Maybe the captain didn't remember. He surely had interviewed hundreds of probationary officers since Jonathan joined the force.

"I don't believe it," Katherine finally said, her voice weak.

Captain Avery's narrowed gaze was pinned on him. He remembered. Jonathan's whole world was about to come crashing down.

"Jonathan's grandma was a sweetheart," Gallagher said. "She wore all black with a long veil. She looked like she came out of another century, but the cookies were terrific. At our graduation, she brought enough orange cream cannoli for the whole class."

"Katherine," Jonathan said, not knowing what else to say. He'd lied, and now it was all out in the open, and the only thing he could do was to appeal for her mercy.

"Tell me this isn't true," she said, her eyes imploring. "You said she died when you were fourteen. That's why you had to go to the Clifton School. She's not dead?"

He couldn't give her the answers she wanted to hear. Watching the last bit of hope drain from her face was the most painful moment of his life. There was no anger or disbelief, just the awful look of disillusionment as it took hold and sank its barbs into her.

"I never thought you would lie to me," she said in a shattered whisper. "I never thought it could be possible."

Everything in him wanted to soothe her anguish, but he was the cause of it. All this was his fault. "I'm sorry," he managed to say.

Her eyes drifted closed. "I don't feel good."

"Shall I send for the doctor?" Gallagher asked.

Katherine turned her face to the wall and covered her eyes. "No. Just go, please. Everyone, please just go."

Captain Avery stood. "Forgive us. We've pressed too hard. Get some rest and let us take things from here." The captain's voice was kind, but his glare lethal as he jerked his head to motion Gallagher and Jonathan to leave the room.

Gallagher obeyed instantly, but Jonathan couldn't leave her like this. He stepped closer to the bed and knelt down. "Katherine . . . I'm sorry."

"Go."

"Let me explain—" he began, but Captain Avery cut him off. "You heard her. Get out of here."

He couldn't leave, not when she looked so pale and sick and it was all his doing. "I'm on my own time," he said, reaching for Katherine's hands, but Captain Avery yanked him back.

"I am *ordering* you out of this room," he bit out. "Stand up, walk through that door, and meet me at the station house in one hour. If you aren't there, consider your employment terminated."

He stood, barely able to comprehend how quickly his life had collapsed. He'd surely lost Katherine forever and was probably about to lose his job as well. He'd built a castle on a foundation of sand, and it was all about to be swept out to sea.

22

Jonathan went straight to the station house to change into his uniform. He'd been wearing street clothes while visiting Katherine, but this was the most important meeting of his life and he needed to look like the epitome of an upstanding New York City police officer. He closed the locker door and braced his hand against the cold metal, praying for mercy.

He could probably sift through the constellation of white lies and half-truths he'd told over the years and come up with a plausible explanation that might work with Captain Avery. Jonathan's father taught him how to lie with a straight face from the time he was old enough to speak. Later, when he fled across the river for a clean and honorable life, it still began with a lie. He couldn't have a fresh start with the Rinaldi name slung around his neck, so he adopted the new name his mother provided. Even after his mother died and Nonna arranged for him to be raised at the Clifton School for Orphaned Boys, he kept up the lie.

It was time to quit lying, but that didn't mean he had to tell the truth. His story was private, and they couldn't force him to talk. A grinding headache pounded in his skull as he navigated the corridors toward the administrative wing. His family shouldn't be anyone else's business, and he could lean on sixteen years of impeccable service with the police force to vouch for his integrity.

His lungs constricted a little more with each step toward Captain Avery's office. He could barely draw a full breath as he arrived outside the door and knocked. A terse command ordered him to enter.

Jonathan straightened his shoulders and lifted his chin before walking inside. He focused on a vague space on the wall. "Reporting for duty as requested," he said in a calm voice.

Captain Avery remained seated behind his wide oak desk, but to Jonathan's surprise, Detective Fiaschetti, the head of the Italian Squad, stood in the corner of the office.

The captain began the meeting. "I've asked Detective Fiaschetti to be here because of some insight Gallagher provided about your history at the Clifton School. It seems much of what we believed about your private history may have been inaccurate. I'd like to hear your side of the story."

This was it. He wouldn't lie, but he couldn't tell them the truth. "My history with the New York Police Department began when I was eighteen years old. I have no private history."

"Don't be evasive," Captain Avery bit out. "You know exactly what we're asking. You gave us the impression you were orphaned at age fourteen and have no family. According to Lieutenant Gallagher, that's not the case."

"Gallagher will do anything to bring me down. You know that."

Captain Avery's mouth thinned. "This isn't about Gallagher; it's about the badge you're wearing over your heart. That badge is a symbol of integrity, and if you aren't worthy to be wearing it, I need to know now. Why were you raised in the Clifton School if you had a living grandmother?"

Jonathan stared at a spot over Captain Avery's shoulder and refused to answer. He'd learned enough about constitutional law to know that he wasn't required to answer the question.

"*Do* you have a living grandmother?" Detective Fiaschetti asked.

He kept staring straight ahead. "I consider my only family to be the men of the New York Police Department."

Captain Avery stood and walked around the desk. "That's not answering the question. I was in the room when Katherine Schneider asked you the same thing, and you implied there was. So tell us the truth. What are you trying to hide?"

"I haven't done anything illegal since the day I took my oath for the police force."

Detective Fiaschetti let out a string of curses and barged forward to stand inches from his nose, yelling with all his might. "Don't give me that hogwash! There is no birth certificate for anyone named Jonathan Birch born in the year you claim. Tell us your real name."

Jonathan remained silent.

The detective rapped out the question again. "Tell us your real name or I'm arresting you right now."

"You can't do that!" he retorted, and Detective Fiaschetti smiled.

Jonathan's mistake crashed down on him. Fiaschetti had fired the order in Italian, and Jonathan answered in the same language.

Being fluent in Italian wasn't a crime. It would take some explaining since he'd always denied knowing any foreign languages, but they couldn't fire him for speaking Italian.

"Let's hear it," Detective Fiaschetti said in English. "If you thought you were standing on thin ice before, please be assured you're now up to your neck in a world of trouble. What's your real name?"

"Rinaldi," he admitted.

Captain Avery launched across the room and slammed him against the wall. Sparks showered before his eyes. He blinked, clearing them away, but the captain hauled him further up the wall by the lapels of his dress coat.

"You're part of the biggest crime family to infest New York City?" he roared.

"I left the family long ago. I don't have anything to do with them anymore."

"Except that Granny Rinaldi still brings you cookies, eh, boy?"

He clamped his mouth shut. Nonna Rinaldi wasn't part of the criminal aspects of the family, but that wouldn't matter to the police, and this wasn't the right time to defend her.

Captain Avery seemed tired as he returned to his desk. "Don't report for duty tonight," he said, his voice no longer angry but sad. "Turn in your badge, your keys, and your gun. Your association with the New York Police Department is over."

Katherine's parents noticed Jonathan's absence the moment they returned, and Katherine was too embarrassed to talk about what had happened. She hadn't even fully accepted it herself, and merely told them that Jonathan had been ordered to attend an important meeting at his station house.

"I hope he bakes us another of those blueberry pies," Lilian said. "I don't care if the sugar rots my teeth, I want more."

"I care," her father retorted. "It would be bad advertising if my wife lost her teeth. No dentist has unlimited powers against the destructive nature of sugar."

They continued making jokes, and Katherine's chest felt even tighter. Her parents had welcomed Jonathan with warmth and generosity, and he had fit into their family like a long-lost puzzle piece. Her mother even started teasing Katherine about planting tulips this fall so they could be ready for a spring wedding.

Lilian would want Jonathan's head on a platter when she learned of his betrayal. Katherine didn't even understand what had happened, and she didn't have the strength to tell them.

It was easier to confide in Midge. The overnight nurse joined her a little after two o'clock in the morning and listened as Katherine poured her heart out. She spoke in a low voice, hoping that Sarge standing guard outside her door wouldn't overhear.

"He's been lying for years about a so-called dead grandmother who is in fact alive and well and baking him cookies. Why would he do that?"

Midge's careworn face was heavy with compassion. "People usually lie for personal gain or because they're embarrassed to admit the truth. Did he have anything to gain by telling you his grandmother was dead?"

"Absolutely nothing."

"Then for some reason he is embarrassed."

Katherine folded her arms across her chest. "He ought to be more embarrassed for carrying on a string of lies all these years."

She felt disloyal for even uttering such words about Jonathan. All through the night she clung to an irrational hope that he would come see her and explain what happened. Each time a footfall sounded in the hallway she startled awake, hoping he would be there with a brilliant explanation for his behavior.

Morning came and there had been no sign of him. When her parents arrived, their first question was about Jonathan, and she still didn't know how to explain his absence.

"I think he's in hot water with his supervisor," she said. "Captain Avery may have caught him in . . . in a falsehood."

A falsehood sounded softer than a lie, and she wanted her parents to keep their good opinion of Jonathan. It didn't matter that he'd done something terrible, she still wanted to protect him.

A little after breakfast, a new officer from the police department arrived to stand guard outside her door, since Sullivan wouldn't be returning to duty. He'd suffered a fractured arm and two broken ribs after falling beneath the galloping horse.

"What has become of Lieutenant Birch?" her mother demanded of the young man named Patrolman Conti.

"He got fired," Conti said.

Katherine gasped, unable to even draw a breath, but Lilian was on the warpath. "The cause?"

"None of us can figure it out," Patrolman Conti said. "He

seemed like such a straight arrow, but rumor has it he lied about his past to get on the police force, and Captain Avery won't overlook something like that."

Oh, Jonathan. This was going to devastate him. The police department was his whole world, but why should she feel badly on his behalf? She was one of the people he'd lied to!

Sober, upright Jonathan Birch. The man who blushed when chorus girls tried to flirt with him. Who took care of baby owls and wanted nothing so much as to be the best police officer in the city. What part was a lie and what was the real Jonathan?

Lilian continued badgering the young policeman for more details, but it was obvious Patrolman Conti didn't know anything more. If he did, Lilian would have drawn it out with a scalpel.

Her lower lip began wobbling, and she clenched a handful of bedsheet, praying she wouldn't start blubbering in front of a stranger. Her father noticed and ushered the young officer from the room, requesting privacy before closing the door.

"Privacy?" Lilian echoed. "I wasn't finished interrogating him. We need to get to the bottom of this."

"He doesn't know anything," her father explained.

"Then I'll go to the station house and demand an explanation," Lilian asserted. "No man shall be allowed to hurt my daughter's feelings and remain unscathed."

Her mother made good on her threat and disappeared for several hours, returning late in the day only to report that other officers at the station house confirmed Jonathan had cleaned out his locker and had been ousted from the department. Nobody knew the precise cause, but Katherine could no longer deny that she'd fallen for a fraud.

Just as they'd done after Paul broke her heart, her parents stepped in to save her. They remained positive and good-humored. Lilian played the harmonica and encouraged the nurses to sing along. Her father pointed out that he'd encouraged his wife to play the harmonica because it prevented her from polluting the world with tone-deaf singing, prompting Lilian to struggle through a mortifying rendition of "Danny Boy."

Her parents' antics gave her something to latch on to, even if she couldn't participate. Acceptance of Jonathan's betrayal was a dark weight smothering all the light and joy from her life.

The next day a box filled with lemony cookies was delivered to her room. The note consisted of only two words: *I'm sorry.*

The zesty scent of citrus and powdered sugar made her mouth water, but she looked away without touching them. "Give them to the nurses," she told her father, and his eyes softened in understanding as he carried them away.

The next day she was well enough to be moved into the general ward with seven other patients. Four cots lined each side of the room with only a single privacy screen that could be rolled between the beds when needed. Her parents, both experienced with people in pain, never believed in treating invalids as weaklings. They made the rounds to everyone in the ward, chatting with people who wanted company, and knowing when to leave others alone.

Her father flattered and joked with the nurses, helping them change bedding and carry water. The nurses adored him, especially the way he made the beds with military precision and flawless hospital corners.

"You're lucky to have such a tidy husband," a nurse complimented Lilian. Her father was within earshot, and her mother wouldn't want the praise to inflate his ego.

"You wouldn't say that if you had to dust the walls of his house once a month for the past thirty years."

"Dust the walls?" the nurse asked in confusion.

"It's the only way to keep paint looking fresh," her father defended.

"Yes, but he also asks me to polish the bottom of his shoes," Lilian added.

"That was *one time*," her father said. "I do it myself now."

By now everyone in the ward had become accustomed to her

parents' humor. Their relentless teasing was one of the reasons her father's dental practice was so popular.

Jonathan bombarded her room with deliveries every day. The hospital had honored her request to stop him from visiting, although the cookies still came. Her parents offered them to the other patients, but she never took a single bite. If she tasted a morsel, she might be like Persephone, thinking a few pomegranate seeds would be harmless, not realizing that they would suck her back into the underworld.

She would never forgive Jonathan. Although excising him from her heart was going to hurt, she intended to do it and never look back.

23

Jonathan spent the week after his termination in painful limbo. Anguish mingled with the shame and embarrassment from being fired, but mostly he was lonely. He lived in a city of millions yet felt entirely alone.

Emptying his station-house locker had been a unique humiliation. All of it fit into a single packing crate: a few sets of spare clothes, a chipped coffee mug, and a shaving set that had been a gift from his grandmother. He'd forgotten to clean out his desk, so his fountain pen was still at the station house, but it would be too painful to go back and retrieve it.

All of his worldly possessions were in his tiny rented room, which wasn't much bigger than a prison cell. He was forbidden from returning to the station house, and his attempt to see Katherine at the hospital had been blocked by the staff. He worried about her health and headed to the nearby pharmacy, where he put a nickel into the telephone box to call Smitty at the station house, needing to know how she fared.

"They say she'll be in the hospital a few more days," Smitty said. "She can't go back to the all-ladies' apartment building, and word has it her parents are taking her away as soon as the hospital releases her."

Please don't take her to Ohio, Jonathan silently prayed. "Where will she be going?"

"Sorry, Birch, I can't say more than that. We're all on strict orders."

"I understand. Thanks and good luck, Smitty." His chest squeezed as he hung the receiver back on its hook. That might be the last time he ever spoke with the young officer he considered a kid brother. It would be selfish to continue pressing others for more information, so he funneled his frustration by baking at the restaurant's kitchen on the first floor of the building.

He'd been using this cramped kitchen for years. The restaurant's owner let Jonathan use the kitchen during the morning hours before the cooks arrived to prepare lunch. The arrangement suited them both. The restaurant bought all the ingredients, and Jonathan baked enough to supply them with desserts to sell. Ever since getting fired, he'd been making enough to send on to Katherine.

So far he'd made lemon citrus cookies, almond pizzelles, coconut macaroons, and amaretti cookies, all personally delivered to the hospital. Today he baked focaccia bread. Maybe she was getting tired of the bombardment of sweets, and a rich loaf of focaccia bread was probably his finest culinary accomplishment. His first batch was already in the oven, the second five loaves having been set aside to rise. He'd baked the bread with olive oil, fresh basil, a little rosemary, and plenty of garlic butter across the top, so the kitchen smelled divine. The sun was beginning to rise when he began kneading the last batch of dough.

The snick of a door opening surprised him, and Jonathan looked up to see the silhouette of a man in the doorway to the kitchen. "I thought I might find you here." It was Howard, Katherine's father.

Jonathan's heart almost stopped. "How is she?" he asked.

"She's doing well," Howard replied. "The doctor thinks she'll be strong enough to leave the hospital soon."

Relief flooded him, and he managed a nod. "Good." He dried his hands with a towel and came around the butcher-block counter to see Howard better. "I've got focaccia bread today. It's one of her favorites."

"Katherine wants you to stop sending her things," Howard said gently, and Jonathan flinched. Sending her things was the only way he knew to apologize, to show her that he cared and thought of her all the time. Now that he'd been ousted from the police force, his relationship with Katherine was the only thing of value he had left.

"I wanted to apologize in person, but they wouldn't let me see her."

Howard gave a sad smile. "I don't think it would have done any good."

Another wave of remorse washed over him. He returned to the other side of the counter and his kneading of the dough. It had been idiotic to believe sending her gifts could have magically bought him her forgiveness. He couldn't meet Howard's gaze. Katherine's father was exactly as she had described him: kind, funny, and fatherly. Nothing like his own father, who had taught Jonathan how to use a switchblade and to lie without flinching.

"If you don't mind my asking . . ." Howard said, hesitation in his voice.

"You can ask me anything," Jonathan said as he kneaded.

"Why did you lie to her?"

His hands stilled, and it occurred to him then that Katherine didn't know his whole story. She knew he'd lied about his grand-mother, but she didn't know his real name or why he grew up hiding it.

Well, there was no reason to hide his past from her and her family anymore. No doubt the news would eventually leak to the other officers on the police force, so his career with the department was over.

"I grew up in a rotten family, the youngest of three sons . . ." Jonathan began.

He went on to tell Howard the truth about everything, making no attempt to justify his behavior or seek forgiveness. Katherine and her parents needed answers, and he provided them, beginning with growing up in Italy until he was seven, then his memories of Brooklyn where his father and uncles conspired to extort honest businesses. It continued until he was twelve, when his father, two uncles, and both his older brothers fell victim to a hail of gunfire.

"After that, my grandmother started wearing black clothes and still does to this day. She lost all three of her sons and two grandsons in one night. My mother had enough. I was her only remaining child, and she would do anything to protect me, even if it meant leaving what was left of the family, which they considered a slap in the face. The Rinaldis are thieving criminals, but they love each other and vow loyalty until death. When my mother broke that tie, there would be no forgiveness."

Continuing this line of discussion sounded dangerously close to a justification for his behavior. Under the circumstances, he could be forgiven for his lies while a child, but when he left the Clifton School for Orphaned Boys, he was a free man. He could have gone anywhere in the world, but he chose to stay in New York and perpetuate the deception.

Howard must have been thinking the same thing. "Was it so bad that you had to live the lie forever?"

Probably not. He could have reverted to his real name and stayed on the other side of the river if he'd taken a normal job in an office or as a clerk somewhere. But he wanted to be a cop, and his ties to a criminal family in the city would have made that impossible.

"I wanted a family, and the police department is a family of sorts," he tried to explain. "They never would have accepted me if they'd known I was a Rinaldi."

He divided and placed the dough into bowls to rise in a warm corner of the kitchen. The loaves in the oven were ready to come out. He wrapped his hand in a towel as he extracted the heavy cast-iron pans and set them on the counter to cool.

"And now?" Howard asked. "Have you told the police department the whole truth?"

"Yeah, they know. And they fired me the moment I told them."

"I'm sorry," Howard said. "It's not surprising, but I'm sorry the life you wanted isn't going to happen."

He set another pan on the counter. "I probably should have expected it."

Yet he hadn't. Getting fired was the biggest humiliation of his life.

Concern crinkled the corners of Howard's eyes. "What's next for you?"

Jonathan had no plans—no prospects, no aspirations, nothing. "I don't know," he admitted. For the past few days, he'd felt like a hurt animal in a cave, licking his wounds. Which was why he'd been baking up a storm. It was something to distract him from the humiliation as he endeavored to win Katherine's pardon. He needed to find a way through this fog of despair. It was time to find a new purpose in life, and yet he still didn't have an answer to Howard's question.

"Surely there are other cities that could use a trained police officer," Howard said.

Jonathan sagged. "There isn't a police force in the country that would hire me after getting fired by the New York City Police Department."

All Jonathan really wanted was to protect Katherine and help guide her out of the physical and emotional pain she was enduring. He reached for a grater to begin shredding parmesan cheese to melt atop the bread.

"I don't think Katherine should go back to the Martha Washington," he said. "She won't be safe there."

218

"I agree," Howard said. "We'll hide her and keep her protected until the men who did this are caught. If that doesn't happen soon, we'll take her back to Ohio."

Katherine didn't want to go back to Ohio. She loved New York, she loved the late-night clinic where she worked, and she shouldn't be made to leave against her will. Yet Jonathan could understand a father's need to protect his daughter from danger. His own mother had done the same.

He lined a basket with cheesecloth. The loaves of focaccia on the counter had cooled, and he now cut them into quarters, put them in the basket, and covered them with the remaining cheesecloth. "Would you take this basket to Katherine for me?" he asked.

Howard's brow furrowed. "She doesn't want to see you again."

"I know. Please give her the bread and tell her I'm sorry. From the bottom of my heart, I'm sorry." He kept the basket extended, but Howard wouldn't take it.

"Son, you need to stop," Howard said, not unkindly. "The two of you are both in a lot of pain. Pestering her with gifts and reminding her of you won't help."

"Then give it to her and tell her I understand it means goodbye. Tell her . . . " A surge of regret swelled inside. If he kept talking, the grief would overtake him and embarrass them both. He set the basket on the counter and pushed it toward Howard, then pulled back and folded his arms across his chest.

Howard waited a few moments before picking it up. "I'll tell her that you're sorry, and this is goodbye."

Jonathan nodded. "Thanks."

Howard returned the nod. "Good luck, son," he said as he turned away and headed back into the restaurant and out the front door.

Jonathan wished he'd had a father like Howard Schneider, but there was no point in wallowing in impossible dreams. It was time to do something useful with his life.

Katherine didn't wish to go back to Ohio or California or any-where else. She'd probably never forgive him, but he still wanted to make New York City safe for her again. He knew how the underworld of New York worked.

Maybe it was time for him to become a Rinaldi again.

24

Jonathan's vow to extinguish the danger surrounding Katherine was hampered by his lack of a badge. He had no allies, no friends, and no family to help. The Rinaldis wouldn't help him investigate a Mafia case, but he possessed their cunning and would use it to start untangling this plot.

According to Dante, the person who bought three dozen Reveille clocks was a Mazzini. That meant there was a Mafia connection somewhere within the Sons of Chaos organization. Jonathan sent an anonymous tip about the Mazzinis to the Italian Squad, but it probably got lost among the hundreds of other tips that flooded the department after Katherine's sketches were published.

The Mazzinis were bad news. The war between the two families had its roots going all the way back to Sicily, and the conflict resumed without missing a beat once they both found their way to New York City. The recent truce between the families gave power over the canneries and fish markets to the Rinaldis, while the Mazzinis took over the cotton and sugar mills in Brooklyn.

But Dante also said that one of them had gone to college to become an accountant and was known to put on airs and mouth off Marxist claptrap. The notes written by Achilles seethed with Marxist class resentment, so the Mazzini accountant was the source to focus on in Jonathan's search for who had bought the clocks.

Going to college and getting certified to be an accountant was the sort of thing that left a record in the books, which compelled Jonathan to head to the New York Public Library to start looking. He gaped at towering shelves stacked with books all the way to the ceiling. Where to begin? The police department had specialists to handle this sort of research, but that avenue was now closed to Jonathan.

He started in the reference department, beginning with the telephone directories. Most accounting agencies had advertisements in the directory, though few listed the names of their accountants. Mazzini wasn't a name that would inspire confidence with the public. The name would more likely send people fleeing in the opposite direction.

A librarian approached with an offer to help.

"I'm looking for an accountant but have no idea how to go about it," Jonathan admitted.

The librarian offered his hand and introduced himself: "Kenneth Kaufman, reference librarian."

"Giovanni Rinaldi."

There was a split-second flinch from the librarian, his eyes widening behind small, round spectacles, but he hid it quickly with a pasted-on smile. Nobody flinched when he introduced himself as Jonathan Birch.

"Are you looking for a company or a specific individual?" the librarian asked.

"An individual."

"You'll want to consult with the Institute of Accountants. They keep a listing of everyone who has passed the certification exams. This way, please."

Ten minutes later, Jonathan had the name of the only accountant in the city named Mazzini, who worked at a large accounting firm in Queens.

It didn't take Jonathan long to cross the river and find the place. The company occupied two floors of a fifteen-story brick building. The directory board in the main office listed at least sixty accountants, with Emilio Mazzini midway down the list.

He approached the woman staffing the front desk. "I'd like to see Mr. Emilio Mazzini, please."

"Do you have an appointment?"

"No, but it's a matter of urgency."

The woman frowned and consulted a large scheduling calendar. "He is not with a client at the moment, so I suppose there wouldn't be any harm. He's in office 515."

Jonathan nodded his thanks and headed up the stairs and through a maze of hallways. The outward-facing offices were larger and had windows overlooking a leafy street, while the ones on the right were more like closets with no windows.

Emilio Mazzini's office was on the right. He was a young man wearing a swanky three-piece suit with a bright paisley tie. Emilio had the same deeply hooded eyes and weak chin as a lot of the Mazzinis, but his smile was wide.

"Emilio Mazzini, CPA," he said with a hearty handshake, then welcomed Jonathan into his office.

The humble office was fitted out nicely, including a fancy walnut desk and matching bookcase with a glass front. A framed photograph of nattily dressed young men rested atop the bookcase, and a diploma from the College of East New York hung on the wall behind the desk.

Jonathan paused to study to photograph.

"My fraternity brothers," Emilio said proudly. The men in the photo wore white seersucker suits and boater hats. Only the well-to-do could afford such clothes. These men came from a world of privilege that was alien to Jonathan.

"You graduated from East New York?" Jonathan asked.

"Class of 1909," the younger man said. "I still get together with some of the fellas to go yachting or to attend a political meeting. Several of them tell me I should run for office someday. I'm sorry, I didn't catch your name."

"Giovanni," he said, slipping into his old identity with ease. "What made you decide to become an accountant?"

Emilio leaned back in his chair. "My family is in the sugar industry. There comes a time in any successful business empire when money can no longer be stashed beneath the mattress. We needed professional management, and I was happy to step up to the plate."

"Sugar." Jonathan nodded. "That's quite an industry. Does your family own the refinery on Kent Avenue?"

A bit of confidence faded from Emilio's expression. "We don't actually *own* the whole refinery, but we do a lot of business with them. What can I do for you, Mr. . . . ?"

Emilio let the sentence dangle, but Jonathan wasn't interested in revealing his last name just yet. He stood before the bookcase, pretending to study the photograph of the fraternity brothers while surreptitiously skimming the well-thumbed books on the shelves. Several were about revolutionary history and anarchist theory.

He needed to steer the conversation to the matter at hand. The only thing they knew about the man whose tooth Katherine had pulled was that his first name was Vittorio. It was time to see if Emilio might know this person.

"You said some of your old college friends suggested politics for you. State office?"

It seemed there was nothing young Mazzini liked talking about more than himself because he preened a little before answering. "I'm not sure political office is the right course to make real change. If anything, the political marketplace needs to be shaken up a bit, and that's best done from the outside."

"Is Vittorio helping you with that?"

Emilio blanched a little. "Vittorio?" he asked in confusion. "Vittorio Lastra?"

224

"Yes, Vittorio Lastra. The pair of you work together a lot." The gamble was paying off, given how uncomfortable Emilio looked. He straightened in his chair and tugged at his shirt cuffs.

"Look, I don't mean to be rude, but what are you getting at? Why are you here?"

Jonathan kept his voice completely calm as he braced his hands on the desk and leaned closer to Emilio. "I want to see Vittorio Lastra, and you're going to tell me where I can find him."

"Who are you?"

Jonathan smacked the desk hard enough to make the pencils in the cup jump. "I'm Giovanni Rinaldi, and I have business with Vittorio Lastra. Are you going to tell me where I can find him, or do I need to tell the guy who owns this accounting firm about how the Mazzinis are stirring up trouble?"

"Whoa, whoa . . ." Emilio held both palms up in defense. "We're keeping our end of the bargain with the Rinaldis. If something doesn't have sugar or cotton on it, we don't touch it."

"Vittorio got his face plastered all over the wanted posters, and that's not good for anyone's business."

"We didn't have anything to do with that," Emilio said. "Lastra is an idiot. Always has been."

A pounding came from the other side of the office wall. "Keep it down over there!" a muffled voice from the neighboring office complained.

Emilio shot to his feet and pointed at the door. "I want you out of here now," he hissed. "If the Rinaldis have concerns, get Dante to come talk to us. We've been minding our own business. We've got sugar and cotton. You stick to the harbor markets."

Jonathan wasn't there to restart the war with the Mazzinis; he was there to find out Vittorio's last name, and he'd just done so.

He casually adjusted his cuff links as he left the office without another word.

Jonathan was no longer welcome at the precinct station house, but now that he had Vittorio's full name, it needed to be handed over immediately. A part of him wanted to track Vittorio Lastra down himself and once again be a hero in Katherine's eyes. Even if they never saw each other again, knowing that he'd been able to do this for her would ease the sting of the way they'd parted.

Trying to personally bring down Vittorio Lastra would be selfish. The police had the resources to get the job done faster and more efficiently, so Jonathan walked the painfully familiar route back to the station house to turn over the name. A newsy he'd known for years was hawking papers on the corner, and Jonathan pulled a nickel from his pocket to buy an issue.

"Hey, Jackie, when are you going back to school?"

"Never," Jackie said as he handed over a copy of the newspaper. "I'm going to be a cop as soon as I'm old enough."

"You'll go further if you graduate from school. In the past few years, we didn't hire a single new officer who hadn't finished school."

"Why should I listen to you?" Jackie said. "You got fired."

News traveled fast. He'd never seen Jackie smirk before. To some, cops were like gods who walked the streets. Now he was just an unemployed man carrying around a world of regrets.

Jonathan fished out another coin, this one a quarter, and handed it to the boy. "Go inside and ask for either Smitty or Jankowski to come outside," he said. "If they're not there, just get whoever is on duty at the front desk."

Jackie pocketed the quarter and raced up the station-house steps. Jonathan watched with envy as the kid barreled through the front door and disappeared inside. How strange it felt to be standing there outside, helpless to walk up those steps and into the place he'd considered his home for the past sixteen years.

A few minutes later, the precinct door opened and Sean Gallagher strode down the steps. "You're not welcome here," he said.

Jonathan grimaced. Vittorio Lastra's name was a gift on a silver platter, and giving it to Gallagher was galling.

It didn't matter. Katherine's safety was what mattered, and Gallagher could be depended on to pounce on this lead if it earned him more glory inside the station house.

"I have a strong lead on the name of the guy whose tooth Katherine pulled."

A competitive gleam lit Gallagher's face. "Spill it," he said bluntly.

Jonathan did, including everything he knew about the Mazzinis and how they'd bought three dozen Reveille clocks. Gallagher quickly scribbled everything onto a notepad.

"Emilio Mazzini is a braggart," Jonathan said. "I think he's a foot soldier in Achilles's army, but he's too cocky and stupid to be Achilles himself. His office is full of books by Karl Marx and other revolutionary claptrap. I have a hunch the Sons of Chaos is an anarchist group, not the Mafia."

"Why is that, Giovanni? Trying to protect your beloved countrymen?"

He ignored the taunt and continued without getting angry. "The guy who cut Katherine's neck was not Italian, so keep an open mind when you question Vittorio Lastra. He could be part of the Mafia, but he's just as likely to be an anarchist. Get his mug shot to show Katherine for identification—if she feels up to it."

"Oh, don't worry about Katherine," Gallagher said. "She'll be up to it. I've been able to provide great comfort to her after all she's been through lately."

"Shut up, Gallagher."

Gallagher adopted a wounded expression. "I thought you'd like to know that Katherine is recovering quite nicely. Just yesterday she and I teamed up to play a round of bridge with her parents. We beat them."

"Keep away from her," he warned.

His words made no dent as Gallagher flipped the notepad closed and tucked it into his breast pocket. "Don't worry. I'll be too busy tracking down Vittorio Lastra."

Envy bloomed in Jonathan's chest as Gallagher vaulted up the steps and disappeared inside the station house. Temptation to take part in the hunt clawed, but love for Katherine meant turning this lead over to someone else. Gallagher had the badge and the resources to make the most of it.

All Jonathan could do was watch from a distance.

25

Katherine's parents helped her move into a suite at the Knickerbocker Hotel after being discharged from the hospital. It wouldn't be safe for her to return to the Martha Washington. The Knickerbocker had around-the-clock security in the first-floor lobby. It also boasted a restaurant, an ice cream parlor, a newsstand, and plenty of comfortable seating in the lobby that felt like a home. She would be as safe and protected as a canary in a cage.

She still tired easily, and the scar on her neck itched constantly. She'd been warned the itching would last for months, so she started wearing a silk scarf loosely knotted around her neck as a reminder not to scratch.

And the scarf covered the hideous scar, which was front and center across her neck, a mass of ugly scab tissue. Someday it would fade into a white scar of raised skin, but she'd be stuck with it for the rest of her life. It was a small price to pay for not dying, but her world would never be quite the same. She'd always been so vain about her pretty neck, but she saw how the hotel staff reacted when she forgot to wear the scarf. They blanched and recoiled, then pretended they hadn't noticed it.

She couldn't leave the hotel until the police captured the entire gang of people behind her attack, and after a week inside she was limp with boredom. She felt like a marble rolling around in a padded box, and it would get even worse once her parents returned back home. Her father made a comfortable living, but this trip to New York had cost him dearly. They weren't the sort of extravagantly wealthy people who could afford to live in a hotel like this forever. If the police couldn't solve the case soon, she'd have to take Edgar's offer of a job in California.

Maybe she ought to leave regardless. A big part of her desire to stay in New York had been Jonathan, and it would be easier to forget him if she was busy carving out a new life in San Francisco. Jonathan was her past, and California might be a wonderful new adventure. If she kept saying that to herself often enough, she might eventually believe it.

The best thing to happen all week was when the police arrived to announce they had arrested Vittorio Lastra and his brother Gino, both of whom had been tracked down to an apartment in Saint Louis.

Lieutenant Gallagher brought a series of mug shots for her to identify. She sat at a tea table in the private parlor of her hotel with her parents on either side of her for support. A tea service with delicate porcelain teacups had been set out, but she was too nervous to put anything into her stomach until this distasteful business was behind her.

Katherine recognized Vittorio instantly in the first photograph. "That's him!" she said, relief trickling through her.

"Are you certain?" Lieutenant Gallagher asked. "We have other images. It took some doing, but one of our guys managed to pry his mouth open so our photographer could get a good shot of his dental work. Take a look."

Sure enough, the wide gap where his mandibular molar used to be was healing nicely. Her father leaned in to scrutinize the dental work. "Did you pull that molar with your left hand?"

"I did," she said proudly because left-handed extractions were always a challenge. Her father reached out to shake her hand.

"Well done!" he congratulated. A professional handshake from her persnickety father was a hard-won prize, and Katherine grinned as she accepted it.

Her mother got straight back to business. "What have you learned from him?" she asked Gallagher. "Who are his associates?"

The lieutenant frowned as he returned the photographs to the file. "I'm sorry to say that we haven't been able to learn much from Vittorio or his brother. They've completely clammed up. We offered them a sweet deal if they pointed the finger at whoever is planting the bombs, but they haven't said a peep."

"Were they the ones who paid someone to attack my daughter?" Lilian demanded.

"Doubtful," Gallagher said. "They left New York the day after the *New York Journal* first printed their sketches two months ago. It took us a week to track them down in Saint Louis."

Hope that this case might be coming to a quick end faded. If the brothers refused to speak, it meant she would be required to testify against them in court, making Achilles even more anxious to silence her forever.

"How did you learn their last name?" she asked while her mother poured Lieutenant Gallagher a cup of tea. He held the teacup aloft as if in a toast.

"I have my ways," he said, brimming with false modesty. He took a sip and set the teacup down with great care. He sobered as he met her gaze. "The Lastra brothers are foot soldiers. The bombs continued after they left New York, and another went off last weekend at Grand Central Station. The Sons of Chaos have taken credit for it."

She looked at him in confusion. "A bomb? I heard there was a huge fire at Grand Central. I didn't realize it was from a bomb."

He nodded. "Not all bombs cause explosions. Some cause a

chemical reaction that starts a fire. What happened at the Grand Central warehouse mimicked what happened on the *Lorna Doone*. A hotly burning fire that broke out in several places."

Gallagher went on to report that the warehouse fire burned for an entire day before firefighters got it under control. It sounded like a bunch of cylinder bombs, the type Jonathan had explained to her during one of their tutoring sessions.

Thinking about Jonathan was demoralizing, and she fought the temptation to scratch her itchy neck. Every man she met for the rest of her life would want to know about the hideous scar, but at least Lieutenant Gallagher already knew about it and understood. It made her feel closer to him, even though she was leery of getting into another romantic relationship. Her judgment concerning men had proved catastrophically bad for a second time. She'd fallen in love with the smoke screen Jonathan created to hide who he really was, but a part of her still cared for him.

"Why did the police department fire Jonathan?" she asked Gallagher, and his response was automatic.

"He lied to cover up his Mafia connections."

"Did you know about it?"

Gallagher shook his head. "I never knew anything about his early life as Giovanni Rinaldi. That whole family is a pack of crooks."

The blanket condemnation didn't feel right. Couldn't a decent person still spring from a corrupt family? Jonathan was a liar, but he didn't seem like a bad man. He blushed whenever the chorus girls teased him. He wouldn't even jaywalk!

"Jonathan isn't a crook," she said, not quite believing she could be defending him. "He won't even take a free doughnut when he goes into a late-night deli."

"Yeah, that's pretty stupid," Gallagher said. "Me, I take all the free doughnuts I can get." He collected the mug shots of the Lastra brothers and prepared to leave, bantering amiably as Katherine walked with him to the door.

She was left with unresolved questions about how she could still be so attracted to a silent, secretive man she could never trust.

———————

Katherine couldn't sleep. The wound on her neck forced her to lay flat on her back, a position she hated. Worse than the physical discomfort was the fear. Each time sleep started to tug, the slightest noise would jerk her awake, and she quaked in terror until the silence of the room assured her she was alone and safe. It always took a while to calm her racing heart and ease back into a restless doze.

Apparently, her body had returned to its night-owl ways. Night had always been the time when her mind expanded and became alive, yet now she was trapped in this gilded cage, struggling to sleep and still nurturing a broken heart.

She missed her old life. She missed feeling useful as she fixed people's teeth or fed the baby owls. She longed for the simplicity of Saturday luncheons with the other night-shift workers of the Martha Washington. She missed the dentists at the clinic, even Dr. Friedrich! He was formal and fusty, but he was a decent man who didn't want to kill her.

Or lie about every facet of his existence.

She sighed, wishing her neck would heal so she could start sleeping on her side again. She stared at the ceiling and tried not to itch her neck. How much longer was she going to be trapped in this hotel room with nothing to do?

She wasn't a coward. She was naive, wounded, and heartsick, yet she couldn't go through the rest of her life wondering why Jonathan hadn't been honest with her.

It was time to do something about it. She rose from bed and headed to the sitting room dividing the hotel suite's two bedrooms. She lifted the receiver from the telephone anchored to the wall, and an overnight operator came on the line.

"Number, please?"

"The wireless office at the Port of New York."

"Please hold." Katherine gazed at the city lights twinkling outside the window as her call was connected. How lively everything was, even at midnight.

"Port of New York, how can I help you?"

"Inga, its Katherine Schneider."

"Katherine!" Inga exclaimed. "How are you feeling? We've all been so worried about you."

"I'm fine," she said. "My neck is still sore, but I'm fine. Listen, you folks still have overnight messenger boys on staff, don't you?"

"Of course."

"Can you have one of them deliver a message to Jonathan Birch for me?"

"I don't know where he lives."

"I do." Expecting Jonathan to be awake and in his room at midnight was a gamble, but Jonathan was a night owl like her. She gave Inga the name of the boarding house where Jonathan rented a room, along with a simple message. "Tell him I'm at the Knickerbocker Hotel and that I'm awake."

"That's it?" Inga's confusion was obvious.

"That's it."

She hung up the telephone, quickly dressed, and left a note on the tea table telling her parents she'd gone down to the lobby. It was time to demand answers from Jonathan.

Downstairs, she paced circles around the brightly lit lobby while waiting for Jonathan to arrive. The grandiose space was vacant except for a few employees. A janitor polished the marble floors, and a doorman nodded to her with each lap she made. A clerk behind the front counter spoke into a telephone, placing an order at the kitchen for a guest who wanted a grilled-cheese sandwich delivered to his room. Maybe she ought to pen a "While the City Sleeps" article about overnight hotel staff. She'd never covered that angle before, and there was quite a variety of staff who worked through the night to ensure the comfort of the guests.

After an hour of pacing, she was about to give up and return to her suite when a disturbance near the front door caught her attention.

Jonathan looked disheveled and haggard as he argued with the doorman, insisting on entry.

"It's okay," she called out from across the lobby. Jonathan sagged in relief as he spotted her. The doorman stepped aside, and Jonathan strode down the marble hallway to meet her.

"Katherine, are you all right?"

"Good evening, Giovanni," she greeted.

His expression became guarded, but he gave a tiny nod of his head. "If you'd prefer to call me that, I will answer to it."

"It's your name."

"Not anymore, but as I said . . . if you prefer to use it, I won't argue."

Why did he have to be so civilized? She wanted to get a rise out of him, not listen to that perfectly modulated voice, so poised, so maddeningly polite that it made her want to smash something. She'd spent the past two weeks trying not to think about him or worry about his fate, and that wasn't fair. *She* was the one who had suffered. *She* was the one who'd been lied to.

Jonathan's gaze dropped to the scarf draped around her neck. Maybe the garish scabs marring her neck would rattle his composure. She lifted it up so he could see.

He winced a little, then nodded. "It looks to be healing nicely."

"Really? Is that all you can say?" Her voice echoed in the silence of the lobby, and the man waxing the floor paused a moment to watch.

"Why did you ask me here?" he asked calmly.

She wanted to pick a fight. She wanted to unleash the bitterness that had been festering since the moment she learned of his deception. In a perfect world he would have all the right answers to soothe the roiling tangle of emotions, but no. He was as calm as always in the quiet of the lobby.

"Gallagher says the Rinaldi family is a pack of shameless crooks."

A hint of annoyance crossed his face, though it vanished quickly. "Gallagher doesn't know everything. You ought to keep away from him."

"Gallagher never spun a full-blown fantasy about his life and pretended it was real."

Jonathan began to glower. Good. He ought to feel a tiny hint of the turmoil she'd been enduring. He took a steadying breath and gestured toward a cluster of upholstered chairs at the far end of the lobby. The grouping was surrounded by potted palms and offered a bit of privacy from the night staff still preparing the lobby for the day ahead.

She lowered herself into the tufted chair beside a coffee table. Jonathan didn't bother with a chair but sat on the coffee table opposite her, their knees almost touching as he leaned in to speak quietly.

"You need to watch out for Gallagher," he said. "He's hated me since the day I showed up at school and gave him competition for the first time in his life."

She raised her chin. "I like him."

"Don't," he snapped. "If he senses that, he'll use you to hurt me. When I was sixteen, he found out about a girl I liked and did everything possible to seduce her. He succeeded. He did it just to prove that he could, and then he lost interest in her a month later. It broke Charlotte's heart."

"Is Charlotte real or someone else you made up to create your fake life story?"

"She was real, and Gallagher took her away just to prove that he could," Jonathan said, raising his voice for the first time. How annoying that after finally getting a rise out of him, it was about some other girl instead of her.

"Fine. I don't know anything about Charlotte, but Sean has always been decent to me."

"*Sean*, is it?" Now his jealousy was blatant.

"Yes, Sean. My parents like him too."

She added that last bit just to be mean because Jonathan adored her parents. He got to his feet and began pacing.

"Your parents are too good to see the jealousy in Gallagher. He'll sweet-talk and curry favor if he thinks there's something in it for him, but all he really wants is the next medal or the next promotion."

Maybe. From the instant she met Gallagher, he had laid on the flattery with a trowel, yet he'd also been shrewd and diligent and helpful. "I know that he's a strutting peacock, but at least he's honest about it. He doesn't try to hide who he is, and I trust him. He's also brilliant. He told me all about the fire at Grand Central and how he's getting close to linking it to the *Lorna Doone*."

"He's not brilliant; he's a braggart."

"I don't believe it," she said.

"That's because you're an open book. Anyone can read you from a mile away."

She stood to confront him. "And you think there's something wrong with that? I refuse to lock down my emotions and withdraw from human society like a turtle in its shell lest someone get a glimpse of the real me. I have nothing to hide and share my thoughts and feelings as part of forming friendships. That's the human experience."

Now Jonathan raised his voice to match hers. "That's the human experience for people who were lucky enough to have been raised by loving parents, who earned an honest living. But for someone whose father was killed while carrying out a midnight shakedown? No, I've never been eager to share my life story, but you wouldn't let it go. You poked and prodded no matter how often I asked you not to."

Her mouth dropped open. "I did not!"

"Yes, you did! You don't know anything about struggling to overcome your past and trying to rise above a lousy upbringing. Your life has been charmed since your first day on earth."

She bristled. "I worked hard for everything I have. Dental school wasn't exactly a cakewalk. While other girls were fixing their hair or attending dinner parties, my father trained me in the principles of oral surgery."

Jonathan faked a little bow. "Pardon me. Your life has clearly been one of great hardship."

Was he taunting her? She lifted her chin, struggling to maintain her dignity. The last few weeks had been the worse in her life, and she refused to let Jonathan take potshots at her.

"Yes, I've had a great deal of hardship over the past few weeks." Her throat choked up, and an embarrassing wobble took charge of her lower lip. "I can't sleep because I have nightmares. I'm trapped in this hotel and going out of my mind from boredom except for when I think about venturing outside, and then I get so scared I can't even draw a full breath."

Jonathan looked instantly stricken. "I'm sorry. Katherine, I'm sorry and take it all back." He reached both arms toward her, but she slid away. "Katherine, please. Let's sit down and talk this out."

She'd rather yell it out, but she'd already stressed the fragile skin on her neck, and it was starting to hurt. She conceded and let Jonathan guide her to a seat.

An avalanche of guilt clobbered Jonathan for the unkind words he'd hurled at Katherine, a woman who had good cause to resent him. At least she let him lead her to a seat instead of smacking him across the face like he probably deserved.

This was it. She was ready to listen, and it might be the last chance he'd ever get to speak with her. Once seated, he forced himself to calm down and think logically.

"I'm sorry for what I just said, and sorry for deceiving you about my past." A silence stretched between them. In the past, this sort of silence between them never bothered him. Now it was excruciating. "Tell me what questions you have, and I'll answer them honestly. I swear it."

She fiddled with the scarf at her neck. "My father already relayed everything you told him."

Not everything, because Jonathan hadn't confessed everything. It was embarrassing, but she deserved to know.

"I didn't tell your father why I waited beneath that lamppost for you, night after night for two years. It was because most of my world covering the overnight shift was walking through the muck of vice and drunks and hookers. And in the middle of all that misery, I saw someone who was so pure she took my breath away. She made me believe in goodness and mercy. She was a fairy-tale princess, a shaft of light in the darkness. She was sunshine on a moonless night, and I wanted to protect her."

Katherine's expression remained carved in stone, and he longed for the time when she gazed at him with admiration. Those days were probably gone forever, but she'd called him tonight for a reason, and he wouldn't give up yet.

He drew a deep breath and met her eyes. "Will you ever be able to trust me again?"

She looked away, her mouth twisted with bitterness. "I doubt it."

He shouldn't have expected anything else, and yet, for a few fleeting moments, he had hoped for more. He hoped she'd say that she wanted a reconciliation, that she understood why he lied, and that he hadn't lost her forever.

"Can I ask you something?" Her voice was cautious in the silence of the lobby.

"Anything." He would lay the world at her feet if she asked it of him.

"Have you ever thought of mending fences with Sean Gallagher?"

If possible, his mood lowered yet another rung into pure misery, but he said he would answer her questions and he'd do it honestly. "Never. You don't understand him like I do."

"I'm sure that's true, but . . ." A myriad of expressions crossed her face as she parsed her next words. "Everybody has a lot of sides to their character. I think you and Gallagher bring out the worst in each other. He has so many fine qualities, but all he lets you see are his bad ones. I think you do the same to him. Do you know why he never learned how to swim?"

He snorted. "Yeah. He has this weird fear about getting his face wet."

"That's because his father used to hold his head underwater if he brought home bad grades."

Jonathan paused, tempted to reject the story. Gallagher was an accomplished liar. Feeling sympathy for him would require believing that the sun could rise in the west. He folded his arms across his chest. "I still won't ever trust him. You shouldn't either."

Katherine continued. "I think the two of you are more alike than you realize. Once upon a time, two complicated, tormented boys were trapped together at the same school. They were wounded boys who would rather fight and scratch for whatever scraps of dignity they could find rather than learn how to cooperate with each other."

A hint of amusement bloomed inside. How could she always, *always* look for the best in anyone? "Katherine, you may be the most trusting, idealistic woman in the world."

She crossed her arms and glared at him. He didn't mean to make her angry, but it looked like he'd just poked a tiger. "I'd rather be a trusting fool than a liar, Giovanni."

It was a slap in the face. He wouldn't retaliate or defend himself. She needed to get it all out, so he waited. Apparently, that was the wrong thing to do because she seemed to get even angrier.

"Aren't you going to say anything?" she demanded.

"What would you like me to say?"

"That you were wrong and shouldn't have lied to me, especially after we grew close. You *knew* about how Paul hurt me and yet you kept spinning your lies."

Every word stung because it was true. Some people might be able to take what he'd done in stride, but not Katherine. She was built of pure sterling silver, and he was a base metal that could only tarnish her.

"I *am* sorry," he said, wishing the words didn't sound so inadequate. "On top of all the fears you've been going through, I made everything worse by adding to your suffering, and for that I'm deeply ashamed."

"If you hadn't been caught, would you have ever told me the truth?" she asked.

It was a question he'd never considered, and he took a moment to think. He'd been so committed to burying his former life that he never thought of reconciling with it or revealing it to anyone. It meant the fear of exposure would always lurk just beneath the surface of any sunlit day, but he would have paid the price rather than risk losing her.

"No, I wouldn't have told you," he admitted. "At least now it's all out in the open. I hope I'll be a better man for it in the long run."

Katherine continued looking at him with a stony expression, and he risked asking a delicate question. "You once said that you'd be willing to forgive anyone, even Judas or John Wilkes Booth. Can you forgive *me*?"

Her spine stiffened, and she looked away from him. Her demeanor grew even colder. "I guess I'm not as virtuous as I thought."

He sagged a little and accepted her answer. "Would you like me to leave?"

She swallowed hard. Several moments passed . . . and then she did the most amazing thing. She shrugged.

He waited, but she didn't say anything else or walk away. She remained silent and motionless, sitting in the upholstered chair with the dignity of a queen. But he understood the message she just sent.

She wanted him here. For whatever strange, illogical reason, she needed him to be here. He watched her carefully. Katherine's chin was pointed at a proud angle, the paisley silk scarf tied around her neck. The scar beneath it was ghastly, but it would heal eventually. Maybe it would take just as long for the wound he caused her to heal, but she had just cracked open the door, offering a sliver of hope.

He strolled over to a neighboring cluster of chairs, where a discarded newspaper lay on the table. He brought it to Katherine and offered her a section.

They didn't speak another word but calmly read the newspaper until two o'clock in the morning. Katherine finally yawned, set down her section of the paper, and left without another word.

Not promising, but a start.

After that night, Jonathan began coming to the hotel at midnight to see Katherine, and she was always there, waiting for him at the same upholstered grouping of chairs beneath the potted palms. Their warm friendship had vanished, replaced by Katherine's chilly disdain, but the fact that she continued coming to the lobby each night gave him hope.

He always brought her something. Sometimes it was a bouquet of flowers, other times a sack of homemade focaccia. One night he brought her a fountain pen that had a barrel made of silvery-white moonstone. "I thought it was appropriate for writing your 'While the City Sleeps' column." He set the pen on the coffee table, and she stared at it, refusing to touch it.

The pen sat there for an hour while they read the newspaper. Reading was a safe activity that required no conversation and couldn't prick still-tender wounds. They never discussed the news, just silently traded sections until inevitably she'd fire a question at him.

"Did anyone in your family ever go to jail?"

It was typical of her questions. She'd pick some aspect of his past she knew he wouldn't welcome and ask a probing question to see how he'd react. No matter how uncomfortable, he always answered honestly.

"Most of the men in my family have served jail time."

"Did your father?"

Jonathan nodded. "Three years for aggravated assault. A fisherman was reluctant to pay 'protection money,' so my father broke his arm."

Katherine's eyes widened in disbelief, but he wouldn't sugarcoat or hide anything from her because honesty might someday win her trust back. The only time it was hard to tell the truth was the time she talked about her scar. They had been meeting for a week when she set the newspaper down and fiddled with a pretty pink scarf at her throat.

"People cringe when I forget to wear a scarf. I suppose I'll have to wear one forever. The scar is so ugly."

She looked him in the eye and waited. He'd rather discuss anything than the brutal assault, but she wanted to talk about it and needed him to be honest. Her scar was a scabbed-over slash that marred the perfection of her neck, and even when it healed, it was likely to be a ropy line of raised flesh impossible to disguise.

He smiled gently and told her the truth. "Your scar is a mark of survival. It happened because you were brave enough to help the police with those sketches, even though you knew it was dangerous. It's a battle scar no different from one earned at Bunker Hill or Waterloo. Don't ever be ashamed of it."

Her eyes widened as he spoke, a little watery in the soft light. "Thank you," she whispered.

Then, as if sensing she'd just lowered her guard, she frowned and picked up a section of the newspaper. Her shield was back up.

He retrieved his own section of the paper but couldn't concentrate while staring blankly at the sporting page. It was late, and he was growing tired. He'd been meeting Katherine each night for the past week, and it never got easier. She hadn't even begun to forgive him, and he didn't know if she ever would.

Katherine sucked in a breath, and he looked over the edge of his newspaper to meet her eyes. "What?"

She smiled broadly. "Our baby owls made the newspaper again." She set the paper on the table so they could both read the story printed there.

The young owls had become celebrities in Midtown Manhattan and were getting ready to fly. A specialist from the Brooklyn Zoo advised the women at the Martha Washington to prop broomsticks outside their windows to let the owls practice hopping from perch to perch. Mrs. Blum was interviewed in the article. *"I am thrilled that my efforts have helped foster the poor orphaned owls,"* she told the reporter.

"'My efforts,'" Katherine scoffed. "Mrs. Blum wanted them tossed into a wastebin!"

Jonathan nodded. "Yes, but every resident of the Martha Washington knows it's the women of the eighth floor who saved those owls."

She continued reading the article with a softly nostalgic expression. It was the second time she'd lowered her guard in a single night, and he ventured for more.

He rose to his feet. "What would you like me to bake for you tomorrow?"

The corners of her mouth turned down. "Nothing. I don't know why you keep bringing me things."

Why indeed? He pondered the question all the way home.

It was three o'clock in the morning by the time he got back to his building, which was the perfect time to start baking for the day. It meant he'd have time for the dough to rise or cakes to cool before heading off to bed at sunrise.

He decided on almond pizzelle cookies. If he moved quickly, he could get two hundred baked and cooled before dawn, but the sugar canister was empty.

The supply room contained barrels of flour and fifty-pound stacks of sugar filling the floor space. Jonathan grunted as he hoisted a canvas sack of sugar over his shoulder and lugged it into the kitchen, carefully laying it on the counter. He grabbed a knife to slice the top open but paused at the name printed on the canvas.

Torricelli Sugar, along with its motto featuring a sugar-plum tree.

Jonathan's heart started pounding faster. Alberto Torricelli owned the largest sugar refinery in the state. He'd been the first victim of a Sons of Chaos bomb.

The *Lorna Doone* had been carrying sugar. The warehouse at Grand Central had been stuffed with sugar.

He laid a hand on the canvas sack and pressed, barely making a dent in the tightly packed sugar inside. Sugar was highly flammable. A large sack like this would make an ideal place to hide a cylinder bomb and get it smuggled onto a ship.

Last weekend's fire at Grand Central shared the same characteristics as the *Lorna Doone* fire. According to newspaper reports, a series of fires had started in a warehouse behind the station, and the Sons of Chaos had already claimed credit for it by flooding the neighborhood with the familiar manifestos with the red border.

Emilio Mazzini claimed his family worked for Torricelli Sugar, and he was an anarchist. The sugar refinery would be a perfect place to plant the cylinder bombs in sacks, which could be planted in a variety of places.

Jonathan put away the baking equipment. The restaurant was going to have to get their desserts somewhere else today, because he needed to choke back his pride and contact Sean Gallagher.

26

The Torricelli Sugar Refinery was a hulking brick building with smokestacks, evaporating tanks, silos, and a grain elevator. The refinery spanned an entire city block with its own cooperage, stables for horses, wagons, and a loading dock. It was on the Brooklyn side of the East River, where barges delivered raw sugarcane stalks from all over the world. Seven hundred people worked at the refinery, which meant seven hundred potential members of the Sons of Chaos. Maybe even Achilles himself worked in the refinery.

Jonathan observed the refinery through a pair of binoculars, his elbows braced atop a chest-high brick wall across the street from the plant. Gallagher stood beside him, looking through his own pair of binoculars. They needed to learn how the sacks of sugar were filled and then identify every man who had the opportunity to slip a cylinder bomb into one of the sacks.

"I thought it would smell good," Gallagher complained. Raw sugar emitted a musty, cooked vegetable stench when it was boiled. The cloying stink was everywhere, although after a few hours Jonathan didn't notice it anymore.

They arrived in time to watch the changing of the shifts at eight o'clock when the overnight crew left and hundreds of day-shift workers arrived. Most of the men worked indoors, making it hard to know exactly what was going on inside, but tracking the outdoor work was easy. Sacks of sugar coming out the warehouse doors were loaded onto massive wooden pallets, then transferred to a barge.

Whenever the workers opened the warehouse door, Gallagher snapped to attention and monitored their activity with admirable intensity. Once the workers returned inside the factory, Gallagher lost all interest and proceeded to give himself a manicure. A manicure! He buffed and filed his nails, then worked with a pumice stone to rub his calluses.

"I'm too valuable to the baseball team to let my hands get bad," he defended.

Jonathan squinted at a trolley loaded with canvas sacks leaving the warehouse. Once the pallets came out the door, some were loaded onto a wagon destined for the Wallabout Market at the harbor, others for one of the New York piers to be shipped elsewhere.

Were the bombs being planted inside the refinery or out? Once the wagons set off, it would still be possible to insert a bomb in one of the tightly sewn bags, but the tampering might be visible.

"One of us needs to get inside the refinery," Jonathan said. "It should be easy enough to land a job and start looking around from the inside."

"Good idea," Gallagher said. "I volunteer you."

"Why me? You're the expert on bombs. I won't know what to look for."

Gallagher kept filing his nails. "Being the lead investigator with regard to the Sons of Chaos, I can't be spared. Besides, it might be a good way to earn yourself a ticket back on the police force."

Jonathan sucked in a breath, all senses on alert. "Has there been any talk of letting me back in?"

"Not that I've heard. Of course, that might change if you man up and volunteer for a sugar-refinery job."

Jonathan would endure any assignment to earn his way back

into the department. He'd rather do something noble and heroic, but if it had to be working in a factory with the hope of gaining some new insight, so be it.

He left Gallagher at the stakeout point in search of a newspaper with a classified ad section. When he returned, he spread the paper open to the job postings. Sure enough, the refinery was hiring a machinist, a packer, an office boy, and a general laborer. Jonathan didn't have the technical skills to operate heavy machinery, and he cringed at applying to be an office boy.

"But you'd be such a good office boy," Gallagher taunted.

Jonathan ignored the comment. "I'll ask about both jobs and aim for whichever has the best access to the production process."

"You're going to stink like a bin of rotten vegetables after a few hours in there."

"I'd rather stink like a man than have a manicure like a lady."

Gallagher pocketed the nail file and grinned. "Don't you have a job to apply for, office boy?"

Not even Gallagher's insults could dampen Jonathan's mood. If he could get himself back on the police force, any job at the refinery would be worth it.

Two days later, Jonathan showed up for work at eight o'clock in the morning, ready for his first shift as a packer in the Torricelli Sugar Refinery. He thought that the most difficult part of the job would be adjusting to a daytime schedule.

He was wrong.

His first day at the refinery was the longest day of his life. Packing sugar was the final stage of a long production line that was a grubby, hot, loud, and physically demanding. After raw sugarcane arrived at the factory, it was chopped, pulverized, and boiled in huge steel vats. That was where the heat and the stink came from. The juice was then purified, condensed in evaporation tanks, and then a centrifugal machine spun the liquid to begin the crystallization process. That explained the earsplitting noise. Conveyor belts took sugar to dryers, where hot air was blown across the drums to dry the sugar. More heat and more noise.

Jonathan's job was to hold canvas sacks beneath a metal chute as a river of sugar gushed out. Once the fifty-pound sack was filled, another man pulled a lever to stop the flow, and Jonathan hefted the sack to the next station. He was tired after only twenty minutes. At the end of an hour, he was exhausted from the hoisting, carrying, and mind-numbing boredom. His eyes grew dry from the sugar dust, and a sticky sheen coated his skin, making him itch.

It didn't take long to conclude that none of the men filling the bags from the chute could have had the opportunity to slip a cylinder bomb inside. Filling the sacks took both hands during the quick-moving job. The men who stitched the bags closed using heavy-duty industrial sewing machines were a different story. They were the only people in the facility who might have an opportunity to plant a bomb and sew it inside a sack of sugar.

Every two hours the crew got a ten-minute break. During those precious ten minutes the men gulped water, jawboned, or collapsed onto benches to rest their sore muscles. Jonathan often pretended to be engrossed in swiping a cool rag across his sweaty skin during his breaks. He stripped off his shirt to stand before one of the large electric fans that slowly moved the air, pretending exhaustion but actually watching and listening.

About half the men were Italian immigrants, and the rest were a combination of Irish, Germans, and native-born Americans. Jonathan paid special attention to the Italians, listening for any clue of a family relation to a Mazzini or a Lastra. So far he'd heard nothing other than complaining about the lousy record of the Brooklyn Dodgers or gossip from back home in Italy.

Jonathan paused as one of the wiry Italian men started talking politics about Italy's ongoing war with the Ottoman Empire. The man's cousin had been conscripted into the Italian navy, and the entire family was angry over it.

Angry enough to become part of a violent anarchist group? Jonathan dunked the rag again and swiped at his neck, standing before the fan while listening. Some of the other men suggested ways the cousin could earn a discharge, but one of the men noticed Jonathan lingering nearby.

"Hey, new guy . . . do you speak Italian?"

Jonathan didn't look up, dragged the cloth over the front of his chest, and leaned in closer to the cooling fan. The fellow packer asked again, still speaking in Italian.

Jonathan eventually looked over, feigning confusion. "Were you talking to me?" he said in English.

"Yeah," the packer said, this time in English. "Do you speak Italian?"

He scoffed. "With a name like Jonathan Birch?"

The other men went back to speaking in Italian, and at the end of their break he headed back to the chute.

Over the following days, Jonathan continued watching and listening, searching for any clue of a connection to the Mazzinis or how a bomb could be slipped into the sacks of sugar.

Aside from the Italians, the one man who caught Jonathan's attention was a shipping manager named Chester Lewis. He was a young guy with a narrow build and a swath of floppy blond hair. His job was to monitor inventory and track shipments sent to customers. Chester constantly circulated throughout the packing area, but instead of gossiping like the others during the breaks, he read the newspaper or a book.

The most interesting detail Jonathan spotted was that Chester had only three fingers on his right hand. Building bombs was a dangerous profession, and it wasn't unusual for a man to have missing fingers, scars, or burns on their face. One morning, Jonathan asked him how he'd lost his fingers.

Chester shrugged. "Factory work takes a toll on the laboring classes."

Chester usually kept to himself, but that changed the afternoon the standing electric fan conked out and the floor supervisor said it would take a week to get a new one.

"Move one of the fans from the boss's fancy office out here," Chester demanded.

The supervisor shook his head. "They have ceiling fans in the management offices. I'm sorry about the heat, but you can bring in a fan of your own if you want, otherwise wait until Monday."

The men grumbled about losing the fan, but Chester smiled. "Watch this," he said after the supervisor was out of earshot. He grabbed a hammer and casually strolled to the other end of the factory floor, where the management offices were located behind a closed door.

Jonathan squinted to see through the haze of sugar dust. A bunch of other workers watched as Chester paced before the door to the management area. Once the coast was clear, he used the claw end of the hammer to tug on the electrical wiring tacked along the wall to power the management wing. The lights above the door flickered, then went dark.

No electricity in the management offices meant no ceiling fans.

Chester adopted a nonchalant air as he strolled back to the group, but his expression was triumphant. "Let's see how much the Torricellis enjoy the stagnant air," he said as he arrived back at the break area.

An Irish immigrant smirked. "I'll bet they cut out after lunchtime." There was plenty of murmurs of approval among the men, who liked the idea of management having to put up with the same stinking hot air as them, but others weren't so sure.

"They're going to know one of us did it," Jonathan pointed out.

"So?" Chester replied. "They knew one of us did it when I threw a wrench in the centrifuge turbine last April. We got a three-hour break while they fixed it."

"None of us got paid for those three hours," someone grumbled.

Chester remained confident. "And the union got twenty new members because they docked our pay. It was worth it."

Jonathan returned to work almost certain he'd found the man he'd been searching for during the sweltering week at his refinery job.

———————————

It was time to learn more about Chester Lewis, although nothing in Jonathan's job intersected with the shipping manager. He wasn't in Chester's department, nor did they work together, but the incident with the cooling fan gave Jonathan a perfect opportunity to initiate a conversation.

At his next break he made a point of stopping at Chester's office, a modest room beside the double doors that led to the loading dock.

"Hey," Jonathan said as he approached Chester's open door. "That thing you did with the management's fan was a stroke of genius. Thanks."

Chester leaned back in his seat and grinned. "Anytime."

Jonathan feigned a nervous glance behind him, as though assuring he couldn't be overheard, then leaned in. "You said something about a union back there."

Chester rose, beckoning Jonathan into the office before closing the door. "That's right." He then explained how to join the union and their plans for getting the upper hand over management.

Jonathan lowered his head and pretended to listen, but mostly he was scanning the office for clues about Chester. The place was a mess, with heaps of supply orders and shipping labels, but the diploma from the College of East New York hanging on the wall was easy to spot. The same college Emilio Mazzini had attended.

"Well," Chester finished, "can we count on you to join the union?"

"Absolutely," Jonathan answered. But he wasn't ready to end the conversation just yet. All he had were vague suspicions that Chester was a powerful man within the Sons of Chaos, but no actual proof. He feigned admiration as he scanned the office. "What did you do to earn a private office like this?" he asked.

"Hey, don't look at me like I'm one of those slacker bosses," Chester said. "I'm just a middleman between the refinery and the merchants. I monitor inventory and direct pallets of sugar either to the railroad or the harbor for distribution."

Outside the window, a crane lowered a pallet mounded with fifty-pound sacks of newly refined sugar onto a barge. Jonathan had personally filled some of those bags. They were about to be sent to the harbor to be loaded onto ships, sailing across the world.

"You don't actually do anything with the sugar?" At Chester's look of confusion, he clarified, "You don't inspect it for quality or anything like that?"

"Nope," Chester said, ushering Jonathan out of the office. "I just monitor the inventory, track the bills, and then send the sugar on its way."

That meant Chester couldn't be slipping bombs into the sacks; that was happening somewhere else. Jonathan had learned all he could here. It was time to start looking for who was planting bombs once the sugar left the refinery.

He met Gallagher behind the station house that night to relay what he'd learned. "His name is Chester Lewis, and he's a true believer in the anarchist cause. He's got two missing fingers that are consistent with bomb-making, and he controls where the sugar goes after it leaves the refinery. He also attended the same college as Emilio Mazzini. He graduated a year ahead of Mazzini, but I'll bet my bottom dollar they know each other."

Gallagher's face was impassive as he absorbed the news. "Good work," he said. "I'll have him watched. If he so much as spits on the sidewalk, we'll bring him in."

"I've learned everything I can from the inside. Now I need to track what happens with the pallets of sugar once they leave the refinery."

When Jonathan clocked out earlier today and stepped into the cool September evening, he breathed a sigh of relief that his sweltering stint in the refinery was at an end.

Gallagher looked unaccountably worried. His brash swagger was gone, replaced by a reluctant look of concern. "I wish I didn't have to say this, but there's no getting around it. Your family has a grocery store. They buy sugar in bulk and sew it into smaller bags."

Gallagher didn't need to finish his train of thought. Thinking the Rinaldis could have a hand in this was something Jonathan had already considered.

"Their sewing machine isn't anything like the industrial monster at the refinery," Jonathan said.

"They're cooperating with the Mazzinis. They have a machine to seal up a canvas bag of sugar, they have access to the Port of New York, and last spring they bought a couple dozen Reveille clocks."

All true. The possibility that his family could be the ones responsible for the bombs made Jonathan sick, and it wasn't something he could ignore.

Normally, Katherine took the verbal jousting between her parents in stride because they had a long history of aggressive but joyful teasing. Today was different. They'd become prickly with each other and had retreated into their bedroom to hash it out.

Katherine suspected it was related to the hotel bill that had been slipped beneath their door overnight. Her parents had been here since the day after she was attacked three weeks ago, and the bill was steep.

She had cost her parents a fortune, and she pressed her ear to the door, listening to her father insist he needed to go home. In addition to the pricey hotel fees, he hadn't earned a dime from his practice in nearly a month.

Her mother wanted him to stay in New York. "Katherine needs you," her mother said in a harsh whisper.

"Katherine has around-the-clock security," her father replied. "If the police can't find the people who want to kill our daughter, we need to leave. *All of us*. We can't afford to live here forever."

Katherine tiptoed back to her room. How selfish she'd been worrying about her disfigured neck and broken heart. Her father made a good living, but this hotel was beyond what they could afford if he was no longer treating patients. She had some savings, but that would dwindle quickly since she wasn't working either.

The problem was she didn't know how much longer this would go on. Jonathan wasn't on the police force and didn't know anything, so that left Gallagher. She sent a message to police headquarters, asking him to come to the hotel.

He arrived at noon and met with her in the hotel's ice cream parlor. She ordered a dish of strawberry ice cream with chocolate sprinkles, while Gallagher's order of a plain vanilla ice cream cone was far more ordinary.

"I'm a purist," he said after ordering. "Now, tell me what's worrying you. You're too kind a person to have a furrowed brow like that."

She swiveled a little on the fancy, padded leather stool. Everything about this hotel was expensive. "I'm afraid my parents are going to spend themselves into bankruptcy if this case drags on much longer. I need to know if the police are getting close to solving my case."

Gallagher gave a reluctant shrug of his shoulders. "I wish I had a solid answer for you."

"Will it be a week? A month? Years?"

"Not that long," Gallagher assured. "With luck, maybe a week because I think we're getting close. An undercover investigator at the sugar refinery in Brooklyn may have identified Achilles. We've now got officers watching the suspect's every move, looking for any chance to arrest him and start the interrogation process. If he so much as litters or jaywalks, we'll arrest him."

"It almost doesn't seem fair to arrest someone for jaywalking."

Gallagher glanced at the scarf tied around her neck. "Is what happened to you fair?"

She fingered the silk. "My mother keeps buying me scarves. I've asked her to stop, but I think buying them makes her feel like she's helping."

Her response seemed to upset Gallagher, who stood and tossed his half-eaten ice cream cone into the metal wastebasket behind the counter. "Look, you need to be prepared," he said. "I think the Rinaldis might be a part of this thing. The clocks on the time bombs were all bought at a store Jonathan's cousin owns."

She gasped. "Does Jonathan know?" He was already so ashamed of his family, and if they were responsible for assaulting her, it would be a terrible blow.

"He knows," Gallagher said grimly. "I've heard that he comes to visit you here every night."

"He does." Ever since the first night when she summoned him, Jonathan continued to come each night at midnight. The strange blend of anguish and anticipation was the only glimmer of excitement in her monotonous days. She had been so cold to him, and yet he still came.

"Does he know you might move to California?" Gallagher asked.

She looked at him curiously. "How did you know that?"

"I swung by your clinic to make sure there haven't been more threats. Some scary German dentist said you've been offered a job in San Francisco."

Her shoulders sagged. "I don't want to move, but if this goes on much longer, I suppose I'll have to."

Gallagher grabbed her hand and kissed the back of it, surprising her with his gallantry. "Then I shall redouble my efforts to smoke these criminals out, because losing you to California would be a tragedy."

The spot where he kissed her hand tingled long after he left. She wasn't attracted to Gallagher . . . was she? He was relentlessly fun

256

and always in a good mood. And yet her attraction to a solitary man who watched over her from afar for years seemed indelibly imprinted on her soul.

Ever since learning the truth about Jonathan, she'd became cold and unforgiving whenever he was near, and it wasn't the kind of person she wanted to be. Indulging in a meaningless flirtation with Gallagher was safer and easier than confronting Jonathan's cool cunning and wondering if she could ever trust him again.

This situation needed to be resolved. She had to either forgive Jonathan and force herself to trust him again or she needed to let him go.

It was time to decide.

27

Jonathan was free to resume his nocturnal ways after quitting his job at the sugar refinery. Tomorrow he would start monitoring Dante's grocery store, but for tonight he continued his quest to foil the next bombing, and that meant patrolling Times Square.

"The gray lady" was surely the *New York Times*, but now that the paper's building was under constant police surveillance, Achilles might plant the bomb somewhere else in Times Square, a five-block area representing the cultural heart of the city.

It was a little after two o'clock in the morning when Jonathan spotted Patrolman Conti making the rounds in Times Square, diligently ticking off check-in points on a notepad.

Jonathan strolled over and gave a friendly wave. "They've moved you to nights?"

"Yeah," Conti said with a good-natured shrug. "I don't like it much, but I'm getting paid extra for picking up the shift. We don't have enough manpower anymore."

Jonathan fell into step beside him and nodded to the notepad. "Are you using the plan Gallagher wrote up?" It was Jonathan's plan, but like so many things, Gallagher was probably claiming credit for it.

"Absolutely," Conti said. "It's nitpicky, but this place gets patrolled around the clock, and it's tight as a drum."

"Yo!" a voice called out from down the block. A well-dressed man jogged toward them. It was Rudy Pane, the night engineer from the electrical substation nearby. Mr. Pane was out of breath when he caught up to them. "Are you the cop on duty?" he asked Patrolman Conti.

"Yes, sir."

"Look, something weird is going on at the substation. The pumps in the basement quit working. I tried to call in backup, but the telephone line is dead. If the pumps can't keep the tunnels dry, we're going to have a serious mess in the subway. I'd estimate we've only got a couple of hours before we have to shut everything down."

"Oh," Conti said, looking pale. The kid was new and didn't know what to do.

Jonathan took over. "What do you need to fix the pumps?" he asked Mr. Pane.

"A hydraulic engineer. We've got one on duty at the powerhouse, but I can't get to him without a telephone."

Jonathan turned to the young patrolman. "Conti, use the police call box at the corner of Seventh Avenue and tell the operator to get that engineer out here. Tell them to send whoever is on call for the Bomb Squad too."

"A bomb?" Mr. Pane asked in appalled wonder. Conti looked equally surprised.

"I don't like the coincidence of the pumps failing at the same time as the telephone line. Get someone from the Bomb Squad out here now."

It might be a false alarm, but knocking out the city's major substation would be almost as big a blow as hitting the *Times* building. If the Times Square substation was blown up, it could knock out the electrical grid, bringing the city's subway trains to a standstill for weeks.

He ran toward the substation, Mr. Pane right behind him. They dashed up the steps leading to the elegant front door. Keys rattled as Pane tried to unlock the door, which took a few tries because his hands shook so badly. As soon as the door was open, Jonathan strode through and into the brightly lit interior. Another engineer was at his post overseeing the control panel that powered the rotary transformers.

"Are the subways still powered?" Jonathan asked.

"Yeah, but the pumps downstairs aren't working."

"I'm heading down to check it out," Jonathan said. "Who else is in the building?"

"Just us," Pane said.

"Can the turbines operate without you?"

Mr. Pane nodded. "For about two hours."

"Then you both should get out of the building until the Bomb Squad gives the all-clear signal. Got it?"

The men quickly agreed. They both hurried down the hallway and through the front door while Jonathan checked out the basement. The power was still on, so there was plenty of light as he descended the concrete stairs, his footsteps echoing off the cinder-block walls.

The sound of a ticking clock was unmistakable, and his muscles froze. He forced himself to remain calm and continued his descent into the basement. Six industrial pumps, each the size of a horse, filled most of the room. Everything was silent except for that awful clock. He crept carefully down the aisle between the pumps, scanning from side to side.

Three bombs had been planted behind the rear pump, tucked into a corner where they were hard to reach and would do the most damage. The bombs were wired together on a metal tray and attached to a clock. The drainage pipe leading into the sewer system had a foot of clearance surrounding it and was probably how the bomber got in and out of the basement, sneaking in like a rat.

Jonathan studied the bombs, memorizing their configuration. They were programmed to go off at three o'clock, twenty minutes from now. He turned and raced up the stairs and into the cool of the night. Luckily, Conti had already returned from reporting the emergency and was waiting outside the substation.

"Run back to the call box and tell them we need the rest of the Bomb Squad," Jonathan said. "We've got three live time bombs and a little less than twenty minutes to disarm them."

Conti paled. "Okay. Gallagher is the officer on call tonight, and he's already on his way over."

"Good." Jonathan nodded. Conti dashed off while Jonathan paced, precious seconds being lost with every beat of his heart.

Two minutes later, Gallagher came jogging toward him, carrying a toolbox in one hand and a half-eaten apple in the other. "What have we got?" he asked, his expression completely calm.

"Three bombs planted in a corner beside a pump, and eighteen minutes before they go off."

Gallagher let out a whistle. "Let's go."

Jonathan led Gallagher into the substation and down to the basement.

"That's a Sons of Chaos bomb," Gallagher confirmed once they stood beside the rear pump in the basement. He took another bite of apple, then tossed the core into a trash can where it landed with a clang.

Jonathan flinched, and Gallagher grinned. "You'll never make it on the Bomb Squad if you get rattled so easily, Sapling." Gallagher then sobered and pointed to a wire joining the trio of bombs to the electrical supply line bolted to the wall. "You see how they wired the bombs to that power line? They're hoping the blast will short-circuit the breakers upstairs."

"Will it?" Jonathan asked.

Gallagher rummaged in his tool kit to retrieve a pair of needle-nosed pliers. It took five seconds to snip the connection. "Not anymore," he said. "It would have knocked out electricity to a third of Manhattan if it worked. Instead, they overloaded the power down here, which is why the pumps failed. Now we need to get this contraption out in the open where I can work on it."

"Conti has already called for the rest of the Bomb Squad. Should we wait for them?"

"Not enough time," Gallagher said as he hunkered down to look more closely at the bomb from all angles, but it was hard to do so in the cramped space. "I'm not sure what will happen once I start moving this thing. You should probably get out of here."

"I'm not leaving," Jonathan replied. Gallagher might need help, and he was the only one here until the Bomb Squad arrived.

"Have it your way," Gallagher said. He started inching the tray of bombs toward the center aisle.

It turned out that Gallagher needed help almost immediately. The tray holding the bombs had been chained and padlocked to the pump. It hadn't been possible to see this until the tray had been pulled back a few inches.

"Find out if these guys have a pair of bolt cutters lying around."

Jonathan raced up the steps two at a time and ran to the supply closet. The substation engineers had everything, yet it still took a minute or so to find what he was looking for. He grabbed the bolt cutters from the top shelf, then hurried back to the basement.

"Thanks," Gallagher said as he took the tool, then sent him a sheepish look. "I can't fit back there. Can you slide beneath the pump and get to the padlock?"

Jonathan crouched down. The barrel-shaped pump had about ten inches of clearance beneath it, and it was several yards long. He didn't hesitate and dropped to the floor. The concrete was cold and clammy as he lay flat and began sliding closer. Once he got there, he held his hand back and Gallagher passed him the bolt cutters.

One snip and the padlock clattered to the floor.

Chains jangled as Gallagher lifted them away from the pump. Sliding backward was harder than moving forward, but soon Jonathan was on his feet again, and Gallagher had the tray of bombs in the center aisle.

"Take cover behind the first pump," Gallagher ordered. "I'm going to start dismantling this thing."

This was the most dangerous part of the process, so Jonathan didn't argue with him. The first pump was ten yards away and came up to his shoulders, but he could still see and hear everything if Gallagher needed help.

Gallagher went to work on the three bombs, all of them together about the size of a suitcase. Jonathan held his breath as Gallagher began cutting the wires, his face drawn in concentration. It seemed to take forever even though Gallagher moved with steady, rapid precision. Then he grunted.

"You okay?"

"Yeah, but this is a thick wire gauge and it's tough," Gallagher said. He shook his hand out, then went back to snipping.

Jonathan glanced at his pocket watch. Eight more minutes before they would blow. Far away, the faint wail of a siren could be heard in the night. The rest of the Bomb Squad was on its way, but they didn't have much time left. The cascade of ticks from the clock mingled with snips as Gallagher continued his work.

"Okay, two bombs dismantled, one to go," Gallagher said. There was more grunting as Gallagher kept snipping, and then he paused. "You should get out of here. I'm not certain what's going to happen when I cut this final wire."

"I'm not leaving," Jonathan said. He was protected behind the solid iron pump, and the Bomb Squad wasn't going to be here in time.

"Have it your way," Gallagher said. Another snip sounded. "Okay, if we survive the next ten seconds, we're home free. All that's left—

A boom and a wall of rock exploded. Gallagher's body went flying, and Jonathan ducked, covering his head as rock and metal and concrete rained down, pelting his head and shoulders. His ears hurt from the explosion, and dust choked the air, making it hard to breathe.

"Gallagher!" he yelled, making his way across the room where Gallagher lay sprawled against the wall. Blood covered his face, but an agonized groan meant he was still alive.

"Where are you hurt?"

Gallagher tried to answer, but all that came out was a clenched whimper. For the first time, Jonathan saw fear in Gallagher's expression. He glanced down. *Oh no!* Gallagher's belly was ripped open. There wasn't going to be any surviving this.

"Oh boy . . ." he said in a shaky voice.

"That bad?" Gallagher choked out.

"Hang on to my hand," Jonathan said. "I hear sirens outside. The rest of the team will be here soon. We'll get you to a hospital."

Gallagher began trembling, his face turning white, making the blood spatter even more grotesque against his chalky skin. "I want a medal for this," he managed to say. Unbelievably he gave a little laugh.

"You're going to get every medal the police department has to give," Jonathan said. "I'll personally see to it."

"G-good," Gallagher said, his voice faint now.

It was the last thing he ever said. Gallagher's hand went slack, and Jonathan made the sign of the cross.

He held Gallagher's hand until the others got to the scene. Two bombs had been dismantled, the third having exploded. The danger was over, but Gallagher was dead.

Katherine had been right. Jonathan was so blinded by the bad in Gallagher that he never gave him a fair shake. Gallagher was vain and pompous and ambitious, but was that so unforgivable? He had still been a good man and a great cop. Jonathan would forever regret not understanding that until it was too late.

Katherine jerked awake.

A loud boom in the distance had awakened her, but the noise

faded quickly and all was silent again. She remained motionless, listening and waiting. All seemed calm, but something *terrible* had just happened.

She threw the sheets back and hurried to the window. Street-lights illuminated the avenue below, vacant except for a horse-drawn street sweeper clopping down the avenue in preparation for the day ahead. She counted several heartbeats but couldn't see or hear anything out of the ordinary.

She picked up the telephone receiver, and the overnight desk clerk immediately answered.

"Did something just happen?" she asked. "I thought I heard a commotion."

"I heard it too," the clerk responded. "Everything is fine down here, and the doorman said he didn't see anything wrong outside. He thinks it must have been an accident up a few streets."

She thanked the clerk before hanging up and returned to bed. She was safe, but someone in the city was dealing with a serious calamity if it had been loud enough to wake her up.

She murmured a quick prayer for whoever was in trouble, then sank back into sleep.

28

The explosion was reported in the newspapers the next morning. Katherine sat opposite her mother at the tea table in their hotel suite. Lilian read the society pages and chattered about an Italian duchess seeking a divorce in New York, but Katherine was stricken from the instant she saw the headline. Her heart pounded as she mutely skimmed the story.

A member of the Bomb Squad had been killed. The newspaper didn't report his name, but the explosion had happened at three o'clock in the morning, precisely when Katherine had startled awake.

Thank heavens Jonathan wasn't a police officer anymore. It was horrible to be grateful for that when somebody else had died, but at least it wasn't Jonathan.

The bomb had been at the Times Square substation, the one she'd toured a few weeks earlier. Maybe this was the bomb originally intended for "the gray lady." The *New York Times* building was now under constant police surveillance, so perhaps the substation was as close as the bombers could get.

The telephone rang, but she couldn't tear her eyes away from the story. Her mother answered it instead. Apparently, the trio of bombs hadn't been strong enough to do much structural damage since two of them had been successfully dismantled.

"That was the front-desk clerk," her mother said after hanging up the telephone. "Jonathan Birch is downstairs and wants to see you."

Katherine abandoned the newspaper. Jonathan might know more about the bombing, maybe even the name of the man who was killed. A myriad of thoughts whirled as she rode the elevator down to the first floor. The police gleaned more information after each bomb, so maybe they could solve this soon and she could go back to her normal life.

The elevator landed on the first floor, and the attendant cranked the doors open. Jonathan stood right outside, his expression bleak. She hurried toward him.

"Gallagher is dead," he said.

"No!" she gasped. Not Gallagher. Not Gallagher with the dashing good looks and inflated ego and a tiny chip in his tooth. She'd just seen him yesterday right here in this lobby. They had ice cream together. It didn't seem possible he could be dead, yet she knew by the shattered expression on Jonathan's face that it was true.

She opened her arms. He stepped into them, and it felt like steel bands clamping around her as he held her. "I'm sorry," she said, even though Jonathan never got along with Gallagher.

"I am too."

People in the lobby looked askance at them, but it didn't matter. She needed the comfort of Jonathan's embrace, and he seemed to need it as well. Thank God it hadn't been Jonathan, but *oh, Gallagher* . . .

"Was it the same bomber?" she asked against Jonathan's shoulder.

"Yes. They used the same type of clock as before."

She extricated herself from his arms and sighed. She never wanted to be the kind of person who knew how time bombs worked or the techniques of anarchists. Exhaustion tugged, and she needed a cup of strong coffee.

She moved like a sleepwalker to the front desk and asked for coffee service to be delivered to the corner table where she and Jonathan always met.

They sat in silence while waiting for the coffee. She tried praying for Gallagher, but bitter thoughts kept intruding. It wasn't fair. Gallagher was a good man whose courage and intelligence had made the city a better place, while the people who had planted those bombs were a blight on society. Gallagher was dead and yet the evil criminals responsible for his demise remained alive and triumphant at this very moment.

A clatter of rattling porcelain interrupted her silent tirade as a waiter rolled the coffee cart to them. She straightened her spine and drew a calming breath as the waiter poured two cups of coffee and set them on the table. The pungent aroma brought a hint of energy, and she took a sip while Jonathan continued to glower.

She set her cup down. "When I read the newspaper account of the bombing, my first thought was relief that it couldn't have been you who was killed. I never even thought of Gallagher; I was just grateful it wasn't you."

Jonathan didn't answer, nor did he touch his coffee.

"Are there any new clues about who did it?"

"No."

That meant more decent people were likely to die before those vile criminals could be caught. There had to be some way to bring Achilles down short of handling his bombs or waiting around for the next strike. She had to *think*. How could they stop the bombs before they were built, armed, and placed where they could kill the maximum number of people?

Gallagher thought the Rinaldis might be involved. It was a delicate topic, but if it was true, Jonathan would be the best person to gain insight into the family.

She carefully framed her next question. "Jonathan, could the

Rinaldis have had anything to do with this? Gallagher told me they sell the same kind of clocks used for the bombs."

If possible, Jonathan's eyes looked even more hollow, "The Rinaldis aren't anarchists," he said in a tired voice. "They extort, they smuggle, sometimes they steal . . . but it's all about making money. They don't care about politics or bringing down the social order."

Maybe, but Gallagher thought it was possible, and Jonathan's complicated history with the Rinaldis might distort his view of them.

"I still think you should check it out," she said.

"The police will look into the family if they think it's warranted," he replied.

"But you would do a better job."

Jonathan's stoic expression cracked. His eyes flashed, and his voice was hard. "Keep out of it, Katherine. The police aren't going to do anything until Gallagher is buried."

Frustration boiled over. "This thing has *ruined* my life. Look at me! I have no job. I can't see my friends or go to church or even walk across the street to get a cup of coffee. Gallagher was a friend, and if these crimes don't get solved soon, I might be following right after him to the pearly gates. This is now my fight too."

Jonathan held his hands up, palms out. "Katherine, you need to calm down."

"No, I won't calm down! Gallagher was the best man to solve this case, and now he's dead and you won't follow up on a solid lead."

Jonathan abruptly stood and tossed a dollar bill for the coffee on the table. "I don't have time for this. Stay here, stay out of trouble, and let me handle things."

She watched him leave, tired of feeling so helpless. Yet she couldn't hide forever. It was time to join the fight.

Katherine's declaration still rang in Jonathan's mind as he left the hotel. She was too sensible to do anything rash like go confront the Rinaldis on their own territory and ask if they might be indulging in a little murder and anarchy as a side business.

While her concern wasn't completely unwarranted, the cops weren't going to follow up on any leads until Gallagher was buried. The funeral was in two days, and Jonathan wanted a medal awarded before that time.

So far, Jonathan had honored Captain Avery's order to keep away from the station house, but not today. Everyone knew of Gallagher's penchant for collecting medals. Nobody knew, however, that Gallagher was still hankering for one with his final breath on earth.

Life appeared to be going on as usual at the 15th Precinct Station House. Workaday business carried on at the front counter, where a restaurant owner complained his trash had gone uncollected for two weeks. The desk officer wore a flat expression as he handed over the necessary paperwork.

Jonathan understood the desk officer's annoyance. It seemed disrespectful to worry about uncollected garbage when a police officer had been killed in the line of duty, his body not even cold yet. And yet life went on. He moved deeper into the station house toward the locker room, where most of the guys were gathered in groups, talking quietly to each other.

A few officers looked at him in surprise. "You heard what happened?" Smitty asked, who looked red-eyed and exhausted.

"He was *there*," Patrolman Conti said.

"Was it as bad as they say?" Smitty asked. "I heard that the bomb—"

The slamming of a locker door cut off whatever else Smitty was going to say. "Can't we talk about something else?" Jankowski growled. "Gallagher is dead. It's done, and I'm sick of hearing about it." Jankowski stormed out of the locker room without looking back.

Patrolman Conti looked taken aback. "That was really disrespectful," he began.

Jonathan cut him off. "Leave him alone. Jankowski and Gallagher were close." Sergeant Jankowski was headed off for another day of patrol where he'd be required to carry on as if it were a normal day. The people on the street would see only Jankowski's professional demeanor . . . the tip of the iceberg, as Katherine would say. Underneath lay a world of anguish he was not free to share.

Jonathan had known only one other officer killed in the line of duty, and reaction in the station house had been split. Some people dwelled incessantly on it and wanted to dissect every detail, while others refused to speak of it. Both reactions were typical.

"I'm looking for Captain Avery," he said to Smitty. "Is he in?"

Smitty sighed. "He's in his office, but watch out. He's in a bad mood. You should think twice if you want to confront him today."

"It's business, and it has to happen today," Jonathan said as he left the locker room and strode to the captain's office door and knocked.

"Come in!" the captain barked. He scowled and rose to his feet when Jonathan stepped inside.

"Whatever it is, I don't want to hear it," Captain Avery said. "I've put up with ten years of you and Gallagher going after each other, and if you think you can nudge your way back into the station house now that he's gone—"

"It's not about that," Jonathan rushed to say. "I was with Gallagher when the bomb went off. I heard his final wishes."

Captain Avery stilled. "And?"

"He wanted a medal," Jonathan said. "The Gold Medal of Valor. He earned it. I want him to have it."

Captain Avery sighed and plopped back down into his chair, paging through the documents on his desk. "He'll get it. I've already started the paperwork, but it's going to take a while to go through the proper channels. There'll be a posthumous award ceremony at the end of the year."

"Not good enough," Jonathan said. He spoke calmly but with the determination to win this battle. "Gallagher deserves it right now. When they put him in the ground, I want him to have that medal pinned on his uniform. It's what he would have wanted."

Captain Avery gave a sad nod because they both knew it was true. Gallagher never had a wife or kids who would want the medal for posterity. He spent his whole life chasing the validation of those around him, and he deserved to wear every single one of those medals when they laid him to rest.

"I suppose I can push the process through to make it happen in time," Captain Avery said. "I'll take care of it. You can go now."

"Sir, the Bomb Squad is down a man. I would like to be appointed in Gallagher's place."

The captain tensed up again. "You never finished the training. You aren't even a cop anymore."

"I never stopped tracking the Achilles case. I know it as well as anyone. If it's the last thing I do, I'm going to track down who killed Gallagher."

Captain Avery lowered his head, an ironic laugh choking him. "Did you know that Gallagher put in a recommendation for you to be accepted on the Bomb Squad?"

It felt like a punch in the gut, and Jonathan could barely breathe. "No . . . I didn't know."

Avery slowly nodded. "He did it just last week. I guess he thought the two of you could get along after all."

They *could* have gotten along, but now it was too late. Life was short, and Jonathan had squandered too much of it by nurturing a bitter rivalry instead of turning the other cheek. Had he obeyed Jesus' instruction to turn the other cheek, it might have helped him to understand Gallagher instead of scheming for ways to get the upper hand. Gallagher's recommendation to bring Jonathan into the Bomb Squad was an act of pure decency, and Jonathan intended to return the favor by finding the men who killed him.

Captain Avery agreed, and an hour later Jonathan was back on the police force.

29

Katherine clenched the note from Jonathan as she paced in the confines of her hotel room. He apologized for being unable to continue meeting her each evening because he was back on the police force as a member of the Bomb Squad.

The Bomb Squad! Katherine hadn't even begun to mourn Gallagher, and now Jonathan was taking his place? This time yesterday, Sean Gallagher had been strutting around the city, charming women, solving crimes, looking forward to the next baseball game between the police and fire departments. All that charisma, all that potential . . . now snuffed out as though he never existed. And the same thing could happen to Jonathan.

How could she stay trapped in this room while Jonathan might be walking toward a literal bomb that could explode at any moment? It was impossible to be still, so she continued walking rings around the tiny open area in her hotel suite.

Her mother chattered nonstop, just as she did whenever times were tense. Her parents' wedding anniversary was coming up, and Lilian filed her nails while rambling about the diminishing quality of the gifts her husband had bought for their anniversary over the years. "He used to put such thought into his gifts," she said.

"Now I have to remind him of the date. You'd think that after thirty years of marriage, he'd remember the date."

"Oh, Mother," Katherine said in exasperation, "Dad brings you flowers every birthday and anniversary without fail."

"Yes, but he never pays for them. Instead of going to a florist like a normal man, he visits whatever church just had a wedding or a funeral, then culls through the leftover flowers to make a bouquet."

Katherine stopped pacing, mildly appalled. "He told you that?"

"He doesn't need to. I *live* with the man—I see and hear everything."

As Lilian continued rambling, Katherine paused, her thoughts taking a turn. It was hard to keep secrets in a family. Did the Rinaldi women know what their men were up to? Instead of appealing to Dante or any of the other men leading the family, what about the women? Jonathan claimed Nonna Rinaldi ruled the roost, and there probably wasn't much that went on in the family that she didn't know about.

Katherine started pacing again, steepling her hands beneath her chin as she wondered why the Rinaldi grocery store would start carrying alarm clocks. The women might have some insight into why the clocks suddenly appeared in their family's store. Most women were peacemakers by nature and would probably hate the thought of Jonathan putting himself in danger. If only she could find a way to earn the trust of the Rinaldi women.

A plate of biscotti sat on the breakfast table. It was ordinary biscotti bought at a local bakery, not the divine chocolate biscotti she and Jonathan both loved.

Katherine smiled. She knew how to approach Jonathan's grandmother.

It took all night and part of the next morning for Katherine to arrange her plan. She considered discussing it with Jonathan but quickly rejected the idea. There was no way he would approve, and besides, he was back on the police force and hard to track down.

All to the good. That meant she didn't have to ask his permission or feel guilty about going behind his back.

She still wasn't so foolish as to embark on the plan without protection. Mr. Hearst quit providing bodyguards after she moved into the hotel, but Alvin Washington, her fellow dentist from the clinic, gladly agreed to accompany her on the trip to Brooklyn. His older brother Jake came as well. Jake was a sergeant in the U.S. Cavalry, currently stationed in Vermont but on leave for a month in New York.

Jake wore his uniform. A cavalry uniform wasn't as threatening as a police uniform, but it still commanded a level of respect that was useful this morning. Having two strong men with her eased her mind a bit. Still, her nerves were stretched painfully tight as they approached the Rinaldi store on the corner. All around her, the air was filled with voices speaking Italian, Yiddish, and other languages she couldn't identify.

She'd taken care to dress modestly with her usual silk scarf knotted around her neck. There was no need to mention the attack, her affiliation with the police, or the investigation into the bombings. She was merely coming as a woman who loved Jonathan, requesting the recipe for his favorite chocolate biscotti.

"Are you sure this is a good idea, Katherine?" Alvin's voice was riddled with concern as they passed a gang of tough-looking boys rolling dice in the alley. The storefront of Rinaldi Grocers loomed straight ahead.

She gripped the handles of her basket filled with biscotti. "I'm not sure at all, but here we are."

The storefront looked prosperous, with crates of fresh produce mounded before the window. Alvin and his brother took a seat on the bench opposite the store to wait. Katherine hoped she wouldn't need their intervention, but knowing they were there within earshot was comforting. The apartments over the store where the Rinaldis lived all had their windows open, so that was one thing she had on her side this morning.

"I've got a healthy set of lungs," she said. "If you hear me screaming . . ."

Alvin gave a nod of understanding. "If I hear screaming, I'll come running and bring the cavalry with me."

It was surprisingly easy to slip through the building's side door, where a narrow, brick-lined stairwell led to three floors of apartments above the store. Which one was Nonna Rinaldi's?

Katherine's heart thudded, and her scar itched. The steps were surprisingly steep, and an old lady surely wouldn't want to live on the third or fourth floor. The second floor would be easier on aging knees. One of the apartments on the second level had its door propped open.

The heavenly scent of warm fruit wafted through the doorway. Women chattering in Italian peppered the air, and Katherine held her breath as she peeked into the apartment. An older lady was perched on a kitchen chair, a younger woman sitting near the lady. The younger woman chopped strawberries while a third woman stirred a pot of simmering jam on the stove.

Katherine tapped on the door. "Hello?"

All three woman looked at her in astonishment. One of the younger women asked her a question.

"I'm sorry, I don't speak Italian," Katherine replied. "I'm looking for Nonna Rinaldi."

Her gaze trailed to the old woman swathed in black and holding a cane between her hands like a queen on a throne. The woman showed no curiosity or warmth, no hint of softening.

What if none of them spoke English? The silence was intensely uncomfortable. Only the noise of a sewing machine down in the alley came through an open window.

"I need to speak with Jonathan's grandmother, and I'm afraid it's very important."

That got a reaction, and the old woman straightened. "Why? What is the reason?" she demanded in a heavily accented voice.

Katherine took another step into the apartment, nervously clasping the handle on her basket of cookies. "My name is Katherine, and Jonathan is fine for right now."

It would be cruel to keep the old woman in suspense. Nonna Rinaldi's body eased a fraction, and Katherine inched forward a little farther. If she could but gain their trust, these women might help her.

"Jonathan and I see each other every night because . . . well, because we care about each other. He told me that you baked chocolate biscotti for me when I was sick, and I came to thank you." She peeled the cloth back from her basket of cookies. "I would like to start baking them for Jonathan, but he swears none of the recipes he's found are as good as yours. Would you be willing to share the recipe with me?"

The old woman rolled her eyes, then waved a dismissive hand and muttered something in Italian. Katherine couldn't understand a word, but the other women looked equally annoyed.

She set the basket on the table and drew a steadying breath. It had been naive to hope that appealing for a cookie recipe would soften the old woman's heart. It was probably better to simply tell the truth.

"A police officer was killed two days ago. It's a dangerous line of work, but still shocking when a young, healthy man is suddenly gone forever. Jonathan is back on the police force as part of the Bomb Squad. The thought of him walking straight toward a ticking time bomb is terrifying. I'll do anything to protect him from that. He thinks the Rinaldis might know something about the case."

The slow, steady scrape of the wooden spoon as the younger woman stirred the jam continued, but outside the sewing machine had stopped.

She kept her eyes trained on the old woman as she continued speaking. "Jonathan doesn't believe the Rinaldis knew about the bomb that went off recently, but the police are starting to believe there's a connection. Maybe you can help."

The old woman leaned back in her chair and crossed her arms over her chest. Her face had grown even colder.

"Please," Katherine said, "I don't want to get a message someday that Jonathan has been blown to bits because a time bomb went off in his hands. If you know something, I'm begging you . . ."

The woman stirring jam was heavily pregnant and started to say something in Italian, but Nonna shot her a glare, silencing her. Then she turned that steely gaze back to Katherine.

"It's time for you to leave," Nonna said.

"Please," Katherine said, then held her breath as Nonna rose to her feet, leaning on her cane with palsied hands.

"You are a foolish, *foolish* woman," Nonna said, her tone like a whip. "Leave now and don't ever come back."

Katherine wanted to wither before the old woman's arctic glare, but she couldn't leave yet, not without getting some sort of insight from the women. "Please," she implored, "if your family's grocery store is involved in this, it needs to stop. For the sake of Jonathan and countless others."

The pregnant woman at the stove dropped her spoon. "Leave now," she said gently. "I don't hate Jonathan, but others in the family do. If my husband finds out you've been here, it will go badly for you."

Nonna Rinaldi grabbed a dishrag, walked slowly over to Katherine, and whapped her across the face with it.

Katherine held a hand to her cheek. *Did Nonna just hit me?* It hadn't really hurt, but no one had ever struck Katherine in her entire life!

Nonna yelled in Italian, then switched to English, ordering Katherine to get out as she banged her cane against the floor. Was it possible to be afraid of a ninety-year-old woman?

Yes, it was! Katherine fled out the door and was shaking so badly that she had to clasp the handrail while hurrying down the stairs. She forgot her basket but didn't care; she just wanted to get away from that awful woman.

Alvin and his brother rose to their feet as she stumbled back onto the sidewalk. "It was pointless," she said. "Let's go. Please hurry."

The Washington brothers moved to either side of her as they started down the avenue. If they weren't with her, she'd be tempted to start crying. The side of her face still stung. Nonna Rinaldi was a horrible woman. *Horrible!* Her scathing harangue echoed in Katherine's ears and raised goose bumps on her arms.

"Wait!" a voice called from behind them.

She turned to see a teenaged boy racing toward them. He was at the gangly stage between adolescence and manhood, and he was out of breath when he reached them. He held a single piece of paper.

"You need to know something," he said, still panting. Both Washington brothers took a protective step closer to her, waiting for the boy to catch his breath.

He introduced himself as Carlo Rinaldi, Dante's oldest son. "You have to believe me," Carlo began. "We didn't have anything to do with making those bombs. My dad got duped with the clocks. We don't know who made the bombs, but we know who printed all those flyers that keep turning up at the bomb sites." He extended the paper to Katherine, and she took it.

It was a receipt from a printer on Foster Avenue, requesting two hundred copies of a document, printed on standard-weight paper with a solid red ink border.

"My dad bought that receipt from the printer for a hundred bucks," Carlo said. "He got mad after the Mazzinis tricked him into buying the clocks, and he tracked down that receipt in case he ever needs to blackmail the Mazzinis."

Katherine studied the signature at the bottom of the page. "Emilio Mazzini, CPA," she read aloud.

Carlo rolled his eyes and scoffed. "Yeah, only an idiot would sign his real name to a receipt like that. My dad says Emilio is a puffed-up snob who can't stop flaunting his fancy college degree."

Katherine studied the document, which contained the entire manifesto written by Achilles. It didn't prove Emilio built or planted the bombs, but it was evidence that he was an accomplice. She met the young man's eyes, astonished by his bravery.

"Thank you for turning this over," Katherine said. "I feel certain this is going to save a lot of lives."

Carlo shrugged as if it were no big deal. But he stood a little taller, and his expression had a hint of pride. "I always kind of wished I could be a cop."

Carlo was far too young to believe doors were closed to him. "Why can't you?" she asked.

He shrugged again. "That's not in the cards for someone like me."

Alvin's older brother stepped forward. "Look at me, kid," Jake said in the firm voice of authority. Carlo instantly obeyed, and Jake continued, "If a Black man like me can grow up to become a sergeant in the U.S. Cavalry, you can be anything you want. My brother is a dentist, and he didn't have it any easier. Don't tell me you can't grow up to be a cop if that's what God tells you to be."

Carlo blinked, his jaw hanging open, looking inspired and intimidated at the same time. "Thanks," he said. A grin flashed across his face before he turned around to sprint back to the grocery store.

Katherine was thrilled by Carlo's brave act of handing over the receipt, but Alvin wasn't. "This might cost that kid his life," he said somberly.

A hint of fear settled over her, but she straightened her shoulders in determination. It was all the more reason to solve this crime.

Jonathan sat in the war room at police headquarters with a dozen other officers assigned to the bombing case. There was no more joking or lighthearted quips at their meetings. One of their own had been killed, and the hunt for Achilles was top priority. Detective Fiaschetti reported that Vittorio Lastra and his brother Gino had been extradited back to New York, but a judge ordered Gino released.

"Vittorio was the only one Katherine heard talk about the future bombings," Detective Fiaschetti said. "There's no proof Gino knew anything, so he's out. And Vittorio is asserting his right to remain silent."

"Give me ten minutes alone with him," one of the Bomb Squad members said. "Nobody else has to be there. I'll get him to talk."

The comment was greeted by rumbles of agreement. Detective Fiaschetti let the men air it out for a few moments, but before he could call the meeting to order again, a clerk slipped inside the room and came straight to Jonathan's side.

"There's a woman outside to see you," he said. "Katherine Schneider. She says its important."

Jonathan pushed away from the table. Walking out in the middle of a strategy session wasn't good, but Katherine wouldn't have come here unless it was urgent. He followed the clerk to the crowded main room, where dozens of impatient people lined up to file complaints at the front counter. Katherine stood near the back, her face tense, a single piece of paper clenched in her hands.

"Thank heavens you're here," she said.

"What's going on? Why aren't you at the hotel?"

Katherine was clearly agitated as she leaned in to speak in a low voice. "I need to speak with you privately. I've got evidence of who paid for the Sons of Chaos flyers, and we can't be overheard."

"Follow me," he said and guided her to the stairway leading to the basement. There wouldn't be anyone using the shooting range at this hour. Once they reached the darkened room, he pulled the lever powering the overhead lights. The clang of the lever echoed in the concrete space, and she jumped a little.

He closed the distance between them. "Okay, we're alone," he said quietly. "What is it you need to tell me?"

"Jonathan, I went to see your grandmother."

"You did *what*?" His voice reverberated in the empty shooting gallery, causing her to flinch.

Surely he misunderstood, but his alarm grew as she continued speaking. "Women always know about what's going on in their families," she rushed to say. "My mother knows all sorts of things about my father's business, and I thought that if I introduced myself to your grandmother and let her know I was your friend, she might reveal something. Woman to woman."

This couldn't be happening. Didn't she know how dangerous Mafia members could be when threatened? No wonder she looked agitated.

"That was incredibly foolish," he bit out. "Let me guess. Grandma summoned the crew and threw you out."

"Not exactly, although she seemed quite angry. She banged her cane and asked me to leave. Ordered me actually."

He started pacing to unwind the tension coiling inside. "You shouldn't have gone behind my back like that. You're lucky they let you walk out with all your limbs."

She pursed her lips. "Now I think *that's* an exaggeration. The women weren't happy to see me, but a young man named Carlo gave me a very good lead. Take a look."

He snatched the document she held out, and his heart started pounding as he focused on Emilio Mazzini's signature, authorizing the printing of the incendiary manifesto from the Sons of Chaos. Katherine kept chattering, saying Dante bought the receipt should he ever need to blackmail the Mazzinis. The receipt was enough to arrest Emilio and crack the case wide open, but anger still zinged inside him, making it hard to form a coherent thought.

"Well?" Katherine asked, hope brimming in her voice. Her daffy idealism rubbed him the wrong way because she still didn't seem to realize that she'd put herself in a great amount of danger.

"Please don't ever talk to my family again."

She jutted out her chin. "I'm fighting so we can be free of this."

"I'm already free," he snapped.

"I'm not. Neither is Carlo. He wants more from life than following in his father's footsteps, and I want more than being trapped in a hotel room."

Guilt warred with anger as he held up the flimsy receipt. "This piece of paper is that kid's death warrant. If news of it ever gets out, the Mazzinis will kill him."

"Why would news get out?"

"The printer who sold this to Dante will sing like a canary if the Mazzinis find out about it."

He started pacing, thinking how to make use of the receipt without putting Carlo in danger. It might not be possible because they didn't have the luxury of time. Carlo was a brave kid.

So was Katherine. Her action had been foolish and ill-conceived yet undeniably brave.

"I'm sorry I spoke harshly, but please don't ever approach my family again. No good can come of it."

He hated everything about this case, mostly what it had done to Katherine. He'd always thought of her as sunshine on a moonless night, but now she'd seen the dark, seedy part of New York he'd always hoped to protect her from. And things were only going to get darker in the days ahead.

30

The bleak clouds hovering over the city were a suitably grim backdrop for Sean Gallagher's funeral. Maybe it was foolish to risk attending the funeral since it was a painfully public ceremony, and whoever was out to kill her might still try to strike, but Katherine needed to attend. Gallagher didn't have any family, and she would ensure there would be someone there to mourn him.

She needn't have worried. The church was filled to capacity by a sea of men in blue uniforms. There wasn't even any standing room, so she stood among hundreds of civilians who had gathered outside to pay their respects. Some were journalists and photographers covering the story, but most were ordinary people of all ages and races. Some wore mourning finery, while others were dressed for work. The firefighters were there in force, gathered near the base of the church steps. They wore their formal uniforms, and the firefighters' baseball team stood together, one of them holding high a flag with Gallagher's number on it.

The church doors finally opened, and streams of police officers somberly exited the building. Katherine searched their faces, looking for Jonathan, but there were so many. The officers gathered into formation in the center of the street. Then the pallbearers carrying Gallagher's casket emerged from the church.

A lump filled her throat as Katherine finally spotted Jonathan, serving as a pallbearer along with seven other men from the 15th Precinct.

The police commissioner stepped forward. "Officers, present arms!"

Hundreds of police officers instantly saluted. Katherine put her hand over her heart, as did every other civilian lining the street as the pallbearers carried the flag-draped casket down the church steps and took a position at the front of the police formation.

The steady beat of a snare drum sounded as Jonathan and the other pallbearers set off for the cemetery, Gallagher's casket on their shoulders.

"Good-bye, Sean Gallagher," she whispered. The police officers began marching behind the casket, followed by the firefighters. The last group was the mounted police, all following at a slow, stately pace.

Katherine had seen a part of Gallagher he hadn't shared with many people, all because she'd spotted the tiny chip in his tooth. Maybe if Jonathan had known about Gallagher's troubled history, they would have gotten along. At the very least, he wouldn't have been so intolerant of Gallagher's peculiar need for recognition.

She caught her breath as shame rose within her. Jonathan didn't have a chipped tooth from his damaged childhood, but he'd been a victim too. She had been quick to condemn him after learning he wasn't the sterling man she thought him to be. She'd offered no empathy, no compassion, just a swift condemnation.

Wasn't that odd? Gallagher had been almost a complete stranger when she extended grace and understanding to an imperfect man. Why hadn't she done the same for Jonathan?

The last of the funeral procession had passed, and the civilian mourners began dispersing. The man beside her slipped an apron over his head and tied the strings behind his back as he headed

toward a restaurant on the corner. A pair of construction workers put on their hard hats and set off down the avenue. Life went
on as usual, but Katherine trailed after the mourners heading to
the cemetery.

She needed to see Jonathan. It was time to apologize, to forgive,
and to set things right between them.

Katherine stood beneath the shade of a linden tree during another short ceremony at the graveside. It didn't take long, and soon
the crowds of people began dispersing through the leafy green
cemetery. A pair of departing officers gossiped about Gallagher's
new medal that had been officially awarded this morning.

"That medal was designed by Mr. Tiffany himself," the shorter
officer said.

"And they buried it with him?" the other marveled. "My wife
would dig me up and kill me all over again if I let myself get buried
with a medal like that."

The shorter officer shrugged. "I guess he didn't have a wife or
kids who would have wanted it."

The men drifted too far away for Katherine to hear any more.
What a shame that Gallagher never had a family of his own, except
a father who had damaged him for life.

Gallagher deserved more. *Jonathan* deserved more, and she
intended to give it to him. When she rejected him after learning
about his past, it must have scorched. He appealed for her understanding and forgiveness, but she bluntly refused. Now that Gallagher's funeral was behind them, they could step forward, side
by side, into a brighter future. It was time to welcome Jonathan
back into her life with open arms.

She peered through the crowd of departing officers and spotted Jonathan at the north gate. He was about to disappear into
the city streets.

"Jonathan!" she called out, hiking her skirts to catch up with him. The lumpy ground forced her to hop around tree roots and scattered headstones. "Jonathan, wait!"

She hurried through the cemetery gate and onto the street, where she glimpsed him heading toward an elevated train station platform. She caught up to him just as he was about to mount the steps and managed to grasp his elbow.

"Jonathan," she said, panting from the run. "I saw the procession. Thank you for being a pallbearer. I think Gallagher would have liked that."

He nodded. "I was glad to do it."

"Have the police been able to do anything with that receipt from Carlo?"

"Things are moving fast. We'll be arresting Emilio this afternoon and see if we can get him to talk."

"Good," she said, because it sounded like Jonathan didn't intend to say anything else. Silence stretched between them, and she scrambled for something to say. "I heard they buried Gallagher with a fancy new medal. Is that true?"

Jonathan nodded. "It's the most distinguished medal they give, and he deserved it."

He turned to mount the steps, and she pulled him back again. This wasn't going as easily as she expected. How lonely he looked. Wounded. Part of his suffering was her fault, and it was time to fix it.

"Jonathan, I want you to know that I'm sorry for being so distant," she began. "I shouldn't have shut you out when I learned about your past. I should have been more forgiving. You should have been honest with me from the outset, but I understand things better now. I forgive you."

There was no change in Jonathan's expression. "Thank you," he said dryly. He didn't sound very enthused, and she shifted uneasily and gathered a breath.

"Well, that's said then. Can we go forward like we were before?"

Jonathan looked into the distance as an oncoming train approached the station. It rumbled on the tracks overhead, the roar making it impossible to keep talking. Gears squeaked and steam hissed as it slowed down. It was probably the train Jonathan intended to catch, yet he made no move to run for it. He turned back to her once the train settled on the tracks and the noise abated.

"I don't know if that's possible," he said, and her mouth dropped open.

"Why not?" How could he prefer the life of a nocturnal loner to one of a family with a partner and hope for the future? A myriad of expressions flitted across his face. It looked like an odd mix of cynicism and humor as he regarded her.

"Because I'm not convinced that what I did was all that horrible. We had only been courting for three weeks when you found out about my past. Was I really supposed to share my life history with you that quickly? I've always tried to lead an admirable life, both when I was Giovanni Rinaldi and now as Jonathan Birch. I think I've done a pretty good job of that, but you think I ought to grovel and be grateful for your forgiveness."

Katherine folded her arms across her chest. "It wasn't exactly a white lie, Giovanni."

"No, it wasn't. It was something that started when I was twelve years old and didn't have any control over. Even now it's a problem because you're likely to bring it up every time I annoy you. Or sneak behind my back to poke into my family business because your good intentions overshadow what I think."

"I wasn't sneaking. I was trying to help."

"You knew I wouldn't want you seeing my family."

"Well, yes, but—"

"So you aren't perfect either, Katherine."

She bristled. "I never said I was!"

"You do it every time you call me Giovanni. It's a little prick, a little jab to point out that you're better than me."

She absorbed the accusation at the same time as scrambling for a way to deny it, but nothing came. "I was wrong," she choked out. The words didn't come easily, and it was especially painful because she knew calling him Giovanni would be hurtful and she'd done it anyway.

Katherine had been born into a loving and wholesome family. It hadn't been hard to walk the straight and narrow because she was born into it. Jonathan had to climb out of a cesspool, and look how far he'd come. He wore his dress uniform with an array of ribbons across his chest, proof of his accomplishments. And among those commendations was the Bomb Squad ribbon, the same blue-and-red ribbon Gallagher had, and it hurt her to see it.

"I'm glad you're back on the police force, but I wish you weren't on the Bomb Squad. I'm sorry I ever loaned you that chemistry textbook or helped with your studies. I wish you would remove that ribbon and walk away from this assignment."

One corner of his mouth quirked, but it vanished quickly. "That's not going to happen," he said, and she had to look away lest he see how much his comment hurt. It felt like a personal rejection. If he cared about her, he ought to be willing to consider her feelings.

"Come here," Jonathan said, drawing her into his arms. She clung to him as he gently rocked her, stroking her back. "Thank you for apologizing," he said against the shell of her ear. "It took a lot of courage."

She squeezed her eyes shut and held him tighter. "But?" she said, because it didn't sound like this conversation was leading where she hoped it would go.

"But I will be staying on the Bomb Squad. It's my calling, Katherine. There aren't many people able or willing to dismantle bombs, and as long as we continue to live in a fallen world, it will require decent men willing to roll up their sleeves to get the job done."

She wasn't the sort of person who could kiss a man goodbye at the start of his shift and pray he would still be alive at the end of it. "Jonathan, no—"

He touched a finger to her lips to stop her from talking. "Thank you for what you said, but today isn't a good time for this conversation. I love you, and I pray we can work things out, but I have a job to do."

Jonathan touched the brim of his cap before hurrying up the staircase to catch the next train. How strange that the first time Jonathan confessed his love, he simultaneously walked toward a Bomb Squad assignment that frightened her down to the ground. She didn't even have a chance to tell him that she loved him back. All she was left with was bewilderment and fear for his future.

Katherine's parents had left for their anniversary luncheon by the time she returned to the hotel. They were celebrating in style, spending the entire day and evening out on the town. It would be their last day in the big city before packing up and returning to Ohio tomorrow.

It meant Katherine's hiatus was over. She couldn't afford to stay at the hotel any longer, and the Martha Washington wouldn't take her back as a resident. Nobody else would rent a room to someone with a price on their head, so it was time for Katherine to make a decision. She either needed to follow her parents to Ohio or take Edgar's offer and move to California. Jonathan hadn't exactly fallen at her feet in gratitude for trying to rekindle their relationship.

Her tangle of conflicting emotions grew so perplexing that she called on her friends at the Martha Washington to join her for lunch in her hotel room. She needed Midge's wisdom and Inga's cheerfulness, but mostly she was looking for someone to agree with her that Jonathan was being unfeeling and irrational.

Katherine paced before the window while Inga and Midge sat at the table, feasting on a platter of muffins, cheeses, and strong tea delivered by the hotel.

"Why does Jonathan have to be on the Bomb Squad?" Katherine

demanded as she paced. "Why can't being a police officer be enough for him?"

"Men are competitive," Inga said. "He wants to be at the top of the heap."

Even Midge wouldn't side with her. "You can pressure him to quit the Bomb Squad, but I don't know if he'd ever forgive you for it."

Katherine sighed. She and Jonathan weren't married or even engaged, so she didn't have the right to object if he wanted to risk his life by being a hero with the Bomb Squad. The brochures Edgar gave her about California were tempting. If she left New York, Jonathan might even be willing to follow her, and they could start over in a new city.

"Look at these," Katherine said, handing each woman a brochure. "I think going to California is my only option. There isn't enough work for another dentist in Hudson, and going to California would be safer." *Safer for Jonathan too*, she silently added. Maybe he would have no interest in following her, but she hoped he would.

Inga slipped on a pair of gold-rimmed spectacles to scrutinize the photographs of towering redwood trees and cliffs hugging the ocean. "It looks quite pretty, but you said the police are close to arresting the people behind the bombs. Why can't you stay in New York once it is solved?"

"Because Jonathan would still be on the Bomb Squad if we stay here," she admitted. "I used to love the idea of how strong and courageous he could be, but that was before Gallagher died. I want a future with Jonathan, and that can't happen if he's determined to spend his life handling bombs."

Midge's smile was sad. "Dearest, please don't stand between a man and his calling. Some men are destined to be happy in a pulpit or a dentist office or teaching school, but Jonathan has been called to be a protector."

"But, Midge, he could die!"

Midge stood, her tall frame still exuding healthy vigor despite her advanced age. "Katherine Schneider, you need to listen to me. Don't ever doubt in the darkness what is true in the light. If God is good and trustworthy in the easy times, you need to trust him during the dark nights of the soul as well. Right now, you are being ruled by fear. The voice of doubt whispering in your ear is leading you astray. Jonathan has been drawn to a noble calling, maybe even a godly one. I don't believe you were put on this earth to interfere with that."

Katherine rocked back on her heels, stunned by the dressing down. Her friends were supposed to be on *her* side, not Jonathan's. Her neck itched, and she fiddled with her scarf, glancing at Inga for support.

Inga was the softie. Surely Inga would back her up.

Instead, Inga glanced at Katherine's scarf. "Your parents haven't ordered you to leave New York, have they? Even after *that*?" she asked, gesturing to Katherine's scarf.

Her parents had been frightened ever since Katherine ventured to New York, but they never tried to stop her, and she would have resented it if they had. Jonathan deserved the same level of respect, but was there a more dangerous job in the entire world than dismantling bombs?

It didn't matter. If God had led Jonathan into a life of dangerous service, who was she to interfere with that? She had no business imagining a future with Jonathan if she couldn't accept his calling and offer him her full support.

The only remaining question to be decided was if she could be strong enough to accept Jonathan's decision.

31

Jonathan's hunt for Achilles had reached a boiling point, and he didn't have time to mull over Katherine's surprising offer of a reconciliation. A few days ago, he would have pounced on the chance to win her back, but the trail leading to Achilles was white-hot, leaving no room for tangling with the guilt and regret that choked him whenever he thought of either Katherine or Gallagher.

Jonathan was fairly certain that Chester Lewis from the sugar refinery was Achilles. Plainclothes policemen had been tailing Chester for days, and last night they confirmed Jonathan's hunch when Chester tracked down Gino Lastra, the big-nosed brother who'd been released for lack of evidence.

The plainclothes officers watched as Chester and two accomplices entered a flophouse where Gino was staying. They dragged Gino into the back alley, pinned him on the ground, and Chester whipped out a knife, preparing to inflict the punishment that made him infamous.

The officers descended quickly. When the lead officer flashed his badge, all three attackers fled and Chester escaped into the underworld.

Now that Achilles knew the police were closing in, he was likely to become more dangerous than ever, using his last days of freedom to score another monumental attack. They searched Chester's apartment and found purchase orders indicating he'd been stockpiling explosives for more chemical bombs, but there was no sign of the chemicals or the bombs in the apartment. Chester could be anywhere by now, and those bombs needed to be found quickly.

Arresting Emilio Mazzini was their best shot at tracking down where Achilles would flee. Jonathan laid out his plan for Detective Fiaschetti at police headquarters.

"Emilio knows me as Giovanni Rinaldi. I scare him. If I offer to sell him the receipt back, I think he'll fall for it and incriminate himself. Once we've got him cornered, he might roll over and lead us to Chester or wherever those bombs are being made."

Detective Fiaschetti agreed, and it didn't take long to put their plan in place. Jonathan would meet with Emilio in his office and offer to sell the receipt for a hefty sum. They didn't need Emilio to take the deal; they just needed him to engage in enough discussion to prove the authenticity of the receipt that would survive challenge in court. Once they had that, they could charge Emilio with complicity in the associated crimes and cut a deal.

The office where Emilio worked had thin walls, so the police stationed detectives and a stenographer in the office next door to Emilio, listening to every word. Jonathan booked an appointment for later in the afternoon under the name he wanted carved into his tombstone: Jonathan Birch.

Mazzini took the appointment, but recognition dawned the instant Jonathan walked into the office. The accountant stood so quickly, the chair toppled over behind him.

"Not you again," he said.

Jonathan held up placating hands. "I'm here to offer a truce. I'm sorry we got off on the wrong foot the other day. That was entirely my fault. I had business with Vittorio Lastra that wasn't pleasant, but I shouldn't have taken my frustration out on you."

Emilio narrowed his gaze. After a tense few moments, he carefully righted his chair and sat back down. But his eyes never once disengaged, nor did he blink. "Can I offer you something to drink?"

"No need." Jonathan casually picked up the photograph of the Kappa Tau Delta fraternity from the bookcase. He scanned the young men and spotted Chester Lewis in the back row almost immediately. "Nice photo," he said, tamping down the surge of triumph as he returned the picture frame to the bookcase, then took a chair opposite the desk.

The fraternity picture would be turned over to a police sketch artist to draw up a wanted poster for Chester as soon as Emilio was under arrest. Tonight's newspapers would be blanketed with it.

"Let's talk business," Jonathan began. "I want to renegotiate the truce between the Rinaldis and the Mazzinis. I've recently acquired a document that will be damaging to your family's reputation. I am prepared to offer it to you. For a modest price, of course."

Emilio sat up straighter. "What do you think you have?"

"I have the receipt from a print shop on Foster Avenue for two hundred copies of a political screed." He held up the receipt with Emilio's signature on the bottom. "You have a very distinctive signature," Jonathan added in a complimentary tone.

Beads of perspiration began to pop up across Emilio's forehead. Jonathan continued the conversation in a deliberately casual tone.

"Did you write the text or was it Chester Lewis? Maybe it doesn't matter because that signature is enough to handcuff you to this document."

Emilio blotted his forehead with a handkerchief. "How much do you want for it?"

"How much can you afford?"

"I can give you a hundred dollars."

Jonathan leaned back in his chair, folding his arms across his chest. Emilio was so nervous that he probably didn't notice the faint rattle of keys in the office directly behind him—a police stenographer recording every word of their conversation.

"A hundred dollars?" Jonathan shook his head. "The city just held a funeral for a cop killed trying to dismantle a bomb, and a stack of these notes were scattered all over town right after it happened. Cops don't like people who kill fellow cops. Neither does the public. Execution in the electric chair is almost guaranteed for anyone involved in Lieutenant Gallagher's death. I think you can come up with more than a hundred dollars, Emilio."

Emilio slammed a fist on the desktop. "Two hundred dollars, and that's the top I'm offering."

"Not good enough."

Emilio stood, upending the desk, and lunged for the receipt. But Jonathan held the paper up high out of the man's reach. With his other hand, he pulled out a pistol and pressed its muzzle under Emilio's chin.

"Hold still," Jonathan warned. "Things are about to get interesting."

Detective Fiaschetti burst into the room, followed by two other officers. It was time to pressure Emilio to tell them what he knew about the bombs.

Emilio, terrified of the death penalty, started to crack shortly after being locked into an interrogation room at police headquarters. Spread out on the table in the stark cinder-block cell were postmortem photographs of men who'd been electrocuted earlier in the year. One of the electrocutions had been botched and was particularly gruesome.

It had the desired effect. Emilio's shirt was damp with sweat, though he still refused to talk. "I want a deal," he insisted. "I didn't kill anybody, but I know who did."

"We do too," Jonathan said. "Where did Chester run to after the cops almost caught him yesterday?"

Emilio looked away. "I don't know."

Jonathan set the photograph of Emilio's fraternity brothers on the table. "You're good friends with Chester, or would you prefer I call him Achilles? Such a clever nickname. I'll bet he'll be furious with you after he learns about that receipt."

A faint whimper escaped Emilio's throat. "I don't know where he is, and I didn't have anything to do with planting those bombs."

"I think it's time for a lesson in criminal law," Detective Fiaschetti said. "You don't have to build the bomb or set the timer to be guilty of murder. You participated when you commissioned those flyers to stoke public fear. We're willing to cut a deal, but you're going to have to bring something very tempting to the table. What have you got?"

Emilio bowed his head, his body curling in on itself. "I know where the next round of bombs is going to blow. I'll tell you, but I want to walk out of here a free man. No one can know that I talked."

"That's not going to happen," Jonathan said.

"The next round of bombs will start going off tonight," Emilio said. "A lot of them. There might still be time to call it off."

Detective Fiaschetti shot across the room and hauled Emilio up by his collar. "Might?" he roared. "You start talking right now if you want to keep that nose of yours in the middle of your face."

Jonathan let the detective engage in a few more verbal threats before calmly interceding.

"Let the man talk, Detective," he said. Jonathan was a master at playing the sympathetic cop after a little bullying, and Emilio played into his hands. After the detective released him, Emilio took a ragged breath and began talking.

"A bunch of cylinder bombs have been packed into bags of sugar and sent to the harbor to be loaded onto ships."

"How many bombs?" Jonathan asked.

"Around a hundred if they all get planted. Chester wants a big show. The biggest show ever."

A hundred cylinder bombs! Jonathan's mind reeled, but he kept his voice even. "What ships have been targeted, and when?"

"I don't know. We've got a guy in the warehouse who figures out which ships to plant them on. The bombs were put together yesterday. Depending on how long it takes the sulfuric acid to eat through the disk in each cylinder, they'll start burning late tonight or tomorrow."

"Which warehouse, and which ship?" Detective Fiaschetti said, enunciating each word like a bullet.

"A lot of ships," Emilio said on a shaking breath. "Chester wants a whole bunch of ships to get hit all at once. He wants the *Lorna Doone* times ten. It's going to be bad."

"*Which warehouse?*" Detective Fiaschetti shouted, shoving his face inches away from Emilio's nose.

Emilio flinched and started weeping. "Chester will kill me if I snitch. Get me on a train to leave the city, and I'll tell you whatever you want to know, but I don't want to die."

Jonathan pushed a photo of an executed convict closer to Emilio. "This guy didn't want to die either. Neither did Lieutenant Gallagher. Neither do the people on those ships that are about to leave port with a bunch of bombs on board."

Detective Fiaschetti took over. "If we miss saving these ships because you were too busy sniveling, I will personally throw the switch when they electrocute you."

Emilio took a deep breath and let it out slowly. "All right. It's the warehouse that services the *Caledonia*. That's the only ship I know for sure has been targeted. The rest will be the luck of the draw."

"Why the *Caledonia*?" Detective Fiaschetti asked.

"It's a passenger ship," Emilio said. "There will be around eight hundred people aboard. Like I said, Chester wants a big show, and Henrik said he can deliver."

"Who is Henrik?" Jonathan asked.

"Henrik Bauman. He's our guy down at the warehouse who is responsible for planting the bombs on the ships. He'll decide at the last minute depending on the size of the cargo hold for each ship. The bigger the better."

Detective Fiaschetti stood and opened the door, speaking to an officer posted outside. "Have someone call the docks. If the *Caledonia* is still in port, order it to be evacuated immediately."

"Yes, sir," the young officer said. "What if it's already left?"

"Send a wireless message to get it back to port." Detective Fiaschetti closed the door and turned to Jonathan. "Let's bring our new friend Emilio down to the harbor. He can help us find Henrik."

"No!" Emilio said, his face turning pale. "I can't. *I can't*."

"Sure you can," Fiaschetti said congenially. "Just pretend that your life depends on it. Because I can assure you that it does."

Hundreds of ships set sail from the Port of New York each day, and a mysterious man named Henrik was the only person who knew which ships had the cylinder bombs on board. Jonathan needed to find Henrik and make him talk.

Emilio's anxiety expanded as the police van drove along the mile-long stretch of warehouses lining the harbor. "Look, I've already told you everything I know. Just take me back to the jail, but don't let anyone see me. Please."

The police van finally arrived at Warehouse 36. Jonathan opened the van door and jumped to the ground. Detective Fiaschetti followed, but Emilio shrank further back into the van.

"I ain't leaving," he said.

"Sure you are," Jonathan said. "You're going to introduce us to Henrik Bauman."

It was easy to understand why Emilio was terrified. The moment Emilio was spotted wearing handcuffs and leg irons while shuffling between police officers, everyone would know he was cooperating with them.

Jonathan tamped down a hint of sympathy at the cringing fear on Emilio's face. Gallagher had been afraid at the end too. People on the ships would be afraid when fires broke out at sea. Jonathan scrubbed his face of emotion and leaned into the van, grabbed the chain linking the handcuffs around Emilio's wrists, and dragged him out.

The waterfront was busy tonight. Dozens of ships floated in the harbor as tugboats guided oceangoing steamers into port. The tugs looked like toy boats as they navigated among transatlantic ocean liners billowing smoke. Acre-sized warehouses were stacked high with tons of cargo. It was the biggest harbor in North America, and Jonathan needed to find a bunch of cylinder bombs, none of which were larger than a loaf of bread.

The sliding doors at Warehouse 36 were open. Pallets of coffee and sugar were mounded beside stacks of lumber and barrels of tar and turpentine. Trollies carrying coal rolled along a maze of railway tracks crisscrossing the pavement. Longshoremen used hand trucks to wheel their loads, while others carried heavy sacks balanced across their shoulders. There looked to be fifty or so longshoremen in this single warehouse.

Jonathan called to one of them, who was busy wheeling a cask. "Hey, we're looking for Henrik Bauman. Is he around?"

The longshoreman straightened. "Yeah, he's in the back office."

Jonathan nodded his thanks, and he and Fiaschetti frog-marched Emilio into the cavernous warehouse. A grubby back office had a window in its door behind which a man wearing spectacles was at work. A chalkboard hanging on the wall outside the office showed a list of ships and cargo due to sail today.

Henrik wore a white shirt with the sleeves rolled up. The moment he spotted the police uniforms, his face blanched. He stepped out of the office, yanking off his spectacles to stare at them in shock.

"Emilio?" he said.

Emilio sagged and nodded. "They're on to us. Just tell them what they want to know. They'll let us go if we cooperate. Then we can both make a run for it."

A flash of anger darkened Henrik's expression, but it vanished quickly. "I don't know what you're talking about."

Fiaschetti's voice was calm and businesslike. "Tell us the names of the ships with cylinder bombs smuggled aboard, and I promise you won't get the death penalty."

Henrik darted into the office, slammed the door shut, and quickly bolted it. Jonathan dropped Emilio's arm and raced to the door. He jiggled the knob, but it was locked tight.

"He's got a gun," Fiaschetti warned.

Was it to kill himself or shoot at them through the window? It didn't matter; he had to be stopped. Jonathan rammed his shoulder against the locked door. Nothing. He tried again, pain shooting through his shoulder with the force of the blow.

Henrik continued loading the gun, then closed the cylinder. Jonathan grabbed a metal chair and smashed it through the glass in the door. Shards flew everywhere.

Henrik put the gun to his temple.

"No!" Jonathan yelled, but it was too late.

The report of a gunshot echoed in the small confines of the office, and Henrik dropped to the concrete floor.

Jonathan reached through the broken window to unbolt the door and hurried inside. The acrid stink of gunpowder tinged the air, and Henrik didn't move. Their best chance for identifying the ships in danger had just been lost.

"Is he dead?" Detective Fiaschetti asked.

Jonathan nodded, his shoulder aching, the crushing weight of defeat almost sending him to his knees.

Fiaschetti cursed and kicked a chair.

The chalkboard on the wall outside the office listed every ship sailing out of port today. Over a hundred ships had already departed, and any one of them could be loaded with bombs. The *Caledonia* left three hours ago. It was too far out to sea for their wireless messages to reach.

A bunch of longshoremen had gathered outside the office, gaping at the dead man sprawled on the floor. Jonathan assumed his calm, professional demeanor. "Who's in charge here?"

A hard-muscled man with a shiny bald head nodded toward the dead man. "He was, but I'm crew chief of the longshoremen here. Name's Jim Tully."

Jonathan motioned for the crew chief to follow him several yards away and spoke quietly.

"Mr. Tully, the police believe a number of bombs have been planted in sacks of sugar stored in this warehouse. The dead guy in the office was picking which ships for them to go on."

Tully looked genuinely shocked. "Bombs?" he gasped.

Jonathan held up a hand. "Calm down. This type of bomb won't cause an explosion but a chemical fire. We need to learn which ships got loaded with sugar, and if there's any more sugar still in the warehouse. Were you here when the *Caledonia* was loaded?"

The longshoreman wiped his brow. "Yeah. We loaded it a couple of hours before it sailed."

"Will the cargo hold allow a member of the ship's crew to get inside the hold while at sea?"

"They can get inside, but the hold is stacked with cargo floor to ceiling, wall to wall . . . just a single aisle down the center. The sugar is behind two hundred barrels of turpentine. Henrik said he wanted the sugar in first, then the turpentine."

Jonathan cursed under his breath. Henrik had ordered the cargo to be loaded in a way that would ensure a massive fire. The sugar would be impossible to get to but guaranteed to cause an enormous conflagration from the turpentine.

They needed to warn the captain of the *Caledonia* to get back to port before a catastrophic fire in the middle of the Atlantic put all eight hundred people aboard in danger. But figuring out how to reach them would take a miracle.

32

Katherine spent the afternoon flipping through the brochures about California. The photographs were beautiful and tempting. Charming shops and elegant hotels lined the streets of downtown San Francisco. It seemed so different from New York. Not better or worse, just different. Could she be happy there?

The ringing of the telephone broke her concentration. She set the brochures aside and reached for the receiver. The desk clerk told her an urgent call had come in, and he would connect her. Seconds later, a panicked voice came on the line.

"Katherine? It's Inga. I'm down at the harbor. Katherine, it's a mess." Inga's frazzled voice sounded so unlike her cheerful friend.

"What's going on?"

"I just got to the wireless office, and the police are swarming all over. There's been a threat, and the Bomb Squad has been called in. You should know that Jonathan is here."

Her breath caught. "Is he okay?"

"He's very worried," Inga said. "I don't understand what's happening, but it's bad. We're calling all the ships back to port. Katherine, I left my spectacles in your hotel room. Is there any way you can bring them to me? It's getting dark in the tower, and I can't see to file the messages."

"Absolutely," she said instantly. Her parents were still out on the town celebrating their anniversary, and whatever was happening down at the harbor was too urgent to wait.

Katherine hired a horse-drawn cab to take her directly to the harbor, but trouble started three blocks from the port. Fully loaded wagons and drays clogged the streets and brought traffic to a standstill.

"The police have blocked off the harbor," the cab driver said. "I can't get you any closer."

Katherine stuck her head out the window and spotted the police barricade at the intersection straight ahead. It didn't matter; she was close enough to walk. She paid the driver and hopped down from the carriage.

Honking horns and angry shouts filled the air. She covered her ears while hurrying between the vehicles stalled behind police barricades. Wagons loaded with barrels and crates blocked her view, making her feel tiny as she wove between the towering walls of cargo, heading for the wireless office where Inga worked. A furious driver whose flatbed wagon was stacked with timber yelled at a police officer standing before a barricade.

"This load is an hour past due," he snarled. "If I can't get it to the ship before it sails, I'm making the police buy it!"

"Nothing is sailing out of the harbor until that mess is cleared up," the police officer said, pointing out to sea.

Katherine looked at where he pointed. Good heavens, a ship was on fire! A coastal steamer with inky clouds billowing from the rear of the ship. A fireboat cast soaring arcs of water directly at the flames. Crew members directed nozzles mounted on iron posts toward the crippled ship, sending jets of water blasting into the air.

She hadn't come here for this. The police manning the barricade were so distracted by the angry cargo drivers that they weren't paying attention to her. She slipped around the hip-high barricades and ran toward the wireless tower at the end of the pier.

Abandoned pallets of cargo were scattered all over the loading area, but everyone was gone. No sailors or longshoremen. The conveyor belts and grain elevators had ceased operation. Only a handful of men near the open doors of Warehouse 36 were busily at work. Two men stood atop a raised platform and poured sacks of sugar into a mesh net below.

Powdery sweetness tinged the air. A fire truck and a few firemen watched as tons of sugar sifted through the net, forming a white mountain on the dirty pavement. Why on earth were they ruining all that sugar?

Katherine craned her neck to see the top of the wireless tower. Inga had given her a tour of the place years ago. Wireless operators sent Morse code over radio waves to communicate with ships at sea, and every additional story of height meant they could cast their signals a little farther out to sea. The tower was five stories high and had antennas on the top.

She hurried to the door at the base of the tower. It wasn't locked so she slipped inside, clutching her handbag with Inga's glasses inside. She was breathless after climbing to the top of the tower, finally arriving at the spacious room with a panoramic view of the harbor. It was so crowded that nobody noticed her arrival. Inga was at a wireless station with headphones covering her ears, her fingers tapping the bar on the wireless transmitter as she sent a message. Two other operators, both men, were just as engrossed in their work.

Police officers crowded the other side of the room, conferring around a table with other men. Some looked like dockworkers, others wearing the uniform of the harbor police. Jonathan and another officer stood at the corner window, staring at the burning ship in the harbor.

Tension crackled in the air, but everyone sounded calm as they carried out their assigned tasks. Inga stood, holding a scrap of paper. "Message from the *Annabel Lee*," she announced. "They've got smoke coming from their hold."

Jonathan turned away from the window. "How far out are they?"

"Fifteen nautical miles."

A man with the harbor police scrutinized a map tacked to the back wall. "Tell them we're sending a fireboat right away."

Nobody noticed Katherine standing in the doorway. She intercepted Inga before the younger woman got back to her station. "Here are your glasses," she said.

"Oh, thank heavens!" Inga gave Katherine a quick hug. "Everything is so frantic. I usually file the incoming messages, but I haven't been able to see well enough after the sun began to set."

Inga went on to explain that someone had planted cylinder bombs on several ships that had left port today, but nobody knew which ships. The wireless operators had been trying to contact all forty-five ships that had been loaded at Warehouse 36. Every one of them needed to get back to port to be inspected.

"We didn't get word to the *Dorset* in time," Inga said with a nod to the ship burning in the harbor. The sun had finally set, making the fiery blaze on the *Dorset* look even more dramatic against the night sky. One of the fireboats must have just gotten the order to head out in search of the *Annabel Lee*. It peeled away and began sailing east while the single remaining fireboat kept drenching the *Dorset* with water.

"Katherine!" Jonathan exclaimed, and she jumped as he rushed to her side. "What are you doing here?"

"I brought Inga her eyeglasses. Can I stay and help?"

"No, you can't stay!" Jonathan said in exasperation. "It's dangerous up here. They're searching for cylinder bombs in the warehouse below. They already found three, and there could be more."

Despite the risk, she didn't want to leave. Instinct compelled her to stay and help out. "You might need an extra pair of hands," she offered, but Jonathan started propelling her toward the door.

"Thank you for bringing Inga's glasses, but you need to leave."

Was he really going to throw her out? It wasn't rational, but she wanted to stay. In times of crisis, there were always people who ran for cover while others ran straight toward the danger. She was tired of being wrapped in cotton. Everyone in this room was doing something noble and heroic, and she didn't want to hide under the covers in her hotel room when she could be helping others.

She scrambled for a reason to stay. "I have medical training."

Jonathan grasped her shoulders and locked eyes with her. "Katherine, you're a dentist."

She smothered a gulp of laughter. "It's still medical training. I'm not squeamish, and you may need me."

"I could use her help," Inga said. "Normally I'm the one who files each communication, but traffic on the wires has been too heavy for me to keep up."

"Let her stay," a voice ordered from the corner. It came from a scowling man wearing a police uniform with a captain's badge pinned to his barrel chest. "Inga, get back to work. We can't have even a single station lying idle."

Jonathan opened and closed his mouth, looking torn. Ultimately he must have decided to let her stay because he drew her across the room to introduce her to the men at the table. "Katherine, this is Captain Duranty, the commanding officer of the harbor police," he said of a dapper man with a handlebar mustache. "And that's Captain Esposito, in charge of the city's marine fire brigade."

Both men gave her quick nods. Jonathan then pulled her aside to fill her in on operations in the tower. They used a nautical map covering the center table to chart the last known location of each ship they managed to contact. The map was littered with quarters, pennies, and dimes. Even a few saltshakers and paper clips were scattered on the map, each token symbolizing the position of a ship at sea. As soon as a tower operator got the current location of a ship, the message was conveyed to Captain Esposito, who updated the map. He'd been tossing the messages on the floor, but now that Katherine was here, she'd file them by ship to track their progress.

A bald wireless operator ripped a page from his pad and handed it to Captain Esposito. "Coordinates for the RMS *Malta*," he said. "No sign of a fire yet, but they're on the way back to port."

Captain Esposito moved a dime to update the *Malta*'s position, then handed Katherine the message for filing.

Katherine scooped up dozens of other scraps of paper on the floor, containing the various ships' coordinates. As she started filing the messages, she became familiar with the curious names of the ships in danger: the *Diamond Bay*, the *Bluebonnet*, the *North Carolina*. Most of the messages contained little besides terse coordinates, but some had a snippet of personality. The RMS *Malta* operator must have had a dry sense of humor when he suggested anyone planting a bomb on a mail ship lacked imagination.

It took twenty minutes to file the initial stack of messages, but after that there was little to do but watch. It was awe-inspiring. So many people, each one fully engaged in the desperate quest to reach the forty-five ships and get them safely back to port.

Everyone was worried about the ominous silence from a ship called the *Caledonia* with eight hundred passengers aboard. It had sailed beyond range of the harbor's wireless by the time the police were aware of the danger. The best they could do was urge fellow operators aboard ships within the range of their signal to broadcast messages farther east. The hope was that by sending out a daisy chain of messages, word would eventually reach the *Caledonia* that their ship was in grave danger and must return to port immediately.

Soon Katherine was assigned another job. The tower room had a single telephone line to keep in contact with the fire departments and police station houses. Normally the wireless operators staffed the telephone, but they were fully occupied, so Jonathan asked her to take over telephone duty.

"All you have to do is place a call when requested or take a message and convey it to the right person," Jonathan said. "Can you do it?"

"Of course."

He cupped her face between his palms and pressed a kiss to her forehead. "Good," he said and turned away to rejoin a group of men studying a blackboard with dozens of ships listed.

Did he just kiss her? Before she could process the meaning of that quick kiss, another batch of messages needed to be filed. The next hour was spent with telephone and filing duties, yet there was plenty of down time to watch ships as they arrived back in port. Spotlights flooded the harbor to guide ships to berths, where their holds could be off-loaded by brave and determined longshoremen, who rushed to carry the sacks of sugar for inspection. They looked so tiny from up in the tower. Katherine admired every single man down below as they carried out their mission.

The panoramic view of the floodlit harbor was amazing, but it was hard to look anywhere besides at the *Dorset*, still battling flames as a fireboat sent arcs of water at the stricken vessel. A catastrophe was unfolding before her eyes, yet she was proud to be here. She was going to remember this night forever.

She kept to the telephone stool and tried to stay out of the way. The spot where Jonathan kissed her forehead still tingled. Everything had been left in limbo after the funeral, but now he acted as though they were together once again.

Another hour passed, and her back began to ache from sitting on the tall stool. Though they still had a long night ahead of them, the urgency of the first few hours had faded. A fourth wireless operator arrived to let people begin to take short breaks. Inga's break happened at one o'clock in the morning. The two of them huddled in the corner, quietly exchanging gossip about the Martha Washington.

"You should see the owls!" Inga enthused. "They're learning how to fly, flapping their wings and hopping between the broomsticks we propped outside our windows. You've never seen anything so cute."

Katherine's heart squeezed. The survival of the owls was a group effort, but she was still proud of her part in it. "I wish I could see them."

"They are most active at dawn and dusk," Inga said, then continued chatting about the other ladies of the eighth floor.

It made Katherine lonesome. Could she ever go back to her normal life? Working in the tower tonight reminded her what it felt like to be part of a team. Good people coming together to make the world a better place.

When Inga returned to the wireless station, Katherine shifted her attention to Jonathan, who was focused on the nautical map. Maybe he felt her gaze because he stepped away from the chart and returned to her side.

"The *Dorset* fire is finally out," he said, "and it is coming back to port to evacuate the crew."

"That's good news," she replied. An awkward silence followed, so she changed the subject. Nudging him with the tip of her shoe, she asked, "Are you ever going to return my chemistry textbook?"

He looked at her in surprise. "I haven't finished reading it."

"I might be moving to California. I want it back." His gaze turned speculative, but not particularly worried. It would be nice if he fought for her or begged her not to leave. At the very least, he could look upset at the prospect.

Instead, all he did was frown at her. "Hmmm."

"What's *hmmm* supposed to mean? Speak in actual words. Or speak in Italian if you'd prefer. I don't understand a word of Italian, but go ahead and use it if it means you'll express yourself instead of expecting me to guess what's going on behind that steel mask you're wearing."

A bit of humor lit his features, but it vanished as he leaned down, his nose tickling her ear as he started whispering in Italian to her. The words were the most gorgeous, lyrical sounds she'd ever heard, filled with lots of vowels and dips and loops. The cascade of words was both melodic and expressive, sending a thrill all the way down to her toes. When he finished, he straightened and gazed out to sea with a stoic expression.

The side of her cheek still tingled from the warmth of his breath. "What did you say?"

"I said your shoelaces are untied."

She glanced down. "They are not!"

He shrugged. "Then maybe I told you how I really feel about your moving to California."

"Oh? Why don't you repeat it for me in English?"

She turned to him so they were nose to nose. They stood in a room filled with people, but it felt intensely intimate as he looked into her eyes. Whatever he just whispered in her ear was glorious. She could sense it.

Inga's terse voice interrupted. "There's a fire on the RMS *Malta*," she called out, triggering a flurry of activity in the tower room.

Jonathan raced back to the map, the others clustering around Inga.

"What's the location of the fire?" Captain Duranty demanded.

Inga kept listening to a constellation of electronic dot-and-dash noises funneling through her headphones. She wrote while listening. "They've got the fire under control," she said. "The bag of sugar was in their kitchen, not the cargo hold."

Katherine sighed as her tense muscles began to unknot. After a few more exchanges, it became plain that the RMS *Malta* had only the single bag of sugar aboard. It was a mail ship, not a cargo ship, so there was no danger of the hold catching fire.

A policeman added another hash mark to the board tracking the number of cylinder bombs found. They'd identified fifty-four of an estimated one hundred bombs. It was anyone's guess how many had been aboard the *Dorset* in the harbor. Most ominously, the still absent *Caledonia* surely held the mother lode of bombs.

"Why would Achilles target the *Malta*?" the fire marshal asked.

"He wants to cause as much disruption as possible," Jonathan answered. "The *Malta* is a British mail ship. He probably hoped the bag of sugar would be stowed alongside crates of mail in the hold. Destroying a ship's mail would anger a couple thousand people all over the world whose mail got destroyed."

The telephone rang, and Katherine hurried to answer it. A police officer on the ground said journalists were clamoring to get inside the tower room to observe what was happening. There wasn't much spare room in the tower, but she passed the message to Captain Duranty, who authorized a single journalist to come up and document the night.

To Katherine's surprise, the man who tromped up the stairs two minutes later was Dennis Keogh, the *New York Journal*'s reporter who was afraid of heights. He looked pale and a little breathless after climbing all the way up to the tower room. With windows on three sides, it wasn't a good place for a man trying to ignore how high off the ground they were.

"Are you going to be okay?" she asked him quietly.

Dennis looked a little embarrassed. "So far tonight I've seen men pull apart cylinder bombs, dozens of longshoremen unload sacks they knew might have live bombs inside, and a fire crew sail straight toward a burning ship. I'll be okay."

Jonathan came over to provide a briefing to the journalist, recounting how many ships had safely arrived at port and which were still at sea. "There's been no word from the *Caledonia*," he added, "a ship with around eight hundred passengers on board. It was too far out to sea by the time the warnings were broadcast. The best we can hope is that another ship that's already gotten the warning will spot it and relay the message."

"What happens then?" Dennis asked.

"The *Caledonia* will need to get to the nearest port as soon as possible. We know it's got a lot of bombs aboard, but Captain Esposito said we can't send the fireboats out that far."

Now that the fire on the *Dorset* was out, the ship had at last made its way back to port. Even from her position in the tower, it was easy to see the exhaustion among the crew as they staggered ashore, their clothing and faces darkened from smoke.

Someone brought up the evening edition of the *New York Journal*, announcing a reward for information leading to the arrest of Chester Lewis, better known by his nickname Achilles. A sketch of a skinny man with blond hair accompanied the story.

"That's what he looks like?" Katherine asked.

Jonathan nodded. "The drawing was taken from a college fraternity photograph a few years ago. A bunch of men with the Sons of Chaos came from that same fraternity."

Dennis scowled. "That kid's parents must be so proud about what he learned in college."

A shiver ran up Katherine's spine. Chester Lewis was a contemptable human being, and unless they caught him soon, he might end up forcing her to move to California.

Jonathan stared out at the harbor, where the *Diamond Bay* was on fire. It had returned to port safely an hour earlier, but smoke began billowing from its hold before the sugar could be off-loaded. Twelve ships had arrived back in port, with hundreds of dockworkers rushing to unload their cargo. Thirty other ships had been contacted and had confirmed they carried no sugar. Those ships continued on their journey, but the damage tonight was bad. There had been fires on four ships, and there was still no word from the *Caledonia*.

Frustration roiled as Jonathan watched the flames. How could so much chaos have been wrought by a group of cynical, evil people? He couldn't hand another victory to Chester Lewis. They needed to use the press to turn the chaos of tonight into a victory for the good people of New York.

His first ally in that cause was right there in the tower. He stood beside Dennis as the fireboats rained water on the blazing *Diamond Bay*. "What you see out there is a shining example of selfless human decency," Jonathan said. "Ordinary people working together to save our city. The Sons of Chaos tried to tear us down, but they only made us more united. We've been forged into something stronger and more valiant than we were this time yesterday."

"I hear you," Dennis said as he jotted on his notepad. "The morning newspapers will sing the praises of the heroes here tonight. And that Chester fellow? He's a nasty piece of work. His precious manifesto keeps misspelling the word *annihilate*. He should have spent more time in college learning to use a dictionary instead of building bombs."

"His downfall is sure to come," Jonathan said, "and soon."

The morning editions of the newspapers would carry news of Emilio Mazzini's arrest and Henrik Bauman's suicide. Chester's grand scheme to sink a dozen ships had failed. He'd managed to inconvenience thousands of people and had cost the shipowners untold expenses, but he had failed miserably.

At four o'clock in the morning, an all-night diner sent over a meal of hot pastrami sandwiches with sauerkraut. Jonathan didn't even like sauerkraut, but everything tasted wonderful tonight. There was a camaraderie among them as they ticked off every ship located, every cylinder bomb found.

Katherine huddled close beside him at the corner table as they polished off the last of their sandwiches. "Thank you for letting me stay," she said.

"Don't thank me. I wanted to throw you out. It was Captain Duranty who thought your medical training might come in handy."

She lifted her chin. "I cared about your health."

"My *dental* health?" he challenged, trying hard not to smile.

316

"I care about your entire health," she said, her fingers curling around his hand. "I care about every drop of blood that pumps in your veins. I care about your big generous heart that compels you to keep the city safe. I'm fascinated by your calm, keen mind. I love you, Lieutenant Birch. And yes, I care about your dental health too."

What had he ever done to deserve a woman like this? He smoothed a tendril of hair behind the shell of her ear. He'd never been very good with words, and she deserved more than he'd given her. "I love you too."

"You do?"

"More than my next breath of air," he said and reached for both her hands to cradle between his. "Katherine, I don't want you to move to California, or Ohio, or anywhere else besides possibly into a home you and I both share. I want to walk you home through moonlit streets at night. I want to wake up beside you. I want to bring you chocolate biscotti and wipe our kids' runny noses."

Her eyes widened and sparkled. "Our kids won't have runny noses. They'll be perfect."

"You are so naive," he said with a little shake of his head. But he said it with affection because he hoped she would always be so idealistic. The world needed people like Katherine Schneider.

The telephone rang. Katherine sprang up to answer it. He joined her, and she tilted the receiver so they could both hear.

"Stay tuned for a long-distance call from Boston," the operator said.

Katherine had her pencil at the ready when a man's growly voice came on.

"This is Dick Summers, harbormaster in Boston," he said. "Do you know about the *Caledonia*?"

"We've been looking for it all night," she said.

"Well, she just sailed into port here in Boston. Your wireless lines have been overloaded, and they couldn't get through to you. The ship is here and is being evacuated. A bunch of guys from the fire department are unloading the sugar from the hold as we speak."

Jonathan stood on top of a chair to announce the news to the whole room. "The *Caledonia* just arrived in Boston. They're safe."

Spontaneous applause filled the tower room. Dennis pumped his fist in the air, and Jonathan hopped down to scoop Katherine into a bear hug. Captain Duranty moved the saltshaker representing the *Caledonia* to Boston. Somewhere, hundreds of miles out to sea, other ships had managed a daisy chain of signals to reach the *Caledonia* with the warning to get to the nearest port.

By six o'clock, all forty-five ships had been accounted for. Chester's plot had crumbled. Now all they had to do was find him before he could strike again.

An hour before sunrise, it was all over. A second shift of police officers arrived, and Katherine was free to walk home. Jonathan offered to escort her, and she gladly accepted. He cradled her hands within his as they rode the subway, heedless of the other morning commuters crowding the train car. She and Jonathan snuggled on a bench together, whispering about the night they'd just survived.

"Inga said the owls are starting to fly," she told him.

Jonathan squeezed her hands. "If I live to be a hundred, I will always remember our late nights together feeding those chicks."

She leaned in to kiss him, feeling the same way. It was hard to believe those wriggly pink, featherless chicks were starting to fly. "Can we get off a stop early to go see them? Inga says they're active right before dawn."

Jonathan agreed. If they got off at the next stop, they would pass by the Martha Washington on their walk to her hotel.

The first hint of dawn lightened the sky as they emerged up on 29th Street and strolled toward the Martha Washington. It had been five weeks since she'd last been here, and it felt like coming home. She grinned at her first sight of the building because dozens of broomsticks stuck out of the windows facing the ally. What a glorious, haphazard mess! They arrived in the alley and craned their necks to scan the broomsticks in search of an owl.

"Look, there's one!" Jonathan said.

Katherine's gaze followed where he pointed, squinting through the gloom. Sure enough, the silhouette of a little barn owl perched on a fifth-floor broomstick. Its heart-shaped face tilted and swiveled to look down at them. She glanced up at the eighth-floor ledge. "There's another," she said. It was in the nest, but tall enough to be seen peeking out over the edge.

Jonathan nodded. "They've grown so big."

"Haven't they?" she marveled. She caught her breath as the chick on the fifth-floor broomstick leapt and flapped its wings enough to land on the broomstick above.

An arm clamped around her neck to drag her backward. "Hello, Katherine," a congenial voice purred.

She tried to jerk away, but the arm tightened and hauled her back against somebody behind her. She yelped, trying to twist away.

"Katherine, don't move," Jonathan warned.

Jonathan's voice was tense with alarm, and then something cold pressed against her neck. A knife pressed at the base of her neck as a man's arm squeezed around her still-healing throat, and it hurt terribly. She couldn't turn to see who held her; all she could see was Jonathan, staring intently at her.

"Chester, you don't want her. You want me," Jonathan said.

"I want whoever will make bigger headlines." The tip of the knife pressed harder. "I don't need another dead cop on my record because I've already got one of those, don't I?"

Katherine whimpered at the mention of Gallagher.

Achilles's tone was conversational as he continued. "I followed you two lovebirds on the subway all the way from the harbor, and you didn't even see me. My plan for sinking a dozen capitalist ships didn't work out as planned, and now my face is all over the newspapers. I've got you to thank for that, Lieutenant Birch. So you're the one I'm going to hurt with my swan song. Frankly, she'll make a more interesting victim than you."

"Take it easy. You don't want to do this," Jonathan said in a soothing voice as he stepped forward.

The knife pricked her! Jonathan froze. Was she bleeding? Whatever Chester just did had succeeded in keeping Jonathan immobilized.

"Stay where you are, Birch," Chester warned. "I'll kill her right here if I have to. But you know what? Another slit throat seems like old hat for her. And I'm kind of famous for that number I can do on the Achilles tendon." He snickered a little. "I'll get more attention if I keep her alive, but crippled. Both ankles! What do you say?"

She couldn't tear her eyes off Jonathan. He hadn't moved a muscle but sweat broke out across his face. He was as scared as she was, yet his voice sounded calm.

"You don't want her," Jonathan said again. "Police officers get more press. Let her go and I'll do wherever you want."

"You're going to do whatever I want anyway. Hey, I heard that little Carlo Rinaldi decided to become a snitch and tattle on Emilio Mazzini. Big mistake. I've already put out the word among the Mazzinis. That kid is as good as dead."

Chester held her before him like a shield. Even if Jonathan had a weapon, he couldn't do anything. Chester started dragging her deeper into the alley. She heard Jonathan say she was going to be all right. How was she going to be all right? This awful man was going to cut her tendons and put her in a wheelchair for the rest of her life.

He wrapped another arm around her middle, freeing her neck but trapping her even firmer than before as he forced her into the alley. Jonathan remained frozen in place, hands up. She didn't want this happening in front of Jonathan. He'd already seen Gallagher killed before his eyes.

"Katherine, your shoelaces are untied," Jonathan shouted suddenly.

She looked down, and the report of a gunshot deafened her. She screamed and leapt away as Chester toppled over.

Jonathan kept his pistol trained on Chester, who lay sprawled in the alley. Blood was spattered everywhere.

"Don't look," Jonathan said, but she couldn't tear her eyes away.

"You sh-shot him," she said.

"Yes, I shot him." Jonathan lowered the pistol.

"Hey! What's going on down there?" A woman on the fourth floor stuck her head out a window, looking down. "Should I call the cops?"

"Good idea," Jonathan replied.

"Should we get Midge?" another woman called down. "She just got back from the hospital, and that guy needs help."

"Don't bother. He's dead," Jonathan called back. He tucked the pistol into his waistband and approached her. "Are you okay?"

She was dizzy and shaky and had Chester's blood on her. But the man was dead, his organization unraveling quickly, and Jonathan had just saved her life.

"Yes," she breathed. "Thank you, Jonathan . . . I'm okay."

She stepped into his arms as they closed around her. Jonathan might look calm, but his heart pounded so hard that she felt it clear to her bones.

Thanks to Jonathan, she was free again.

33

Jonathan felt no guilt after killing Chester. He had only a few seconds to decide between Katherine's life and Chester's, and it hadn't been a hard choice. Now that the kingpin behind the Sons of Chaos was dead, the men already in custody were willing to roll over on the other members of the anarchist group, and the police rounded them up in short order.

More important, the threat to Katherine was over. With the entire group in custody, Katherine had nothing left to fear, and Jonathan helped her move back into the Martha Washington. Soon she would return to her job at the clinic. Jonathan had already resumed his position on the night shift and was continuing his training to become fully qualified to serve on the Bomb Squad.

The only part of life that wasn't returning to normal was the fate of the Rinaldis because Carlo now had a price on his head. The Mazzinis would never forgive the young man for turning over the receipt that led to Emilio's downfall. Carlo's only hope of survival was to flee the state.

To Jonathan's surprise, the entire Rinaldi clan decided to leave with Carlo. After almost thirty years in New York, the family was pulling up stakes and heading to California for a fresh start.

It was time for Jonathan to say goodbye. He'd never fully cut ties to his family in the past, but this time would be different. Nonna was ninety-one years old, and soon she'd be on the other side of the country. Today would be the last time he'd see her in this life.

"Don't you think this would be better handled privately?" Katherine asked as they walked toward the departure platform at Grand Central Station.

He squeezed her hand as they walked. Katherine would never admit it, but she was terrified of his grandmother. He wanted to change that. In all likelihood, he and Katherine were going to grow old together and create a family of their own. He wanted her to have a good opinion of Nonna, the woman who had saved his life.

"She'll want to meet you properly," he said as they angled around a porter wheeling a luggage cart.

Katherine scurried to catch up to him. "She kind of hates me. The last time I saw her, she hit me in the face with a dishrag."

"She doesn't hate you, but the Rinaldis don't mess around when they sense a threat. Look, there they are."

At the far end of the platform, two dozen Rinaldis gathered together. They wore their best clothes, with baggage and steamer trunks mounded around them. Some of them looked excited, others anxious. They were about to embark on a new chapter, and Jonathan prayed it would be an honorable one. A wave of bittersweet memories surged because there was a time when he loved all of them. This was going to be harder than he thought.

Dante stood in the middle of the family with a toddler in his arms, his pregnant wife at his side. Carlo was there too.

Jonathan raised a hand as he approached. "Dante!" he called.

His cousin turned to look and gave a single, brusque nod. Dante didn't look happy about leaving. He was walking away from a mighty empire here in New York. Leaving the city for the sake of his son spoke well of him.

"Good luck in California," Jonathan said. "You'll write once you get there?"

"I'm sure somebody will," Dante said noncommittally.

Uncle Mick barged in, grabbing Jonathan in a big hug. "We're proud of you, Giovanni," he said, and there were plenty of nods of agreement and only a little grumbling. "It's okay with us if you want to be a cop."

Jonathan let go of Mick and leaned over to shake Carlo's hand. "You've got a bright future ahead of you," he told the boy. "California is a fresh start, and the world is wide open."

Then came the moment he dreaded. Nonna stood to the side, as erect as ever, but tears had begun pooling in her eyes.

His own eyes suddenly stung. "Don't cry, Nonna," he murmured in Italian, but two fat tears slid down her wrinkled face. His stalwart, tough grandma who'd saved his life by getting him to safety all those years ago. This was the last time they would see each other, and they both knew it.

Nonna gulped back a sniffle. "Here," she said, shoving a balled-up scrap of paper into his hand.

It was the recipe for chocolate biscotti.

"Grazie, Nonna," he choked out.

The tough old woman raised her chin and fixed her gaze on Katherine. "That woman is an idiot," she said in Italian. "She walked into our house and expected me to start talking family business."

"She's a brave woman," he said, continuing to speak in Italian, "and I love her. I hope to marry her soon, and I would like your blessing."

"I concede that she is brave," Nonna finally said. "You could do worse."

He kissed the old woman on both cheeks. "Thank you, Nonna. For everything."

Uncle Mick pulled Katherine into a hug and congratulated her in Italian because the old man had never learned English. Katherine looked bewildered at the loud and effusive compliments as others circled around to embrace her. Jonathan got a good deal of ribbing from the men, and the women gushed with congratulations, all until Dante's wife noticed one critical detail.

"There's no ring!" Dante's wife said, looking pointedly at Katherine's left hand.

"Hurry up and marry her," Uncle Mick said. "She's a dentist, so I'll bet she makes more money than you."

"Lock down the deal!" someone else hooted, and heat gathered beneath Jonathan's collar. He never liked being the center of attention. All the women looked at Katherine, some impressed, some horrified at the prospect of a woman working in such a profession.

"What's going on? What are they saying?" Katherine whispered to him.

"They're saying that you're too good for me," Jonathan replied. He might never be as virtuous as Katherine, but he was a better man when he was with her. Yet he would not embarrass her before his family by failing to propose. He wished he had a speech prepared and a proper ring. A grubby railway platform wasn't the ideal place for this, but it was time.

He sank down onto one knee and reached for her hand. A chorus of good-natured heckling came from the men behind him.

"Katherine, I love you. We've come through storms and—"

"And idiocy," Dante hollered in Italian. "Asking Nonna for the biscotti recipe is a prime example."

"Shhh!" Nonna said. "Giovanni, proceed."

He tried to hold back a grin but failed. Katherine was smiling too. Beaming actually. She didn't understand Italian, but she knew his family gathered on the platform supported what was about to happen.

He squeezed her hand. "Katherine, we've just received my grandmother's approval, and that's not easily won. I loved you from afar, and then I loved you through every moonlit walk home for the past two years. I will be the happiest man in the world if you would agree to be my wife."

"Oh, yes, Jonathan," she said, her voice vibrating with happiness. "Yes, yes, *yes!*"

He shot to his feet and swooped her up into his arms, swinging her around as his family cheered. Soon the Rinaldis would be on their way to California, but he had found the perfect woman to create a family of his own right here in New York, the city they both loved.

34

Two Years Later • Autumn, 1915

Katherine hurried alongside Jonathan, anxious to get to the Martha Washington. They were running late for Midge's birthday party because Jonathan had baked a huge batch of chocolate biscotti that took longer than expected.

Their apartment's kitchen wasn't all it could be. The stove was ancient, and the oven had hot spots that continually burned food. Their icebox was so small that they had to visit the market daily, and water barely dribbled from the faucet. Jonathan hankered for a better kitchen, so they'd be moving soon. But she would always treasure the memories of their first years of marriage together in their cozy apartment, where they bumped elbows, battled drafts, and burned countless dinners on the old cast-iron stove.

"I'm not sure we should have even baked for Midge," Katherine said as they rushed across 29th Street. "She's so fussy about healthy food, she'll probably turn her nose up at the biscotti."

Jonathan tossed her a look. "You're not still mad at her, are you? It's been two years!"

"I wasn't exactly *mad* at her," Katherine clarified. "I just didn't like the way she encouraged you to join the Bomb Squad with such enthusiasm. And now you might have to go to war!"

"Nobody is going to war," Jonathan said, staring straight ahead as they strode closer to the Martha Washington.

"Tell that to Inga." While it was true that President Wilson promised to keep them out of the dreadful war in Europe, Inga had gone overseas to work for the American ambassador in Berlin. It seemed as though the war crept closer every day, and Jonathan had explosives training. If America joined the war, men like Jonathan would be among the first called up.

She forced the gloomy thoughts from her mind as they stepped through the front doors of the Martha Washington. Memories came rushing back. Some of the best and worst days of her life had been spent right here in this building, but with time the bad memories had begun to fade, replaced by the good.

The party was in full swing at the rooftop café. Dozens of women mingled and laughed. Katherine immediately spotted Midge, standing by a potted palm tree.

"Happy birthday, Midge," she said, passing her the basket of biscotti. It was Midge's seventy-fifth birthday, and she still worked the overnight shift at the hospital. Her decision to keep working wasn't out of necessity but from the desire to keep engaged with the world.

As expected, the party consisted mostly of women, though a few of the doctors and hospital staff where Midge worked had come too, most of them men. Jonathan naturally drifted toward the men to talk politics while Katherine huddled with her old friends.

"Mrs. Blum is worse than ever," Delia confided. "She wants to start inspecting hemlines to make sure our ankles are appropriately covered. Can you believe it?"

Unfortunately, it was very believable, but Katherine didn't want to waste time nattering about Mrs. Blum.

"How is Inga?" she asked. "Has anyone heard from her?"

Delia brightened. "We received a letter just last week, and you would not believe it! The Americans at the embassy socialize with the staff from all the other neutral embassies. It sounds like they are having tons of fun with the Spanish, the Swiss, and the Norwegians. She accompanied the ambassador to a weekend hunting party and saw three of the German princes galloping through the Black Forest."

"No!" Blanche gasped. "Which ones? Are they married?"

That triggered a flurry of excited discussion about other letters Inga had written over the past year, most of which mentioned touring the grand museums and tree-lined avenues of Berlin.

Midge seemed skeptical as she listened to the dazzling reports of Inga's life in Berlin. "Can it really be that glamorous?"

Blanche was defensive. "The American ambassador is famous for his parties, and the fighting hasn't come close to Berlin. Of course I believe her!"

Midge wasn't convinced. "I worry about her, but I'm sure she'll come home if America ends up going to war."

And if that happened, Jonathan would probably change his uniform from police blue to army green. She drew a steadying breath and calmed her racing heart.

Jonathan would be okay. It was becoming increasingly clear to her that he was following where God led him, even though it might be toward a hard and dangerous path. God was good, and that meant she could lay all her worries and fears and what-ifs at his door. The world was going to unfold according to his plan, not hers, and that was all right with her.

Katherine looked to the other side of the roof, where Jonathan stood with a couple of other men. How proud she was of him! As always, he was more of a listener than a talker, and she loved watching the quiet intensity of his expression as he absorbed what the others said.

He met her gaze. A hint of a smile tilted the corner of his firm mouth as their eyes locked. Unspoken words flowed between them like an electrical current, carrying the promise of warmth, adventure, and anticipation. It wasn't possible to know what tomorrow held, but for tonight her life was good. It was more than good—it was *blessed*.

And tomorrow? That was in God's hands.

Historical Note

The people in this novel are fictional, except for Dr. Edgar "Painless" Parker (1872–1952) and Lieutenant Michael Fiaschetti (1882–1960). Edgar Parker legally changed his first name to Painless to avoid lawsuits for false advertising. He has a mixed reputation in the history of dentistry. He got his start traveling with circuses, where he pretended to pull the teeth of lions and tigers to fool the crowd with his painless techniques. He exaggerated his abilities, wore a necklace of human teeth, and took out billboards proclaiming himself "the greatest all-around dentist in this world or the next."

Although the American Dental Association branded Dr. Parker a "menace to the profession," he was a remarkably forward-thinking man. He sponsored informative essays in newspapers and magazines, instructing the public on how to care for their teeth to avoid unnecessary trips to the dentist. He sold inexpensive toothpaste and antiseptic mouthwash in his clinics. He had low prices, hired dentists who represented the ethnic composition of the local community, and kept his offices open at nonstandard hours to accommodate working people.

At the height of his career, Dr. Parker employed two hundred and fifty dentists in several states across the nation. Painless Parker ultimately became a multimillionaire and retired to California. His infamous human tooth necklace is on display at Temple University's Historical Dental Museum.

Michael Fiaschetti was born in Italy, moved to the United States as a child, and was an early member of the NYPD's Italian Squad. The team's founding member, Joseph Petrosino, was assassinated in 1909, and Fiaschetti was appointed as his replacement. Although many suspected Fiaschetti might suffer a similar fate, Lieutenant Fiaschetti enjoyed a long career with the police department before leaving to work as a private detective. Many of the methods he helped develop for the Italian Squad are still practiced by law-enforcement agencies today.

The Martha Washington Hotel was established in recognition of the growing number of professional women without respectable housing options in New York City. Contrary to the contemporary meaning of the word *hotel*, the Martha Washington was primarily a residential apartment building. When it opened in 1903, all five hundred apartments were immediately leased, and a waiting list of two hundred women signed up for future vacancies.

The Martha Washington remained a women-only apartment building until 1998. The building has since changed ownership several times, but as of this writing, it is known as The Redbury Hotel. In 2012, the building was designated a historical landmark for its architectural and historical significance.

Questions for Discussion

1. Katherine left Ohio fleeing a failed romance. Do you think she would have become a dentist if Paul hadn't broken her heart? Can there ever be an upside to having a dream not work out?

2. Much of the novel deals with people reinventing themselves. Jonathan, Painless Parker, and young Carlo Rinaldi all try to become someone different. What are some challenges that come with a complete transformation of a person's life?

3. What was your opinion of Sean Gallagher? Did learning his backstory and watching him during his finer hours make you reconsider his character? Have you ever known someone whose history helps explain questionable behavior in the present?

4. Could Jonathan and Gallagher have ever become friends?

5. Have you ever worked a night shift? If so, did you notice

a different culture and mindset among your nighttime co-workers?

6. At one point, when Katherine is fearing for Jonathan's service on the Bomb Squad, Midge tells her, "Don't ever doubt in the darkness what is true in the light." What did she mean by this?

7. Many professions in law enforcement, the military, or first responders are inherently dangerous. What input should the spouses of such people have in asking them to step back from the job?

8. Katherine tries to help Jonathan understand the enmity between him and Gallagher by saying, "Sometimes people show you their best side, but sometimes they only let you see their worst." How common is it for people to behave differently depending on who is present? What explains such behavior?

9. Jonathan doesn't warmly accept Katherine's offer of forgiveness after the funeral. Why do you think he hesitated?

10. At the end of the novel, Katherine returns to the Martha Washington and reflects, "Some of the best and worst days of her life had been spent right here in this building, but with time the bad memories had begun to fade, replaced by the good." How important is it to be able to set aside bad memories? Is this an admirable trait or one that should be resisted?

Read on
for a *sneak peek* at
the next book of the

Women of Midtown series

by Elizabeth Camden

Available in the spring of 2025

Inga Klein has just arrived in Berlin as the newly hired secretary for the American ambassador to Germany. As the threat of impending war looms over Europe, the ambassador has asked Inga to keep an eye on his chief of staff, the infamously stern Benedict Kincaid. This scene opens as Inga meets the kitchen staff at the house, along with the rest of the embassy staff.

"Benedict lives like a monk," the cook said as she refilled Inga's mug. "He is an excellent chief of staff, but he's got his quirks, and whatever you do, don't touch his *Encyclopedia Britannica*."

"He's reading it cover to cover," the cook's assistant said. The way Nellie gushed made it clear she held Benedict in awe. "He underlines passages and circles things and writes in the margins. I think he loves that encyclopedia more than his firstborn child."

"Not that he has a child," the cook rushed to say. "But if he did, the poor mite would be a distant second in his affections to that set of encyclopedias."

Inga startled as a door slammed down the hallway, followed by the arrival of an imposing man striding into the kitchen. His finely drawn features and windblown hair gave him an impression of dark, brooding vitality. He directed a penetrating gaze at her while tugging off a pair of riding gloves. His intense focus made her uneasy.

"Benedict!" Nellie said. "Come meet the ambassador's new secretary. Inga brought us drunken cherries."

"Drunken cherries?" Benedict asked as he eyed the bowl of cherries on the breakfast table. The two words were laden with enough disdain to form icicles in the warm kitchen.

"Brandied cherries," she clarified. "I bought them in Hamburg, and they're delightful on waffles or porridge. I'm Inga Klein. I'll be working for Ambassador Gerard as his new secretary."

She offered her hand, but he made no move to accept it. His gaze sharpened as he scrutinized her, then tilted his head a little closer, as though listening for something. "Do you have an *accent*?"

She smiled. She'd been told she spoke English so well that she barely had an accent at all anymore, but he had obviously spotted it. "Yes," she said brightly. "I'm originally from right here in Germany. A little village in Bavaria that's famous for its shoes."

Benedict's face went very still, and a cyclone of disapproval whirled behind his cold, sculpted features.

"Hmph" was all he said.

It was amazing how so much censure could be packed into a single syllable that wasn't even a real word. No wonder Ambassador Gerard didn't like him. She had been prepared to grant Benedict the benefit of the doubt, but how could she warm up to a man who brought an arctic blast into the cozy little breakfast room?

Benedict gave a brief nod to the cook, then left the kitchen and strode down the hallway, disappearing into a side room. The door slammed behind him.

"Don't let it worry you," Nellie said. "He doesn't like anybody and always acts suspicious until he gets to know you."

"That was still rude," the cook said. "Inga is new here, and there was no cause for that."

At least Inga had managed to soften up the surly cook, and perhaps she could make progress with Benedict Kincaid as well, but it should be done quickly. It was vital she establish a decent rapport with the second-most powerful man at the embassy, yet her sour feelings were already snowballing. She needed to nip this in the bud.

"Excuse me," she said to the cook, then hurried down the hall to follow Benedict. What a relief that the hallway smelled only of lemon polish rather than fire or brimstone.

She needed to quit thinking of Benedict as the enemy. Winning him over would be her first step toward soothing tensions between the ambassador and his chief of staff. She rapped quietly on the door.

"Come in," Benedict said from the other side.

She entered the room, which was obviously a library. Floor-to-ceiling bookshelves covered one wall, while the rest of the space was furnished like a sitting room. Morning sunlight filtered through the leafy shrubbery outside the tall windows, making the entire room shimmer with an amber glow. Benedict sat behind the desk like a king, a hefty tome opened before him.

She drew closer to peek at the book, and a bubble of laughter escaped. "I heard rumor that you're reading the *Encyclopedia Britannica* from cover to cover, but I didn't believe it."

"It's true," Benedict said dryly.

"Do you ever skip the boring parts?"

"There are no boring parts."

Oh, good heavens, Ambassador Gerard was correct when he claimed his chief of staff was allergic to fun. Benedict still hadn't looked at her since she entered. "You haven't introduced yourself," she pointed out. "Shall we try again? I'm Inga Klein, the ambassador's new secretary. And you are?"

"I'm reading," he said. "We are just getting to know each other, so perhaps you are unaware that Saturday mornings are one of the few times I have for recreational reading, which I look forward to all week, and which you are currently interrupting."

She couldn't imagine anything more tedious than reading an entire encyclopedia cover to cover. "Aren't you ever tempted to skip ahead to the good parts?"

"And what would those be?"

She shrugged and flashed a teasing grin. "Oh, you know, juicy scandals like Lucrezia Borgia or the Salem Witch Trials. But no, it seems you'd rather read about—" she leaned in to look at his current article—"the pollination behavior of insects."

She said it in a playful tone, but his voice was utterly serious as he replied, "One third of the world's food supply depends on insect pollination, but Miss Klein finds it beneath her. Interesting."

She sighed. "It seems we've gotten off on the wrong foot, and I'd like to change that. For a start, I hope you'll call me Inga."

Benedict settled a bookmark in place and closed the heavy volume with a slow, deliberate motion. He stood to face her, and for the first time a hint of softening eased the sharp planes of his face. "Miss Klein, although it is no fault of yours, I don't like the fact that you are German."

It felt like a slap in the face, and she took a step back. "That sounds rather small-minded."

"No, it's called diplomacy. Right now, the whole of Europe is balancing on a knife's edge. War between Germany and the Allied Powers is almost inevitable, and don't believe the newspapers. This war won't be a cakewalk that will be over before Christmas. My goal is to keep the United States out of a pointless, bloody war. To do that, our embassy needs to maintain a reputation for strict neutrality. Your presence endangers that."

"I'm only a *secretary*."

"You're someone who has the trust of the ambassador, and that puts our reputation for neutrality in jeopardy with the French and the British, both of whom will be suspicious of your influence over Ambassador Gerard. Please don't be offended, but I'm going to ask the ambassador to send you back to America. I don't want you here."

She exhaled sharply. No one had ever come after her so aggressively, and it rattled her. "Ambassador Gerard won't send me away. He needs me and obviously has no concerns with my being German."

"That's because he is still a novice in diplomacy. James Gerard is the public face of the American Embassy, and his behavior must be flawless. If he stumbles, it's my job to clean it up."

"You answer to the ambassador, not the other way around,"

she pointed out, yet it made no dent on the ironhard expression on Benedict's face.

"Ambassadors come and go with each new administration," he said. "The diplomatic corps stays, and we will be here long after Gerard is gone. We know how to get things done, how to swim beneath the surface and leave no ripples in our wake. If you are to be part of that team, you need to understand the rules."

"Fair enough," she said. "What are the rules?"

"Every person who works at the embassy is considered part of the diplomatic corps. That means you must be patient, respectful, and resist taking sides. Right now, most nations are forming their alliances, and they'll attempt to drag the United States onto their team. Don't let them."

"Of course not! Just because I was born in Germany doesn't make me disloyal. I'm an American now."

He looked at her for so long, a frisson of tension began gathering along her spine, and it was hard not to shrink beneath his piercing scrutiny.

"None of this is going to be easy," he cautioned, and for the first time his voice actually had a note of compassion. The unexpected kindness sent a tiny shiver down her arms. "My goal is to have the American Embassy serve as a peace broker," he continued. "Both sides need to trust in our neutrality. If someone punches you in the jaw, you can't lose your temper and retaliate, or it endangers our reputation for neutrality. We won't be able to advance our cause with anything but our intellect, and one wrong foot can topple that. Miss Klein, you are a wrong foot."

She took a moment to digest that statement before responding with equal resolve. "I am a wrong foot who is going to remain firmly planted at this post."

"If I fail to persuade the ambassador to send you home, you need to be aware that Berlin is filled with spies. You must be on guard against that."

"I repeat. I'm just a secretary—"

"Who has no idea what she's stepping into or else you wouldn't sound so baffled. Miss Klein, you are the worst possible secretary for an American ambassador."

The coffee in her stomach began to sour. She was coming to understand why Ambassador Gerard disliked Benedict so much. She didn't yet understand the diplomatic landscape but was smart enough not to wade into an argument she couldn't hope to win with a seasoned and sophisticated diplomat like Benedict Kincaid. She glanced at his encyclopedia.

"Forgive me for interrupting your Saturday morning," she said. "I'll let you get back to the fascinating world of insect pollination."

Inga couldn't escape the room and Benedict's disturbing presence fast enough. She needed to report back to Ambassador Gerard immediately.

Elizabeth Camden is best known for her historical novels set in Gilded Age America, featuring clever heroines and richly layered story lines. Before she was a writer, she was an academic librarian at some of the largest and smallest libraries in America, but her favorite is the continually growing library in her own home. Her novels have won the RITA and Christy Awards and have appeared on the CBA bestsellers list. She lives in Orlando, Florida, with her husband, who graciously tolerates her intimidating stockpile of books. Learn more online at ElizabethCamden.com.

Sign Up for Elizabeth's Newsletter

Keep up to date with Elizabeth's latest news
on book releases and events by signing up
for her email list at the link below.

ElizabethCamden.com

FOLLOW ELIZABETH ON SOCIAL MEDIA

Author Elizabeth Camden   @AuthorElizabethCamden

More from Elizabeth Camden

When lawyer Patrick O'Neill agrees to resurrect an old mystery and challenge the Blackstones' legacy of greed and corruption, he doesn't expect to be derailed by the kindhearted family heiress, Gwen Kellerman. She is tasked with getting him to drop the case, but when the mystery takes a shocking twist, he is the only ally she has.

Carved in Stone
THE BLACKSTONE LEGACY #1

Natalia Blackstone relies on Count Dimitri Sokolov to oversee the construction of the Trans-Siberian Railway. Dimitri loses everything after witnessing a deadly tragedy and its cover-up, but he has an asset the czar knows nothing about: Natalia. Together they fight to save the railroad while exposing the truth, but can their love survive the ordeal?

Written on the Wind
THE BLACKSTONE LEGACY #2

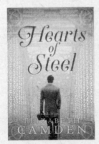

When successful businesswoman Maggie Molinaro offends a corrupt banker, she unwittingly sets off a series of calamities that threaten to destroy her life's work. She teams up with charismatic steel magnate Liam Blackstone, but what begins as a practical alliance soon evolves into a romance between two wounded people determined to beat the odds.

Hearts of Steel
THE BLACKSTONE LEGACY #3

BETHANYHOUSE